WHAT EVERY BODY IS SAYING

Carla Vermaat

Also by Carla Vermaat

Tregunna

WHAT EVERY BODY IS SAYING

Carla Vermaat

Published in Great Britain in 2016 by
Carmichael Publishers, Cornwall
Copyright © Carla Vermaat 2016

A CIP catalogue record for this book
is available from the British Library

ISBN 978-0-9933339-3-4

Typeset in Meridien by Varwig Design
Cover Image © Carla Vermaat – Design by Varwig Design

Printed and bound in Great Britain by TJ International, Cornwall

Carmichael Publishers
www.carmichaelpublishers.co.uk

For my family

PROLOGUE

His mind seems to have got stuck in a loop. Head hanging low, he walks back to the small grassed picnic area dotted with wooden benches, only one of which bears the remains of a meal. A fly drifts in Holly's plastic beaker, still half filled with pineapple squash, her favourite. Paper plates are weighed down by cutlery. Crumbs are picked at by a sparrow, which cautiously watches his every movement. The basket, so thoughtfully packed by Justine before they left the holiday cottage that morning, is still on the bench just next to where she sat. On one end, Holly's tiny jacket hangs over the arm; a tea towel, smudged with crushed strawberry, lies crumpled on the other end.

His gaze drifts off, not wanting to look where they had sat not so long ago, where their dreams had been shattered in just a few moments.

Turning on his heels, his mobile vibrates in his pocket, but he ignores it. The only person he would like to speak to is Justine and he knows it won't be her.

He hesitates, stops, not knowing what to do. Or what not to. A weathered signpost points in the direction of a public footpath that disappears into a wooded area on the hill. Flies sit on dog litter next to the wooden style. A hand-painted sign reads: 'Dogs on leads please'.

All of a sudden, he finds himself shaking, his skin chilling as if he has been touched by a thousand tiny ice-cold hands. Incredulously, he stares down at where Holly had run in the grass less than half an hour ago, giggling happily, chasing bees and butterflies. Her bare arms and legs shining with sun cream so thoughtfully applied by Justine, her cheerful voice mixed with the sound of birds chattering in the shrubs and the gentle flow of the river beyond them.

Those last moments were so intense, so deeply etched in

his memory that he can clearly picture the scene again, hear their voices, feel their happiness.

Insects buzzed. A buzzard circled above a prey invisible to the human eye. The water in the river, slow and dark, sluggishly moved with the tide, for an instant disturbed by something under the surface. The bright white feathers of an egret were reflected in the shallow water. The smell filled the air with a sense of mud and decay.

But above all there was Justine. Her pretty face lifted up towards the sun, strands of hair the colour of honey had come loose from under her baseball cap, wafting around her head like seaweed swaying with the waves. The gentle curve of her body as she leaned on outstretched arms, legs crossed, wiggling her toes in bright blue sandals.

And Holly. His thoughts pause. Rewind. Play.

Their lovely little Holly, with a crust of a sandwich in her small chubby hand, too impatient to sit quietly with them, getting up, running off in front of them, laughing at their lazy warnings to stay away from the busy cycle trail. Holly, running towards the edge of the river with its cracked banks of dark mud. The water gently flowing towards the deepest parts, to the point where it merges with the salty water of the estuary. Holly, warming his heart, making it burst with pride and love, waving her hand as though she was about to spread her wings and fly away. Like he knew she would in maybe fifteen years time.

If only he hadn't reached out for Justine, her arms and shoulders bare and warm in the sun. Perhaps everything would have been different now. His life wouldn't be so brutally disturbed and everything would still be normal and happy, with future and full of promises. Like that new life, still so precious and tiny growing in her belly.

If only she hadn't turned to smile at him and he hadn't pulled her towards him, laughing at her faint attempts to protest, feeling aroused by the scent of her. For a few seconds the world had come to a halt and there had been only the two of them, an unbreakable bond, two hearts and two souls merged into one.

He can still feel the sun on her lips, smell the grass on her fingers.

And he can still hear the scream.

It seems ages before a police car pulls up. Two police officers get out, looking around as if they cannot believe their eyes. One, in her mid forties, wears the expression of someone who is trained to put off anyone who may even be considering wasting her time.

'You are Mr Walker? Charlie Walker?' she asks.

He scratches his head as if he has to find the right answer. 'That's me.'

'You made the call?'

'Yes.' His hand moves to his pocket. Then it dawns on him that it will be ridiculous to show her his mobile.

She produces a warrant card but his eyes are too watery to read her name next to her picture.

'Are you all right, Mr Walker?'

No, he isn't. How can he be, after what he's seen? After what he felt on his fingertips?

'Yes.' Unconsciously, he wipes his hands on his thighs.

Passing cyclists slow down, and some even stop to look around, curious at catching a glimpse of the police car parked on the grass verge, and to listen to the conversation between a police woman and a young man whose shoulders are slumped and his face is ashen.

The other officer joins them for a brief moment to introduce himself as Constable White before he motions the bystanders to get moving.

'Everything is under control. Please move on.'

'What's your full name and address please, Mr Walker?'

He stares at her, stunned, unsure suddenly how to respond. His planning had involved calling the police like a responsible citizen, but he hadn't thought further than that.

Now he is regretting everything. It would have been so much easier to forget about the whole thing, pick up his hired bike and leave this place.

'What's that got to do with anything?' He asks curtly, overwhelmed suddenly by the sense that he shouldn't have made the call.

Her face is blank and she repeats the question, producing a small notebook from her chest-pocket. She writes down his details, seemingly unnerved by his earlier message on the phone. Her colleague is younger, perhaps the same age as him, fulfilling the task of keeping curious passers-by away with a stoic face, every so often glancing at his older colleague as though he expects an encouraging smile or even a tap on the shoulder.

'Were you alone, Mr Walker?' With her toe she touches an empty carton of Justine's fruit juice, a wasp buzzing around it in an attempt to find an opening to absorb the sweetened remains.

'My wife's gone ahead. To the car.' Thinking of Justine, her face so pale, it was almost translucent, all he wants now is to run away and be with her, find comfort in her arms, in her presence. Give comfort to her in return. He reaches out, wanting to grab the police woman's arm and quickly pull her through the high grasses and bushes to what lies in the mud on the river bank.

She raises one eyebrow, not moving. 'Can you tell me what happened, Mr Walker?'

He almost wants to laugh, hard and loud. Perhaps this isn't the reality after all, but just a horrible nightmare. Perhaps he will wake up in a few minutes, cuddle up against Justine's warm body and tell her about it. She will take his hand between both hers, look at him with almost the same expression as when she looks at Holly, that specific look he sometimes secretly envies their daughter for. Together maybe they will smile and wonder about dreams and their possible meanings, which, in this case is quite obvious: his uncertainty about his ability to look after his young family, to protect them from all the evil in the world.

'Mr Walker?'

'I've already explained everything when I called the police station.' He is getting annoyed, his impatience to get away from this place growing with the certainty that there will be no quick escape, not even an easy way out. They will require more, much more than he can possibly give. Only they don't know that and they will keep trying until ... who knows when.

'It would help if you could tell us too.' Kind words that don't come simultaneously with her high-pitched voice.

'I just want to go. Please. I cannot leave my wife on her own. She is ...'

'Please answer my questions, Mr Walker.'

He stammers as he delivers the story, reliving it in all its horror. The moment he saw his daughter's chubby little hand. The moment when her white cotton dress with its printed coloured butterflies disappeared from sight. Her thin voice trailing behind her, singing incoherent shards of a nursery rhyme. Bees humming, the mixed colours of flowers, the sound of the rippling water from the river, the dark salted mud smelling as it dried in the sun. He is sure he won't be able to enjoy those simple things of life any more.

'Did you go after your daughter?'

'Of course I did!' They both notice the hesitation.

She frowns. Her radio crackles. She receives instructions from a voice which keeps breaking up after confirming that I am still here, that she's taking my statement now, and that her colleague is securing the place. She seems unnerved by the messages, but PC White jumps into action with a nervous expression on his face, and opens the boot of the police car to retrieve a roll of blue and white police tape.

'Shall I ...?'

'Wait a mo, Lee, we don't want to make fools of ourselves, do we?'

11

'I guess not.' He stands awkwardly, one foot on the cycle track, seriously considering putting the tape back into the car.

'So you went after her,' she resumes.

'Yes.'

'Your wife too?'

'Not straight away.' With a growing sense of guilt, he remembers his reluctance about leaving Justine, about closing his eyes, enjoying the pressure of her warm and sweet lips on his, her hands teasingly creeping under his shirt. 'She was clearing the table.'

'And then, Sir? What happened, please?'

Tears are blurring his vision, both police officers are lost in an impenetrable mist. All he can see is the top of her blonde hair as Holly disappeared behind the shrubs.

He swallows. 'She … she waved at me.'

'Who did, Sir?'

He can't believe that a woman, any woman, can be so insensitive. She's a policewoman for heaven's sake, trained to deal with all sorts of circumstances, trained to remain calm, soothing those who need comfort, implacable towards suspects. Act like a human being, not like a robot.

'Go on, Mr Walker.' Her colleague nods in encouragement, an expression of pity and compassion in his eyes that suddenly puts all the afternoon's events into perspective.

Unconsciously, he straightens his back and shoulders, as though he has finally come to a decision. 'As I said, she was waving at me. Well … incredulously, that's what I thought. Ridiculous.' His voice breaks in a half-sob, half-laugh. He swallows back a sour, burning blob of nausea. 'I'm sorry. I … I need to be with my wife. She's pregnant.'

The police woman sighs and he expects to see a flash of anger but she quietly gestures him to go on, a hint of sympathy in her brown eyes. 'Of course, Sir. We fully understand, but for now …'

'We need you to tell us everything, Mr Walker,' her young colleague interrupts.

He nods, defeated suddenly, realising that there is no point in trying to hurry them towards the riverbank. It is too late anyway.

'All I could see was her hand sticking out of the mud.' His voice almost fails him. 'Only her hand.'

1

If anything, I wish I had paid more attention to the screen when my mobile rings. DCI Jason Guthrie is very close to the bottom of my contacts list. Professionally, I can't delete him, which is the only reason why he is still on it. Most times I do check, let the phone go to answer phone as soon as I know it is him.

'Yes?'

We rarely exchange how-are-you's or any other informal greetings. Between us exists a mutual hostility that allows us to be as curt as possible, if and when we can't avoid one another.

'Tregunna, listen, I'm a bit short of staff …'

Beside me a monitor erupts in a single high-pitched bleep. I hesitate, waiting for Guthrie to go on, meanwhile letting my eyes wander to the equipment beside the bed. There are plastic pouches hanging from a metal pole on wheels, transparent liquids drip slowly into tubes that are the vital link between life and death. The monitor keeps careful watch that this lifeline remains intact. A green light blinks, rows of coloured lines track slowly across the screen, then disappear and the next set appears. Some of the lines are almost flat, others jump up and down like a landscape of a distant mountain range.

'Where are you?' Guthrie demands.

I look at the face on the pillow. The deep ebony of her hair, half shaven where she's had surgery when they removed the bullet, looks even blacker in dramatic contrast to the white marble of her skin. I can see the blonde line of her roots, which suddenly makes me think about finding a hairdresser. Her eyes are closed. She doesn't notice when I'm here, she won't notice when I go. Or perhaps she does. In a vegetative state like hers, who can tell?

'I'm on my way home, Sir.' The lie is as blunt as his outburst.

I am well aware that this makes him none the wiser. I could be travelling from anywhere in the country, with many hours ahead on my drive back to the southwest.

'Right.' He stops, not asking me again where I am, which tells me that he is preoccupied with something more important than our conversation. I hear noises in the background. Legs of cheap chairs scraping on the lino floor, the clacking of keyboards. Voices, curt, to the point. No silly remarks, no cheerful banter, no laughter, only a distinctive sense of urgency.

'How can I help, Sir?'

'I need you to do an interview.' We both sense the underlying emergency, otherwise he wouldn't have admitted to needing me.

'What about Jennette?'

'Who?'

'DC Penrose.'

'Oh. Yes. She's busy with something else. Ehm ... they found something suspicious on the other side of the coast. She's dealing with that.'

'Okay.'

He mutters something to someone else, then his arrogant voice hits me once more. 'Listen, Tregunna. I have no time for bullshit. I have more important things to do than deal with a nutcase.'

'I'm sure you have, Sir.' My sarcasm is lost on him.

In contrast, I have plenty of time. Even if it is for what he calls a nutcase. Although my consultant hasn't officially declared so, I am fit for work, and ready. At least, I think so. Perhaps it is not the entire truth but I am fed up staying at home and doing little else than staring at the ceiling and becoming addicted to soaps and quiz shows and repeated episodes of decades old comedies. But having my superior offering me the discarded crumbs from his job is only adding salt to my wounds.

'Sir, I ...'

He interrupts. 'Listen, Tregunna, this man is pestering me. He's calling me about every five minutes. And I don't like that at all.'

'Perhaps it is important.'

'Whatever his reasons, he won't give up. I've told him that he'll be taken care of as soon as possible. But right now, I have no time to deal with him. Not at this very moment.' He stops for breath, or rather, he waits for my reaction.

'What is going on?' I ask.

He tries to suppress a sigh. 'Believe it or not, we are dealing with a serious terrorist threat. Which, I hope you'll understand, is top secret information for the moment. The message was received in Exeter, but the threat is right on our doorstep. And it is really serious, Tregunna.' Even in these circumstances, he still manages to sound pompous and conceited. He's already having visions of being called the hero of the day, for dealing with terrorists and bomb threats, and successfully averting lots of deaths and casualties.

Fixing my eyes on the silent figure in the hospital bed beside me, I straighten my back. The comfortable chair that was standing next to the bed during my previous visits seems to have gone awol. Instead, I am sitting on the unforgiving hard surface of a three-legged stool.

A nurse passes in the corridor. I've come to know most of them here, sadly, and I imagine that I know exactly which one of them is now humming and softly singing a repetitive tune. I am certain from the sound of her footsteps that it is the blonde girl with a puffy round face and a fair chance of future problems with obesity.

'Where exactly is the threat?' I ask.

'The more people who know at this stage, the more chance we'll have to prevent an outbreak of panic.' Guthrie's arrogant reply is prompt, letting me know that any further questions are wasting his time.

A terrorist threat is the worst case scenario for a policeman. For a brief moment I don't envy him the task ahead. 'Okay.'

16

'Between you an me, it's at White River in St Austell.'

'I see.' White River means it's really is a serious threat. A modern shopping centre built not so long ago to attract visitors from all over the county and beyond. A perfect place for terrorists to target and cause as many deaths and casualties as possible to make their point. Whatever that point may be.

'I presume you'd like me to work on something else?'

'Of course.' He doesn't even have the decency to show his relief that I am willing to take over an undesirable task. 'I'll have someone text you the address. Listen to the man when you get there, no doubt you will be able to quieten him a bit.' He manages to make it sound an accusation rather than a compliment. 'Explain to him that you are no less than my right hand officer. Whatever. But don't let him call me any more.'

'All right.' A perverse part of me is considering saying that I will do what he wants as long as he says 'please'. But I sense that this is not the time for silly jokes that will cause his blood pressure to rise sky-high.

'Good.' He sounds very close to thanking me, but there appears to be someone else who is in need of his attention and he disconnects abruptly.

Seconds later, I receive a text message with a name and an address on the outskirts of Newquay. No further details, not even an inkling of what it might be about.

'Everything all right?' Tall and skinny with spiky black hair and a stud in her nose, one of the nurses stops in the doorway, pointing at the silent body in the bed beside me. Her plucked eyebrows, more like thin lines, rise as she sees me with my mobile, but she just shrugs. Under her uniform are signs of a preference for gipsy clothing. Or perhaps she is a hippie in her spare time.

'I guess so.'

She observes the patient with a faint smile that pulls the corners of her mouth into a less grumpy expression. 'No changes?'

I shake my head, wishing I can tell her otherwise. We both know that every day means less hope for recovery. The bullet that went into the patient's brain has been taken out, but she is still locked in a coma. Her heart is pumping and she breathes without the assistance of a machine, but other than that there is no activity.

'I'm sure it's all going to be okay.' The nurse sounds unconvincing, but we let the words hang in the air. She straightens the sheet across the bed, gently touching a motionless hand. On her chest pocket is a badge that tells me her name is Mirabelle. It makes me wonder what her parents were expecting, or hoping, when she was born.

'Yes,' I say obediently. 'She's doing great.'

'She'll love your flowers.'

She gestures and I turn. I did notice earlier that there was a fresh bouquet of mixed pink and white flowers in a glass vase on the window sill, but I haven't given it much attention. Rising to my feet, I reach for the little white card that is attached to one of the pink roses, opening it with my thumb. 'Get well soon, my darling.'

A shiver runs down my spine. 'When was this delivered?'

'I don't know. I just assumed that you brought them for her and …'

'I didn't.'

Her gaze tells me that I should consider the possibility that the patient in the bed may well be able to hear us. She is warning me not to say things that may cause distress, that may set the monitors off bleeping in alarm. Or worse, cause a sudden fatal pressure on the brain.

'Well, then someone else must have brought them in.' As she leans towards me, she reads the message on the card. 'Hmm, nice one.'

Although it isn't signed, I know who sent the flowers. I am tempted to tear the card from the bouquet, but I decide to wait and do it as soon as the nurse has gone. She won't understand the situation and I don't feel like explaining it to her.

I take the white hand in mine, pressing it gently with my fingertips, hoping that there will be a response. There isn't. Not today, but maybe tomorrow ...

'I'm sorry, Becca, but I'll have to go,' I say, both to Mirabelle and the patient. Becca. I find it easier to call her by her real name than by the name she used when we met. 'I will be back, I promise.'

As though we are expecting some reply, Mirabelle and I both stare at the white face. Even the lips are deathly pale. I think I see her eyelids flutter, but Mirabelle doesn't react, so I guess it must be a trick of my imagination. I kiss her forehead just under the bandage and leave the room without looking back.

I find it unnerving that a person can be dead and alive at the same time.

Penmarric Drive is a long street that twists through a bleak-looking housing estate like an octopus that finds itself trapped in a glass bottle. There are side streets off it that end abruptly in small parking areas and dried out ditches, creating perfect escape routes for anyone on the run. All the streets are lined with modest, identical terraced houses, adding to the confusion. The whole estate is depressing and claustrophobic. I drive round aimlessly, returning to what looks suspiciously like the corner I have come across at least two times already. There seems no logic to the numbering of the houses. A block numbered 36 to 43 is facing a similar one with numbers 221 to 231 whilst the next block of houses is numbered 84 to 92. The Satnav isn't helping either as Penmarric Drive shares one postcode.

I stop on a small car park facing what must have been a playground for young children when the estate was built years ago. A single car tyre dangles from a rusty frame that has room for at least three proper swings. A mother stands patiently with a pram, a toddler running around her in circles, arms wide spread as though the child is imagining being a bird or an airplane.

Hanging around the remains of what appears to be a bus shelter is a group of youths varying in age from ten years old to young adults. They follow me with their eyes full of suspicion, exchanging what feels like insults aimed at me. Scenes from American police films spring to mind and for a moment I consider offering them money to protect my car. The thought makes me smile, but I am still not sure if I will find my car in one piece when I come back. I may be prejudiced, but it is how I feel when I stop close enough for them to realise that I am addressing them.

Opening the window a few inches I say, 'I am looking for

Lobb. Any idea where I can find him?' I make a vague gesture towards a block of detached houses, half of which have broken windows and front doors boarded up.

There is a ripple of sarcastic laughter.

'Who wants to know?'

I cast a quick glance over my shoulder. 'If it isn't the bloke behind me, then it's me.'

Less laughter, a bit more fidgety, as though each of their brains is contemplating the next move forward. One of them steps closer. The appointed spokesman. At five foot two he downed by the others, but that doesn't make him less important. Perhaps the opposite. He is wearing low-slung jeans that reveal the brand of his underwear, which is neither expensive nor impressive, and a faded green sweatshirt. His bare feet are encased in grubby trainers with broken laces. The sides of his head are shaven, with a tuft of dark brown hair kept into place with gel.

'Looking for trouble, mate?'

'I am trying to find Patrick Lobb.'

'Why?' he asks, chewing gum without closing his mouth.

'That is between Lobb and me.' I'm already fed up with this pointless display of masculinity.

He gazes at me, not sure how to react, feeling his superiority slip away. He nods. 'All right, mate. But no trouble, hey?'

I shrug with an air of indifference, which appears to be accepted as an appropriate response.

'There.' The youth points with his tuft. 'End of that block. With the yellow door.'

'Thanks.' I turn and drive the short distance to where he's pointing. Getting out of my car, I'm half expecting to be punched and robbed of my phone and wallet as soon as my back is turned. Smug laughter follows me, but that's all. Slightly ashamed all of a sudden, the thought comes to me that my prejudices are probably completely unfounded.

A concrete path bordered by unkempt grass, littered with

daisies and dandelions, leads to a yellow front door, slightly ajar. I can smell fish and chips and cigarettes and hear music mingled with the dull bleeps of a computer game. I knock hard, wait a minute with no response, then count to ten before knocking again.

Then a voice calls out, 'The door is open!'

A narrow hallway is lined with coats on cheap hooks, shoes and boots in all sizes scattered underneath. A staircase with a threadbare brown carpet leads to where the computer sounds are coming from.

'In here!' someone shouts.

The living room has three huge sofas against each of the walls. One is beige with brown cloths on the armrests presumably to cover stains and cigarette marks. One is dark green faux leather and the third is navy satin, printed with pink roses. In each corner is a wooden cabinet with glass doors on top and a display of bric-a-brac on the only shelf. A fake fireplace dominates the other wall, and above it hangs a large flat-screen TV showing a cheerful weather lady announcing a yellow alert for torrential rain and gale force winds.

A man is sitting in the middle of the dark green sofa opposite the TV, a remote control in one hand, a bottle of beer in the other. He is clearly tall and heavy, if not overweight, with thinning hair and a grey stubble as if he is not sure whether to grow a beard or not.

'Mr Lobb?'

'Who are you?' He doesn't move. The weather lady has finished her warning of a potential deluge and is replaced by a commercial with a man shouting so loudly that I can only imagine this will lose rather than gain any custom.

'I am Detective Inspector Andy Tregunna.' I show him my ID. 'You called the police station.'

'I did.' He nods, gazing at the remote as though he's wondering what it's for. He doesn't press a button to mute the sound, let alone turn it off. On the TV, happy families now come down huge slides at some very sunny resort, one of those popular UK holiday attractions where the entrance fees cost as much as a week's holiday abroad.

'Sorry, I think I expected more of you to come than just one,' the man says disapprovingly.

'I'm sorry.'

'You're not wearing a uniform.'

'No.' It don't think it's time to tell him that I'm not even officially on duty, that I'm only here because of a heavy workload and lack of staff. And because Guthrie has more important issues to deal with.

'Elsie? Police are here!' he shouts, a sense of urgency in his voice. A split second later a woman appears in the doorway. Hands clutching the front of a flowery apron, her eyes are red and her bottom lip trembles. Fear is etched on her face and she cannot hide the tremor in her voice. 'Are you here to tell us ...?'

Inwardly, I curse Guthrie. At least he could have had the decency to tell me why he sent me to this family. Clearly, the couple are in distress and I haven't a clue what I'm supposed to say or do. Guthrie is a snob and no doubt he has already decided that the couple is of zero importance. The bomb threat is evidently top of his priority list. Understandable in a way but, in his position, he should have dealt with other matters in the same manner. Sending me is perhaps his way of showing his superiority, but it also indicates his lack of professionalism.

I clear my throat, hesitant and embarrassed. 'Actually, I've been sent to you for some questions.'

'Questions?' Lobb rises with surprising fitness and elegance. He is even taller than I expected and I have to look up at him as he stands opposite me. His steel blue eyes stare cold and menacingly between his ruddy fat cheeks and bushy brows. 'Questions? How about you answer our questions?'

I don't know what to say. As far as I am concerned the page is completely blank.

'Have you got any news?' the woman wrings her hands. The desperate plea of a worried mother.

'Not yet, no,' I manage to say. 'Do you mind if I sit down and you tell me everything you know?'

Elsie Lobb drops her head and disappears to the kitchen after having offered me the inevitable cup of tea. Her husband gestures me towards the flowery sofa and then kneels in a corner to open a cupboard and retrieve a tattered shoebox. He grabs a handful of photographs from the box. Most of them seem to be taken at school, children posing for the camera, boys and girls alone, in pairs or groups. Photos in all sorts of sizes are shuffled around as he rummages through them, until he freezes to a sudden halt when he finds the one he is looking for: a school portrait of a young girl with curly red-blond hair, blue eyes as pale as his. A gap between her front teeth.

'That is our Leanne.' His voice suggesting that I am now fully briefed, I look for words to say in turn that I am none the wiser, but cannot find any.

'You can take it with you, but we would like to have it back,' he adds. 'It is the most recent we have.'

Picking up the photo between my thumb and index finger, I get the sinking feeling that Guthrie got it all wrong and has sent me here to compensate for his own inadequacies. My efforts to find the right words are interrupted by Elsie, carrying a tray with three cups and saucers. Tea spoons rattle in a small glass.

'Would you like a biscuit, inspector?' she asks absent-mindedly, lowering herself onto the edge of the sofa without waiting for my response. As her eyes lock onto the photo, her lips silently form a single name. It could be a silent scream or whisper of shock.

'What happened?' I ask.

It seems an acceptable question.

'She was going to Newquay, yesterday. Se was supposed to be going to school-friend's sleepover party.' Lobb's sigh is loud and deep. 'Only there wasn't one.'

It sounds like he is reading mechanically from a slip of paper, which somehow makes them emotional. His wife is now sobbing quietly, shoulders dropped in defeat. She is already thinking the very worst.

Gathering my thoughts, I ask cautiously, 'What time did you last see her?'

Nodding, he gestures with his large hands. 'Elsie did. Yesterday morning. Before she left for school. Elsie saw her out as she and our Janice went to catch the school bus.' He stares at the photo as though apologising to their daughter. 'I didn't see her at all. I had an early shift. They were all still asleep when I got up and left at half past five.'

'What do you do for a living, Mr Lobb?' I ask, attempting small talk to make him a bit more comfortable.

'I'm a butcher.'

'Do you have a shop somewhere?'

'No.' His expression tells me that he would have loved to have been able to say yes. 'No. I work for a big company.' The passion long gone, he probably just works to get bread on the table for his family. Nothing more.

Glancing briefly at her husband, Elsie speaks, her voice low and husky with despair. 'She didn't go to school today. Our Janice is two years younger than Leanne. She discovered that Leanne was not there and called us.'

She starts sobbing again, her fear etched on her pale, tired face.

'Do you have any other children?'

'Janice and three younger boys.'

'Where are they now?'

Elsie sniffs, dabbing a propped handkerchief printed with tiny flowers against her nose. 'At me sister's. She lives down the road.'

If this is as bad as my feelings tell me, I'll have to speak to the children as well, but for now it will have to wait.

'Does it happen often that she's not at school?'

'Certainly not. She never misses a lesson. She wants to be a lawyer.' Patrick Lobb cannot hold back a chuckle filled with a mixture of embarrassment and pride. Then tears begin to fill his eyes, but none escape down his cheeks and through his stubble.

'I mean … did you check at school?'

'Of course we did. We wouldn't bother calling the police unnecessarily. Janice needed something from Leanne so she went to her classroom. She called us immediately. Well, she alerted Elsie, as I was at work. Elsie called the school and they confirmed she wasn't there. They assumed she'd been taken ill.'

'Was she at school at all yesterday?'

'Oh yes. She was there and we thought she had taken the bus into town, where that other girl lives. Carensa. We've spoken to her on the phone but she didn't know anything about a sleepover party.'

'So Leanne went to school yesterday as usual, she left the school but instead of going home, she went somewhere else and you believed she was at that friend's house, but she never arrived there.' I hope this is not as frightening as it sounds.

Lobb nods, catching his wife's haunted gaze, revealing what the last hours must have been like: exhausted with fear, not knowing whether to wait for her to come home and beat the hell out of her, or go out and look for her, not knowing where to look, hopes fading, scared of what they might discover if they would find her.

'Did she do that often?' Mentioning the word 'lie' at this stage wouldn't be a wise move, but it must have dawned on them already that the girl wasn't always telling the truth.

'Never.' He shakes his head, then adds hesitantly, 'Not that we're aware of anyway.'

'What is the friend's full name? The one with the supposed sleepover party?'

'Carensa Pencreek. They're in the same year.' Looks are exchanged, a conversation unspoken.

'We've tried to call Leanne's best friend, but that is kind of difficult. Her family won't speak to us.' His mouth has tightened and there is a sudden flare of anger in his eyes.

'Siobhan,' Elsie says by way of explanation.

'And you're sure that Leanne hasn't stayed the night with her friend Siobhan instead of Carensa?'

'Definitely not.' It is Elsie who answers, fury has replaced her anxiety for a few moments. 'Look here, inspector. My husband's a butcher. I clean offices. We live on a council estate. We are true honest people, but Siobhan's parents have made it clear that they don't like it at all that our girls are best friends. We're not good enough for them. Siobhan is not allowed to come here, Leanne is not at all welcome at theirs.'

Nodding, I make a mental note to come back to this point later. For now, it clouds their objectivity and more so, their ability to answer my questions with full concentration. They have called friends and relatives, schoolmates and other parents, they have talked to neighbours and even to the youths that seem to have adopted the bus shelter as the main place for their gatherings.

'How old is Leanne?'

'She's just turned fourteen.'

A dangerous age. Trapped in no man's land between child and woman. Vulnerable. Innocent. Susceptible to persuasion and temptation. An easy target for predators.

'Did you talk to anyone at school? Did anyone see her get on the bus? Or where she got off?'

'Not that we know of.' His eyes tell me clearly that I am supposed to find out all of this for him. My job is to find his daughter.

Elsie frowns, her eyes fixed on her clasped hands. In front of her, the tea is growing cold, the biscuits forgotten. 'A cousin of mine saw her on the bus to Newquay. She doesn't know Siobhan, or Carensa, so she didn't know if Leanne was with anyone. The schoolchildren normally go on the top of the double decker bus. They make such noise that other people stay downstairs.'

The picture clear, I know the feeling. 'But your cousin didn't notice there was someone ... acting suspiciously?'

'She would've told me if there was.'

'Did your cousin see Leanne getting off the bus?'

'Sadly, no. She got off earlier.'

My questions seem to give them some relief because they're no longer alone in this. But at the same time, they become more anxious as the realisation is dawning on them that one of any parent's worse nightmares is becoming a reality.

'Okay.' I clear my throat, trying to sound neutral and professional. 'I'll need names and addresses. As much detail as you can remember.'

Once more exchanging glances, Lobb retrieves a sheet of paper from between a pile of newspapers and magazines on the floor next to his feet. It is a list in a neat and tidy handwriting. 'Elsie's done that already,' he says with a strange, sad smile. 'We've talked about it all the time.'

A small lump in my throat makes it impossible to answer. I see hope flutter across their faces. Eyes like a loyal, trustful dog's left tied to a deserted post because its owners can or will no longer keep it.

Retrieving my mobile I wonder what to tell Guthrie.

3

The waiting room is crowded with the smell of warm bodies. An electric fan on the reception desk is attempting to make the atmosphere a little less close. Mostly couples, or patients supported by a relative or friend, sit and wait, quietly or talking softly, comparing their ailments, and bracing themselves for what is to come once they're called in to see the doctor. Good or bad news, giving fresh hope or shattering it, the waiting is always nerve-wracking.

I choose the first available vacant seat, close enough to the exit to take full advantage of a burst of fresh air when someone enters or leaves. Or perhaps the truth is that I like the idea of being able to run away quickly, without causing a stir, without raising too many eyebrows.

Noticing that I seem to be the only unaccompanied patient, I am perched between two women. Both are in their late sixties. One is accompanied by her husband who seems to be dozing, or attempting to doze; the other has her daughter with her who is obsessed with her mobile phone and ignores the sign with a polite request not to use phones inside the hospital buildings.

Two volunteer ladies are trying to negotiate a trolley between the tangle of patients' outstretched legs, and bags full of with unnecessary items: extra jackets and cardigans, books they won't read, spare glasses. The trolley is carrying an irregularity of mugs - one full of rattling teaspoons - a plastic milk bottle, a glass bowl with sugar cubes and a Celebrations tin. Chatting away cheerfully to one another, the volunteer ladies are keeping a close eye on the newcomers, addressing them with a warm and understanding smile and offering hot drinks and biscuits.

'Would you like tea or coffee?' Her badge tells me her name is Florence, representing a cancer charity.

It feels like I'm faced with Murphy's law: if I accept a drink, I will be called in to the doctor straight away and won't know what to do with my mug, and if I decline, it will probably be ages before I get called in.

'Thank you,' I decide and the daughter with the mobile phone says, 'Tea please,' without even noticing that the offer didn't involve her.

Dressed in a black skirt and a pink-and-white striped knitted pullover, a woman opposite me starts a conversation with the woman by my side as their husbands nod and smile briefly in recognition. Appearing to be regular visitors here, an exchange of rather detailed medical information follows, duly listened to by me and other patients. I am suddenly anxious that the conversation will extend to me and that I will be asked to share my specific medical details and experiences too. Quickly picking up a magazine, I flick through the pages and try to concentrate on articles about luxury holiday cruises around the world and glamorous interior home designs that most people can't afford. Perhaps these magazines are so popular because people like to have unrealistic dreams, especially in a waiting room of a cancer ward.

A nurse enters the waiting room. Her eyes drift across our faces, as if she's trying to work out who'll be her next victim. Glancing at a sheet of paper, she calls a name. Edgar Harries rises from his seat, glancing nervously at his pink-striped wife, who also makes a move to get up. Sounding self-assured, presumably due to experience, the nurse tells Mrs Harries to wait here and her husband will be back in a minute: it's only for a blood test. Mrs Harries nods. Her eyes are like deep ponds, dark and full of fear.

We fall into a conspiracy of collective silence. Mrs Harries shifts uncomfortably, as though the departure of her husband has deprived her of the ability to talk. Without a word, lips pursed and eyes downcast, she gets up and sneaks out of the waiting room, leaving the rest of us in an even more unsettled silence. We glance furtively at one another, uncertain and slightly nervous. The woman next to me, her new companion gone, seems to be casting around, looking for a new victim. As her eyes settle on me, I squeeze mine shut quickly, dropping the magazine on my lap to appear to be dozing off.

My thoughts wander towards the missing girl. Leanne. Somehow it feels wrong to be sitting here while I should be looking for her. Leanne is out there somewhere. By choice, on an illicit trip with her best friend or with a boyfriend she hasn't told anyone about? Or something else, the unthinkable, has happened to her? For all I know, she might be right here in Treliske after an accident, or an attack. Hurt. Wounded. Unidentified.

The two vacant seats are soon taken by another couple. Anxiously I recognise Mr Wood who had his operation the day after I had mine. For a few days we shared a room, allowing us an intimacy that seems to make us both embarrassed now. I stare at his stomach, trying to detect the bulge of his stoma bag under his baggy shirt. He glances at me in the same way and we nod a mutual greeting, silently agreeing that none of the other people need know about our shared history and circumstances. Unfortunately, Mrs Wood thinks otherwise. Her mouth opens. I can see all the revealing questions being formed in her head but before she can emit the first one, the appearance of Mr Cole draws her attention in a different direction. Caught by several wary pairs of eyes, he has a smile for all of us, but his eyes dart over the tops of our heads, not seeing the individual patients. Leaning towards the nurse behind the desk, who hands him a patient file, he looks up when Mrs Wood clears her throat and says, 'Mr Tregunna.'

Mr Cole turns his head and nods briefly in my direction. I try telepathy to make him call my name, as he looks down at the file in his hand. He does call a name but not mine. Margaret Brookham. Nervous suddenly, the woman next to me fumbles with the buttons of her coat, unsure whether to undo them. Picking up her handbag and holding a scarf that tries to slip down off her shoulder, she drops a walking stick. It falls on the lino floor with a clatter like gunshot which forces her daughter to drag her attention away from her mobile phone. With pursed lips and eyes like daggers, she bends to pick up the walking stick, stuffing her mobile phone in her pocket, reluctantly following her mother.

'Mrs Wood.' I nod in reply, not sounding encouragingly.

'How are you, Mr Tregunna? We had good news, didn't we, Roy? The tumour appears to be shrinking. But ...' She hesitates with a frown, uncertain whether it would be appropriate to go on. 'That's what they say. Then why, we wonder, does he still need treatment with ...'

'Carole.' Roy Wood pokes his elbow in her side.

'Andy Tregunna?'

Not saved by the bell but by a young nurse. Her warm grey eyes are full of sympathy. A pair of dark-rimmed glasses sits on top of her forehead, strands of blonde hair stand upright around them. For the briefest of moments I contemplate whether to pretend it isn't me she has called, as if Mr Tregunna hasn't showed up for his appointment. But Carole Wood is staring at me like a schoolteacher who knows what her pupils are up to, and her husband inclines his head, reading my thoughts.

I follow the dancing blonde hair along corridors with green lino on the floor and strip lights on the ceiling. One light is flickering intermittently. Framed prints of sunny seascapes on the walls attempt to improve the gloomy atmosphere. We pass beech wood doors with green plastic handles. One of them is open. I peer inside and see the examination couch is empty, while Margaret Brookham and her daughter sit quietly in the corner, one staring into oblivion with fingers nervously adjusting the zipper of her handbag, the other leaning forward, elbows on knees and tapping the screen of her mobile phone as if it's her last chance to make a connection with the rest of the world. Further along the corridor, we come across a male nurse standing at a water cooler, a pink folder under his arm, balancing two plastic cups in one hand as he fills a third.

'Here we are, Mr ...' She needs to check her sheet. '... Tregunna.'

The examination couch against the wall in the room I am ushered into is covered with a white paper sheet. A tray of empty test tubes sits alongside a box with hypodermic needles and bandages on a small side-table. Gesturing me to sit down, the nurse closes the door behind us. The walls are painted a pale yellowy-green, the only decoration is a framed poster of a desert scene: Bedouins sitting stoically on camels, the outline of a pyramid just visible in the distance. Perhaps someone chose the picture as a reminder of a happy holiday, but I suddenly feel the cruelty of it.

Questioning me about my health and well-being, my diet and toilet habits, my physical state in general, and my mental state, the nurse listens, frowning her thin arched eyebrows. Yet the smile plastered on her face remains intact: she's too young to understand what lies behind my answers.

Once she has ticked the relevant boxes on the sheet on her clipboard, I am weighed, measured and then relieved of so many tubes of blood that I almost suggest she should weigh me again.

She tugs her clipboard under her arm. 'Have you brought someone with you?'

I feel like a child facing the teacher having forgotten my homework. 'No.'

Studying my face for a few seconds, she shrugs. 'Please don't hesitate to ask for assistance if you require anything, Mr Tregunna. We're here to help and support you.'

She sounds like the messenger of very bad news.

'Thank you.'

'Mr Cole will see you shortly.'

She disappears with a smile, her notes and my blood. Thinking of the nurse's last words, I regret that I haven't told Lauren about the appointment. I didn't want her to get too involved. I couldn't face her sympathy, her pity. But I would have loved if she'd been here with me now.

Ten minutes later the same nurse emerges, letting me know, regretfully, that Mr Cole has had an emergency call; a patient he operated on in the morning urgently requires his attention. Her smile tells me that she's unable to detect my mixed feelings of relief and annoyance. Staring at her clipboard again, she tells me the options: I can wait - but it will probably take a while - or make a new appointment at the desk.

'Either way, I think it's best to make your way back to the waiting room.' Broadening her smile, she adds persuasively, 'There are magazines and papers and I'm sure the ladies with coffee and tea are still there.'

And other patients, I think. Nevertheless, I follow her obediently along the corridors as if I'm unable to find my way to the waiting area. The nurse at the desk is speaking on the phone, chewing the end of a pencil and staring at her computer screen. Every once in a while she looks up nervously, wondering how to finish the call quickly but politely. Instead of joining the queue, I follow the woman who is struggling back with the walking stick and her daughter still typing messages in her phone. Holding open the door, I accept Margaret Brookham's warm and earnest smile but receive not even a glance from the daughter. There are much more important things in life than offering a polite smile.

Five minutes later, I walk between the maze of hospital buildings which make it look more like a small village of scattered, partially renovated buildings than a place where people are born and die, and anything in between.

The Air Ambulance helicopter, its blades still and quiet, is parked in front of the A&E department. Briefly wondering whether Leanne's body has been found, I dismiss the idea instantly with a fleeting optimism that she'll probably be home by now. Safe. Unharmed.

As if on cue, my mobile vibrates in my pocket. Half hoping that it's Patrick Lobb to tell me the good news, I look at the screen. It isn't him. I recognise the number.

'Lauren. Hi.'

'Hi.'

I pause one or two seconds too long. It's probably my guilty conscience.

'I hope I'm not interrupting anything?' she asks.

'No.' My reply is curt, guilt undisguised.

When I went for the result of the first scan after surgery, Lauren had invited me to her home afterwards to share the news with her. Good or bad. At the time, it seemed like a good idea, but it wasn't. When I gave her a brief summary of what I'd been told, her face crumpled and I saw pity in her eyes. And regret.

It wouldn't be fair on her to take our growing friendship further. Not even with tiny steps. I knew it, but I didn't act on it. I was, and I am, a coward when it comes to feelings.

'It's only ...' Her voice is a tad lower. 'The boys ...'

I can hear her ten-year-old sons in the background. They are identical twins. According to statistics, they can read each other's mind, finish their sentences and break an arm on the same day. Surprisingly, Stuart and Joe seem to argue a lot.

'Stu! Please! Can you be quiet for a moment? I'm talking to Andy.' Mentioning my name seems to have the opposite effect. More noise and shouting.

'Andy? Sorry, are you still there?'

'I am.' A car with a blaring radio passes.

She listens, uncertain. 'Or shall I call you back later?'

'No, mum! Ask him now!' Stuart or Joe shout back.

'You promised, mum!' The other one whines. At least they seem to agree on something.

'Okay. Andy, ehm ... Friday is my birthday and I was wondering ...'

She stops when she hears the siren of an ambulance approaching behind me. I can sense her brain ticking as she wonders, realises even, where I am. The ambulance's siren stops abruptly as it draws up opposite the Air Ambulance, where two men have just climbed in, gesturing teasingly, and laughing at the arriving colleagues.

'Go on, Lauren,' I say softly.

'It's Joe's idea but ...'

'No mum, it's mine!'

'Oh, will you two stop it now?' Her voice is high and there is a tremble in it. I can hear regret also. 'Andy?' She composes herself. 'Sorry, I shouldn't have called.'

'Mum!' Two excited boys are by her side.

'Andy?' A young voice.

'Yes.' I sigh. 'Make it quick please, whichever of the two you are.'

'I'm Joe.' He chuckles. 'Mum can't hear the difference on the phone either.' Another chuckle. 'Stuart's taking mum into the kitchen, because we'd like it to be a surprise.'

'Okay.'

'Its mum's birthday on Friday and we're off school.'

'Why is that?'

'Mums birthday?'

'No. You being off school on Friday.'

'Something to do with our teachers.' It doesn't interest him in the slightest. All he cares about is the extra day off.

Muffled sounds in the background again. Lauren, still embarrassed, half-objecting to Joe speaking to me.

'We would like to take Mum out to the Lobster Hatchery in Padstow.'

'And you think she will like that?' I ask, suppressing a smile.

He takes a deep breath. Considers. 'And take her out for lunch.'

'And you are inviting me as well?'

'Yes. No. We thought … that you can invite us for lunch. I mean Mum. For her birthday.' There is a long pause. Joe speaks first. Taken aback all of a sudden as he clearly expected more enthusiasm from me. 'Ehm … it was just an idea.'

Behind him a door is closed hard. 'Joe! I warned you! Give me the phone!'

It's so easy to picture her, with her ginger curls cascading down her shoulders or tied up on top of her head, her eyes blue and pale against her face, flushed with embarrassment.

'Andy?' She sounds breathless. 'Andy, please ignore what

Joe just said to you, please.'

'Lauren, about your birthday,' I say gently, 'I'll pick the three of you up on Friday at ten, if that's okay with you?'

'I didn't mean …'

'I know. But your son has just invited me to your birthday party.'

4

'Is it possible to meet, sir?'

As usual, DC Jennette Penrose is curt and to the point, not wasting time with unnecessary pleasantries. She calls me when I park at a superstore, drawing up a mental list of groceries. I can hear her fingers tapping her keyboard. Phones ring in the background. Voices of colleagues. Muttering. Disconnecting with a grunt or careful excitement. It brings a pang of jealousy as I think of the camaraderie in the busy working environment. Perhaps it is more appealing when you're not part of it any more.

'No problem, Jennette. Any news on the missing girl?'

'Not that I've heard.' She wants to move on to her own topic.

'The terrorist threat at White River?'

'That's been dealt with.' There is an edge of irony in her voice and she takes a moment to explain. 'Apparently it was some nutcase having picked up information from the internet on how to produce a bomb. Nowhere near anything that could possibly cause any damage. Though the video made it look very serious.'

She has lowered her voice. I presume DCI Guthrie's mood hasn't improved. It has forced him to reconsider options and opportunities, high and low risk, setting his priorities. He got it wrong. He must have realised by now that calling Patrick Lobb a 'nutcase' and handing Leanne's disappearance over to me, wasn't a very clever move. Yet, in his shoes, I would probably have prioritized the two cases in the same way. A missing girl isn't to be neglected, but you can never ignore a terrorist threat.

'He was just after attention, I suppose,' Penrose analyses. 'But ... ehm ... can we meet, sir? There is something else I'd like your opinion about.'

Inwardly I sigh. The meeting with the surgeon cancelled, I haven't had the chance to ask his professional opinion about going back to work. He hasn't officially declared me fit for work. Guthrie and now Penrose seem to take the liberty of persuading me to do odd jobs for them, knowing very well that I won't refuse.

'I could do with your help, sir,' she adds as an afterthought.

When I came out of hospital, I was definitely unable to work. Still shell-shocked about what had happened to me and with such short notice, I felt a loneliness I'd never experienced before. I found myself in desperate need of a goal in my shattered life. I needed something to distract me from my darkening thoughts. Penrose prevented me from becoming depressed. Unaware of this, she kept any thought of suicide at arm's length by providing me with detailed information about an unsolved murder case I had been working on. She produced files with secretly copied statements and supplied me with updates and new information. We used to meet in cafés, like spies in a badly scripted movie.

'Is this about a current case?' I ask gently.

Patches of blue sky are growing smaller as pewter-coloured clouds are gathering above my head, as if in harmony with the way I am feeling. The wind picks up and the first big drops land hard on the window, transforming it into frosted glass.

'Ehm ... That too, sir.'

She doesn't explain further, sounding hesitant and secretive, which is probably why my curiosity takes over.

'My time is unlimited, as you know,' I say wryly.

She doesn't reply immediately, unsure whether a response is needed. 'Where and when, Jennette?'

Clearly, thinking that I'm at home, she suggests meeting me in a recently opened café in Trenance Gardens, a stone's throw from my flat.

'In half an hour?'

'Yes.' She hesitates, almost changing her mind until she remembers the urgency and adds, almost formally: 'I appreciate it very much, sir.'

Putting my phone in my pocket, I wait for a heavy shower to pass. Big raindrops crash sideways onto the windscreen, sending curly streams down the bonnet. In the rear-view mirror, I watch a couple in their late fifties pass behind me. Head down, the woman is rummaging in a big handbag. Her husband, I presume, pushes a large trolley, filled with grocery supplies enough for at least three months; yet I guess they're on their weekly shopping outing. Seemingly oblivious to the rain, he negotiates his way around rapidly growing puddles. Lips pursed tightly, the woman opens the passenger door of a tattered blue vehicle and gets in, shaking raindrops from her dull grey hair and leaving her husband to struggle with half-filled plastic bags and loose groceries. Water drips from the boot door onto his shoulders, his face sullen and stoic while his wife issues instructions with rapid hand gestures, safely warm and dry inside the vehicle. With sagging shoulders, he looks like a man trapped and defeated.

My phone rings. It's my mother, sounding careful, never certain about my reaction. 'Are you coming over for tea, love?'

'No. sorry, Mother, I'm working on a case.'

Outside the man has almost unloaded the trolley. An empty plastic bag escapes and is lifted by a gust of wind, then, weighed down by the rain, gets stuck in a small tree bearing a handful of yellowing leaves. His wife is shaking her head disapprovingly. Despondently, he pushes the trolley into a bay, apparently not minding the rain. Maybe he prefers remaining outside for a bit longer.

'Are you back at work? That's good news!' My mother asks cheerfully.

'I'm only helping out. They're a bit short of staff.'

'Oh.' Her sense of disappointment creeps into my ears. She has never been very good at hiding her feelings. 'You read about cuts everywhere, so I guess that applies to the police too.' Voice lowered an octave, she rattles on nervously about the current economy, the country falling apart as a result of bad management and how on earth normal people can keep up with everything.

'Mother, I have to go.' I interrupt her.

'Oh. Are you in your car?'

'Yes.' Inside the blue car the man is adjusting his seat belt, joining his wife in staring out of the window. Not speaking. It makes me wonder about the last time they touched. Kissed. Made love.

'Not driving, I hope, Andy? Not while you are on the phone?' My mother's instincts tell her accidents are likely to happen any moment. Especially to me, her only child.

'It's safe, Mother.'

'Oh. Well. Ehm ... I meant to ask you something, but ... I guess it can wait. How about tomorrow? Tea time? We haven't seen you for a while and your father is ...'

The line seems to break off, but the connection remains in place, albeit with cracks and hisses.

'I'm sorry, Mother. Not tomorrow.' Sensing her disappointment, I settle quickly for Sunday lunch and she disconnects, already planning a menu in her head.

It's ten minutes later when I pull into the car park at my flat, half debating whether to put my groceries in the fridge and change my stoma bag before I meet Penrose in the cafe. The weather – or the location - interferes with my phone signal and there is no other way of letting her know. She is too impatient to risk it.

The café is decorated in a trendy modern style with different shaped seats and tables, a small settee with a dozen bright cushions and shelves with all kinds of unusual artefacts. Vintage tea pots. Cups and saucers. Vases. Most of which I remember from visits to grandparents and old aunts. Useless memorabilia. Yet it creates a warm and cosy atmosphere.

'Thanks for coming, sir.'

She has chosen a table furthest from the entrance door as though she's trying to hide from the world.

'No problem, Jennette.' I offer a smile, wondering which of us needs the other more. She's my lifeline with my job. She is my mental anchor. I am hers. She has the overall feeling that her colleagues don't take her seriously and treat her accordingly. She can't see that confidence works both ways. Or find a way out of her general negativity.

Only two of the other tables are taken. Closest to the door are four young women, chatting and giggling away. By the look of the amount of empty mugs and saucers in front of them, they've been here for quite a while. Next to the window is a couple in their fifties, talking animatedly like they haven't seen each other for ages. Quite the opposite of the couple in the supermarket car park. You don't often see couples of that age so upbeat together and I wonder if they recently met on a dating site and have a lot to catch up on.

Penrose is already sipping weak tea in a glass mug, staring over the rim as though we're having a blind date and she's disappointed in my appearance. I order a black coffee and sit opposite her, hiding my stoma bag behind the lining of my unzipped jacket.

'Much appreciated, sir.'

I've tried hard to make her call me Andy, especially as we're meeting in private, but somehow she can't. I've now stopped trying.

'Perhaps it's best to start at the beginning, Jennette?'

'It's just … men!' The outburst produces two round red spots on her cheeks. There is a look of surprise in her eyes and I realise that it isn't what she meant to say. 'Guthrie of course, but Maloney in particular.'

Since I had to take compassionate leave for my operation and Maloney came in as my temporary replacement, the two men seem to have joined forces. Not so much as friends, but it's more like they need each other to cover their backs. For certain, Maloney needs Guthrie for a next step on the career ladder. He has never made it a secret that he'd rather see the back of me and still has hopes to be offered my job on a permanent basis. As a result, Guthrie has him more or less in his pocket. Whenever Guthrie calls, Maloney jumps up like a little dog keen to please his boss, waiting for a pat on the shoulder. For his part, Guthrie is more interested in the financial credibility of his team than taking an interest in most of the cases and he seems quite happy with a loyal side kick.

'They make it impossible for me to do my job.' Penrose declares over-dramatically.

'It can't be that bad.'

'They won't even listen to me.'

I don't give an immediate reaction, wanting to get her back on track rather than listen to her launching into a tirade of complaints and insults. Part of her frustration is based on her belief that life has cheated on her, physically and professionally. I wish I could make her look in a mirror and see what other people see: when she smiles, it's like the sun breaks through the dark clouds. Sadly, the smile is rarely on offer.

'What can I do for you, Jennette?'

She shrugs, deflated suddenly, staring gravely in her half-empty mug. 'Tell me what I'm doing wrong, I guess.'

'Okay.' I keep my face straight, but she narrows her eyes seeing my expression.

'I'm on this case ...' The door opens and she is quickly distracted. A young couple enters the café, bringing in a gust of wet wind along with a swirl of leaves fallen from a nearby tree. They avoid each other's eyes like they are still in the aftermath of a row. The cold breeze has coloured the girls' face and her blue eyes are sparkling with life. The young man's face is much paler, his mouth tight as though he has difficulty keeping his suppressed anger inside. They sit next to our table and Penrose has to lower her voice when she picks up from where she started.

'This case is much more complicated than I thought. I guess than everyone else thought. But still the DCI doesn't take me seriously and Maloney belittles me as if I am a silly schoolgirl.'

'That doesn't sound very professional to me.' I say neutrally.

'Exactly. The thing is, ehm ... Andy ...' Her gaze drifts

towards the young couple. Across the table, the girl has reached out her hand, a peace offering. Her companion isn't ready for it.

'At first every eye was on that bomb threat in St Austell, now it's the missing girl. Poor family. I know it's important that we find her alive and safe, but all the same ...'

An outburst of laughter fills the café with joy and happiness. The four young women seem in a different world where everything is coloured pink and life is an on-going party.

Drumming her fingertips on the edge of the table, Penrose can barely control her annoyance, yet she understands that she will need to if she wants to have a career in the force. Turning her head towards the source of laughter, her face is a mask of defiance and regret having suggested meeting me in this café.

'Perhaps you'd better tell me everything about this case, Jennette,' I say gently.

She stirs, taking in a sharp breath. I know how keen she is to get on with the job. She has such a huge lack of self-confidence about her qualities as a police offers as well as her physical appearance that she's always walking on tiptoes, trying hard to get recognition, which she won't receive from Guthrie or Maloney.

Shaking her head as though making up her mind that a fight will definitely make her feel more satisfied than retreating in defence, she delivers what she clearly perceives as good news: 'Forensics have come back to me about the foot.'

'I'm afraid I'm not with you, Jennette. Whose foot are you talking about?'

She frowns meaningfully but when she sees my face, she offers a wry smile: 'I thought you'd heard about it.'

'I've hardly been at the station this week.'

'Right. Well. To cut a long story short, an older couple celebrating an anniversary went for a scenic drive around the castle at Pendennis Point in Falmouth. They found a shoe.

Nothing special about that, but the upsetting bit was that they discovered that the foot was still in it.'

'Not a pretty sight.'

'Indeed not.' She offers a smile. More relaxed. 'I was ordered to deal with this case. Not a very inspiring or interesting one, as Maloney reminded me kindly. Apparently, fishermen seem to find hands and feet on a regular basis. Comes with the job of working at sea. Cut off when not working carefully enough with ropes and chains and things like that.'

The waitress appears at our table. A device that looks like a mobile phone in her hand, ready to take our next order. 'Can I get you anything else?'

'No.' Penrose scratches at her wrists.

'Another black coffee for me, thank you.' I hesitate. 'And tea for the lady.'

Penrose blushes, not arguing, waiting for the girl to disappear behind the counter. Then she leans back, tucking both thumbs into her belt. Her eyes find her mobile which she put within eyesight on the table between a tiny vase with two red flowers and a small bowl with sugar cubes. She's thinking about checking her messages.

'But you have your suspicions about the foot?' I ask.

She nods, concentrating again, eyes alert, lips a thin line. 'Yes. Forensics are still working on it, but there was something very distinctive about it. Even to my untrained eyes.' She pauses and waits, to add to the drama. 'The foot wasn't ripped off, like what would happen in an accident on board a ship. It was cut off.'

'Cut off?'

She smiles briefly, staring at me for a long time, her expression unreadable. 'With some sort of saw, I'd say.'

I breathe in slowly, sensing why she is so tense about this case. She's been given the task to investigate, but really only to file statements and dismiss the case afterwards as an accident. If the appearance of the foot turns out to be suspicious, if, in her opinion, it becomes a more intriguing puzzle to solve, she won't be able to keep the case. She's well aware that Maloney will be quite keen to take over when he finds out that the foot wasn't a result of a straightforward accident.

'How did Maloney react?'

'He told me I was seeing bears on the road, a dead body in every closet. That kind of stuff. He suggested that I talk to a fisherman.' She is silent for a few moments. 'Basically, he didn't believe a word I said. Or it was more like he wouldn't listen to what I told him.'

'He made you feel silly.'

'Exactly. Only I know that I am right.'

'Did you talk to a fisherman?'

'Yes.' A rueful smile. 'I did what Maloney told me to do.'

Shifting uncomfortably she relives the encounter which clearly wasn't all that pleasant as she is naturally uncomfortable with men.

'What did he say? The fisherman?'

'When I showed him the photo? He couldn't stop laughing.' A mixture of anger and self-pity crosses her face.

'Why?'

'He openly doubted my abilities as a police officer. As – his words – anyone with an IQ above 10 can see that the foot didn't come off by accident.'

'So he confirmed your suspicions.'

She looks at me blankly. 'More than that, sir. He promised me he'd look out for the rest of the body.'

5

In his late thirties, Gerald Davey has curly dark hair cropped to the shape of his skull. A V-shaped scar sits over his left ear. He is Leanne Lobb's mentor at Tregarrett School and Maloney has arranged for me to meet him.

'Sorry you had to wait.' He says unconvincingly, blinking rapidly five times, closing a door behind him to stop me casting a quick glance into a room where teachers and assistants are gathered for lunch break: a TV is switched on a news channel, its sound subdued, and a handful of people sit with half-forgotten cups of tea and their eyes glued to tablets and mobile phones.

'No problem.' I show him my warrant card which he scrutinizes with care, but I don't yet explain the reason for my visit. He doesn't ask.

'Lunch time's almost over. They'll be back before you know it.' He can't hide a hint of despondency.

Following him into an unusually quiet school, he rubs his hands together as if they're cold. He opens a door and we enter an empty classroom with desks in neat rows and sheets of black paper with graphic designs in primary colours pinned on one wall. Motioning towards the chair behind his own desk, he leans back on the edge of the desk, not managing to appear casual.

'Is there a problem?' Another five blinks.

'I hope not,' I say mildly, realising that he's got the wrong end of the stick. Sometimes the most honest and innocent people can behave like the guilty party as soon as they're faced with police officers. It can be difficult to work out whether Gerald Davey is one of them or he has reason to think he is in trouble.

'You are the mentor of Leanne Lobb's group?'

'I am.' A small frown settles on his forehead. More blinks.

'Are you aware that Leanne Lobb isn't at school today, Mr Davey?'

'I haven't seen her group yet,' he says defensively, blinking again.

One of the designs on the wall grabs my attention. A bright red spiral with a green dot in the middle. It feels like an endless way down, a bottomless hole, drawing the eye with a haunting effect. I have difficulty pulling my gaze away.

'I'd like to ask you a few questions about Leanne Lobb, Mr Davey.'

Five blinks. I wonder if he counts them or isn't even aware of his habit. His long and narrow fingers start fumbling in a pile of papers on his desk, retrieving a pink folder.

'I'm sorry. It's a bit of a mess. ' Childish pride forms a smile at the corners of his mouth. 'But I can find this folder everywhere because of its colour.'

He opens it and slides his thumb down a list. 'Of course everything is recorded in the computer, but I find it handy to have it on paper too.' His thumb stops. He frowns, wondering if he has missed something, then adds thoughtfully, 'Oh, yes, Nicky, the girl who answers the phone, asked me about Leanne earlier today.' He scratches his dark stubble as if checking whether he needs a shave.

'May I ask what's going on, inspector?'

'Leanne Lobb is missing. She didn't come home last night.'

Eyes shocked, his face grows pale. 'Do you mean ... is there something wrong? I mean, really wrong? Has her body been found?'

'She is currently missing.' I say, suspecting his question is raised from the point of view of someone who is a keen watcher of police series on TV.

'Oh. But that is ... terrible.'

'I'm sure we will find her, Mr Davey.' I give him a smile to take the edge of his shock.

He stares at the list again. Blinks. 'How can I help?

'I have some questions for you.'

'Yes. Yes of course. Ask. Anything.'

'We are obviously looking for her, which involves retracing her last known steps. I suppose yesterday afternoon was the last time you saw her?'

He stares into nothing, not even blinking this time. 'Every morning the senior staff meet the students as they come through the doors and in the afternoons we escort them to their buses. We do this because we take every opportunity to say something friendly and to be available for support to each of our pupils whenever needed. Our policy.'

In my day, staff came out to make sure we got on the right buses and that we didn't annoy the school's neighbours by running around, yelling loudly and carelessly leaving rubbish that would end up in their gardens. They may call it a friendly school policy nowadays but I doubt there is much difference between then and now.

'Did you notice something unusual?'

'With Leanne? No, I don't think so.'

'She wasn't upset about something? Maybe she had a row with a friend? Or any other ... unpleasant encounter?'

'There was nothing that springs to mind.' He looks up, choses a pen from a chipped mug and starts clicking it nervously. His blinking rhythm has been disrupted. Replaced. 'I can't think ... I'm sure I would remember if there had been something out of the ordinary.'

He clicks his pen with short intervals, as if he is sending a message in Morse code. Silent for a few seconds, perhaps formulating a response in his mind, he continues, 'You mean, like she might have been bullied? No. No way. Not Leanne.' He straightens, smiles, finding himself on safer grounds.

'You seem certain.'

'I am.' He opens a cabinet behind his desk and retrieves a blue ring-binder containing plastic sleeves to protect A-4 sized paper. 'There are others, of course, which is inevitable in an environment with 900 pupils. But we all keep a close eye on that, inspector. We aim to stop it before it escalates. Before more serious harm is done. Of course, we can't rule it out, but we do our best.'

Opening the blue binder he turns the pages quickly, stopping when he reaches the one he is looking for. He pulls out a photo and lays it on his desk. It shows the same background as the current wall, with two girls in front of the black designs. One is tall and skinny, with long blonde hair, shoulders sloped in a hooded red sweater, hands hidden within the long sleeves and a shy smile on a pretty face. The other is red haired with a round face, smiling confidently, hands folded together in front of her stomach. I hadn't noticed on the photo her parents showed me, but Leanne looks rather chubby in an unforgiving grey hooded sweater. With red hair and overweight, she would be a perfect victim for bullying.

'Leanne doesn't care about her looks.' Gerald Davey smiles proudly as though this was due to his input. 'She claims to be happy in her own skin.'

'Why was this photo taken?'

'We had a little competition added to a project. It seems to encourage them to work harder.' Casting a quick glance at his watch, he gestures towards the wall. 'The project was to design a logo and letterhead for a fictional company. Siobhan and Leanne's design had the most votes and we are showing the photo on the school's website. Sometimes we are approached by companies which can't afford a proper designer and we kind of help both parties. You could say it's our way of promoting our pupils' skills. I'm sure you are aware that it isn't easy for them to start careers down here in Cornwall, but we try to encourage them to stay in the area. It would be a shame to lose all that talent.'

I stare at the photo. 'Does Leanne have one particular best friend?'

'Oh yes. Definitely. Siobhan. Siobhan Carter.' He points to the other girl on the photo. 'That's Siobhan.' He smiles fondly, his concern forgotten for a few seconds. Perhaps he has become aware of his nervous habits; the blinking has stopped, so has the pen clicking. 'Inseparable, those two. Shame the parents are ... unhelpful. Discouraging their friendship, I mean.'

Pushing the blue binder to the side, he stares down at the pink folder, his mind wandering about the significance. 'Actually, I think quite a few pupils called in sick today. I remember Nicky saying how unusual it was to have four pupils sick in the same group, and only the odd one in most of the other groups. Well, that may be a little exaggerated of course, but I must admit it is a bit strange. It's not like we're in the middle of a flu epidemic.'

'Do you know the names of those four?'

'No, but I can find out for you.' He grabs a phone from the wall and presses his index finger on the 0. Waits for the connection and repeats my question to Nicky. Disconnecting, he grabs a blank A-4 sheet stained with a pattern of coffee rings, and tears off a corner. 'I'll write it down for you. Sally Pollinger, Kevin Watson and Siobhan Carter. And Leanne Lobb of course.' As he gives me the scrap of paper, there is serious concern on his face all of a sudden.

'Siobhan Carter isn't here today either? And she is Leanne's best friend?'

'Yes. They are close. Like twins. Siamese twins.'

Once again I stare at the photo. Both girls look young, shy and innocent, hardly the type to have boyfriends or involved in other youthful distractions. 'Does either of them have a boyfriend that you know of?'

This makes him chuckle. 'Not those two. I've got some pupils who are ... how can I put it, ahead of their age? There was a girl not so long ago who got pregnant. Fifteen. Around Christmas time it was. But not these two. They are just two young teenagers, inspector, they work hard and Leanne especially is adamant to have a career. She wants to find a good job and make a lot of money to support her parents. She has a younger sister, and I believe there are two or three other younger siblings.'

'Three little brothers.'

'Yes. Well, she wants them to have a good education too.' Shaking his head, he closes the folder as if saying that he's finished with the subject. 'It is very rare that pupils that age are so outspoken about the future, inspector. Most of them believe school is only to have fun but Leanne is rather serious.'

'So you don't think there's any reason Leanne might be a victim of bullying? Are you sure?'

'Everyone likes her, inspector. Siobhan is a bit more shy and quiet, but with her background ... I mean, she comes from an affluent family.' Slightly annoyed with himself, he wonders briefly about the relevance of what he's said, whether saying too much will bring him in trouble. 'Leanne would protect Siobhan if something like that happened to her.'

I nod, changing the subject. 'Did you escort Leanne and her friend to the buses yesterday?'

'Ah ... yes. I did. Part of a mentor's task.' His eyes drift to the photo. The blinking resumes: there is something he is not telling me.

'Do Leanne and her friend normally use the same bus?' I ask, making a mental note to find out where the other girl lives and visit her at home.

'No. They live in opposite directions, but sometimes Siobhan goes home with Leanne.'

'Were they together yesterday?'

'I'm not sure.'

'And what about the other two? Sally and Kevin?'

'Sally has recently moved house. I believe she lives with her grandmother. I'm sorry, I'm not sure where. She might get on the same bus as Siobhan though. I'll have to check that for you. Kevin Watson is always picked up by his mother in her car.'

'Do you have any idea where Leanne may have gone to? Did she mention anything? Like going to Truro for some shopping. Or meeting someone?'

'Not that I can remember.' He shifts uncomfortably, balancing from one foot to the other. Five blinks.

'What about Carensa Pencreek?'

'What about her?'

'Is she one of Leanne's friends?'

'I suppose. The girls in that group are quite close. There are 19 boys in that group, inspector, and only 8 girls.' He pauses as if he has lost his train of thought. 'I'm sorry I can't be of more help, inspector. I guess Nicky can help you with the addresses.'

I offer a hand. His is warm and sweaty. 'Thanks for your help, Mr Davey. Please call me if you remember something else that can help our investigation.'

'Absolutely.' As I turn towards the door, he seems to search for his confidence. 'Do you think Leanne will ...?' He blinks. Three times.

'Most missing persons show up within 24 hours, Mr Davey, and most situations turn out to be innocent, due to a misunderstanding or minor incident. But, of course we always have to take these cases seriously, especially with children.'

'Of course.' He smiles, confidence fully regained. 'I'll come with you to the desk in case Nicky is worried about privacy regulations.' He gives a wry smile, lifting his chin as the sound of young feet in the corridors grows louder. 'We do abide by the rules, inspector, but I don't see the point in withholding the addresses of those three other pupils, you'll probably find them in the phone listings anyway.'

'You've been very helpful, Mr Davey.'

'I'd like to help, inspector. But at this moment, lunch break over ...' His expression is serious when he touches my arm. 'I can't imagine anything happening to any of my pupils. And that group ... they're good. All of them. Bright and willing, not a single rotten apple, if you know what I mean. And ...'

He stops, a hint of surprise colouring his cheeks. 'Now that I think about it, inspector.' He stares at me like someone who has the nasty feeling that he's been conned into signing up for PPI. 'There was something. Yesterday afternoon. We've just started a new project and I put them into small groups to work together. They had to draw up ideas for an advertisement campaign for a chocolate business. The idea is that a third of the groups aim the campaign at young people up to twenty-five, another third aims at the between twenty-five and sixty year-olds and the remaining third aims at the over 60s. It makes them aware of different age groups and its implications for advertisement campaigns, but hopefully it also helps with other matters in life.' He seems proud of his own ideas. 'Leanne and Siobhan were in one group of course. With Sally. Sally Pollinger. The fourth girl was Abbie Mitchell. A new girl. She moved into the area about six months ago. No history whatsoever with Cornwall. Not that it matters. Nowadays there are less Cornish pupils in school than so-called 'foreigners'. But it matters to Abbie. I suppose she feels a bit lonely and, if you ask me, she's a bit too keen on finding friends. Anyway, she's set her mind on becoming friends with Leanne and Siobhan, but as I told you, those two are inseparable. When they were all working on that project, I noticed that the three were whispering and giggling and Abbie clearly felt left out. After class I heard her saying something about it and Leanne took pity on her and claimed that it wasn't personal. It was just a little secret she shared with Siobhan and Sally.'

'Did you find out what the secret was?'

'No, inspector, and at that moment it didn't bother me in the slightest. I felt sorry for Abbie, but it's just something she has to deal with. It's what happens all the time, don't you think? Even at our age. Acceptance and rejection. It's part of our lives. I keep an eye out, though, to make sure that people like Abbie don't get too depressed, but in this case she seemed okay afterwards.'

'You reckon that Abbie knows something about that secret?'

'I doubt it very much, inspector, perhaps you'd better ask Sally.' He glances at me with uncertainty. 'Maybe it doesn't mean anything, but isn't it a coincidence that those three girls aren't at school today? Leanne, Siobhan and Sally?'

I nod, half expecting him to disclose his thoughts and suspicions. Instead, he waves me towards the door and walks with me to the administration area at the entrance. The corridors are filling with pupils finding their classrooms for the afternoon lessons, glaring at us dismissively. Gerald Davey has a kind word for some of them.

'Do you have children yourself, Mr Davey?'

He blinks. Five times again. Looks away, as if he's heard something out of the ordinary. 'My partner has one of each. We live together, so, in a way, yes.'

Arundel Close is a cul-de-sac in a new area on the outskirts of a rapidly growing village, now almost merging with Newquay. Similar semi-detached houses are scattered alongside the new tarmac road which ends in an oval circle of grass. On either of the longest sides are wooden benches that have already become victim to graffiti sprayers. Not by artists, but by vandals.

A woman in her early sixties opens the door of number 11. Her apron is scattered with greasy stains, but her hair is nicely done and her face is powdered, lips red and smiling. 'Yes?' I catch the smell of fish and chips on her breath.

'Does Sally Pollinger live here?'

She nods, nudging a brochure for conservatories with the toe of a fluffy pink slipper. 'What do you need our Sally for?' She makes it sound as if my explanation had better be acceptable, otherwise there will be repercussions.

With an inward sigh I show her my ID. 'I'd like to ask her some questions about one of her schoolmates.'

'Is she in trouble?'

'Sally? I don't think so.'

The door opens an inch wider, but not to invite me in. It is to show me that she has placed her hands on her hips and that she has no intention whatsoever to let me anywhere near her granddaughter.

'Do we need a lawyer?'

'No. There are a few questions I would like ...'

Somewhere in the house a door opens and shuts with a bang. Snatches of arguing voices on TV are replaced by loud periodic retching.

'Nan?' A small boy peers from the living room, tugging at her apron, big blue eyes looking up at her in anguish. 'Mum's taken my plate and ...'

The sounds of someone being sick drift from inside. Wiping her hands over her apron-hips, the woman mutters something under her breath, annoyance and concern etched on her face.

'Ask Sally to help you, Bradley.'

'But ...'

'I said: ask Sally!'

The boy obeys reluctantly, giving me a quizzical look before opening a door at the far end of the narrow hallway.

Before he can shut it behind him, a young woman stumbles out, wiping vomit from her chin, vacant-eyed. Her grey tracksuit looks filthy and she has a big stain of spilled liquid on her chest.

The woman still holding the front door open doesn't know what to say, where to look first. 'Bekah ... please?'

The young woman has landed on her hands and knees, shaking her head as though she doesn't know what she's doing there. 'I am so sick!'

'We can see that,' the older woman replies wryly, not taking her eyes off me. 'Perhaps this moment isn't convenient, inspector.'

I feel sorry for her, but she has too much dignity for my pity. As she steps back to close the door in my face, the woman on the floor looks up, panic in her eyes that are as blue but more closed than the boy's.

'Inspector?' she yells, wildly gesticulating for the older woman to shut and lock the door immediately. 'Is he police?'

'He wants to speak to Sally.' It doesn't sound as reassuring as it is meant to be.

'How could you, Mum? How could you? Call the police! It's as if you think I've committed a crime! I only had a few drinks! Don't you see how bad this is? Now they'll come and take my kids away from me. And this is all your fault. You should never have called the police.' She's yelling the place down, choking in between, drops of saliva and yellow slime dripping onto the new carpet on the floor and staircase.

'Bekah, you're only making this worse!' Her voice has a dubious tone as she considers letting me in only for the sake of setting things right. I'm about to promise that they needn't worry about me, that I won't alert Social Services, when a girl appears.

The woman on the floor stretches out her arm. 'Sal, get me some paracetamol, please. I am ... so sick.'

'You'd better go to bed and sleep it off,' says the older woman sarcastically. 'I doubt if you'll be able to keep the paracetamol in your stomach anyway.' She gazes at me, making up her mind. 'Okay then. Sally, this man would like to speak to you. He's police. It's about one of your friends at school.'

Glancing at me suspiciously, the girl shrugs. Grabbing a hooded sweatshirt from the coat rack, she pulls the zipper up to her chin. 'I know. Bradley told me.' She nods and begins pinning her dull dark blonde hair up onto her head, a plastic band ready between her teeth.

'Perhaps it's best if you come outside,' I say gently.

The older woman screws her eyes half shut, still uncomfortable with the whole situation. 'Okay, but only for ten minutes. And you stay within my sight, Sally. Understood?'

'Yes Nan.'

We take a seat on a bench almost opposite the house. The grass is short and thin, recently sown and cut showing bare patches. A nearby bin is overflowing with plastic bags, and dog waste is dumped at the foot of the pole.

'Is this about school?' she asks, which reminds me that she didn't go to school today and there is clearly nothing wrong with her health.

'No.'

'My mum's not always like that,' Sally says apologetically, sitting down and pulling her feet up, hugging her knees and resting her chin on the faded fabric of her jeans.

'I'm not here to talk about your mother,' I say slowly.

'Am I in trouble? Or Mum?'

'Have you done something illegal?'

'Nope.'

'Then you needn't worry.' I smile reassuringly and see her bright blue eyes soften. 'It's Leanne Lobb I'd like to talk about.'

'Oh.' Her face turns red, and I notice a vein begin to throb in her neck.

'I don't know anything about Leanne, sir.'

'I think you do, Sally. I'm told you are her friend.'

'No. Siobhan is her friend. They are always together.' Hurt has long ago mixed with acceptance of the inevitable.

'Sally, Leanne wasn't at school today. She didn't go home last night. Do you have any idea where she might be?'

She hesitates long enough to suggest that she knows something. 'No, I don't.' A pause. 'What does Siobhan say?'

'I haven't spoken to her yet.' I try to sound casual. I called Siobhan Carter's address but there wasn't anyone at home. Along with the school's rather odd policies, I wasn't offered mobile phone numbers. 'You weren't at school today either.'

'No.' Her head drops and she doesn't answer. Instead, she changes the subject completely.

'I don't like it here. I don't like it here at all. They think we're filth.' She looks round accusingly, gesturing at the semi-detached houses similar to that of her grandmother. Most drives are vacant and none of the net curtains have moved since we sat down on the bench.

'You've recently moved here, haven't you? You must give them a chance.'

'They don't give us a chance!' An outburst of hurt and fury.

As if on cue, a neighbour appears from behind a garage. He doesn't look in our direction but I'm sure he's seen us. He is with a dog, black with a white spot round one eye, like he's wearing a white patch. He looks as though he's going to crush anything he can set his teeth in, preferably a living creature or a human body part. Pulling the leash, the man is barely strong enough to keep the dog at bay. I look at Sally, who still has her feet up on the edge of the bench, wishing I could do the same.

'He's one of the worst.' Sally speaks with a subdued voice. I'm not sure if she means the dog or its owner.

As I gather my thoughts to find a way to tackle the reason for this conversation, I watch the dog dragging his owner along, rather than the other way round. He is sniffing the ground, stopping to lift a leg at each post holding a letter box – front doors are too many feet away for postmen to efficiently and quickly deliver the mail.

The dog halts on the pavement. The owner, forced to stop with him, looks away to pretend not to notice that the dog has crouched down to relieve himself.

'And he thinks we are filth,' Sally says, emphasizing the fourth word with a mixture of anger and disgust. Her voice is loud enough for the man to hear her. 'He doesn't even clean the mess.'

The man moves on, carefully avoiding the dog mess in the middle of the pavement. No poo bag is pulled out of a pocket, not even to scoop it up and move it towards the gutter.

'I hate it here,' Sally continues. 'I liked it better when we lived on the estate.'

'Which was where?'

'Near Leanne's.'

'Penmarric Drive?'

'Yeah.' She nods gravely, pointing with her chin towards her grandmother's house. 'Mum got arrears with the rent.' A statement rather than an expression of hurt or shame. 'We couldn't stay there. We barely had time to take our stuff when Col came to collect us.'

'Col?' I would like to change the subject again and find out about Leanne's possible whereabouts, but Sally is fidgety and nervous and I don't want her to run off.

'Uncle Colin.' She shrugs indifferently. 'We have to call him uncle, but he's our Nan's new man.'

'Your step granddad?'

Her smile lights up her face and I can see beauty lurking. 'They're not married, thankfully. He's two years older than my mum. He could be her brother, says Mum, so that's why they think it's more appropriate for me and Brad to call him uncle.' The flatness in her voice speaks volumes. It explains how her life must have been to date, why she doesn't seem impressed by her changed circumstances.

'He has his own room. Uncle Colin. A fitness room. He spends hours in there, but I think he watches porn films rather than use his exercise machines.'

'Does he have a job?' I ask sympathetically.

She shrugs. 'They say that our Nan once won the lottery.'

'I see,' I say, wondering whether she overheard someone and hasn't understood it was meant as a euphemism.

'We're in the spare room,' she continues in the same flat tone. 'Mum, Bradley and me. I sleep on the floor on an inflatable mattress that deflates about three times each night.' She stops to show a rueful smile. 'If I'd known that, I would have carried my bed on my shoulders.'

I glance at my watch. Her grandmother strikes me as a strict woman who sticks to her own rules. Sally was only allowed ten minutes. Eight have already gone. 'Tell me about school yesterday. Did you hear anything about any plans Leanne might have had? A secret perhaps?'

'No. I'm sorry.'

'So you have no idea where Leanne went yesterday after school?'

'No.'

'Do you have any idea where we can find her?'

'No.' She pauses, staring at her tattered trainers. They have bright yellow laces. 'Have you looked on … like Facebook?'

It hasn't even crossed my mind, but I realise that it would be the first place to find out about someone nowadays. Especially with teenagers. More likely one of my younger colleagues has already been investigating Facebook.

'I'd like you to tell me.'

'I can't help you, sir. You'd best speak with Siobhan.' Avoiding my eyes, hers follow the man and his dog disappearing into a back garden, the proof of their outing still present on the pavement.

'If there is anything you remember, or if you hear something, please call me, Sally.' I hand her my card and, without a word, she slides it into her trouser pocket.

'Mum had a bad day,' she says slowly, not meeting my eyes. 'My Nan said I had to stay with her, clean up, make sure she didn't come out of our room.' The statement holds no emotion, not even an inkling about her real feelings.

Then there is a small girlish giggle. 'I had to make sure Mum kept quiet. My Nan's bridge friends came this morning, you know, Mum would be too much of an embarrassment.'

7

The sky is filled with rain when I pull out of the cul-de-sac, leaving Sally on the bench, staring at me. I turn on the radio and just pick up the tail end of live coverage of a terrorist threat in the White River shopping centre in St. Austell, which turned out to be a false alarm. A 34-year-old man has been arrested on suspicion of wasting police time. Two relatives, a couple of about the same age, are being questioned.

Before she disappears from view as I turn the corner, I see in the rear mirror that Sally has lowered her feet and is swinging her legs frantically. Her body language suggests guilty relief. She couldn't tell me anything useful about Leanne, but I can't dismiss the feeling that she hasn't told me everything she knows.

By the time I drive into Newquay, it is raining. Hard. The air is cold. Wipers sweep full speed. Tyres splash through puddles and headlights of oncoming vehicles seem to evaporate in the spray that creates a mist above the tarmac.

The car park at the rear of my apartment is almost empty and I park as close to the entrance as I can. I have to negotiate a shopping bag with too many items in it and an umbrella that has two broken spokes and flips inside out with every gust of wind. Water drips down inside my collar, trickling down my spine. There is a smell of autumn in the air already, although it is only the beginning of September.

I've always liked autumn but now I feel like I've missed out on something. Perhaps it's because this summer hasn't been good to me. The shock of the disease, surgery and its aftermath, the murder case that involved so many more deaths than I had anticipated, the girl in the hospital, her murderer waiting for the first day in court. If it ever comes to that.

My flat is cold and damp, the windows are obscured by gusts of wet wind. Turning on the heater, I wake my laptop from hibernation and find a different phone number of Siobhan Carters family in BT's directory. Victor Carter. The name sounds slightly familiar, but I can't remember how or why I have heard of him.

Sally mentioned Facebook. Newspaper articles spring to mind. Notifications shared by hundreds of so-called friends, sending open invitations to parties while parents have gone out for a weekend break or a well-earned holiday. Binge drinking parties, drugs and whatever is in fashion, making a mess of the parent's home, damaging property, leaving a mess.

Leanne is fourteen, her friend is one year younger. I'm not sure if I'm too old to think that the girls are too young for that kind of behaviour. Somehow, Leanne's parents and her mentor at school gave me the impression that she is young and innocent, but perhaps that vision is clouded by too much parental and adult love. I presume it depends who her friends are and how much she is influenced by them.

I've spoken with Sally in person, which seems a bit silly now that I recall that people, especially the young, tend to use social media – Facebook, Twitter, Instagram – to tell everyone what they're doing. Some people warn of the dangers of doing this, claiming that every detail of our lives is now stored somewhere in the digital warehouses of numerous databases. Waiting for disasters. We may all be concerned about our personal privacy, but that doesn't seem to exist in the virtual world. We perceive it as unreal, which makes us careless about the potential dangers.

But to find out more about Leanne, I decide to register online on some of these websites and make contact with new 'friends'. I find that daunting in itself. I don't have many friends in real life and I've never seen the point befriending strangers for no other reason than that they're somehow connected to other people I vaguely know. Perhaps I'm cynical, perhaps I have seen enough in my police career to be wary and careful.

Eventually, I find Leanne through Sally's list of friends. She calls herself Leanne Jayne, not Leanne Lobb. She has 367 friends, varying from friends from school to family relatives – and a lot of others I can't place straightaway. Her profile picture is a selfie, face cut off at the chin, the shape slightly distorted because of the angle, making her forehead large and her eyes and nose bulge. I recognise her from the little gap between her front teeth. Other pictures are very much alike. Almost all are selfies, cut off randomly, either with or without Siobhan Carter. None with a boy or a young man that might be a reason for her disappearance. I scroll through her 'posts', 'likes', 'shares' and 'comments'. People tend to post and share interesting or funny information. I find most of them irrelevant and boring. Cats that can sing, dogs running round chasing their own tail, a video of a parrot in a cage cursing the life out of any normal human being. Poems and sayings, clothes and shoes. But there is also a world of information about a fourteen-year-old schoolgirl. I have never met her, but I know her taste in music, what clothes and shoes she would love to own, where she went on holiday the last few years, the fact that her 6-year old rabbit died two months ago. But there is nothing to help me to find her.

Feeling somehow that I have failed, I call her father, hoping that she has come home and that he is now too embarrassed, having made a fuss in calling the police, to let me know she's safe and sound.

'Not a word from her, inspector.' His voice is low as if he's already given up hope.

'Police are looking for her, Mr Lobb,' I say, feeling the weight of responsibility on my shoulders. 'I have no doubt we will find her sooner rather than later.'

'I hope so.' He doesn't believe it.

'Do you have a Liaison Officer with you, Mr Lobb?'

'Yes. Isabel Ward. She's very helpful. Elsie's gone to her sister for a while.'

'If there is anything I can do for you …' I try to sum up statistics about missing persons, how many actually return safely, almost always with quite innocent explanations about where and why they went, but he can only think of what he's seen in TV and read in newspapers: dead bodies in ditches, hit by a car, or worse, victims of rape left to die alongside a deserted country lane.

'She's been gone for hours, inspector.' His next question, unspoken, hangs in the thin air between us: why haven't the police found her yet?

'We will find her, Mr Lobb,' I say but somehow I don't sound convincing, I know it's not very professional, but I feel emotionally involved, as if I knew and care for the girl personally.

Returning to my laptop, I get her Facebook page back on screen and scrutinize it again, eventually finding what might be hidden secrets in comments on previous posts. And there it is: a brief comment on someone else's post about a new song by a recently discovered talent in pop music. 'I am soooo excited!!' Leanne responds.

The comment was posted at ten past four on the afternoon she disappeared, about an hour after she left school. Which tells me that at that moment she was safe and happy. Excited.

The only person I can think of who might shine a light on this for me, is her best friend, Siobhan Carter.

8

Although many people have cancelled their landlines and only rely on mobile phones and internet connections, I haven't and don't. I'm from a slightly older generation and as mobile phones don't always work in my area, not even at home sometimes, I still have a landline and an old-fashioned answer phone. I push in the number of Siobhan's home and although the phone is picked up by someone almost immediately, there is no accompanying voice to respond. I hear heavy breathing, a click, hissing and whispers, and eventually a voice.

'Hello?' Curt and loud.

'Is that Mr. Carter?'

'Yes?' His voice drops to a whisper and I can hear his footsteps loud on a laminated floor as he is taking the phone somewhere more private.

'Who is this?'

'I'd like to speak to Siobhan.'

More footsteps, muffled voices and the quick clacking on a keyboard. A silence follows and I wonder briefly if I've dialled the wrong number. Then there is another click. Dry and crisp. He has put me on speakerphone.

'What do you want?' His voice echoes vaguely against the walls.

I have seen his picture on the website of his company: a man in his early forties, a friendly smile that creased alongside his eyes. His eyes, invisible on the photo as he narrowed them against the light; gave the impression that they too were soft and friendly. Hearing his voice changes my first impression of him abruptly.

Deciding that I'd better come to the point quickly before he cuts me off, I assume that I am speaking to the right person.

'Mr Carter, I have information that your daughter is …'

'Wait!' He clears his throat like a smoker who every

morning gets out of bed and has to deal with lungs half blocked with phlegm. 'Wait! Ehm ... my daughter?' He sounds as though he is unsure he has a daughter.

'Siobhan.'

There is a long silence. I hear subdued sounds in the background, someone opening a door, a high-pitched female voice asking if anyone wants more coffee or tea. It feels like I have interrupted an important meeting until I hear a woman's voice, breaking, 'Oh my God!'

'Who is this?' he barks in my ear.

I can almost imagine him pacing up and down, hands on his back, every so often gesticulating to express what he means. He is like a caged tiger, impatient and with suppressed frustration by nature.

'Is Siobhan at home?'

This time the silence lasts so long that I almost believe the connection is lost. 'Hello? Mr Carter?'

'Who are you?'

'I really do need to talk to Siobhan, Mr. Carter. It is important.'

'She's ... No. You can't.'

'Is she ill?'

'Ehm ... yes.'

'But this is an important matter, Mr Carter. A matter of life or death. Police are ...'

'No. Police got nothing to do with it.' A brief silence, heavy uncontrolled breathing, arguing voices in the background.

'Listen, mate, stop calling me and wasting my time.'

I suppress a sigh. My annoyance with the man increases with each second. 'Mr Carter, I'm just checking if ...'

'Checking, huh? No need for that, I can promise you. I keep my end of the deal, you keep yours, understood?'

Deal? My silence is filled with his frustration and anger, then there is another bark, 'Who are you?'

I hesitate. Something is preventing me from disclosing the fact that I am a police officer. He doesn't sound like the most cooperative of people and I'm convinced he will cut me off as soon as I tell him I'm a police officer investigating the disappearance of a girl he ignores and despises only because of her background.

'You haven't told me who you are.'

'Haven't I?' I feel like a recalcitrant teenager, bending words and sentences for my own comfort and for the sole reason to annoy him further. 'Ehm ... I'm Andy. Can I have Siobhan's mobile number?'

A gasp and I hear a woman sobbing. Papers rustle. Quick footsteps. A door closing.

'Listen, Andy, if that is your real name. Who are you? What do you want with my daughter?'

'As I said, I would like to ask her some questions.'

A discussion follows. Raised voices, sadly not understandable.

Then he blurts, 'Are you a reporter?'

I contemplate this. There must be something wrong there. Carter is a business man, and, according to information I retrieved from several websites, an important one in the local business community. Perhaps he's involved in some business deal he doesn't want to release to the press yet.

'No, nothing like that, sir. But this is kind of an emergency. Or rather, it could be. I believe your daughter might be able to tell me about the whereabouts of her friend.' I am hesitant to mention Leanne's name. Lobb told me how strongly Carter feels about the friendship between the girls and I'd rather not jeopardize their secret meetings and get-togethers.

'Her friend? Is that what this is all about?'

'Yes. This is about one of Siobhan's friends, Mr Carter. I am a police officer. My name is Andy Tre...'

'What?'

'I am a police officer of Devon and Cornwall Police. I am investigating the disappearance of ...'

'You've got a nerve!'

'Sorry?'

He doesn't reply. The line is dead.

9

Early morning, and the sun is rising behind the hills. Newquay is almost deserted. Delivery vans are parked in the shopping street, drivers are whistling cheerfully or looking grumpy. The sun hasn't risen high enough to shine over the harbour. I shiver in my jacket, wishing I'd put on a jumper.

The tide is coming in, but not yet far enough to fill the harbour. Birds pick in the muddy sand for a breakfast treat. The drumming sound of an engine is background music to the cries of the seagulls hovering above the fishing vessels that are moored up in the shallow waters. The *Anna-Louise* is standing upright on her keel, steadied by struts which are secured in the sand. The first ripples of seawater are gently lapping it. As soon as the tide is high and lifts the vessel afloat, she will be away for who knows how many days.

I stop at the water's edge, my feet between thick rusty chains that are attached to the fishing boats lined up on the beach along the tide line. 'Mr Trebilcock? Clem Trebilcock?'

I look up at the boat, hearing someone moving something. The sharp shrieking of steel on steel. A short ladder leans against one side of the boat.

'Mr Trebilcock?' I call again and a man's head appears from above the bow. 'Yeah?'

'Do you have a minute?'

'Not now.' He chuckles.

'So when …?'

'Whenever we're back.' A second man emerges from behind him. Younger, curious. His body has the same shape as the older man. Shoulders as wide and strong, although the older man's face has been more often exposed to the elements.

'It is about …' I almost explain the reason for my visit, but suddenly I am aware that there are other fishermen preparing to leave the harbour. 'It's about what you discussed with Jennette Penrose.'

'Ah, the lass, hey?'

His grin is mischievous and I'm glad that Penrose didn't come with me. She wouldn't have appreciated his reaction, or the tone of his voice.

'About the foot?'

Then, I notice someone peer from the deckhouse of another fishing boat, and I realise how silly I am in trying to be secretive about what seems to have become common knowledge amongst all the fishermen.

'Yes.'

He thinks about it, lifts his head to feel the wind on his face and to scrutinize the sky for signs that there may be a sudden change in the weather. Then, quickly making up his mind, he exchanges a few words to the younger man whom I presume is his son, and surprisingly quickly comes down the ladder.

He's wearing a grey woollen hat, a black home-knit woollen jumper. His yellow oil skin trousers are stuffed into long yellow boots.

'I'm sorry to keep you,' I start, but he dismisses my apology with a short nod. 'Got time for coffee?'

He points at the long building which houses a busy café in the season, but is now more or less closed, although there is a lone board on the sand promising pasties and soup of the day.

The building is perched between the beach and the cliffs that rise up to the town above. Next to it is the entrance of the Treffry tunnel. A vital piece of Newquay's history, often overlooked by tourists and passersby, the tunnel once provided a link between the packhorses delivering Cornish minerals along the tramway and the harbour where the minerals were shipped for smelting elsewhere. Today, the remains of the tunnel are used to house the Rowing Club's Pilot gigs.

Tables and chairs are stacked up to one side, only a few are available for possible visitors. Trebilcock opens the café's door, shouting a greeting and an order for two coffees and grabs a chair, placing his so that he can keep an eye on the tide, the weather and his boat.

'I knew you were police,' he says matter-of-factly, lowering his big body onto the seat that seems too small for him. He has a thick Cornish accent.

'My name is Andy Tregunna.'

He narrows his eyes. 'Cornish?'

'Born and bred.'

He nods approvingly, making me feel like I've passed the test. 'Why do you want to speak to me?

'PC Penrose told you about a man's foot that was found at Pendennis Point earlier this week.'

'She did. She showed me a photo.' From behind long bristly eyebrows, his sea grey eyes sparkle with amusement. 'I told her that a foot cut off like that, can't possibly have been caused by an incident on board. Does your forensics confirm that?' Without waiting for my reply, he jerks his head towards the window. Smaller boats moored at the quay are floating on the gentle waves rolling in from the ocean. 'Alf, from the *Evening Sun*, had his arm cut off. It happened twelve years ago, but I can still see in my mind what it looked like when I took off his coat. I'd never seen anything like it then and I haven't seen anything like it since. It was all flesh and bones and blood, inspector.'

'You saved his life.'

He shrugs. 'We were together, out at sea. In the distance, we could see the harbour, but I knew we couldn't waste any time. He wouldn't have survived if he'd been on his own.' He interrupts my next thoughts, which remain unspoken. 'What is it exactly you're after, Mr Tregunna? I told that lass. Incidents like she described and showed me on the photo don't happen on boats like mine. It wasn't anything like Alf's accident either, that's for sure.'

He stops abruptly when a tall and slender woman brings us two mugs and a handful of biscuits, each wrapped in red and gold cellophane. He nods by way of a thank you and she replies with a smile that suggests that they know each other outside the harbour as well.

'Do you know who the poor man was?'

'Hard to tell.'

'I'd have thought that forensics are clever enough nowadays.'

'I'm sure they'll do their utmost.' I pull an envelope from my pocket. 'You told my colleague that you would call her if you found the rest of him.'

'So it was a man then?'

'Just a manner of speaking. I haven't seen the post mortem report yet.' At least that fact is true. I look up at him. 'What made you say that to her?'

'What?'

'About the rest of him.'

Narrowing his eyes, he studies me for a long time. 'Isn't that obvious, inspector? The foot was cut off. Or should I say sawn off? It must have belonged to a dead person.'

'What happened to the arm of your mate? Alf?'

He shrugs. 'It went overboard. No point in trying to rescue it. We were at open sea. It was rough enough as it was. I could barely apply a tourniquet and steady a man conscious enough to know what is happening to him.'

'He was conscious?' I ask incredulously. I can only but try to imagine what it must have been like: two fishermen in a small fishing vessel dancing on the waves of the Atlantic, both panicking, one desperately trying to help keep his mate alive, the other already seeing his life passing before him.

Trebilcock nods. 'He was. All the time. Never forgotten his face when he looked down at where his arm was a few seconds earlier.'

'He must have been in a hell of a lot of pain.'

'Pain comes afterwards. In the beginning you feel nothing.'

I'd rather not speculate if it is true. 'Is he still a fisherman?'

'Of course. Fishing is in his family, his blood, his genes. He can't live without the sea.'

Retrieving a printed photo which Penrose emailed last

night, I push it in his direction. He studies it quietly. His face has no expression. 'Is this what I think it is?'

'A torso. Yes.'

'I thought so. Same person?'

'Results haven't confirmed it, but we're working on the assumption that it is one body.'

He pushes the photo back to me. 'What do you want from me?'

'I hope you can make me understand why the foot was found at Pendennis Point near Falmouth and the torso in a rock pool on the other coast, at Treyarnon Bay.

He whistles through his teeth. 'Other coast, hey? Now there you got a problem, inspector.'

'That was my thinking exactly, Mr Trebilcock.'

He grins, again mischievously. 'I hope you're not here to ask me where to look for the rest?'

'It did cross my mind.'

'Have you heard about the containership that lost part of its cargo?'

'Container ship?'

'Hmm. You must have heard about it, inspector. What was it, sixteen, eighteen years ago? A containership was caught by a huge wave and fifty-something containers washed into the sea off Lands End. One of the containers contained millions of pieces of Lego.'

'How is Lego related to body parts?'

'That is precisely my point. It tells you that we don't understand the sea at all. We can send people to the moon and launch rockets that take a decade to reach another planet, circle around it and send back photos and charts to us. But we can't predict what the sea does. A bit, yes, our maths can tell us about tide times and such, but that is more or less all. When you think about it logically, the containers should have sunk and still be lying somewhere on the seabed near Lands End. Even if the container was ripped open, you would expect that the Lego bricks would also remain on the seabed. Lego doesn't float. It's made of ABS plastic which is heavier than water so it will not float naturally. Some small bricks will float initially as small bubbles cling to their surface but they will all sink eventually. Then how is it possible that the Lego pieces wash up all around our coastline? And beyond. They say the pieces are even found in the USA.'

I shake my head, slightly taken aback by his response. 'Fishermen use sophisticated equipment nowadays,' I say slowly. 'They can detect shoals of fish. They don't rely on the so-called 'huer's' any more, to call from the hut high on the rocks and wake the whole village as soon as he notices a shoal of pilchards,' I add, referring to the rich history of Newquay harbour. From here, I can't see the white painted 'huer's hut' on the cliffs, but I know it's there, albeit nowadays only for the purpose of tourists photographing it with the spectacular sea view and hazy headland beyond.

'Technology may have improved, inspector, even for us fishermen, but it's still not as straightforward as you think.'

'Maybe not. But coming back to the original subject, Mr Trebilcock, you know the sea better than me. You understand the sea.'

'I wouldn't dare to claim that I know and understand the sea, inspector. I respect it, I respect its powers. I fear and admire it. I love and hate it. I can't live with or without it. My life depends on it in many ways. The sea may be peaceful and blue to you on a summer's day, but it can be mean and cruel and a devil as well.'

'Are you saying that you can't help me?'

'I wish I could.'

I know he is serious and not shunning my questions. Yet I feel disappointed.

'But I know someone who might be able to help you, inspector. I say might ... be able to help you.' He picks up his mug and gulps down its contents. 'She's a carer, but also a keen amateur oceanographer in her spare time. She also belongs to a group with like-minded souls who are involved in currents and tidal electricity at the moment. If she can't help you, I'm sure she knows someone who will.' He grins as he rises to his feet, towering over me, almost blocking the light like in a full eclipse. 'But don't expect her to know the sea, Mr Tregunna.'

I follow him with my eyes as he takes both our mugs and places them on the counter. A woman shouts a thank-you and I follow him outside where the beach has disappeared by a few meters and some of the fishing boats are already afloat, pulling at ropes and chains.

'There is one thing I do know, though, inspector,' he says earnestly when I shake his calloused hand. 'It wasn't as clear on the photo of the foot in the shoe, but by the looks of it the torso can't have been in the water for too long. I'm not one of your forensic specialists but I'd say about 24 hours, not much longer. And I'm pretty sure the foot and the torso weren't dumped in the water at the same point.'

'Are you sure of that?'

My ignorance amazes him. 'That container foundered 20 miles from Land's End. It took the Lego bricks about eighteen years to wash up on our beaches. And they still do. It's impossible for a torso and a foot to travel such a distance in a couple of days.'

'So you're saying ...'

'Yes inspector, in my opinion it's pretty clear that someone disposed of those body parts at different places. I'd say you're dealing with a shrewd murderer.'

I watch him climb the ladder getting back on board of the *Anna-Louise*.

Mid-way back up the steep road into town I have to stop and gulp for air. Leaning against the low wall and looking down on to the harbour I see him arguing with his mate.

It suddenly occurs to me that he didn't mention the possibility of the body parts being thrown overboard from a boat. Or a fishing trawler.

The incident room is cold and damp. Or perhaps it's the frosty atmosphere that drops on each of us like an invisible veil when Maloney comes in, lips pursed and wearing an air of misguided self-importance.

His eyebrows rise when he spots me and he is about to say something, most likely to enquire what I'm doing here, when a voice says sarcastically: 'Morning, sir.'

In reply he only nods, not even wondering whether he's being mocked. He frowns as Penrose rushes in, face flushed, and finding a seat nearest to the door, as her escape route. 'Now that we're all here, let's get started, shall we?'

He summarizes and analyses the current cases, listening to shortened reports and suggestions, issuing instructions for house visits, updates and new leads. If any.

Much to my surprise the case of Leanne Lobb's disappearance seems to be more or less closed. She has come home. Reports are being written and documents filed. It occurs to me that Guthrie's initial view on this case had been right after all: Lobb wasted our time.

As soon as everyone has left the incident room to find the coffee machine and start work – in that order - I read the report of PC Isabel Ward who had been appointed as the family liaison officer when we all feared for Leanne's safety. She was there when the fourteen-year-old appeared out of the blue as if nothing had happened. She hasn't wasted more time on the report which is curt and devoid of details.

I find her blocking the door to the Ladies talking to DC Champion, who is half her age, offering a recipe that involves different variations of seaweed. I half listen to her explanation of red, green and brown algae in vegetarian dishes, thinking I'd prefer a medium rare steak. I'd better not say that to either of them if I don't wish to make enemies.

'Andy?' She smiles as Champion closes the door behind her.

I lean against the wall, trying to appear casual. 'You were there when Leanne Lobb came home?'

'Yes.' Her plucked eyebrows lift with the corners of her mouth.

'What happened?'

She opens her mouth as if to suggest I should read her report but she thinks twice. She knows me well enough to understand that I'm after the details, the unspoken words, the body language.

'Sorry, Andy, I'm on my way to meet someone.' She stares at me and adds: 'You can come with me if you like. I'm all yours in the car.'

Her expression shows only kindness, but I sense from her words that she too feels that there is more to Leanne's return than her report suggests. I nod, not asking where her appointment is.

'Why your interest?' she asks as soon as she starts the engine and turns of the instant blaring music.

'Loose ends.'

'Something nagging you?' She checks her lips in the make-up mirror, flaps it back.

'Perhaps.'

'I know what you mean. I have exactly the same feeling.' She pulls out of the car park, waiting patiently for a gap in the traffic that's moving slowly behind a recycling truck. Men in bright orange jackets and grubby trousers are collecting waste for recycling from the pavements, emptying coloured bags with plastics, paper and carton into the different compartments in the truck.

'They say everything is being dumped on the same pile anyway,' she says with a hint of cynicism. 'Let's hope that isn't true.'

The truck rounds the corner and we gain a bit of speed until we approach a set of temporary traffic lights installed near a crew of men filling potholes in the road. Several of the men have mobile phones in their hand instead of a work tool. I glance at Isabel's face; by now Penrose would be agitated by the hold up, venting her frustration loudly about road workers. Men in general. In contrast, Ward is stoic, unemotional.

'Janice came home first. She's Leanne's younger sister. Elsie's sister had collected the three younger boys from school and they were still there. As usual Janice walked from the bus stop on Treloggan Road. Elsie was standing at the window. She didn't want to go out, in case there was news. She was scared that her other daughter wouldn't come home either.'

'Understandable.'

'In a way, yes. As soon as Elsie saw Janice, she went to open the front door. Embraced her as if they had been separated for weeks. Janice was quite .... embarrassed by her mother's affection and pushed her away. It wasn't weird or odd; it was just the reaction of a teenager thinking she's too old for a hug.' A brief pause. 'You know.'

'Hm.'

'Anyway, that was why Elsie didn't notice that Leanne was following her sister at a short distance. The front door was still half open. Janice stamped up the stairs angrily, or whatever her feelings were, and Elsie was starting to cry. The front door was pushed open. From where I was sitting on one of those three sofas, I had a clear view of the street. I saw Leanne approaching up the path and recognised her instantly. She was dressed in the same clothes as those that had been described when she disappeared, carrying her school bag as though she'd just got off the school bus with her friends and school mates.' Isabel frowns thoughtfully. 'It was kind of odd.'

We pass the boating lake. For no particular reason, I look across towards my flat. Waiting for a few horse riders trotting along the dried overgrown banks of the Gannel river, we turn left and leave Newquay behind us.

'Patrick had barely moved since I arrived there. All the time, he was staring at the TV screen, not seeing or hearing anything. He said he wouldn't move until there was news about Leanne. We ran to the hallway and he was just quick enough to catch Elsie, almost fainting when she heard Leanne's voice behind her, saying, 'Hi Mum.'

'That's what she said? As if she hadn't been away for twenty-four hours?'

'Exactly.' She smiles approvingly.

'Patrick grabbed his daughter and his wife in the same embrace. I said it would be advisable to get Leanne's clothes into plastic bags to send to forensics, but I was ignored. Not deliberately, mind you, it was just that Patrick was holding them so tight. He was crying. Elsie was staring over his shoulder, looking at me incredulously. She clearly couldn't believe it. I could see that she didn't want to move because she was afraid that it was only a dream.'

I can almost picture the situation: a frozen image of three people holding each other, clinging to hope and relief, fears already dissolving.

'What was the first thing Leanne said?'

Isabel Ward cast me a sideways glance. 'You're really into this case, aren't you, Andy? More than usual, I'd say.'

'Perhaps,' I say reluctantly. 'It was a strange case from the beginning. Guthrie calling and asking me to see the Lobbs, just because he thought Patrick was an attention-seeking nutcase.'

'Hm. I see what he meant, though. From what I saw of Patrick, I think that he is one of the most stubborn people I have ever met. His constant calls to the police must have been a nuisance. I can partly understand that it put the call handlers off.' She sighs. 'But, answering your question, Leanne's first words were: "Hey, what's this all about?"'

I let these words sink in. 'Like she came home from school like on any other day?'

'That was my impression.'

'She must have thought that her day off school hadn't been noticed.'

'Which is hardly likely because her sister goes to the same

school. Still, she thought that she was in the clear, although that thought was short-lived. She wriggled out of her parents embrace but I could see her struggling to maintain an air of self-confidence. She realised that things wouldn't be so straightforward as soon as she saw me in the doorway. She tried, though, saying "What's up?" at which point her father kind of recovered from his shock and, as happens with parents, his relief about her safe return was replaced with anger.'

Isabel stops talking, slowing down and concentrating on the traffic, waiting behind a bike rider before overtaking after a bend in the road. Then she continues: 'He shouted at her: "Where the hell have you been? Don't you understand that we have been sick with worry? How could you have been so selfish? What the hell were you thinking?" Meanwhile Elsie started to sob and she clung to her daughter as if she thought she needed to protect her from Patrick's fury. Then Janice came down from upstairs. "Where have you been?" she asked Leanne and that seemed to set things in motion. They were all quiet for half a minute and I suggested to Janice that she should make us a big pot of tea and we could all go into the living room. Luckily, they did what I told them to do. Elsie drew the curtains and Patrick turned his back on us. I asked Leanne to take off all her clothes and put everything in evidence bags so Janice went upstairs to collect fresh clothes for her and then she made us all a cup of tea. I called the station and told Guthrie as Maloney was out of reach on his mobile.'

'So that was the end of her disappearance,' I say slowly.

Isabel continues, 'I tried to question Leanne without the presence of her father, but he simply refused to leave us. He demanded to hear everything. He was clearly suspicious that there was a man involved and he was already thinking about revenge, but unless I called the station for help to physically remove him, there was nothing I could do. Besides, I didn't think it was so important because Leanne started telling us what had happened before I could ask her any questions.

She said nothing bad had happened to her. She hadn't been victim of a child abuser. She hadn't been assaulted or raped. There was no need to see a doctor, not even a nurse. She was perfectly healthy and in good shape. She was only very, very tired.'

'Did you believe her?' I ask.

'Yes. Well, I did think she wasn't telling the whole truth, but she looked alright. Her clothes didn't show any sign that she'd been assaulted and clearly she wasn't in distress as if she'd been raped. She hadn't been crying either. At that point, I thought she only looked very tired.'

'Where had she been?'

'To Plymouth. To see a gig by some pop star. I checked and the event had actually taken place.'

'Has someone seen CCTV images to check if she'd really been there?'

'No. I reckon Maloney won't be that keen on wasting time on that. She wouldn't lie about it.'

'How did she get to Plymouth?'

'She got on the school bus to Newquay. We'd already established that she and her friend Siobhan went to Newquay, supposedly for a sleep-over party with Carensa Pencreek. But instead of going on to Carensa's, Leanne took another bus to Plymouth. She must have changed her clothes at the bus station. She arrived in Plymouth, got something to eat in Subway's and went to the gig. So far, everything seemed to go as planned. It was only because the pop star – I forgotten his name now, Tam or Sam or something – joined the fans, including Leanne, after the gig and had a drink with them. That's why she was late and missed the last bus back to Newquay.'

'Don't tell me she spent the night with the pop star.'

'No. There was a girl, Stacey, who lives in Plymouth and she said Leanne could go home with her. She didn't want her parents to know about the gig either and so she sneaked Leanne into her room. They had to wait the next morning until Stacey's mother went to work, which was why Leanne was unable to catch the first bus and arrive at school in time as she had hoped so that nobody would think she'd been anywhere other than staying with Carensa, as her parents had thought.'

We drive in silence for a while. I try to put the events in the right order. It all sounds pretty logical and credible to me, but something is nagging at me. Leanne might be back safe and sound, but there is something not quite right about her story.

'Do you believe her?' I ask finally.

'It seems that everything is all right. Leanne was certainly smitten with the pop star. She couldn't resist going but she knew her parents wouldn't let her go if she asked them. It makes sense that she tried to get her own way.' She shakes her head when I open my mouth to interrupt. 'Come on, Andy, we've all been fourteen. We've all lied to our parents when there was something which, to us, at least, was a matter of life and death. I sneaked out with my best friend to be with a group of friends in a barn in a nearby farm. We did nothing except talk and tell each other ghost stories, but the attraction was that we were there illegally, so to speak. In hindsight, I think that my parents probably knew ...'

I raise my hand. 'What did you just say, Isabel?'

'I said that we told ghost sto...'

'Not that. About your friend.'

'Oh. Yes. Of course I would never have been so brave to climb out of my bedroom window if I'd been on my own. We only did that when my best friend was staying with me. I would have been too scared and ... wow, Andy, I see what you mean!'

I nod pensively. 'Does Leanne strike you as a girl who would travel all the way to Plymouth on her own? Coming back late in the evening? On her own?'

'No. she doesn't.'

'Someone is lying. Which is why I wish to speak to

83

Leanne. And to her best friend, Siobhan Carter.'

Sensing her looking at me several times, Isabel doesn't remind me that the case is closed. She doesn't ask why I feel I can't let go of this case.

I wouldn't have known the answer.

11

Andrea Burke is a forensic scientist with a strong preference for the colour red. She has dyed ruby red hair and a pair of red-rimmed glasses. I have never seen her wearing anything else other than clothes in shades of red. Even when she is dressed in a white forensic suit the dominant colour red shines through it.

She butts in almost before I can answer my phone. 'Tregunna?'

'Yes?'

Isabel has dropped me off and I am walking back home, passing the zoo, then under the railway bridge and through Trenance Gardens. The trees are yellow and auburn and an autumn smell hangs in the air. In front of me is a procession of two dozen young schoolchildren accompanied by a teacher and probably volunteer parents. One of the adults has started a song and the children are joining in.

'Sorry, I can't hear you,' I shout back at Andrea Burke, trying to block out the singers as I press the phone to my ear.

'I said: I have some interesting news for you. Sir.' As usual, the last word comes out as an aftermath, sounding almost like an insult.

'About?'

The singing has finished, followed by a ripple of laughter and a young voice yelling out a suggestion for the next song. Someone else shouts in protest, but the singing starts up again.

'Where are you?' Burke asks, hesitating.

'Within earshot of a group of school children.'

'I can hear that, Tregunna.' She can be curt and even rude sometimes, but one of her better habits is that she rarely loses her temper. 'So you're not at the station?'

'No.' I say, wondering why she called me. We have one of those relationships that cannot be described. She is neither a friend nor an enemy. She just seems to react either way however the mood suits her whenever we meet.

Two songs down and the school children have had enough. The boating lake comes into view and their excitement increases. Young feet move faster and I slow down.

'A little bird told me you were in the harbour early this morning.'

'I was.' As if on cue, a male blackbird with a yellow-orange beak appears from under a shrub and whips in front of me on the path, every so often stopping to peck at something invisible to the human eye, and to keep an eye on me.

'So I gather you were enquiring about those body parts.'

'Your little bird has been busy.'

She makes a noise in the back of her throat that sounds like a combination of a chuckle and a giggle.

'Right.' She falls silent. I can almost hear her brain ticking over while she makes up her mind. 'Do you want to hear this or shall I call Maloney?'

'Okay,' I offer. 'What's up?'

'It's about those body parts.'

I hesitate. As a human being I find the thought of the body parts horrifying and unnerving, but as a policeman I am intrigued. I almost envy Maloney for leading the case.

'It's not my case. I'm officially not even working.'

'I know. But I thought you'd like to know.'

'Hm.'

'Just admit it, inspector.' She giggles mischievously. I can hear someone in the background and I imagine that she is sharing a joke at my expense.

The school children have reached the edge of the boating lake where you can hire a boat. A man in his fifties with a lopsided grin and one leg that is significantly shorter than the other, is limping to and fro trying to please everyone at the same time, handing out life jackets and instructing the adults how to adjust them, meanwhile keeping an eye on three boisterous boys who are already climbing into one of the boats. The outing might have seemed a good idea to the teacher at first, but now she seems to be finding it all very stressful keeping the children at bay.

'Maloney is dealing with this case,' I reply to Burke.

'Yes. I know.' There is a brief silence. 'He is a prick.' Clearly, she's in one of her sulky moods. And she is certainly not in the mood for sharing her information with Maloney. Yet I can't understand why she picked me instead.

The shouts of the children are increasing.

'Are you somewhere near a school?'

'I'm more or less following a group of seven-year-olds who are going out on the boating lake.'

'I didn't know you had children.'

'I don't.'

'Oh. Okay. We ran DNA of the foot and the torso through the system. They're the same body.'

I can hear her rummaging through papers. Footsteps and a man's voice in her vicinity.

I wonder again why she called me. She isn't a person who likes to speculate, nor disclose any information before she is certain of its accuracy from the many tests she runs.

'I thought so.'

Ignoring the hint of sarcasm in my voice, she continues, 'Do you remember that we found a hand six weeks ago? In August? In the Camel River beside the Camel Trail near Padstow? Stuck in the mud?'

'It wasn't my case, but I do remember.'

She chuckles. 'It was a man's hand. Approximate age between 25 and 40. Nobody came forward missing a hand.'

'Hardly to be expected.'

She is silent for a moment, contemplating how to continue. 'Well, believe it or not, I had a flash of inspiration, if you like, and I've just compared the DNA results of the foot and the torso with the hand. A perfect match.'

Whether on purpose or not, she has managed to silence me for a few seconds.

'You mean the hand and the foot and torso belonged to the same body?'

'That is exactly what I'm saying.'

'Are you sure?'

She laughs by way of reply. 'Did that make your day, Tregunna?'

She has a sense of humour that doesn't exactly match mine. 'Yes. Well, that's incredible.'

'Yes. Given the fact that the hand was found ... let me check ...' Her voice is suddenly serious and professional, devoid of any mockery. 'On the 4th August ... which makes it about six weeks ago.'

12

The sky is pink, turning the green hills across the River Gannel a dirty brown and where sheep can be seen grazing in the fields divided by old stone walls. I hear shouts of young children running alongside the lake, and two sets of teenagers in hired rowing boats, roaring with laughter as they attempt to have a race on the lake which becomes an uncontrolled circling in one spot, then ending up in a crash of bows.

My landline rings. My mother. She rarely calls me on my mobile, unless she's tried my landline first several times.

'I'm sorry to call you at this time, Andy.' She starts with an apology as though it's too late for a social call. 'But I …'

She sounds upset and I interrupt her abruptly. 'Are you okay, mum? Is everything all right with father?'

'Well, yes. I suppose.' She's a bit taken aback by the sudden urgency in my voice, as if she never expected me to be worried about either of them. In her mind, parents worry about children, not the other way round.

'Andy, listen … ' She tries again, slightly out of breath. 'I can understand it if you don't feel up to going to the hospital, but …'

'The hospital? Why?'

There is a pause. 'Well, I don't want you to feel sad or anything, with unhappy memories and all that.'

'It doesn't bother me, mother.' She doesn't know anything about my weekly visits to Becca in Treliske; I doubt if she's even aware of her existence. Of course, she knows what happened but I never gave her any details – and she never asked.

'Do you need me to drive you to the hospital, mother?' I am wondering if she or my father, have an appointment with a consultant about some issue with their health, without letting me know about it, just as I didn't tell them about the tumour in my bowel before I had my operation. The irony of this catches my breath when I stifle a nervous half-laugh.

She guesses what I'm thinking, and replies, 'No, no, nothing like that, love. It's not about me. Or about your father. It is about ... do you remember Mr Grose?'

'From Treworran Hill?' Although it's years ago, I've never forgotten Mr Grose.

'Yes, that's him.' She sounds surprised. She hasn't expected me to even remember the address. 'I might have told you that he was taken to hospital a couple of months ago.'

'Not that I can recall.'

'Well, actually, it may have been around the time that you were in hospital yourself and I didn't want to tell you.' A most likely explanation for withholding from me such otherwise useless information.

'Okay,' I say warily. I cannot imagine that she's still upset about Mr Grose. Unless he died recently and she now feels emotional about it. Regret, perhaps too.

'He had a fall a while ago,' she continues, as if reading my mind again. 'They took him to Treliske and found out that he had suffered a stroke. He had a couple of strokes later when he was still in hospital and ... well. He's still in there. I visit him every now and then when your father needs something from Truro.'

My poor father, finding an excuse to go shopping in Truro rather than being dragged into visiting people in hospital he barely knows.

'I feel rather sorry for Mr Grose.' She rattles on. 'The poor man hasn't got a soul in the world. He never had children and he and his wife were without siblings themselves.'

'I had no idea he's still alive,' I say, filling the silence.

'No, I suppose you didn't.' She sounds disappointed somehow, as though she's been telling me about him several times and discovers that I haven't listened.

'He's soon to me moved to a care home.' She pauses for a cynical chuckle. 'Bed blocking, that's what they call it, isn't it? A disgrace! To think that Mr Grose fought for his country in the war and that he helped rescue us from …'

'Mother?' I reprimand.

'Sorry dear. Well, they found a suitable place for him in a care home and he will be moved out of the hospital at the end of this week. Everything seemed to be sorted, but now someone has asked about clothes and other personal belongings. Photographs, paintings or other mementos. Perhaps a small piece of furniture. You know, to make his room look more … recognisable to him. I don't really know why he thought of me, because, you know, he's never been very … close to me, but … anyway, the nurses in the hospital kind of knew that I have a key to his house. I clear the mail and keep an eye out for him, you see. But now they've asked me to get some more clothes for him. And choose some personal items which he may appreciate having around him in his new room.'

I think of Mr Grose's house and can't help a shiver. 'Why are you telling me this, mother?'

'Well.' She clears her throat. 'I saw Mr Grose and I asked him if he could think of anything that he wants me to collect from his home. I didn't think it was a big thing to him because he seemed all right about going into the care home. But, well, he got rather … upset about it.'

'Perhaps he realizes what it means.'

'Yes, maybe so. But the thing is, Andy, that house has always given me the creeps. I let myself in to check his mail and all that, but I never stay one minute longer than I need. You know, with that kitchen door locked all the time. And besides, well, to my relief, to be honest, he was quite adamant that he doesn't want me to go there.'

'Perhaps his memory has gone and he's forgotten what he owns. Maybe he got upset about that.'

'No, no, nothing like that! In fact, there is nothing wrong with his memory. Well, obviously he doesn't remember what date it is or what he had for tea yesterday but, for instance, he remembers everything about you. In fact, he would like to see you. He said he will tell only you what he wants from his house. He insists that nobody else but you goes in.'

Another shiver runs down my spine. 'I'm surprised he remembers me. I've only met him maybe three or four times. And that was years ago.'

'Indeed.' I can picture her pursing her lips together. Remembering.

My mother used to visit Mr Grose regularly as part of her volunteer job for a charity that aimed to assist the elderly and less gifted people, helping with odd jobs in and around their homes and giving them general support. She tried to limit her duties to the minimum during school holidays, but for that one day when the bottom part of Mr Grose's set of false teeth broke in two halves and there didn't seem to be anyone else available to collect them from his house and take them to a dentist for mending. I can't recall now what she told us about it at the time, but I do recall how shy and reluctant I was to have to go with her and how I felt when I was about to meet him for the first time. My mother didn't seem all that keen either, but there was no other option than to take me with her. I'd never even seen him before but, admittedly, I became curious about him from what my mother told me about him. His wife had died in front of him, at their kitchen table, a trauma that changed his life and couldn't be wiped from his memory. The sight of the mess of food and blood mixing on her dinner plate, then dripping onto the floor, never left him and from then on he associated her death with everything that was remotely dirty. Inevitably perhaps, he developed a phobia. Misophobia, a morbid and irrational fear of being contaminated with dirt or germs. In hindsight, I suppose, in his case it was also a fear of dying as suddenly as his wife had.

I have no recollection of my mother saying that she liked or disliked him, but she always spoke of him with a certain amount of fondness. She knew, of course, that his wife had died. Perhaps she felt sorry for him. By that time, his phobia had developed and he wouldn't go out of his house any more.

He can't have been as old as I thought he was but, at the time, I thought he must have been about a hundred years old. If not older. He had wavy grey-blonde hair that stood up from his skull like an electrostatic halo. I remember staring at his huge ears and believing that with ears like that, you could hear everything from miles away. Wearing a brown velvety dressing gown over a neat pair of dark trousers and a white shirt, he looked like a character that appeared in the books I read, and then subsequently in my dreams and fantasies. Or rather, in my nightmares. I was eight years old and, to me, he was the bogeyman who snatched away naughty children.

I was so nervous, I had to use the toilet as soon as we arrived, my mother raising her eyebrows disapprovingly; making me wait with crossed legs until she'd wiped everything in the bathroom that I might possibly touch with my fingers. When I had finished in the bathroom, I heard her humming upstairs, quickly changing his bed for him. My mistake was that I didn't wait for her to introduce me to Mr Grose properly. I stood in the hallway, looking up the stairs, but then I couldn't take my eyes off it when I noticed a padlock on one of the downstairs doors. The padlock hung on two strong metal rings screwed into the frame and the door itself. It was open. It was like Pandora's box. There was nothing more interesting for a boy like me. I just had to open that door and find out why someone had put a padlock on a door inside his home.

Mr Grose found me a few minutes later, as I stood in the open doorway gazing at the drawers and cupboards with missing fronts, and trying to avoid looking at the kitchen table in the middle of the room. There she was, his deceased wife, wearing a pretty pale dress, sitting behind her dinner plate piled up with food, and some other stuff which I didn't care to examine, still holding a knife and fork in each hand as if she was about to eat.

'Don't disturb her,' a voice whispered in my ear, startling me to a near heart attack. Mr Grose gently touched my shoulder and closed the door behind of me, clicking the padlock into place to lock the door with a key that dangled on a gold chain around his neck.

I don't remember that there was ever another word spoken about it, not even when my mother came down from upstairs and looked at us suspiciously. Obviously, she noticed my pale face and shocked expression and she demanded to know what had happened as soon as we left the house. But I kept my head down and didn't look back because I knew that Mr Grose was standing at the window and he was following me with his eyes. He never said anything of the kind, but he willed me with those eyes not to say anything about what I'd seen.

It was about two weeks later that I finally gathered up the courage and asked my mother if she'd ever been in his kitchen. Or seen what was in it. She hadn't. Previous volunteers had tried to open the door and were subsequently refused to enter the house with the threat of a lifetime ban for trespassing. My sensible, practical mother, however curious she may have been, never tried.

After the first time, Mr Grose asked her to bring me to his house again. I didn't want to go, but good Samaritan as she was, my mother thought it would be rude to ignore the wishes of a very lonely man. If I'd made a point of it, I'm sure my father would have stepped in but, in truth, I was curious and intrigued also. I had told my friends about what I'd seen in that kitchen, but they had laughed at me, calling me a 'silly sod' and 'insane', which, gradually convinced me that, whatever I'd seen in that kitchen, I must have misinterpreted it.

'I can't imagine what he wants from you, Andy, but I can no longer ignore his requests,' my mother said, looking me straight in the eyes as though hoping I could explain it to her. 'And I will stay with you and keep an eye on you, of course. I won't leave you out of my sight.'

At that time, I only had a vague idea about abuse, least of all of a sexual kind, and I had no idea at all that it could happen to children, yet the situation made me blush and I couldn't make myself ask her what she meant exactly. I doubt if she would have replied in all honesty.

So I sat next to him on a foot stool and I listened. He wasn't used to dealing with children and he spoke to me as an adult. He never explained about his kitchen, but he did mention that he barely ever set foot in there. Which didn't surprise me at all. He'd bought a kettle and a microwave and had someone place a large fridge-freezer in the hallway where his coat rack used to be, and stacked it with frozen meals. Every day, he had one of the meals for his lunch and one for his tea. He wasn't a stupid man. He watched TV and when he realised that he wouldn't stay healthy or even alive without going outdoors he bought a computer and had a WIFI connection installed to be able to order online everything that he needed. He set up an online bank account as soon as the service was available and someone brought him some cash for tips for the delivery men.

For my part, I answered his questions about my life at school, my friends and family while my mother busied herself with a dust cloth and wet wipes. She didn't hoover the place because she was afraid that she wouldn't be able to hear me over the sound. If she had ever thought that my relationship with Mr Grose was of a dubious nature, she would never have said so. But after three or four times, she never took me to him again. I always wanted to ask him about the kitchen, but there was never the right opportunity. And he'd never given me a second chance to have a look.

'Andy?' I become aware that my mother hasn't stopped talking until she is now waiting for a reply.

'Sorry, mother, I was miles away.'

'Will you go and see Mr Grose, please? I know it means a lot to him.'

'Yes, I will see him.'

That night, lying alone in my bed, I think about love and death. Mr Grose never got over his wife's death. After that, he was a sad, lonely, mostly disturbed soul. Mad in one sense, if you had to put a label on him. So, young as I was, I understood that life isn't always without pain. Or grief.

Trying to wipe away the memories of him, I stretch my arm and open my hand. I imagine Lauren's body beside me, an image so strong that I can almost feel her breath against my face, her heartbeat against mine. Reaching out beside me, I find only a cold and empty place. I close my eyes and feel the darkness of my mind reaching out to me instead. I turn onto my back and let my fingers run down my chest and belly, avoiding the fresh stoma bag on one side, until I reach my groin. I touch myself, thinking of Lauren, wanting her, needing her. But nothing happens. I haven't had an erection since I had surgery. Months ago. Mr Cole tried to reassure me that it is only a matter of time. I'm not sure if he was telling the truth. All I know now is that I am not in a position to offer a new future to Lauren and her sons.

I shouldn't have agreed to take her and her sons out for her birthday tomorrow.

13

The weather has let us down. The forecast sounded promising, but there is no sign of the sun and it is too chilly and windy to spend a few hours on the beach. Instead, Lauren has requested a visit to Padstow. There are shops with the inevitable items for tourists. Made in China. Queues outside pasty shops that now offer much more flavours and fillings than the traditional Cornish recipe, like Thai curry pasty's, or blue cheese and chickpea fillings for the vegetarians. In the sheltered harbour are small boats and larger sailing yachts amongst the fleet of fishing vessels. The Jubilee Queen is waiting for the tide; she will soon depart for a trip around the rocky islands off the headland, with passengers hoping to spot seals, dolphins or a shark.

Joe and Stuart follow in our trail, sulking and trying to remind their mother that it's a day out for them as well. I buy them all a pasty and an ice cream, and a green silk scarf that contrasts beautifully with Lauren's red hair. We watch strong young men launching a gig, listening to their banter as we watch passengers board the ferry to Rock across the estuary. The sun breaks through the clouds and I suggest a walk up the beach which stretches out towards the dangerous Doom Bar.

Joe and Stuart share a look and nod in agreement as though they are doing me a favour, rather than the other way round. The sand is surprisingly warm beneath our bare feet. Lauren has wound her new scarf around her head, strands of red curls wave around her face. She is carrying two pairs of sandals in one hand, laughing as her son's feet sink deep into the soft sand, making it difficult for them to run. It brings a warm and loving smile to her face and I almost envy the boys.

'Perhaps it was a mistake dragging them to Padstow,' she admits.

I shrug. 'Why? We are here to enjoy ourselves and if that

means one has to give in to the other, then so be it.'

'Is that how you feel today?' Her voice is serious and a small frown creases her freckled forehead. 'Are you trying to please me and the boys, but not yourself?'

'No, that was not what I meant.' How can I explain that every detail of this day is a precious gift to me? That I like the company of her twins almost as much as I like hers? That it makes me feel as though I belong to someone, that I'm not alone.

'I'm enjoying myself, Lauren.'

Something in my voice makes her turn away. A silence settles between us, but it's not uncomfortable. I try to say something, but nothing comes. Then the moment is gone. The boys have found something. An empty bottle made of green glass, its aluminium cap weathered by salt.

'Is there a note in it?' Together with Lauren, I bend to look at the 'treasure' in Joe's hands. There is sand on his face and in his hair.

'A note?'

'Like a message in a bottle.'

'What sort of message?' Stuart asks seriously.

'Well. Suppose you are the only survivor of a sinking ship and you end up on an inhabited island. And you want to go back home but obviously you have no landline, or mobile phone, or anything else to make contact with. But if you have a bottle, you can write a message on a piece of paper, put it inside the bottle, throw it into the sea and hope that someone will find it and rescue you.'

Joe nods, the idea appealing to him, but Stuart cocks his head and looks at me, eyes thoughtful. 'What if you have nothing to write on? No paper, no pen?'

'Perhaps you could find a large leaf from a tree and scratch the message onto it with your finger nail. Or you could scratch the message onto a pebble.'

'What if the pebble doesn't fit in the bottle?' He mentally measures the top of the bottle.

'But what if you don't have a bottle?' asks Joe, following his brother's train of thought.

'You'll have to wait until one washes up on the beach,' I say, suppressing a smile. 'Like the one you've just found.'

'Perhaps we can write a message and throw it back in the sea?'

'You could do that.'

The conversation results in Lauren emptying her bag on my jacket spread out on the beach and we search through its contents for a pen and a piece of paper. Eventually, we decide on a supermarket receipt because it already has the date and address printed on it. The boys edge away from us, making sure they're out of earshot, as they prepare a message for their bottle. There are giggles and sniggers. In a ceremonial manner, Lauren – as it's her birthday – has the honour of launching the bottle into the sea as if it's a brand new yacht being launched on her maiden trip. We watch it bopping on the waves until it drifts off with the retreating tide.

There is something white in the distance and the boys are guessing what it may be. They roar with laughter as their suggestions grow wilder and unlikelier. A big white shark. A sailing yacht washed ashore with a lone survivor. They don't seem to notice how difficult it is for me to keep up with them, my feet sinking in the soft sand. I feel my legs weaken with every step, my heart pumping loud and fast in my chest. Demanding the ultimate from my muscles and legs.

Lauren stops when I halt to gather my breath. 'Are you all right, Andy?'

'Out of practice, I guess.' I stutter between breaths.

'Boys! Joe! Stu! Wait for us!'

'No Lauren please. Let them go on.'

She hesitates, torn between love and concern for her boys and sympathy and anxiety for me.

'It's just the aftermath of the operation,' I admit, glad to have my breathing under control again. 'You go with them, Lauren.' I look up again. 'I'll follow, I promise. And you can rest assured that I'll get there in the end.'

She smiles. 'Before or after dusk?'

'Before. Absolutely.'

But Lauren insists on a break. She has soft drinks and chocolate bars in her bag and we sit in the sand, enjoying the sun and the breeze which is gentler now than in the morning. The white sand of Doom Bar is almost translucent in the sun, stretching out in sweeping furrows towards the middle of the estuary. I tell them about a Cornish folk legend which says that it was a mermaid who created the Doom Bar as a dying curse on the harbour after she was shot by a local man, but another story, about all the ships having been wrecked on the treacherous sands on stormy nights, appeals to Joe and Stuart more.

Jumping up and down, they are like foals in spring, or cattle just being released after spending the winter in a barn. Faces flushed and eyes sparkling, they haven't got the patience to sit in the sand and enjoy the sun.

'This is fun,' Joe exclaims as he throws his arms in the air. 'Come on, Stu, let's race.'

They run, using their arms as wings and swirl around like sea gulls gliding on the wind. Lauren makes herself comfortable with her head on her bag and I sit next to her. Wondering. Thinking. Dreaming.

'Were you at Treliske hospital when I called?' she asks hesitantly, quickly adding: 'And I don't mean to see Becca. I mean for you.' She hasn't opened her eyes.

'Yes.' There's no point in denying it. 'I had an appointment with Mr Cole. The surgeon.'

'Everything all right?'

'I suppose.'

A flash of irritation appears in her eyes as she opens them and looks straight into mine. 'I'm sorry for asking, Andy. I'm only … interested in your wellbeing. Forgive me for that!' She snaps. 'But if you'd rather not tell me …?'

'The appointment was cancelled. The surgeon was called away on an emergency.'

'That's not the point I was making.'

'It's not that I don't want you to know,' I say miserably. 'I don't want to think about it.'

'There's no point in hiding your head in the sand.'

'I know.' I look away. There's a wall of silence between us. She's no longer a friend, she has become an enemy. I wish I could bury my face in her arms. And cry.

'But you do.'

I don't respond. I can't find any words. I feel utterly inadequate to deal with this. Every time I think about it, it stirs up a fear in me, a fear rooted in something I prefer to avoid talking about, despite knowing full well that I need to. Not to everyone, but at least to her.

'I'm sorry, Lauren, but I ...'

Her face has softened. Anger is replaced by pity. I don't know what I hate most.

One of her sons is shouting, his voice driven towards us by a gust of wind. She looks up, shielding her eyes against the sun. I see them running through the puddles in the furrows formed by the swirling currents. Water splashes up beside their bare feet. I envy them for their youth, their innocence, their carefree life.

'It looks like it'll take a while to catch up with Stu and Joe.' She points, quickly tossing the remains of our little picnic in her bag.

'We've been lazy.' I smile and stretch out my hand to help her rise to her feet. I can't help it, but I guess I am holding her hand just a split-second too long. Her face is close enough to kiss her. She turns away from me, gazing past my shoulder, eyes searching for her sons.

'Let's make a move then,' I say, trying not to show my disappointment. I offer to carry her bag, but she shakes her head.

We walk in silence. The wall between us is beginning to crack. At least, I hope it is. The beach seems endless. The distance between us and the boys grows wider. It doesn't seem to bother her any more as long as she can see them.

They are heading for the white object we saw earlier. It's close to Hawkers' Cove, a small hamlet nestled in the arm of the headland. Where it once must have been a lively little place with trading vessels and a lifeboat, it is now almost deserted, as most of the houses are holiday homes and only a few are permanent residences. It used to have a quay where boats anchored to load and unload their cargo, but nowadays there is so much sand washed in from the ocean that it has silted up and become impossible to keep it open. It's hard enough to keep the channel open for access to Padstow harbour without constant dredging.

A harbour patrol vessel passes by with a noisy engine, two men on board grabbing the handrail to keep their balance as they head for the open sea. Or that's what I think they're heading for. There's a flash of something bright yellow and it suddenly dawns on me what's happening beyond Hawker's Cove, what the white rectangle in the distance is.

'The boys ... we can't let them go there.' I blurt out, startling Lauren.

'What's wrong?' she asks, panic already low in her voice.

'I know what that white shape is,' I say, shaking my head. 'We can't let the boys go there.'

'Why not?'

I swallow hard. 'It's the police.'

She gasps and I don't need to look at her to see that she knows, that she remembers the white tent that was erected by police to shield off the crime scene at a supermarket car park. It was months ago, but it must still be very much on her mind.

'The boys ... not again.' Her eyes are open wide with shock and disbelief.

'Exactly.' I take her hand and keep up with her as fast as I can.

We reach Stuart and Joe at sufficient distance from the police tent. They have stopped, standing motionless. Stuart turns his head as we approach, searching my face for a denial of what is obviously going on in his mind. He wants my reassurance; he wants me to tell him that it's not what he thinks it is. Somehow I can't. Instead, I gently reach out and pull him close to me, draping one arm around his shoulders, reaching for Joe with the other. He doesn't move, probably amazed and embarrassed by my touch. I feel him looking up at me, but it isn't me he sees.

'What is it?' Joe asks.

'What's happening?' Stuart asks.

Fortunately, we are too far away to see anything clearly. Five months ago, the two boys found a woman's body wrapped in plastic. Memories of that horror and fear float over their identical faces, and then on Lauren's. I want to shield them, protect them, but it's too late. A police car stops next to the others, as close to the shore as possible, blue lights flashing but no siren. The harbour patrol vessel is pulled onto the sandbank. Men in yellow fluorescent jackets walk in a slow line along the side of the hill with their heads down, eyes scrutinising the ground. Every so often, one of them stops and raises an arm. Bends down. Shaking his head. False alarm.

'What are they looking for?' Laurens voice is raw and low. She looks up at me. The dark flecks in her eyes seem to float like spilled oil on water. Our eyes meet for the briefest of moments, and I want to put my arms around her, close her eyes to create a barrier between her mind and the horror she has already recognised. She seeks reassurance which I can't give her.

'Come on, we'd better go to the Lobster Hatchery before it closes,' I say, in a vague attempt to distract them. But none of us is in the mood so we head back to the car and Newquay in silence.

14

It's still light outside. I pour myself a glass of water and lean over the balcony and try not to think about the day with Lauren and her sons. Some things can hurt too much. It's better to concentrate on work, however little there is to think about. Leanne Lobb is safe at home with her parents and I haven't heard about the progress with the body parts. I have called the station, but the woman at the desk is new. She isn't going to disclose any information to someone she doesn't know. My suspicion that another body part was found today on the rocks between Hawker's Cove and Stepper Point remains unconfirmed.

Restlessly, I wake my laptop and find a few emails that were sent about an hour ago but didn't appear in my inbox until now.

Penrose has emailed me with several attachments. The first is the statement of Charles Walker, a young man who saw a hand sticking out of the mud on the bank of the Camel Estuary and briefly feared it was his little daughter, reaching out for her father's help. When he saw her standing on a piece of solid rock beside him, waving at the hand, he burst into tears, panicked, grabbed her under his arm and hurried to the picnic table where his wife Justine was still sitting in the sun, sipping fruit juice and staring into oblivion with dreamy eyes. They had just found out that she was pregnant.

In the second attachment, I find the latest post mortem report along with Andrea Burke's findings confirming that all three body parts belong to the same person. The last attachment is a brief statement of enquiries made after the discovery of the hand by local police, summarised that, in the absence of the rest of the corpse, and albeit unlikely, it was believed that the person had survived. The file had ended up in someone's bottom drawer.

The photo of the hand reminds me of my conversation with Clem Trebilcock and I pick up my mobile phone, pulling it from the charger.

'Can I call you back?' Joan Walters answers the phone after the fifth ring.

'Is it possible to have a word?' I say after I've introduced myself.

'I'm driving.' I can hear traffic. The radio in her car crackles.

'I can call you back. What would be a convenient time?'

She doesn't answer. Instead, she asks cautiously, 'What did you say this is about?'

'I didn't. I got your name from Clem Trebilcock. He's a fisherman from Newquay.'

'Oh. And?'

'He recommended you. He says that you know everything about tides and currents.'

'I wouldn't say that,' she replies, nevertheless pleased with the compliment.

'I'm pretty sure you know more than I do.'

'Okay. Sorry. My traffic light's turned green. I have to cut you off. If you send a text message to my phone, then I'll try and call you later.' A lady who certainly knows what she wants.

I return to the balcony. The sky is pale blue, and the clouds drifting in from the ocean are bright pinks and oranges. The air is growing colder and I go back inside, closing the door behind me. I sit down and switch the TV on. Coronation Street is working itself to a climax, making sure viewers will want to watch the conclusion of the conversation between two sisters having fallen for the same man. The programme is followed by a police drama based in the fictional county of Midsomer. Probably written with a huge wink to the police, it has an extraordinary average of three deaths per episode. Nevertheless, I enjoy watching it, although I wouldn't admit it to my colleagues.

My landline rings. It takes me a few moments to realise that the sharp sound isn't coming from the TV, where Barnaby and his sidekick are today dealing with the murder of two prostitutes, a car dealer and a homeless man. Barnaby picks up the ringing phone on his desk, but the ringing continues.

'Tregunna.'

'O hello Andy. This is Cindy, from Sunrise in Treliske.'

Sunrise sounds lovely, but it is also the oncology department. My first instinct it to put the phone down. Bury my head in the sand.

'Yes Cindy?' She's one of those nurses who always seems to have time for everyone and replies to every question in the most honest and truthful way, choosing her words carefully so that nobody can get too upset.

'You had an appointment with Mr Cole this week, when he was called out for an emergency.'

'Correct.'

'You didn't make a new appointment.' It is a statement but it feels like an accusation.

'No, there was a queue at the desk. I thought it would be better to call.'

She doesn't remind me that I haven't called.

'That's okay, Andy.' She makes it sound as though she knows exactly what's going on in my head. 'Can I then put your name down for next week? Wednesday?'

I can't find an excuse to postpone the appointments much further ahead.

'Feeling like a schoolboy caught in some naughty act, I scribble the details on the edge of a magazine.

I empty the glass of water and pour a large whisky instead. I guess it's one of those days that one needs something stronger than water. With the glass in my hand, I force my attention on Penrose's notes and Charles Walker's statement. Walker said he told his wife to pack their things and get on the hired bike with their daughter, and ride back to their holiday cottage in Wadebridge. She didn't ask why, just looked in his eyes and quietly obeyed. When he was alone again, he kneeled on the small stony beach to keep an eye on the hand, not daring to touch it as by that time it had occurred to him that there must be a body attached to it. It was only at that point that he took out his mobile to call the police, finding there was no signal. Hoping that nobody else would make the same horrible discovery as he had, he raced to the old iron railway bridge across a tributary of the river.

The recording of his message confirms that he was there when he made the call. The woman who took the call had difficulty hearing him because the wind was whistling through the bridge. He then hurried back down to the little beach and waited for the arrival of two local police officers.

By the time the police had everything in place to examine the body and remove the rest of it from the mud, the tide was coming in and only the dead person's fingertips were visible above the surface. Charles Walker was so upset by everything that he was taken to a local doctor and given sleeping pills.

I pace up and down my flat. I think about the hand. Leanne Lobb. Lauren. Mr Cole. No, not Mr Cole. Sally Pollinger. My mother. But not Mr Cole.

I've almost lost my appetite. Guiltily, I look at the fresh vegetables; they'll have to remain in the fridge. Retrieving a frozen meal from the freezer, I read the instructions and place it in the microwave. While the plate rotates behind the glass door, I look out of the window and stare across the lake. The colourful sunset has turned to dull grey. The first leaves have already blown off the trees that surround the boating lake. A tall skinny man walks slowly along the path, hands tucked deep into his trouser pockets, a small white dog on a lead making its owner's life difficult as it twists and turns around poles and shrubs and trees. A woman, also with a dog, hurries away from him as though he has somehow scared her. I have seen both of them many times before. The woman lives in one of the bungalows opposite me beyond the lake; the man always disappears under the huge brick pylons of the railway bridge that spans over the valley. He's one of those people who make others wary and suspicious because of his grubby appearance.

His dog has stopped near a silver grey car parked on the side of the road, lifting its leg to pee on the front wheel of the car. The man waits patiently, not in the least bit bothered by his dog's actions. The microwave pings that my meal is ready but a movement in the corner of my eyes stops me from turning away from the window.

The driver of the car has climbed out, blocking the dog owner's path. I follow the brief encounter. Not so much a conversation with words, but with body language. The driver is angry; the dog owner shrugs indifferently pulling at the lead. Although I can't see it, I presume there is someone else in the car, as the driver bends towards the opened window and shakes his head. Grabbing the opportunity, the dog owner swiftly moves away. A real life soap episode in a nutshell.

I go back and sit down again at the table which is now covered with papers. On the left are my original scribbled notes about Leanne Lobb and the copies of my reports and emails to colleagues to keep them updated. On the right are copies of Penrose's case. I reply to her email, thanking her for her efforts, letting her know that I have made contact with Joan Walters, an amateur oceanographer, as Trebilcock had suggested, and invite Penrose to come with me to meet her.

Her reply comes straight away. She's too busy. There's been a development: the head of a man has been found near Steppers Point at the entrance to the Camel Estuary.

I am starting to imagine things. Like there is still someone sitting in the car that has survived an attack from a little white dog. It's too far away to see clearly but I am convinced that I can see movement behind the side window. Why would anyone sit inside a car for forty-five minutes?

I shut the blinds. Dust whirls off them. They're rarely used. I have no neighbours across from me and my floor is too high up for passers-by to peer in. I contemplate sneaking out and walking round the lake, past the car to check if anyone is inside, and make a note of the licence plate.

Ridiculous thoughts. Yet, I can't get rid of them.

Peeping through the blinds, I notice a flicker of orange light. Although we're not supposed to smoke in our own cars these days, I wonder if the driver has lit a cigarette. I consider searching for a half-forgotten pair of binoculars when it strikes me that this is exactly what I can see: the orange light of a lamp post is reflected in both lenses of a pair of binoculars which is pointing right at me. Then I remember my heated up meal in the microwave but neither this nor the rain will stop me any more. I change into darker clothes, put my navy blue jacket on and find a woollen hat in a drawer amongst my socks and underwear. With my phone in my hand in one pocket of the jacket, I sneak out of the building and head for the shadows of the hedges that mark the line between the road and the park. At the far end of the lake, opposite the River Gannel and its faint smell of mud and decay, I turn and go back the other way. There's a stretch of pavement beside the road, and a path that winds its way round the boating lake. I choose the latter, regretting it almost instantly because at this hour, and in the rain, every person without a dog looks suspicious. For that reason, I use the next gate to get back onto the pavement.

There's a camper van parked behind the silver grey car. I stand a few feet behind it, peering through the back window. I half expect to find a courting couple in the car, not two men. Making a mental note of the licence plate, repeating it several times to myself, I move forward as if in a hurry, with my hands in my pockets and my head tucked under my collar as if I am sheltering against the cold air and the rain.

Approaching the side of the car, I bend over and knock on the window on the driver's side. He has a pair of binoculars in his hand. As he presses the button to open the window, he tries to hide it out of sight but he's not quick enough.

'Sorry,' I say. 'Do you need any help?'

He is in is early thirties, with spiky blonde hair and a black stud in his eyebrow.

The smell of fatty chips drifts towards me through the few centimetres of open window.

'Help?' He asks incredulously, still fumbling with the binoculars.

I take out my mobile, holding it up as though to illustrate what I'm referring to. 'I suppose there's no signal?'

The passenger leans over towards his driver. He is older, dark skinned with straight black hair and a flat nose. I'm not sure if he's recognized me, but he narrows his eyes as he looks up to peer through the open window. 'Why?'

'Sorry.' I shake my head in confusion, holding up my mobile again, wondering if I dare be bold enough to take a photo of them. Perhaps that isn't such a good idea.

'I thought you needed help. Mobile signals are a random thing here in Cornwall I'm afraid. Even rain can interfere with connections sometimes,' I say casually. I press my finger on the screen and there is a flash of light.

'What the …?' The driver shouts.

'Sorry.' I quickly slide my mobile into my pocket, stepping back with one foot. 'My mistake.'

'What are you on about, mate?' The passenger is fumbling with his seat belt which is still strapped across his chest.

'Sorry,' I say again, shaking my head as though astonished by my own stupidity. 'I thought you had a flat tyre and were waiting for help. I thought you may not have been able to call the RAC or Green Flag or something, because you lose connection so easily round here, with the lake and the hill and the river and all that.'

'A flat tyre?' His angry voice interrupts.

Too late, I realise that I have now managed to do what I had tried to avoid in the first place: that one of them, or both of them, will get out and inspect the tyre. The passenger, a pack of muscles, moves to open the door.

'No, it isn't flat after all,' I say hastily, but he climbs out. 'Your tyre. I'm so sorry.'

He is standing on the pavement, staring at me as I step away from the car.

'I didn't see it very well in the dark. It looked like a flat tyre, but it isn't,' I repeat. 'Honestly. I'm so sorry.'

'Oh.' He still looks incredulous, as if a stand-up comedian has told a joke and he is the only one in the audience not laughing, asking himself where and why he missed the point.

'No worries,' I grin stupidly, backing off further, but taking too much time for my own liking to decide whether to make a run for the gate or continue on the pavement. I hear the engine starting when I opt for the first option where the path leads to a small bridge across the stream that supplies the lake with fresh water. On the other side is an overspill system constructed to release water from the Gannel to keep the lake at the same level all the time.

I reach the bridge, gasping for breath, heart pounding. Slowing down, I take a quick look over my shoulder and almost laugh out loud. The car has gone, the sound of its engine is dissolving in the clatter of rain on the tarmac path.

15

It is amazing how the hospital always feels and looks different depending on why you have come. Finding my way through the long main corridors that are intermittently obstructed by fire doors, I dread the sight of the place when I come for X-rays or scans, or even to have my blood taken, let alone to see a consultant to hear the results. But when I come to see Becca, however sad it is to see her lying motionless and vacant in her bed, I always feel relieved. I am free and able to walk out of there whenever I choose to whereas she can't.

Mr Grose is in the Neurology ward. The nurse at the desk recognizes me. Smiles. Her cheeks are pink. I remember her name when I look at her name badge. Rosie.

'I've never seen you here on a Saturday morning.'

It takes me a while to realise that she assumes that I have come to see Becca. It's incredible that I didn't grasp that Mr Grose and Becca are almost in adjacent rooms.

'I saw her a few days ago. I'm here to see Mr Archibald Grose.'

Her smile shows a hint of sadness. Neither Becca nor Mr Grose has many visitors.

'Are you family?' she asks, making conversation as she studies a blue screen behind her on the wall.

'My mother is a … friend. He asked to see me.'

'He sleeps a lot. Don't worry about it too much if he falls asleep. He probably won't even remember that you came to see him.'

'Thanks for the warning,' I say but I ask for his room number.

'Room 12.' She smiles. Frowns. 'Will you be seeing Becca as well?'

I didn't intend to, but for some reason I can't admit it. It'll probably make me feel guilty when I leave without seeing her. Even though she won't be aware that I'm there. 'As soon as I've seen Mr Grose.' I turn on my heels. 'Why do you ask?'

She looks a bit uncomfortable. 'One of the other nurses, Bethany, suggested putting some bunting up in her room. Balloons. Cards. Nice smelling flowers. But we thought we'd ask you first.'

'Why?' As soon as I hear myself asking why, I realise that she is misunderstanding me. She thinks I don't see the point in celebrating the birthday of someone who will not be aware of it, let alone able to enjoy it. I don't tell her that I'd completely forgotten about the birthday.

'It's not that I don't think it's important,' she says hesitantly. 'People wake up from comas after several years. Decades even. But with Becca ....' Her voices tails off. Then she takes a deep breath and continues a bit more optimistically. 'All the same, we can only make a wild guess about what coma patients can hear or feel or sense. If she is aware of anything, perhaps it would be a nice gesture to celebrate her birthday, if you agree?'

'Yes,' I reply, but I'm not convinced. Neither do I welcome the feeling that I'm expected to be in charge of everything. I am not Becca's relative. To a certain extent we might have been acquaintances, rather than friends, although she would probably disagree with that.

'Perhaps you could have a word with Bethany when you come back from Mr Grose?'

'I will,' I say, feeling as though I have become a rather unwilling member of their team.

The room is for two patients. The patient closest to the door has left perhaps for some treatment or a fag. A pile of magazines and folded papers are on his bedside table, about two dozen cards on the board above his head.

Mr Grose is sitting in a comfortable chair beside a hospital bed piled high with pillows with a bed trapeze lifting system dangling over it. Across his legs is a pale blue hospital blanket that reminds me of my time in hospital after my operation.

He doesn't look much older than the man I remember; I've always thought of him as a very old man.

He's had several strokes and is paralyzed on one side. His right arm lies at a strange angle on the armrest of his chair and it takes me a while to notice that it is strapped on with black Velcro. His mouth is askew and slightly open on one side, allowing a trickle of saliva to run down his chin. Every so often he uses a blue check handkerchief to wipe it away with a look of disgust on his face. No matter how much he has been deprived of by the strokes, his dignity is still in place. I see sadness in his eyes when he sees me looking at him.

'I never expected it to end like this.' His speech is slurred and soft and comes out with great difficulty. I have to lean closer to hear him.

'I'm sorry.'

'It's not your fault, boy.'

I wonder if he realizes that I am much older than the boy who sat next to him and listened to fond memories of his wife.

'My mother said you asked to see me.'

'Yes.' A tear wriggles its way through the creases on his face. 'I'm not going back to my house.'

It suddenly occurs to me that he had never spoken about it as his home. Perhaps it wasn't his home any more after his wife's death.

'Ever.'

'No.' There is no point in arguing about it, although a lot of people, as sensitive and hesitant as my mother, probably would.

'Someone needs to deal with my house.'

'Would you like me to call your solicitor?' I ask gently.

'No. The official papers were taken care of years ago.' He vaguely shakes his head and wipes his chin too late. Saliva drips onto the lapel of his dressing gown, leaving behind a dark wet stain. 'My house ... you've been in my kitchen.'

'Yes.' I can still feel the horror of that day and I feel sorry for the boy I was then, not understanding what had happened.

It took me a long time to be able to fall asleep without thinking about it.

'I can't deal with that now,' Mr Grose says sadly.

'Is it still like it was ... all those years ago?' I ask incredulously.

'She's aged, you know, falling apart. As the years went by, I wanted ... I knew I needed to do something about it, but I couldn't.' The good side of his bottom lip trembles. 'You'll have to be very careful.'

I'm stunned. Of all the things I expected from this visit, I never thought he would ask me to deal with the body in his kitchen.

'What would you like me to do, Mr Grose?' I hear myself asking. The idea of going back there already gives me goose bumps.

'I can't bear the thought of ... people touching her.' His eyelids are drooping and it seems to be more difficult for him to keep his head up. He's getting tired.

'I see.'

'I'd like you to go there and ... take her away.'

I feel like I have jumped off a bridge and landed in some sort of conspiracy. A joint enterprise. However reluctant I am to take part in it, I don't seem to be able to ignore it. I am involved, no matter what or how or why.

'Where would you like me to take her?'

A tear has formed in one eye. 'It doesn't matter any more, boy, you decide.'

Closing his good eye, while the other one remains half open, he stares at me between grey eye-lashes but without seeing me. He seems to have used all his energy.

I get up, gently taking the handkerchief from between his fingers and wiping a drop of saliva from his chin. He murmurs, knowing, appreciating the gesture, nonetheless I feel I shouldn't have done it.

I leave his room without looking back, knowing instinctively that I will carry that last look of him with me for a long time. Instead, I try to retrieve from my memory the image of the man who was the first to treat me as an adult, the man who shared his biggest secret with me. In one sense, I have always seen him as a friend, a person I could trust if I needed someone.

There is sadness in the air as I walk through the corridor and approach the nurse's desk for the second time. Rosie is now in the company of two colleagues. A man in his early thirties with a stud in both ears, a tattooed ring around his neck, short dyed blonde hair and a gentle smile. A badge says that his name is Les Dunwell. Staff nurse. I have never seen him before. The other colleague is Mirabelle, who recognises me. 'Mr. Tregunna!'

I wish I hadn't said that I would come back to discuss Becca's birthday. I feel more like running away from this depressing ward where, in some cases, you can tell that life is ebbing away by the shallow breathing and the frail, skinny limbs laid out on the beds. Nobody wants to end up like this and it makes me wonder what the purpose of life is. How would Becca feel if she knew about her condition? Does Mr Grose realise what has become of him and why does he still cling on to life? Is he still hoping that one day, against all odds, he will be able to go back to his life or is he just quietly waiting, praying that he won't last much longer?

I have spoken to the consultant about Becca's situation and life expectancy, but he simply stated that, legally, he is restricted to dealing with her next of kin. Which is undeniably a difficult approach because there is only her sister, and her mother. I urge myself to stop here. Dorothy Trewoon is a chapter in a book that I don't like opening. A book I would destroy if I could.

'Has Bethany mentioned that we'd like to put bunting and balloons up in Becca's room?' Les Dunwell asks me almost cheerfully.

'She did.'

'What do you think? Would it be a good idea? Shall we have a cake as well?'

I stare at him. I can't believe that he's serious and actually means a proper birthday cake. Judging by his expression, I think he is.

'Why not?' Perhaps the nurses need something to cheer themselves up. It can't be easy to work on a ward, especially at this end of the corridor, where life and normality are seeping away from formerly proactive human beings. People do recover from strokes and brain damage, but it's the ones who stay here much longer that you notice. And remember.

'Leave it to us,' Rosie nods with more confidence than I can muster. 'If you can come in around coffee time in the morning, we will have everything ready.'

'Okay.' They are looking at me expectantly. I pull out my wallet and give them a few notes.

'Thank you, sir.' Rosie puts the money away in a cash box in a drawer. 'Will you invite anyone else?'

Sadly, there isn't anyone. 'Like who?'

'Well, her mother …'

'No.' My tone is sharp and uncompromising. They exchange glances. Surprised, Shocked. I expect when a nurse comes on duty, they don't read everything in a patient's file. Only the relevant things necessary for their treatment and their prognosis.

'She hasn't got a mother.' Somehow I find it difficult to think of Dorothy as Becca's mother. It makes it too close. Too intimate. I still think it's unbelievable what a mother is capable of doing to her own child.

'O, but I thought …' Intimidated by my fixed gaze, Rosie looks at her colleagues for moral support.

'It's a bit difficult to explain, Rosie,' says Les Dunwell gently. 'But Becca's mother won't be coming for her birthday.'

'Or her sister,' adds Mirabelle with a sideways glance at me.

'That's right.' I've had enough. Turning on my heels, I enter Becca's room, pushing the door shut behind me, aware of the tenseness in my shoulders. I stand still at the foot of her bed. I listen to the bleeps of the monitors, a dripping tap making a dull plopping noise in a mug placed in the wash basin. I look at the tubes that are inserted into her body to keep her alive. Her breath is shallow, but stable. Her face is pale, with only a hint of blood colouring her cheeks. The nurses are right, she deserves a birthday party but it's very sad that the nurses and I will be the only ones attending.

16

The weather forecast has attracted the last tourists of the season to flock into the county. The A30 is blocked at Temple, where the new part of the dual carriageway still hasn't materialised. Traffic has slowed to snail pace. Yellow speed camera's are too conspicuous to be ignored. Drivers of oversized four-wheel drive vehicles, which they treat as too precious to get scratched on stray brambles in the overgrown hedges, refuse to reverse on the narrow lanes.

Joan Walters is about my height, slightly overweight, with straight hair cut to shoulder length, dark but with tell-tale streaks of grey, and a long thin face. She isn't pretty, but her smile is warm and pleasant. She's wearing black jeans and a bright blue padded jacket, zipped up to her chin. It's hard to put an age to her.

When the appointment was made, she didn't give me her address but suggested I get on the little passenger ferry from Padstow to Rock. Feeling the tremors of the engine beneath my feet, the wind in my face, I look down the river to where Stepper Point and Pentire Head are guarding each side of the entrance to the estuary. I'm reminded of the day out with Lauren and the boys, which started with a promise and ended in an anti-climax. I haven't spoken to her since I dropped them of at her home.

Joan Walters is meeting me on the slipway where the ferry stops. A cautious woman, who makes me think she lives alone, but once had an abusive husband, from whom she escaped and who still appears in her nightmares and darker moments.

'Sorry, Mr Tregunna,' she says, smiling and shaking my hand with a firm grip, instantly making me change my mind about her. She isn't the type to become the victim of any form of abuse. 'I'd invite you home, if it weren't for my father. He isn't feeling very well today.'

'Is it okay to see me? Should you be with him?'

'No, no, it's fine. Honestly.' Following the other ferry passengers up the slipway, she makes a vague gesture towards a car park. 'Do you mind if we have a walk?'

'No.'

'Are you sure?' She looks me over, her eyes roaming from the top of my head down to my shiny black shoes. 'I mean … you're not exactly dressed for a walk on the beach.'

'It doesn't matter.'

'It's just … because of my father.'

'I'm glad you agreed to see me in the first place.'

Now that the head of the body has been washed up too, it's all the more important to know where all the body parts were first dumped. The fact that three of the four parts have been found around Padstow has significantly increased the likelihood that they were dumped near there. The foot though, is a different matter. It seems highly unlikely that it drifted along the coast and washed up at Pendennis Point. The assumption that the foot has been chucked in the water on the other side of the coast to cause confusion, seems more plausible and I hope Joan Walters can confirm these thoughts.

If there had been any suggestions that this was the result of an accident, they have all dissolved now into the certainty that we are dealing with a murder. I think of 'we', although I am not officially working on the case, which is both a relief as well as a frustration.

I follow Joan across the car park which, surprisingly, is almost full. In the corner is the entrance to a coastal path which follows the slope of the sand dunes.

'At low tides,' she explains, 'it's easier and quicker to get onto the beach.'

'Okay.' We stop for a few moments to watch the ferry head back to Padstow, passengers clicking with camera's and pointing to something dark that drifts just under the surface. I can almost feel the disappointment as the object turns out to be a bundle of seaweed.

'My father is … confused sometimes.' Joan Walters offers me a sad smile and I'm instantly reminded of Mr Grose, half slumped in his chair, the muscles on one side of his body useless, no longer able to be controlled by his brain. I nearly ask her what's wrong with her father, but I've heard too many sad stories this week already and I don't feel like hearing any more.

'Today is not one of his better days,' she continues with a tiny smile, not reading my thoughts. 'I'd rather not want him to see you. Nothing personal. Any visitor will upset him, make him feel paranoid.'

'Is he old?'

'No.' Sensing my discomfort about implying that she is old enough to have a long retired father, she smiles widely. 'Not really. But he's been diabetic almost all of his life. He's recently lost his leg. It has made him … moody. In denial, I guess.'

'Sorry. I just assumed … I saw an old acquaintance of my mother in hospital this morning. I guess that sparked the idea of …'

'It's all right, inspector, I am forty-two.'

She chuckles, waiting for me to walk next to her as the path widens out.

'How did you find me?' she asks.

'Clem Trebilcock suggested I talk to you.'

A faint smile flits over her lips. 'So you said.' She shrugs as if she doesn't understand why he would have mentioned her.

'He says you are an oceanographer.'

'I wish. I'm only an amateur.'

'I'm sure you know much more than most,' I reply, trying not to be patronising. She's the type of woman who takes everything seriously.

Burying her hands in the pockets of her padded jacket, she explains. 'Oceanography is a scientific study of oceans, the life that inhabits them, as well as their physical characteristics including their depth, their movement and chemical makeup. But also the topography and composition of the ocean floors.'

'A wide range to study.'

'Indeed. I'm part of a local amateur group based in Falmouth. Nowadays it's an even wider subject than it was a few decades ago, as it now involves things like how to harness the power of the ocean to generate renewable energy, but things like that are too technical for me.' She grins with self-mockery. 'My main interest is in the movement of the water. Tides and currents. Why and how, for example, rip tides occur and in which circumstances. Which is how I know Clem Trebilcock. Sometimes I go out with him to do my research while he's busy with his nets and lobsterpots and stuff. It's interesting to see how he uses his GPS system, how it traces shoals so that he can follow and catch the fish. How this relates to currents, mostly.'

'I can see why he recommended you to me.'

'I hope so.' Her eyes narrow as she cast me a quick sideways glance. 'Is this a professional matter? Police?'

'Not officially.' I don't really want to explain my situation, but she waits, as if our meeting is meant to be an exchange of information and not just one way for my benefit.

'You've probably heard that we found human body parts,' I say, gesturing towards the river with a tilt of my head. 'About six weeks ago someone found a hand. This week we discovered a foot and a torso.'

She nods. She's read about it in the papers or heard from her oceanographer friends. 'Horrible things to find.'

'Yes. The latest find was yesterday. A group of four young men walking along the coastal path made the discovery when they came down from Stepper Point to have lunch in the tearoom at Hawkers Cove.'

'Unbelievable. Almost on my doorstep.'

'Not exactly. One foot was found at Pendennis Point.'

I show her a map of the county with four red dots on it. She studies it, following the coastline from Falmouth right round to Padstow as though she is considering walking it herself and estimating how long it will take her.

'Falmouth?'

'That's why I'm here.'

She hasn't taken her eyes off the map. 'How long between the findings?'

'The hand in the Camel was found six weeks ago. The other parts were all found this week.'

'All of them? Even the one in Falmouth?'

'Yes.'

'And you are certain that it's the same body?'

'Yes. Although it can't have been easy to retrieve enough material to run DNA-tests, once we have the results it's pretty accurate.'

She shakes her head, frowning. 'Impossible, inspector. Of course, I can't give you the exact timing, but it would take at least a few months for those parts to travel as far apart as that. Where did they enter the water?'

'I was hoping you could tell me that.'

Her frown deepens. 'That would be an interesting project to study, but I think it would be very unlikely that I could give you an area small enough to work on.'

'I was afraid you'd say that.'

'Hm. Say the poor soul fell from the cliffs near Land's End, and his body was so damaged that it … fell apart … it is possible that those parts got separated and drifted along both sides of Cornwall's coastline.'

It hasn't occurred to me before but the suggestion that Lands' End was a possible place where the body parts were dumped, seems to be quite logical.

'The body parts were cut of,' I tell her, after a hesitation.

'It wasn't an accident?'

'No.'

She stops where the path splits. Points. 'Shall we walk on the beach? I'm sure we can find a sheltered spot to sit. Or would you rather stay on the path?'

'The beach is fine.'

She nods, relieved, and almost runs down in front of me, like a horse, sniffing the fresh air of spring after being held in stables during the winter.

I catch up with her on the beach. We are both slightly out of breath. Smiling like excited children. 'If I tell you where these body parts were found and when, and how long forensics believe they have been in the water, is it possible for you to tell me where they come from?'

'I would need more details. Was it a man or a woman? What height? Weight?'

'A man. The foot was still in the shoe.'

She nods, her face serious and business-like. 'That is useful information. I would need the brand of the shoe. Whether it was leather, or a plastic sandal. I will need as much detail as you can get.'

'It was a trainer.'

'I'll need the brand. The make. The model.' She opens her mouth, closes it. Pauses. 'I can't promise anything.'

'I don't expect miracles.'

'Was there any clothing left? Apart from the shoe?'

'No.' I'm intrigued by her questions,, which seem professional to me. 'Why do you ask?'

'It can make a difference, to keeping afloat, I mean. Do you remember your swimming lessons? At one point I remember, I had to jump in the swimming pool with my clothes on. If you close your jacket high up and cross your arms in front of your chest before you jump, you create a pocket of air and you would float for a while. The same can be the case with other clothing. Depending on the fabric, the air can remain in place for a shorter or longer period.'

'I thought it would be a matter of currents helped by the tide.'

She smiles. Amused by my ignorance. 'Sports shoes have air chambers in the soles. It makes them float. In general, they are light. Leather shoes are heavier, usually with solid soles and heels. If there is a leg attached, or a part of a leg, it's possible that it will help it to float as well. And whether a body part has been floating or not, can make a lot of difference to where it ends up. '

'I don't follow you.'

She shakes her head, finding a sheltered corner with half a dozen rocks, their tops smoothed by wind and water. Perfect to sit on, but we stand. I'm not all comfortable on hard surfaces these days, and her explanation seems to stop her from relaxing. On the contrary. Her face is flushed as she picks up pebbles, throwing them in the water as though she is forcing away her darkest thoughts.

'I'm saying that I can give you some indication of the direction the parts would have drifted, but not the exact point where, say, the torso was thrown into the sea. Besides, I suppose it will not be very useful to you anyway, because it will be hard for you to prove. Tracking currents is like tracking ghosts, inspector - you can't see them and they leave no evidence. You can only observe where flotsam started and where it ended up. Afterwards we can. We learn from that, but we can't predict exactly what will happen.'

She's on a roll now.

'We can release 100 table tennis balls into the water at one side of a headland and we will find most of them back, but there will be a certain percentage that will drift off and we'll find them sometimes miles away along the coast. A small percentage may even never turn up. We have some statistics on this, but basically we don't know for certain why one ball ends up miles from another.' She smiles to soften the blow. 'It's like a duck race.'

'This may be useful that it might tell us not to not proceed with this line on investigation,' I say to reassure her.

'Not so fast, inspector. I will discuss this with our group and perhaps we'll come up with something useful for you after all. But don't hold your breath.'

'Okay.'

She isn't finished. 'I'm sure you heard about the Lego bricks.'

'Clem Trebilcock told me about it. I've looked it up on the internet.'

Oceanographers and amateurs have been investigating what happened to the Lego bricks after they were spilled from the container, trying to solve the mystery of where the pieces ended up. And how and why. So far, the ocean hasn't revealed its secrets. Instead of sinking and remaining on the bottom of the ocean, as was expected, the bricks have not provided any insights to the mysterious world of currents and tides.

'Yes. The container fell of the ship years ago off the coast at Land's End. Why did a considerable percentage of bricks wash up at Perranporth on the north coast and not so many on the south coast? When you study the map, beaches like St Ives and Hayle are much more likely places for them to wash up. But that didn't happen.'

She shakes her head, following her own train of thought and subsequent worries. It makes me wonder whether scientists worry more when they learn about the threats to the environment, or whether they start learning more because they have their concerns already. She continues. 'The most important lesson we've learned from the Lego bricks is that things which sink to the bottom of the sea don't always stay there, as you would expect. They can be carried around the world, seemingly at random, but more or less subject to the oceans' currents and tides. Children may think it's fun to comb the beaches to find the Lego pieces but when you think about it, it's a threat from an environmental point of view. Forget the one container with the Lego pieces in it. Occasionally you hear about it in the media, because people think it's fun. But what happened to the other containers? What was in them? Have their contents damaged our waters and our coastline?'

She stops to catch her breath.

'All sorts of items wash up our beaches. If possible, we get in touch with companies whose products end up on the shoreline. Plastic in the sea is not going to just decompose and go away. Plastics are deadly in the sea, poisonous for birds, a catastrophe for wildlife.'

When we walk back later, she urges that I should not set my hopes too high.

'We have to look at every possibility to find what happened to this man,' I reply gently. 'So far, we haven't even established his identity. His age is between twenty-five and forty, so it's quite likely that his parents are still alive. Perhaps he had a wife or girlfriend. Children. They have a right to know that he's dead. And what happened to him.'

Once more, she shakes my hand in a firm grip when we are back at the slipway waiting for the ferry. 'Well, inspector, I'm glad that Clem gave you my name. Although the circumstances are sad, I have enjoyed talking to you and I will certainly look into this case.' She chuckles. 'Otherwise I would have been stuck in the house with my father, listening to him grumbling when he knows perfectly well that he can only blame himself for not sticking to his diet and not being more careful with his medication, blaming me and my sister.'

I offer a smile. 'He doesn't blame you. He blames himself.'

17

Mr Harradine Curtis lives in the flat next to mine. He is a fifty-odd years old sod who works for Newquay town council. He deals with claimants who are living on the poverty line, sometimes as poor as those in some third worlds countries, or claimants who are trying to get benefits when they have undeclared income from undisclosed sources. That's what he told me in a half-defeated tone when I came to live in the building and I very much doubt that he's changed his job since. Although he seemed to despise his work, he is simply not the type to part from a good job and try something else. Creature of habit, any new, fresh start would involve too much effort and uncertainty for comfort.

We had brief conversations in the beginning but other than the fact that we were both living alone, we didn't seem to have much else in common. He had outspoken, rather out-dated opinions which I rarely shared with him. As a result of a rather pointless issue about parking spaces, there is now a cold war coming between us.

It started when I parked my car in the parking area for residents. Admittedly I had noticed a wooden sign, perched in the surrounding wall and covered in ivy. It had numbers and letters on it, but I never asked myself what it was meant for. It emerged that it was there since he owned a car and he'd more or less claimed that specific space to park. I didn't realise this before he pointed it out to me, as he had recently bought another car, second hand, and couldn't be bothered to change what turned out to be his car licence number on the sign because everyone else knew it was his.

'You wouldn't mind parking somewhere else, Mr Tregunna?' His voice was polite, but with an obsessive undertone.

'I'm sorry, Mr Curtis, I wasn't aware we have designated parking spaces.'

'Well, we haven't, officially, but this dates from years ago, before your time. The rule is still in place.'

I was sure the estate agency dealing with the residents on behalf of a landlord who seemed to have moved to Spain, would have told me if it was. Clearly, Mr Curtis abided by his own rules.

'I didn't know,' I offered. 'I will move my car now. It won't happen again.' Even though I thought he was trying it on, I couldn't be bothered to argue with him.

'Everyone knows,' he said, frowning accusingly.

I soon found out his reasons for his childish, self-made rule: the space he claimed for himself turned out to be about the only place that wasn't under the trees, and therefore not under attack by birds' droppings. My irregular hours in the police force, however, meant that on one particular day I had arrived before Mr Curtis came home, and as it was the only free space at that moment, I parked on it. He was one of those people with a constant fear of police and, as by then, he was well aware of my job, he daren't argue this time and although I rarely park on that acclaimed space, he hasn't spoken to me since, nor does he return my greetings. Not even the slightest nod to acknowledge me.

Now, he is sitting on a bench near the lake, staring at a young mother and a little girl feeding breadcrumbs to the ducks. He looks up when he hears my footsteps and I wonder briefly if the young woman might be his daughter. I've never seen her before. It wouldn't surprise me at all if they'd previously been estranged.

Much to my surprise he looks up and offers a shy half-smile. 'Good day Mr Tregunna.'

'Good day Mr Curtis,' I say, slowing my pace for an exchange of polite chit-chat about nothing in particular. But he has other plans in mind.

'You are a police officer, am I right?' he says rather timidly.

'I am.'

He looks at the young woman, shifting uncomfortably.

'Would you mind having a word?'

By the looks of him, this must be an act of desperation rather than a peace offering.

'About a police matter?'

'You could say that.'

'In that case, it may be better if you go to the police station. Best to do it the official way.'

I am not really judging him for his previous behaviour. I'm just tired and I need to change my stoma bag. Besides, I don't believe he has anything more serious in mind than silly things like leaves or bird droppings on his second-hand car.

'Will they believe me?' he asks rhetorically.

The little girl runs away, nearly tripping over his feet, being mock-chased by her mother. Both giggle. Mr Curtis lifts his lips disdainfully. I'm almost relieved that he isn't the young woman's father.

'They might think I am crazy. A nutter.'

Suppressing a smile, I briefly consider telling him that he won't be taken seriously by anyone when all he does is complain about nothing at all really.

'I'm sure they will listen to you, Mr Curtis.'

'Maybe so.' He shrugs, unconvinced. 'But ... I thought ... if I could put the case to you first? Before I make a formal complaint?'

With an inward sigh I watch the little girl run away, giggling and chuckling, and I wish I could be so innocent again. And run away like that. I can only hope that Mr Curtis isn't planning to involve me in some silly complaint about one of our other neighbours. Or that he wants me to sign a petition to the council to get them to remove the trees.

'Ehm ... I haven't got much time.'

He nods as if he's expected this. 'I do understand that you are a busy man, Mr Tregunna. But I'd appreciate it very much if you would listen to me for five minutes.'

Most of our neighbours would probably walk away at this point – he isn't anyone's favourite around here – but I can't. In a weird sort of way, I feel sorry for him.

'Okay.' I glance at my watch.

'It won't take longer than five minutes, I promise,' he says with a vague smile, interpreting my glance at my watch as me making sure that he doesn't take more than five minutes of my time. Then I make the mistake of sitting down next to him as though we are going to have a long conversation. As if we're acquaintances. Friends.

'I've told one of my colleagues about it, but she said quite bluntly that I am acting like someone with mental health problems.'

Perhaps he has parking issues at work as well.

'She says I'm paranoid.'

He pauses, gazing across the lake. I presume following the young woman with his eyes. She is pushing the pram with little girl, exhausted, almost asleep in it.

'But I'm not. I'm not imagining things.' He hesitates. 'Which is why I dare to suggest that you listen to me.'

Shaking his head, his hand disappears into the pocket of his blazer and he retrieves a tattered notebook that looks like he's had it since his childhood. Opening it, he licks his thumb before turning each of the pages. I see columns divided by straight lines, small, tidy handwriting.

'Here you are, Mr Tregunna. These are my observations.'

With a rather sad smile, he offers me the notebook. Accepting defeat, I take it and open it where a pen is wedged into the spiral binding in the spine. I am not sure what he expects. Nor am I sure if I am interested in his weird little concerns anyway.

'Look!'

I look. On top of the page is today's date, the left-hand column has hours, divided in quarters. The other four columns seem randomly filled with A,B,C or D.

'What is this, Mr Curtis?' I ask, regretting it.

He doesn't answer immediately. Instead, he checks his watch. It is gold-coloured with a matching strap. By the looks of it, it's one that needs winding up every so often. Carefully, he pulls the pen out of the spine and adds an A and a question mark in the relevant column beside the current time. Pushing the pen pack into the spine, he straightens his back. 'Being a policeman, I thought, you may have access to … certain resources.'

'If this is anything serious, Mr Curtis, then you really ought to go to the police.'

I know at least one of the desk officers is brilliant with time wasters. I am tempted to offer to make an appointment for him with that officer in particular.

Ignoring me, he says, 'Don't look straight away, sir, but on the road opposite the lake is a car parked. A black VW Golf. There are two men in it. Sometimes there is only one.'

I stare at him incredulously.

'At this very moment there are two,' he continues without taking his eyes from the parked cars. He's forgotten me.

'They have been here almost constantly for a few days now. The licence plate is …' He flicks through the pages and taps on one of four long rectangles filled with numbers and letters that form number plates. Four of them. Colours added behind them: silver, blue, black, silver grey.

'What is this about, Mr Curtis?'

'These men are acting rather suspiciously.' He gestures with his chin in an unspecified direction. 'In my opinion, it is certainly not normal that there are one or two men watching this area almost constantly. With binoculars.'

'Since when have you been watching them?' I ask, feeling a shiver running down my spine.

'Well.' He shifts uncomfortably, eyes down in embarrassment. 'Since that bomb threat in St Austell. Yes, I know very well, inspector, that it was a false alarm, fortunately, but we can't ignore that these things happen, can we? That man in St Austell may have been a sad lunatic who wanted some attention, but all the same, he might have been a genuine terrorist. We have to be careful at all times, inspector.'

'I don't believe those men are terrorists, Mr Curtis.'

He shrugs. Opens his mouth for the next best option. 'Then they're looking for children. There are so many threats nowadays. Technical things. Perhaps they can make videos with binoculars. I mean, let's face it, Mr Tregunna. Nobody would be bothered by someone using binoculars, but if they were filming other people, it would be a different matter all together. Like filming young children. Like the young woman with that little girl we saw a minute ago. I mean, it's not right, is it, inspector?'

'But not strictly illegal,' I say slowly.

He nods. 'But it's certainly not generally accepted in our society.'

'True.' I stare at his notebook. 'What would you like me to do with this, Mr Curtis?'

'Well, I don't really know. I thought maybe, if you can find out who these men are and then send some officers to talk to them, perhaps they'll be scared and … not come back.'

Once more I stare at the pages, half covered with his boyish observations. 'I will see what I can do for you, Mr Curtis.'

'That's all I ask, Mr Tregunna,' he replies almost cheerfully, but definitely relieved that he won't be dealing with the matter alone any more.

He tears a blank page out of the notebook and writes the four licence plate numbers on it. Without a word, I slide the page into my pocket. If Mr Curtis is paranoid, then I must be suffering from the same condition.

I've recognised one of the numbers. The silver grey one. It's the same car that was parked at about the same spot as it is now, when I flippantly pointed out a flat tyre.

I have already checked the number plate at the police station. The car is registered in the name of Victor Carter.

18

Hidden amongst high autumn-coloured trees, Camellia House is perched on the sharp bend on the road from Newquay to St Columb Major. A high boundary wall, overgrown with ivy, has a narrow entrance way giving access to the front garden, and a drive, covered in grit and broken shells, leads to a parking area at the back. It would look attractive and welcoming if it wasn't for the rather forbidding wrought iron gates, supported by two stone pillars. One has a black marble plaque engraved with the name of the house, the other has a white, less friendly sign, instructing visitors to wait. A small metal strip above it has narrow slits and a tiny microphone. Two cameras attached to iron poles behind each of the pillars rotate slowly as they monitor every inch of my car, zooming in on my number plate, and probably on my face as well.

A metallic-sounding voice crackles from above the waiting sign. 'Please hold your identification card here.' Approaching it, I say, 'Can you open the gates, please?'

'Please hold you identification card here.'

'Is Mr Carter in?'

The same words are repeated again and it occurs to me that I'm having a one-sided conversation with a recorded message. Then a different recording crackles through the microphone. 'Thank you.'

I wait. Nothing happens. I've had my chance. I walk back to my car. Get in. More annoyed than I was already. I stare at the gates. Nothing seems to be moving except a strip of brown paper that has got stuck in the ivy.

I get out again, walk back to the sign, acknowledging defeat. After all, showing my ID-card isn't such a big deal. Stubbornness won't help me here. The cameras are following every inch of my movements. Wait here. I wait. Nothing happens. The computerised programmes behind the system have already rejected me. I'm not welcome at Camellia House.

I walk round the boundary wall, considering its height and my chances of climbing over it. I'm not fit enough. Besides, trespassing will probably do me more harm than good. The decision is no longer mine when I notice the rusty barbed-wire fence half hidden behind the ivy.

Getting back into my car, I get my mobile out, not really knowing what to do next. I feel flustered with anger and frustration. I'm even more determined to get access to this house and reveal its secrets. There has to be another way.

As I start the engine, move the car into gear and turn on the space which is obviously designed for that reason, one of the gates slowly swings open and a man appears, holding the leash of a black dog that seems eager to have a go at me.

His head shaven, and with a wide black moustache carefully curled upwards, the man is wearing a black suit and white shirt, top button open, no tie; it looks like every piece of clothing is at least one size too small. He observes me with a neutral expression, waiting until I half get out of my car, one hand still on the steering wheel, the engine humming softly.

His gaze is blank. 'Mr Tregunna?'

I nod. I didn't need to identify myself after all.

'Follow me.' His head jerks to the side as he steps back. The dog jumps, pulling at his leash and showing his teeth to me by way of a serious warning. The man doesn't give any further instructions and as the left-hand gate remains closed, I turn off the engine and follow him and the black dog on foot, keeping a sensible and safe distance. Mr Carter must be directing proceedings from behind closed curtains.

The front garden has a rectangle of shortcut grass with a polished stone sundial in the middle. Neatly trimmed hedges run along the borders in straight rows making it look so meticulously tidy that it has probably involved a surveyor with a theodolite measuring it out precisely. This is the artwork of a control freak.

The white-painted front door opens as we approach up the drive. A young woman is waiting in the half-opened doorway. She's in her late twenties, with dark hair tied at the back of her head with a black plastic clip, wearing a black dress and a single string of small pearls around her neck.

'Can I take your coat, sir?' The man and the dog have somehow disappeared.

'It won't take long.'

'Can I take your coat, sir?'

She avoids my eyes demurely. I wonder if she's been instructed to repeat the words one more time. Like the recorded pre-programmed message at the entrance.

'What's your name, sir?'

She sounds as though she's half expecting that I'm a salesman with a range of products nobody really needs.

'My name is Andy Tregunna. Police. I'm investigating the disappearance …'

'Your ID, sir?'

I retrieve my ID from my pocket and she takes it without checking it. She has clear instructions about how to act in such circumstances. Inviting strangers into the house is never an option.

A door behind her in the hallway opens and she is pushed aside by a tall and muscular man, his broad shoulders squeezed into a black suit which makes him look like a square block.

'Cum'in.' His head jerks to the side as he steps back, lacing his fingers as though preparing for a fight. His knuckles make a frightening cracking sound like warning shots from the gun of an invisible enemy hiding in trenches beyond my sight. The young woman disappears with quickening steps.

'Mr Carter?'

Without a word the man closes the front door behind me, trapping me in a big hall with shiny black marble tiles and white walls covered in colourful modern art canvases in black frames. A wide black marble staircase is cantilevered off the wall as though it's floating in mid-air. The ground-floor doors are all closed, except for a large double door which is slightly ajar. I can hear men's voices behind it, arguing, both sounding forceful: two stags having a clashing of power.

'Sir?' The square block pushes open the double doors. 'Mr Tregunna.'

Two men come forward with an urgency that gives the impression I'm the person they have been waiting for. One is a tall and slim man with a light beige suit, a pink shirt and burgundy scarf, dark blond hair and blond brows in a tanned and freckled face. The other man is a generation older and bears so much resemblance to the younger man that I decide they must be father and son.

The younger one is holding my ID-card, tapping it thoughtfully with a fingertip. 'Detective Inspector Tregunna.'

My gaze drifts through a modern-style living room. Again, black tiles and white walls, and in here the furniture is also black and white. Leather and glass and chrome. The work of an interior designer, it lacks identity with its expensive look, its quality. About two dozen satin cushions in different, bright colours are scattered on the sofas to lift the monotony of the monochrome décor.

'What!? Police?'

Without acknowledging me, the man turns towards the older man while emptying a crystal tumbler with a considerable amount of gold liquid.

'I thought we agreed we'd have no police involved!' The father's blotched cheeks turn to a darker shade of pink. His eyes express anger and surprise.

'Careful, dad. I didn't invite him.'

'Then why is he here?'

The younger man shrugs. 'I guess we're about to find that out.'

Making a show of pulling my phone from my pocket, quickly sliding my finger over the screen, I read out one of the licence plate numbers supplied by Mr Curtis.

'Is that your car, Mr Carter?' I smile casually. 'I take it one of you is Mr Carter?'

The older man shrugs and pulls back two steps. The other frowns annoyed that I don't appear to know him.

'I'm Victor Carter. This is my father.' He sounds like he is addressing his favourite pupil who finally managed to push him towards the very edge of his patience.

'Nice to meet you, Mr Carter,' I say flatly. 'Is that the registration number of your car?'

He shrugs with badly acted indifference. 'I have several cars. You'll have to check with my secretary.'

'Why is this car parked at Trevemper Road in Newquay?'

'Is it?' Amusement in his eyes.

'Why?'

'Trevemper Road. Near the Gannel?'

'That's correct.'

'It's a public road. With a parking area, I believe, Mr Tregunna. Free parking.' He holds out his hand and I take my ID-card. 'Is there a problem?'

'I wonder why that car seems to be parked there all day throughout the evening, with two men in it and a pair of binoculars.'

He shrugs. 'As I said, I have several cars, Mr Tregunna. I also have several men working for me. They're the ones who use my cars. At work and in their free time.'

'Are you saying they are sitting there in their spare time?'

'I'm afraid I can't think of any other reason.' He turns to the other man, who is pouring a drink from a bottle with an expensive whisky label. 'Can you, dad?'

'Are you sure?' I ask.

'Do I look like I'm stupid, Mr Tregunna?'

'This has no relevance whatsoever to the disappearance of your daughter?'

It's a shot in the dark, but it hits the bull's eye with great precision. A deep silence sets in. They look at me, stunned, shocked. There is movement at the double doors and from my peripheral vision I notice that the taller one of the body guards is standing in front of them, arms crossed across his chest and legs spread. He'll stop me from running away.

Carter Senior gulps down his whisky, including half-melted ice cubes. They rattle against his teeth and his eyes widen as he swallows them bravely.

'How do you know my granddaughter?' His voice is low and anxious.

'I'm here in relation to her disappearance and ...'

Turning towards his father, Victor presses his index finger onto the other man's chest. 'What is this? I've told you exactly how we're going to deal with this and I insisted that the police wouldn't be involved. And I definitely don't want them in my house!'

'Vic, I promise, I don't have anything to do with this.'

Clearing my throat and stepping forward, I sense that the man behind me at the doors also moves. Once more his knuckles make a threatening crispy sound.

'Where was your daughter Wednesday night, Mr Carter?'

Victor Carter has put one hand in his trouser pocket. I can see him clenching his fist as he moves restlessly through the room, occasionally picking up folded papers and dismissing them instantly, briefly pausing near the window to look out over a garden surrounded by overgrown walls that block the view along the valley.

'At home.'

'According to my information she had ... a sleepover party with a friend in Newquay.'

'Ah, yes, I'm sorry. Wednesday. That's correct.' He won't win an award for acting. 'What about it?'

'Is it possible to have a quick word with Siobhan, Mr Carter?'

Carter lifts his chin offensively, narrowing his eyes. 'What about?'

'Just a few questions, sir. Mainly about Leanne Lobb, her ...'

'About whom?' he interrupts brusquely.

'It's in relation to the disappearance of your daughter's friend, Leanne Lobb,'

'Leanne ... who?' Carter Senior asks coolly, not wasting time.

I'm aware of a strong undercurrent, as if everyone around me is in a conspiracy that I know nothing of, but about which I am supposed to be briefed.

'Leanne Lobb. She is Siobhan's best friend and she is ...'

'My daughter is not a friend of that ... girl.' Victor Carter's voice is laden with ice. His mouth moves with disgust. 'My daughter is not involved with those people ... who live on an estate like that.'

'So you know Leanne and you know where she lives.'

'I think you'd better leave now, Tregunna.'

'I am informed that Leanne is Siobhan's best friend.'

A flash of anger colours his face, his eyes are gleaming with a mixture of disgust and something I can't fathom.

'Certainly not!' He blurts, and then swallows and takes a deep breath. 'As I said, I think you'd better leave now, Tregunna.'

'All I want is to ask Siobhan where they were on Wednesday night.'

'I told you, Mr Tregunna, Siobhan was in Newquay for a birthday party with that other girl, Pencreek.'

'Why lie about it? Mr Carter? You know as well as I do that there was no sleepover party.'

He moves forward quickly, waving his index finger in front of my eyes. 'What else do you know, Mr Tregunna?'

'I know where the girls were. And who with.' It is slightly untrue, but I don't care any more. The man is frustrating me to the core.

'And are you going to tell me?'

'I'm here to ask questions.'

He chuckles uncomfortably. 'Is this some sort of game, Mr Tregunna? Like Cluedo? Is it my turn now to make a guess? Where and how and by whom?'

'I find it strange that you don't seem to want to know the truth, Mr Carter. Why are you lying?'

'Is it a crime to protect my daughter? If so, arrest me if you like.' With a dramatic effect he holds up his wrists as if challenging me to cuff him. His father mutters something in protest and it occurs to me what is happening when the patio doors are pulled open and a girl appears on the doorstep. She stops mid-step, staring at me, face flustered and eyes wide. Accusingly. Angry. Scared.

'Siobhan, would you mind? Can't you see that we are in a meeting?' Victor Carter smiles, but not with the warm gaze of a loving father. Then he turns his back on me, gesturing to the bodyguard with his thumb. 'Accompany Mr Tregunna to his car, please, will you, Tony?'

'Yes sir.'

Reluctantly accepting defeat, I nod. I have nothing on him and he knows it. Only in this case, I'd prefer to have the benefit of the last word.

'You haven't told me why your men are watching the building where I live, Mr Carter.'

'Goodbye Mr Tregunna.'

19

Mr Grose's house at Treworran Hill seemed a big and impressive building when I was eight years old, but it's really a normal size family home which sits between two similar-sized houses, albeit each one set higher up the hill than the next. Throughout the years, different occupants have tried to adapt their homes to their own style and taste. The house on Grose's left has light pink paint on the original granite bricks, with similar painted pots of geraniums lined up on both sides of the four steps that lead to the front door. The house on the other side has been updated recently, the walls plastered and painted white, the original wooden frames replaced by plastic ones.

Mr Grose's house looks old and gloomy with its weathered granite bricks, paled remains of brown paint that must have been the original colour on the wooden window frames decades ago, and unwashed windows with curtains closed behind them.

Vehicles stop behind me, waiting for the traffic light on top of the hill to change. An impatient driver hoots. Fumes of burnt diesel carry through the street. I smile a little sadly when I climb the four granite steps that lead to his front door.

Memories float through my head as I use my mother's key and go in, for a few moments standing still in front of the kitchen door. It has a big padlock, for which Mr Grose entrusted me with the key before I left him in the hospital.

I weigh the key in my hand and, picturing the eight-year-old boy who pushed open the kitchen door without knowing what he'd find, take in a few sharp breath before opening it. When I do, I can't make myself look at the table in the middle. The kitchen, with the cupboards and drawers open and empty, and Venetian blinds at the only window, is surprisingly clean. There is some dust gathered over the months since Mr. Grose has been in hospital but it is not at all as bad as I feared. I had visions of being in a horror film, threads of dust clinging to every surface, brushing against me as I force my way to the middle of the room, where the remains of his wife sit motionless at the table.

The first thing that strikes me is the smell. A faint hint of disinfectant mixed with the sweet smell of roses. Wiping the dust from the seat I sit down opposite her and take the plate with paled food away, dumping it in one of the bin bags I brought with me. The knife, still resting in her hand, clatters on the hard Formica surface of the table, startling me as it falls. Gently, I remove the fork from the other hand. Only then I look in the face. It's a horrible grey colour under a brown wig. Blue eyes are staring at me intently as if she is debating whether to tell me her secret. There's a smile on her lips that resembles her expression in a framed discoloured photograph on the window sill behind her. It adds to the morbid atmosphere.

I sit there for several moments, reliving my first view of her, sensing the dread and fear, yet stricken by the anti-climax of it now. I rise to my feet. Somehow I must have knocked the table as I get up. Her arm falls aside and a hand crashes on the floor shattering into a pile of pieces. A gold wedding ring, half hidden, is still smooth and shiny.

Seeing the small pile of bits on the tiled floor spurs me into action and frees me from the sense of secrecy. When I lift her head from a wooden frame that has been made to keep the rest of her together, one of the eyes falls on the table with a dull thud. It's a glass eye like those used for teddy bears or dolls, a strip of metal glued onto the back to keep it in place. The wig is still attached to the head, even as it crumbles at the touch of my hands.

Mr Grose once told me he would love to have been an artist. Sculpture being his favourite. I remember very clearly how I had sniggered behind my hand. Artists were a bit odd to me then. I thought of them as bohemian dressed in strange colourful clothes and spending all their time in bars or their studios with naked women lounging on sofas. Now I feel a bit ashamed about my ignorance.

Seeing the accuracy with which he had sculpted his wife's face, I can't deny my admiration for him and it makes me feel sad that I never really knew him. In hindsight, I would have liked to have visited him more often. Get to know him.

He would have been a great sculptor. He had made from dull grey clay a perfect replica of his wife, at least of her head and hands. The rest of her was made of newspapers, now more than thirty years old, to form her shape beneath her clothes.

It takes two bin bags to remove Mrs Grose from where she'd been seated all those years. Then I make a phone call to the police station and ask the desk officer to stick a note on the crime scene board in the incident room, to find an artist of some sort to create a facial reconstruction of the head that was found near Hawkers Cove on Lauren's birthday.

I climb the stairs for the first time in my life. Check Mr Grose's bathroom, empty his dirty laundry bin, clear his bed and chuck the sheets in a third bin bag. Whoever will be dealing with the task of emptying his house won't be finding dirty socks and pants. I will always remember Mr Grose as a proud and dignified man.

When I lock the front door behind me, three black bin bags at my feet, a woman emerges from the porch of the pink house next door. She is small and skinny, with a long and narrow face and a pronounced chin. Her dull brown hair is cut too short across her forehead which makes her look as if she's been trying on a wig for a fancy dress party and forgot to take it off.

'Are you his son?' she asks suspiciously, taking an e-cigarette from between her lips and planting her hands on her hips.

'No, I am ...'

'Then who are you?'

Her voice has the sharp edge of someone short-fused.

'I'm Andy,' I say, trying to sound friendly. 'And you are ...?'

She points at the pink house. 'Neighbour. When's he coming back?'

I open my mouth to tell her that she wouldn't need to ask that question if she had bothered to see Mr Grose in hospital but he might not be grateful for her visit. All the same, she deserves some kind of truthful answer.

'I'm afraid he won't be back. He's ...'

'Dead?' She interrupts bluntly.

'No, no, he is still in hosp ...'

'Very good.' She seems to have the annoying habit of interrupting every sentence at the most crucial word. 'He's a weirdo.'

I freeze. 'What makes you say that?'

She shrugs, her lips drawn in a thin, tight line. 'Me kids. He always stared at them ... like ... you know.'

'No.'

'I have always ... what?'

'I said: no. You'll need to explain what you mean by implying that he's a weirdo.'

For a few moments she is speechless. Perhaps the conversation has become too difficult for her to comprehend. 'Who are you?'

'I'm a police officer.'

A shrug is followed by a self-confident smile. 'Oh. Police. So you do know what I mean.'

'I'm sorry?'

Offering a smile for the first time, albeit a wry one, she arches an eyebrow and cocks her head to one side. 'I understand that you lot don't want to talk about it. Which, to me, is outrageous! Those' - she jerks her head in the direction of Mr Grose's house – 'people get more protection from police and society than the poor victims.'

'Mr Grose did nothing ...'

'Is he on the list?'

'What list?' I know what she means but her behaviour ruffles my feathers. Putting Mr Grose's key in my pocket, I pick up one of the bin bags, wondering if she's ever peered through a tiny gap in the curtains and spied on Mr Grose – or his wife.

'The list of sex-offenders and paedophiles.'

'Mr Grose is on no such a list.'

She snorts. 'If you say so.'

'Do you have any reason to believe he should be on that list, Mrs ...?'

'Foster. Jill Foster.' She jerks her head. 'That's what they say. We keep an eye on him. For the safety of our kids.

'How long have you known him?'

'Not long. We moved in here about a month before he ... left.' She shrugs. 'Someone said he was taken to prison. Just as well, I thought. A relief for the neighbourhood.'

'Mr Grose is a respectable man. He isn't a weirdo or a paedophile, or whatever people want to believe.'

She isn't convinced. 'Is that evidence?' she asks, pointing and staring at the bin bags.

'Evidence? For what? The poor man is in hospital. I'm just clearing some stuff ...'

'You said you are police.' She sounds like she doesn't believe me and is putting me in the same category as Mr Grose.

'I am,' I say curtly, aware that I am slowly losing my temper. 'If you had any grounds for suspicion, why didn't you go to the police and make ...?'

'What would they have done? They'd rather protect him, not our kids.'

I take a deep breath. 'How many kids do you have?'

'Three. Two girls and one boy. It's the boys he's after, I am sure of that.'

'Has he ever done anything to your son?'

'No, but I recognised his type as soon as I saw him and I've made sure he couldn't do anything to hurt my Dan.'

'So there is no reason whatsoever why you believe Mr Grose is a paedophile. What made you ...?'

'I knew, Officer,' she interrupts again. 'First time I saw

him, I went to introduce us. Me and the kids. He didn't even look at the girls, only had eyes for Danny. Asked how old he was and when Dan said he was eight, he said he once knew a lovely boy of eight years old, but he disappeared from his life.'

A lump comes to my throat and I feel a shiver between my shoulder blades. 'You may have misunderstood what that ...'

'I've got eyes and ears, officer. I'm not stupid. I know men like that. They behave like normal people, but they have dark, secret thoughts.'

'I'm sure if you had ...'

'What will happen to the house?'

I pick up the second bin bag, remembering the fondness in Mr Grose's eyes. Whether or not he was ever involved in sexual abuse, he never laid a hand on me and I can't believe he has done anything to other boys. Still I make a mental note to ask my mother if there had been any such suspicions about Mr Grose years ago.

My mobile vibrates in my pocket and with shameful relief I retrieve it and answer the call. Maloney.

'Tregunna. You called.' He sounds tired and annoyed.

'Yes.' I look at Mrs Forster. She hasn't moved and doesn't seem to be bothered about listening to my conversation. 'I think we ought to find an artist who can do facial reconstruction.' I stare at Mrs Forster. 'Of the skull.'

Her mouth falls open and her eyes are immediately drawn towards Mr Grose's house.

'In which decade are you living, Tregunna?' he snorts. 'We don't need artists to do that. We have experts and computer programmes to do that for us. Much quicker and cheaper, and more accurate.'

I have my doubts about the last bit, but know better than to correct him. He is right though about the costs; I must have been side-tracked by Grose's unexpected sculpturing skills.

'Anyway.' He hesitates. 'I think you are right in this case, Tregunna. I see no point in waiting for people to come forward on the basis of a rather vague description. In the end, the cost of having a facial reconstruction done by some computer nerd, will be less than wasting our time following up useless leads.'

'Okay.'

'What's going on?' Mrs Forster demands, before I have put my mobile back in my pocket. 'What did you say about a skull?'

'It's got nothing to do with Mr Grose, Mrs Forster.'

'Are you sure?' Her eyes widen. 'Was it true then what they say? About that eight-year-old boy who disappeared?'

I am still grinning when I drive to the cemetery, to fulfil Grose's last request. In the distance I can see the blue-grey smoke from the old steam train that has been reinstated by train fanatics and now runs through the valley from Bodmin to Wenford Bridge for the benefit of the tourists and hobbyists.

There is a funeral going on. There are men in black suits, white shirts and grey ties, the women dressed in black skirts and matching stockings. The odd one is wearing a white blouse, but generally they are all in black. Clearly, they are the deceased's family. Another group is made up of friends, with long hair and beards, wearing leather jackets and trousers, and knee-high boots, carrying black helmets with logos hand-painted on them. The groups don't mix. They belong to different worlds, which makes me wonder how the deceased would feel if he knew.

I turn and I gaze at a weathered headstone. A branch with two roses is engraved above the name: Elizabeth Amy Grose-Liddell, beloved wife of Archie. The date of her death tells me she'd already been dead for two years when I first saw her in that cold kitchen.

Without looking over my shoulder for prying eyes, I kneel down and bury Mrs Grose's wedding ring in the soil of her grave.

20

Sunday. The day stretches out endlessly dark before me. I have called my mother that I had to decline her invitation for an old-fashioned Sunday roast after all. Work. I wish I hadn't, but it's too late now to change my mind. I can't go to Lauren's either. I desperately want to, but it wouldn't be fair on her. Perhaps Ray Campbell, one of the pathologists, will have time for a drink in the pub later. He is perhaps closest to being a friend than anyone else. I can call him. Invite him for a pint. I consider this, then discard the idea with one of the worst excuses: I wouldn't want to ruin his wife's plans for the day. Ray and I occasionally met for a drink before he got to know his wife and his lifestyle changed gradually. I suppose they do their best. Every so often they invite me to their house parties, most of which I decline politely. I shouldn't have done that. There is a limit to the number of invitations you receive when the response is always the same. I'm no longer on their guest list. I need to put my name back on it. In one way, I desperately want to talk to him, share my worries and concerns with him, and listen to his reassurances that I am seeing problems lurking round every corner. On the other hand, he will probably lecture me about being more open to people, talking openly about my cancer and stoma. He means well, but he can be so scarily truthful, not hiding behind senseless clichés, that I fear his words before they're spoken.

Work. Concentrate on your job.

From day one Carter has lied. And I want to know why.

The girls planned the trip in advance. They invented the sleepover party at a classmate's home in Newquay, using Carensa Pencreeks' name for the sole reason that she lives in Newquay, which gave them the opportunity to travel to Newquay without being questioned. They pre-planned Sally Pollinger's home as a safe place to spend the night with the intention of going to school the next morning as usual. It could have worked. No questions asked. What went wrong was the fact that in Plymouth they missed the last bus back.

Leanne's story that she slept at Stacey's house becomes less believable when I think it through. Her claim that she had to wait for the girl's mother to go to work in the morning before she could leave herself, doesn't add up either. If she had been so desperate about getting back to school in time, she would have sneaked out early in the morning, even before the girl's mother woke up. She would have caught the early bus, thinking there was still a fair chance that her trip would have remained unnoticed.

And there is Siobhan Carter. I must find a way to speak to her. I simply can't believe that Leanne went to see the pop star on her own. Her best friend would have been part of it. Both Sally Pollinger and the teacher, Gerald Davey, said that the two girls are inseparable. Siobhan must have been part of the whole plan. Or at least she knew about it in detail.

I call the station and ask the desk officer to text me a phone number. The message comes up almost instantly. Still not convinced that I'm doing the right thing, and more importantly for the right reasons, I press the number and wait.

A voice with a laugh in it answers. Some people enjoy a free Sunday, a day to relax and do lazy things without feeling guilty. I can't do that any more. Walls are closing in on me. Eating away at me. I would stay in bed all day, staring into oblivion and thinking about my life and subsequently sink deeper and deeper in the all too familiar swamp of depression and self pity.

I clear my throat. 'Mrs Pencreek. I'm sorry to bother you, but I am in the process of closing the file relating to the alleged disappearance of Leanne Lobb. Ehm ... Can I ask you a quick question?'

'Sure, inspector. Happy to help if I can.' A giggle. A low voice. She's having a lay in. I remember the details vaguely: divorced, her only daughter, Carensa, is with her father every other weekend. She must have a new man in her life, one who is making her happy and giggly.

A lump sticks in my throat. Regret. Envy.

'Mrs Pencreek, on the day that Leanne Lobb appeared to be missing, you received a phone call from her parents.'

'I did.' A rustle of bed-clothing. A grunt. 'Elsie called me several times. I think she didn't believe me. She seemed certain that the girls were staying over with Carensa.'

'Were you called by anyone else?'

A pause. 'Yes.' She sounds surprised. 'By Mr Carter. Siobhan's father.' She pauses. Thoughtful. No giggles this time. 'He called a tad later, so I already knew more or less what was going on. I'd given Carensa a bollocking about it. How dare those girls tell lies like that!'

I don't see the point in reminding her she'd probably done the same at that age.

'And you told Carter the same as you told Elsie Lobb? That there was never a sleepover party arranged?'

'I did.'

I thank her, wondering why, even several days later, Carter is still lying.

He lives behind walls with barbed wire on top, he has cameras installed and presumably a sophisticated system to scan, scrutinise and identify every visitor. In case that system fails to identify the visitor, a different system will automatically come into play and one of his body guards will make sure anyone will be dealt with according to Carter's private security rules.

Leanne and Siobhan went to Newquay together. The next day, Janice Lobb noticed that her sister wasn't at school. She phoned her mother. At some point, Patrick or Elsie Lobb called Carter. Or his wife. They were ignored. Yet, at that point, Carter must have realised that something was wrong.

Two girls were missing. Only one pair of parents called the police. Astonishingly, Carter didn't. He didn't even speak to Lobb, however despicable such contact would have been in his eyes. Wouldn't a loving father have overcome his prejudiced opinion if his daughter was missing?

The case is closed. The girls are safe at home, yet something is still nagging at me.

So I call the manager of BarZz, where pop star Sammii had his gig. I've seen his picture and YouTube films, heard his music. It made me feel old. Pale and dangerously skinny with badly hidden acne and droopy eyes, his music is monotone, loud and aggressive and there is nothing that makes me remotely understand why girls like Leanne and Siobhan are so smitten with this boy who thinks he's the new idol the modern world has been waiting for since the Beatles and the Stones stormed onto the scene.

BarZz's manager answers with 'Jack' and sounds as if he's just gone to bed. He gives the shortest possible answers but after three questions, he has enough. My request to see his camera images falls on stony ground. I can't. End of. Police? In that case, I'll have to show him an official request. I try to sound officious and argue that it is only a matter of elimination but he cuts me off with a brusque, 'Okay. I'll see you with the right paperwork.'

There is no way I can get it. Jack knows his rights. To carry out a search on the premises, I must have reasonable grounds for suspecting that there is evidence relating to an offence. I don't even know if there is an offence, I have only suspicions based on instinct and vague assumptions.

I open Google Maps, find the centre of Plymouth and turn to Street view, searching the street of BarZz's location and the surrounding buildings. As usual Google's street images are in sunshine. Cars and bike riders, pedestrians on the pavement are pictured at intervals as I move forward and back again. They disappear and emerge with each camera movement. The images are dated several years ago. Double-checking the address, I stare at the fronts of a hardware shop, a grocers and a window boarded up with plywood and covered in graffiti. Since then, someone has bought the three premises and reshaped the lot into the well-known BarZz, with several bars and dance floors.

Perhaps not so surprisingly, the news agency across the street is still there.

A man with a foreign accent answers my call while helping his customers at the till. I hear the ping of his cash machine and the clatter of coins in the drawer. He is unable to send me his CCTV images over the email, but I am welcome to come and see them. His system is rather old but it does the job for him and he sees no point in spending money on a modern, sophisticated version.

I understand what he means when Mirek Schmidt lets me into a small room behind his shop two hours later. In his early fifties, he is originally from the former East Germany. He has a wide face with pale skin and warm brown eyes. Lost his twin brother in a car accident. Married a Scottish girl. Divorced. Went back for a family visit to his home town and returned to Plymouth with his primary school lover. She couldn't or wouldn't adapt to his new life and left him. Divorced again. He has two sets of identical twins in Scotland and half a dozen grandchildren, also two sets of twins and three grandchildren in Germany. He is in contact with none of them. A life in a nutshell.

The room is cluttered with opened half-empty boxes and discarded display material. A kettle is perched on a table in the corner. No tap or sink. He has water in a plastic container like those people use on campsites. A washing up bowl has half a dozen dirty mugs in it. He offers to make me a Nescafé and I accept more out of politeness, trying not to think about his cleaning habits. He fills two clean mugs, moves a dozen boxes to one side and finds a plastic chair stained with smudges of blue and white paint – the colours of the walls in his shop – and I sit with what looks like a 20-year-old portable TV set and a video player.

He has a collection of videotapes lined up on a shelf under the deeper shelf that holds the TV and video player. Tattered cases with old films, cartoons, soft porn. Action movies. He explains that he can't buy new tapes any more. Instead he goes to charity shops and buys three films for a pound, hoping that no one has broken the seal to prevent the movie accidentally being taped over. Explaining with a lopsided grin that I am lucky as he refreshes the tapes every week on Monday evening, he picks up a relatively looking new version of 'Beauty and the Beast' and slides it in the machine. The camera offers a view of the till and the shop entrance. Straight across the street is the entrance of BarZz.

However old and tatty, his surveillance system is accurate. He winds the tape forward and presses 'Play', leaving me with images of a queue of mostly teenaged girls waiting at the entrance of BarZz for the doors to open. Leanne and Siobhan were certainly not the only ones to have fallen in love with young Sammii.

I recognise them almost instantly. They are almost at the front of the queue, laughing happily and giggling behind their hands. Four other girls in front of them. Two young men behind them, but they all seem so friendly to one another that I am unable to work out if the two girls were alone or with the two young men. Unfortunately the streetlights are dimmed and the shop windows next to BarZz are dark and I can't see clearly enough to be certain that I see the girls leave.

I freeze some of the images on the screen and photograph them with my mobile and thank Mirek after more mugs of Nescafé and a shared tuna sandwich and bag of crisps. When I drive back to Newquay, I wonder if the trip has been worth the effort. All I have achieved is that I have proof that Siobhan was with Leanne, but I doubt that Carter will admit it, even when he sees the pictures on my phone.

Yet my mood has lifted and with the prospect that I can go straight to bed and sleep into the new week, I drive towards the setting sun.

21

At her request, I accompany Penrose to Truro, where the post mortem is held of the latest part of the corpse, the head. She has already attended the examination of the torso and tells me truthfully that she'll need some support for the examination of head.

The odd mixture of the smell of death and antiseptics seems to have penetrated through the wall of glass that separates the viewing area from the post mortem room. Sunlight filters through plastic blinds in front of frosted glass windows and the bright tube lights on the ceiling are reflected in the tiled floor and stainless steel tables.

Penrose is beside me with her eyes downcast, shifting restlessly and uncomfortably, staring at the tips of her shoes, dull and grey, as if she can't wait to give them a good polish. Clearly, not one of her most favourite things, and all the less desirable now that we are here. I understand exactly how she feels when David Jamieson, the pathologist, stretches his fingers in his latex gloves and uncovers the head on the stainless steel slab. Jamieson is more of a showman than Ray Campbell. Whereas Ray sticks to the facts, interpreting them carefully, Jamieson enjoys having an audience and tends to build everything up like a scene in a suspense movie. I suppose he feels he doesn't have enough victims of suspected crimes to work on.

Once more stretching his fingers, he points at the body part in front of him. It is neither a head nor a skull. It is both, with some parts where the tissue is almost in tact, and other parts torn off by something I'd rather not think about. Penrose takes a sharp intake of breath, then remembers to breathe in and out slowly in order not to faint. Or hyperventilate.

With a neutral, professional tone, Jamieson sums up the facts and details, his voice as cool as his work environment, both in room temperature and compassion. 'It is now officially confirmed that the foot, the hand, the torso and the head belong to the same person.'

'Surprise,' Penrose mutters, only audible by me.

'A man between 25 and 40 years old,' the pathologist continues. 'We don't have his dental or medical records to confirm his identity as yet.' He sounds like he is building up to the climax.

'One of the forensic experts has been assigned to create a facial reconstruction.'

I nod, reminding me briefly of my visit to Mr Grose's house, his kitchen now cleared of any evidence of his wife's existence.

'… which will be released to the press soon. As far as we can, we have checked but this man doesn't seem to appear on the national list of missing persons, so we are hopeful that he will be recognised by someone.'

'I really don't understand what we're here for.' Penrose's gaze remains fixed on something on the floor, her face one or two shades paler than usual.

'We can however, now establish the cause of death,' Jamieson continues, apparently unaware of Penrose's contempt. 'We've already ruled out possibilities like suffocation or a heart attack.' He glances in our direction, amusement as well as understanding in his eyes when he lingers briefly on Penrose's face. 'To cut a long story short, and in layman's terms, this man has been hit on the head with a blunt object. The blow caused a brain haemorrhage which eventually led to his death.'

'Can it have been an accident?' I ask, knowing how unlikely it is.

'Hardly.' He is almost pleased with my question that gives him the opportunity for an explanation suitable for the likes of Columbo. 'It wasn't so obvious when we examined the hand and the foot earlier this week, but I have already mentioned in my report the number of haematomas on his torso. There are some on his face as well. It wasn't just one blow which, in theory, could have been caused by an accidental act. This man received more than one blow. He was lying on his side, possibly in a foetal position, when he died. We also found marks on his torso to indicate that he has been subject to beating and kicking prior to his death. Presumably after the blow on his head that killed him, he also received some kicks to his head. Not with the same object that caused the fatal blow, but more likely from shoes. None on his face though, which confirms the foetal position he was in. Clearly, he was trying to defend himself, but we found no usable fibres under the fingernails of his hand. Any traces had been washed away after being exposed to the water.'

He points at the head, but I stare over it in a failed attempt to banish the image of it from my mind. It isn't a pretty sight.

'The most sad, but also the most interesting bit from your point of view, is that it wasn't the first time.'

Penrose wakes from semi-hibernation with a start. 'First time for what?'

Jamieson nods, pleased that he managed to increase her interest in his performance. 'He's been beaten and kicked before this. We found multiple old haematomas on his torso, broken ribs, and now also on his head. At one point in the past, his left bottom jaw has been broken.'

'So what does that mean for us?' Penrose asks sceptically. 'That he was a fighter?'

'More likely a loser,' he replies flippantly.

'Is that all you can tell us?' she asks, grimly ignoring his wink.

'Well, then we have of course our ideas and assumptions about what happened to him afterwards,' Jamieson says stoically. 'For instance, I doubt that there was a mess at the actual crime scene. If he was bleeding, it can't have been a lot. Unfortunately, we can't establish the time of death more precisely than that it has to have been between the last confirmed sighting of him and the finding of the hand.'

'Very helpful,' Penrose whispers under her breath.

'You may not like coming here, Jennette,' he continues seriously, 'like most of your colleagues, but this can be quite an interesting part of my job. Dead bodies speak to me, you see. No, I'm not a weirdo or a lunatic. I rely on facts. Even these individual body parts can reveal a lot more about the poor man's life and habits than appears on the surface. We can see, for instance, that he must have had a tattoo. It is not on his torso, so most likely it was on one of his arms.'

'It would be very helpful if you could tell us the name of his wife or girlfriend or children tattooed on his arm.'

He chuckles in good humour. 'Very funny. No, but I can tell you that the tattoo was in black ink.'

'So you're saying that even these parts tell us a lot about his life.'

'Whether that's useful for your enquiry or not.' He nods. 'The evidence we have here doesn't lie. Bodies, or body parts, don't lie. Both his hand and foot tell us about the way he looked after himself, for instance. Mind you, these are reasonable assumptions that can be helpful for you.'

He's on a roll.

'His fingernails were neatly cut and maintained, but he didn't bother so much about his toe nails. Some were long, some were broken.'

'Which tells us?' Penrose interrupts sceptically.

'That he made sure he looked good for the rest of the world, but not in his private life.'

'He lived alone?'

'I can't answer that question, Andy. But if he had a girlfriend or wife, or a partner, she didn't suck his toes.'

He offers a wide grin, more so at Penrose's disgust and discomfort than his own private joke.

'Anyway, back to the facts,' he resumes with a look at the clock on the wall. 'Someone used a chainsaw to cut up his corpse in into bits. My assumption is that you may find his other hand and foot. However, it's less likely that you'll find his arms and legs. Physically, they won't be so easily recognisable as human body parts. Who can tell the difference between a piece of a man's leg and that of a pig? Like a piece with marrowbone you can buy at the butcher's to make stock for your soup?'

'I'm glad you came with me,' says Penrose, when we climb in the car. She's holding the prints of the pathologist's reports against her chest as if she's creating a hidden barrier between her and the rest of the world. Her eyes are drawn and she looks like she's going to cry.

'Are you all right, Jennette?'

'Sure.'

'Jamieson can be very straightforward sometimes, honest and cynical, but I believe it is his own way of dealing with the horrors of his job.'

'You're saying I'm not the only one he treats with such …'

She stops abruptly bending over to put the key in the ignition, hiding her face.

'Contempt?' I finish her sentence . 'He's not that kind of person, Jennette. He does that to me, occasionally. Depends on the victim on his table, I guess. Or his mood.'

'I suppose.' She shrugs, unconvinced. 'You are always so … understanding.'

It sounds like she's accusing me of bad habits. 'You listen to people. It's like what Jamieson said about those bodies talking to him. You do the same. You don't listen to what people say, you read their body language.'

'I do listen, Jennette.'

'Of course. That's not what I meant.' She blushes guiltily. 'I'm not suggesting …'

'I know, Jennette, ehm …' I point at a car; the driver is drumming his fingers on the steering wheel, waiting for us to pull out. 'Shall we let him have our space?'

She puts the car in gear with so much vigour that for a

moment I fear for the gear mechanism. We jerk forward and she pulls out of the car park, her face flushed and her eyes enraged.

'Those body parts … that head… it unnerves me, I guess,' she admits several minutes later, as we merge with the traffic that's held up by traffic lights. A small tractor is moving alongside the road, digging a trench for cables, the driver concentrating on the job. His two colleagues are watching.

'I find it incredible that we are dealing with … a person … who can actually cut someone's corpse into pieces and chuck them away somewhere.'

'Some people don't function like most other people do.'

'That doesn't make it right,' she snaps, almost driving into the back of the car in front of us.

'No.'

She's silent for a few minutes, frowning, analysing the conversation. 'That is exactly what makes you and me so different,' she says finally, a tiny bit more relaxed. 'You just sit there and accept that those mad people exist.'

'What else can I do? They do exist, Jennette, although fortunately there aren't as many as you seem to think there are. It's better to accept that they are amongst us, so that we can be on the lookout and try to prevent some of the damage they cause. Rather that than blinding yourself from the reality. Learning to understand them, will give us the best chance to catch them and put them somewhere safe.'

'I'd go mad if I could understand them!'

I don't answer, but let the silence speak for itself instead. She seems to relax, her shoulders are less tense, the knuckles of her hands on the steering wheel are no longer white.

'It'll help if we know the victim's identity,' I say casually. 'We can make more progress as soon as we know more about his life. I'm sure it will lead us to the person who did this to him.'

'Man,' she corrects, angry again. 'Not a person. A man. I can't think of any woman who could do such a thing to anyone.'

160

22

The street outside the school is cluttered with cars lining up on both sides. I manage to park behind a tattered red car with a surfboard tied on its roof with pieces of rope that look so weathered I wouldn't trust any of my precious property to be held by it. Before getting out I check for messages and missed calls, but none is important enough for a reply.

I find Gerald Davey in a large room on the first floor. Windows overlook the playground and entrance way. His smile is friendly, his eyes alert.

'I'm still not convinced if this is the right thing to do, inspector.' He's in blinking mode again.

I don't respond. We've had a long conversation on the phone. Eventually, I persuaded him to let me come to the school and have a word with Leanne. He isn't quite convinced that speaking to Siobhan is a desirable option from his point of view. Her father is an influential man. Bold. Someone who won't hold back when something angers him. Acknowledging his point of view, I have postponed to come to the school. Until now. My earlier attempts to have a word with Leanne have failed. Her claim that she didn't feel well enough to talk to me were confirmed by her parents, who don't seem to be as cooperative any more either. Whereas Leanne, being the eldest of their five children, has led a reasonably free life, being treated more or less as a young adult, but they are now watching her with eagle eyes and treating her like a young bird that is too eager to fly before her wings are strong enough.

'I appreciate your help, Mr Davey.'

'I guess there is no other way,' he says, shrugging.

'If you have second thoughts?' I query, hoping he hasn't changed his mind. Allowing me into the school to talk to Leanne Lobb whilst knowing that her parents are, for some reason, reluctant to let me speak to her in private, might well cause him trouble. But he doesn't really believe in the latest code of conduct, and thinks that some government rules regarding safety and privacy have gone way too far.

'If I stuck to the rules, I wouldn't be able to teach them anything,' he complained to me earlier, when he brought up the subject. 'Oh well, all right, inspector. But let's make sure that we keep it indoors.'

I'm not all that sure Leanne will agree to see me, but it doesn't seem to occur to him that she may be the weak link in our little conspiracy.

He rises from behind one of two desks with a small table in between, on which are a printer copier and a tray with a pile of blank paper. His laptop is open and I see a familiar logo on the screen.

'Are you on Facebook?'

My question catches him off balance. He blinks. Caught using social media in working hours. Who doesn't nowadays? Everyone lives with a mobile phone glued to their hand, convinced that without being digitally connected life will come to complete standstill. When you drive past road workers, you sometimes wonder who is actually working and when the multiple potholes will be filled. And customers go through the aisles of supermarkets with one eye on their phone as if they are checking their shopping lists.

'Part of the job,' Davey says with a sheepish grin.

'How's that?'

He looks around him as though he expects his colleagues to pop out from a hiding place shouting 'Boo!' Lowering his voice, he continues, without blinking, 'You're not supposed to know this, inspector, but I use an alias. I need to know what my pupils are up to.'

'That's illegal.'

'Maybe.' He shrugs, meaning that he won't change his mind, whatever I say.

'You are not who you pretend to be. A peeping Tom?'

'I don't do any harm, inspector. I just want to know what

goes on in my pupils' minds. I want to protect them from other people on the internet who are less trustworthy than me. We both know how vulnerable young people in that age group can be. Think of radicalism, drugs, suicide.'

'If you find our something ... what do you do with that information?'

'That depends.'

'Have you ever seen such information? Do you have examples?'

His mobile vibrates on his desk, moving towards the edge. He frowns, blinks and picks it up looking at the screen. 'Excuse me, inspector, I'll have to take this call.'

'Of course.'

He turns his back to me as if to let me know that the conversation is strictly personal, yet his voice is loud enough for anyone to hear him.

His responses are curt and sharp, cutting the other person off as he or she, apparently, wants to say something.

'No, no, please listen to me. - It's going to be all right. - Just leave it to me. - No, Simon, just go to bed and sleep. – Everything will look better once you've done that. - No, listen mate.' He waits several seconds, minutes, listening. 'So you're considering it now, are you? Good for you, mate. - I love you. - Yes, of course I will support you. No problem mate, but please don't do anything foolish. – Do nothing you will regret once you're ...'

Once again he is quiet for a long time, then turns to me with a sheepish grin. 'Hung up on me.'

'Is everything all right?'

'I hope so.' He blinks and slides his phone into his pocket. 'My cousin. He drinks. A lot, these days. I kind of try to keep him on the right track, but it doesn't always work. Sad story really. He's the eldest of my Nan's grandchildren. He used to bully me and our other cousins. Hard to believe as it's quite the opposite now. He married the most beautiful girl in our town. She has a better job, earns more money, popular with everyone. Basically, she's superior to him in many ways.' He pauses. Thoughtful. 'He started drinking because he got depressed about it. Lost his job. Now, his wife despises him, thinks even less of him. I guess she would rather be rid of him but since he hasn't been able to find a new job, it's now up to him to look after their children. I presume it's much cheaper than paying for child-care. Catch-22 really. He's in a downward spiral and calls me every so often when his wife has kicked him out - and I mean literary kicked him out. He stays at ours for a while to sober up until she's full of regret and apologies and begs him to come back.' He smiles ruefully. 'The classic situation, if you ask me.'

'It's good of you to help.'

'We all do what we can, inspector. Now. You were saying?'

'I wondered if you can disclose further information about the use of drugs and alcohol, or other irregularities related to the school.'

'No. Well, yes inspector, but let's say it is a hypothetical case, shall we?' I don't respond but he continues anyway. 'I'm a member of a student Facebook group and they believe I'm one of them. One day I noticed a post from someone offering drugs in the school playground. We caught him red-handed.'

'You can say that, Mr Davey, but how can I be sure that you to catch those students? You could be buying and selling those drugs yourself.'

'I'm not a user.' His eyes are wide open. Not blinking. Eyelids not even fluttering.

'Most drugs dealers aren't.'

'Are you suggesting that I deal in drugs?'

'No. I'm saying that what you do is not right. It's illegal. And it can bring you trouble.'

'I'm protecting my pupils.'

He looks sincere enough to believe him, but you can never tell whether someone is telling the truth. There are scientists studying body language and they can be ninety-five per cent right, but the other five per cent is all the more worrying.

'Suppose I knew about Leanne's secret trip to that pop concert,' he argues. 'What would you say I should have done? Say nothing and let it happen? Or step in?'

'Step in,' I say, too quickly.

He grins. 'There you are, inspector.'

'Leanne is under age. She isn't even allowed to miss a day at school. Her parents can be fined for that.' I look at him. 'Mr Davey, did you know about their plans?'

'Of course not.' He looks genuinely offended. 'I would have told you the first time you were here!'

'Did you find any ... suspicious messages afterwards?'

'No.' He hesitates, making up his mind. 'Okay. There is something, inspector. Not from Facebook or Twitter or what have you. Something happened today and I don't really know what to make of it.'

'Try me.'

He nods, his face serious. 'Girls like Leanne are not likely to be bullied. My view is that, in a way, some people are almost asking to be bullied.'

'That's quite an observation.'

'Maybe. I know I'm generalising. I know it's not in all cases, but I strongly believe that people sometimes allow others to bully them. Anyway, that's a by-the-by. Leanne is not the type, not to be a bully or a victim, although she is vulnerable in a certain way, with her being a bit overweight. Siobhan Carter might be an easier target because her parents are quite well off. Bitterness, jealousy, things like that. Yes, I know, it sounds unbelievable, and awful, when it comes out of the mouth of a teacher, but believe you me, inspector, these things happen here at school more often than you wish to know.' He stops to inhale. 'Anyway, this morning I noticed something that made me think. Most pupils have their own lockers. I saw Leanne and her friend as Leanne was opening hers. Two older boys were next to her. Nothing out of the ordinary. I believe the boys were only teasing each other, possibly even unaware of Leanne and Siobhan. Anyway, somehow the two girls got separated and Leanne was moved into the corner. One boy pushed his mate and he was slightly off balance and half fell towards Leanne. He didn't touch her, inspector, nothing like that. But there was something in her face. Fear. Panic. I'm very sure that she felt trapped in that corner and I could see how scared she was. And I mean really scared. In normal circumstances, she would simply have pushed the boys away, but not this time.'

'What are you saying, Mr Davey?'

He hesitates too long. Five blinks. 'I believe that Leanne is not the same girl she was before she went to that pop concert, inspector.'

I stare at him, trying to read his thoughts. 'What are you not telling me?'

'I have the feeling that there is something wrong here.'

'What about her friend? Siobhan Carter?'

'I haven't noticed anything different in her.'

He points at his laptop. 'When I saw Leanne like that ... I thought you may be right in wanting to see her, Mr Tregunna. It was also the reason that I was signed in on Facebook when you came in.'

'Have you found anything?'

'No, but I can only see messages that are classified as public. I can't see the private messages the girls are exchanging.'

'So you think I should talk to her again?'

He nods seriously. 'That was my thinking, inspector. And I know I'm completely out of order, but that's the reason why I agreed you come here. I believe you need to talk to her alone.'

I nod, seeing in his eyes what he doesn't want to say: without the presence of her parents.'

23

The desk officer has a wealth of information. He absorbs and stores everything he hears and sees, whether along official lines or from gossip or eavesdropping, intentional or not, retrieving every snippet for everyone's purposes whenever it's needed. His name is Rob, but someone rightfully renamed him Sponge-Rob.

Behind the glass partition, he's just making a phone call when I enter the police station, his eyes fixed on someone who has turned his back to the entrance. Maloney is leaning on the desk with one elbow, making sure that Sponge-Bob will notice his annoyance and finish the conversation abruptly. When he becomes aware that Rob's eyes drift automatically towards me, he turns and his brain shifts into a different gear immediately. By the look on his face, I will soon regret that I didn't come in a few minutes later. Or not at all.

'Tregunna! Just the man I want to see.' Maloney intercepts me as I cross the entrance hall. I halt obligingly, staring at him and hope no one has whispered in his ear that I had an illicit meeting with an underage schoolgirl behind the sheds of the school. In hindsight, a very bad decision to meet her there if you think about the possible consequences it could have. Besides, Leanne, albeit in my view a young and vulnerable teenager, stuck to her story and wouldn't tell me anything about the boys behind her in the queue at the pop concert, barely admitting that Siobhan had been with her. Which she could hardly deny because I showed her a photo of the two of them in the queue with the sign of BarZz clearly visible in the window behind them.

'Yes?' Reluctantly, I stop.

'I have to tell you something.' Maloney sounds severe. Adding to the fact that his hand has landed on my shoulder, it makes me seriously wonder if I'm going to be made redundant.

After all, I'm only adding weight to the pay roll and however much I try to help out by doing odd, boring jobs, it doesn't necessarily mean I'm an asset to the force.

'Shall we find a bit of privacy?'

Even Sponge-Rob's eyebrows rise and I see concern in his eyes when Maloney indicates one of the interview rooms. I glance up at the windowless, bare grey walls and almost feel like a suspect in the process of being interrogated by powerful men who are convinced I'm guilty and will turn over every stone to prove it.

'Well, I know this is still a … sensitive subject for you,' he begins, sitting down opposite me. He leans his elbows on the table as if he wants to bury his face in his hands. Or perhaps he's just tired.

Maloney has never struck me as a man who can read between the lines. When I don't immediately ask what he means, he becomes shifty and restless.

'Err, about that shooting a while ago, I mean.'

'Are you talking about the day Dorothy Trewoon shot her daughter because she was having a go at me?' I say bluntly.

'Or her sister. Yes.' He is taken aback, avoiding my eyes. Instead, his eyes focus on the bulge on my stomach and as he becomes aware of it, he is even more uncomfortable. I feel sorry for him. Almost.

'What about it?' I ask.

'Well, I am aware that Dorothy Trewoon has made a request to visit her daughter in the hospital. Next week. You declined.'

'I did.' I say slowly, my body stiffening as I search his face for signs that he's trying to wind me up.

'Is there a specific reason that …'

'It wouldn't be safe,' I interrupt brusquely. 'After all, Dorothy shot Becca in her head. The bullet almost killed her.'

'It was an accident.'

'So she says.'

'But?'

'No but. It is a fact.'

'She was attempting to shoot you. Not her daughter.'

'Nevertheless, her intention was to kill. And I wouldn't be her first victim. Dorothy Trewoon is a dangerous woman, Maloney. She can appear to be nice and friendly, but deep down she is nothing more, or less, than a psychopath. She's killed several times.'

He shrugs. 'She hasn't been convicted yet.'

'You give her the benefit of the doubt?'

'In criminal law, each person is innocent until proven guilty. The burden of proof is on the prosecution and as police officers, it's our job to provide evidence to the prosecution and make sure that the suspect is sentenced accordingly.'

'Nicely said, Maloney, but does that make her innocent?'

'I can't …'

'Neither can I.' I interrupt, getting annoyed. 'What is your point?'

'Well, after you declined her request, she has sent in another one.'

'Another request?' I ask, with a sinking feeling.

'Apparently it's her daughter's birthday next week. Dorothy Trewoon has put in a second request to be allowed to visit her in hospital.'

'You can't be serious.' I say through gritted teeth.

He shrugs, avoiding my eyes.

'Obviously, this second request shouldn't be granted,' I say, but my voice doesn't sound very convincing.

He shifts in his seat, casting a glance at his watch as though hoping the scheduled time is over. 'Guthrie asked me to tell you that he has agreed to her request.' Clearly, Maloney has fallen victim to Guthrie's ability to size men up and get them to do his dirty work.

It's like I've entered a cold fog and everyone around me is barely visible, their voices muted. Allow Dorothy to visit her daughter? How the hell could anyone grant that request? After Dorothy attempted to kill her? The doctor in the hospital had made similar suggestions in the beginning, perhaps for the benefit for Becca, his patient, and I could see his point that Becca might wake up from her coma hearing Dorothy's voice, but the doctor's request was refused by higher authorities because, after all, Dorothy is still charged with attempted murder. If I knew for certain that Becca would want her mother to visit her, I would agree to it.

'So you are the messenger of bad news, Maloney?' I say.

He pauses, and with the first hint of humour, says, 'You could say that. She'll be escorted, of course. There will be no chance whatsoever for her to smother her daughter with a pillow or pull the lifelines out of her body, let alone poison her by inserting a needle into her veins.'

'You watch too many TV-series.'

'I'd thought I'd mention those things for that reason, Tregunna. It just won't happen like it does on TV.'

'I'm more concerned about Becca's mental state.'

'She's barely alive, Tregunna, but yes, I understand what you're thinking.' He is more serious now. 'You worry about what might happen?'

'Dorothy Trewoon is a very dangerous, manipulative woman, Maloney. In some ways, she's a genius. An actress worthy of winning an Oscar. I hope nobody has fallen for her little insincere smiles and feels sorry for her.'

Maloney offers a smile of sympathy. 'Perhaps it would be a good idea if you could be present, Andy, when she arrives.'

'She tried to kill me.'

'You're not scared of her!'

'Of course I'm not. I am more concerned about if and how it will affect Becca. We can't tell if she can hear anything. Perhaps she's capable of listening and understanding, but she has no control of her muscles and there is no way she can communicate. If she does hear us, it must be as frustrating as hell not to be able to respond.'

'I'm sure she will be monitored at all times, Tregunna.' He gives a short nod, as if sealing a business deal.

My mouth is dry. 'What time will she be there?'

'Trewoon? I'll have to check that for you. I'll let you know.'

He doesn't know about my regular visits to Becca, and I'd like to keep it that way. He opens his mouth to say more, then thinks better of it when he sees the angry glance I flash in his direction.

'I wasn't involved in this matter, Andy,' he adds as an afterthought, using my first name as if to suggest that he is on my side. 'I'd have asked your opinion, but Guthrie approved the request before I could talk to you.'

It wouldn't have made any difference and we both know it. Guthrie makes his own decisions and he strongly believes he doesn't need anyone else's input. 'Thanks .... Maloney.' I can't remember his first name. He knows. Smiling dryly, he rises from his seat awkwardly as if his rare offer of friendship has been rudely denied.

'I'm off now.' He pulls a face that is intended for everyone to believe that he hates going off duty. He opens the door and I follow him with a sense of relief.

'The wife's parent's wedding anniversary. We're going to Rick Stein's in Padstow with the family,' he says, mostly for the benefit of Sponge-Rob.

'Hm. I'd better be good, then, the meal,' Rob says, duly impressed. 'It'll be very expensive.'

'But very good.' Maloney nods suggesting he has lots of experience of eating there. 'Anyway, Andy, if it's not interrupting my main course, and if you find something important, let me know. I'll keep my phone with me.'

He's not only wanting to show off to Rob and me, but also to his family. He'd love to receive a phone call interrupting his expensive dinner, to demonstrate his importance.

'Good luck, Andy.' He waves jovially.

'Enjoy your meal ... eh ... Philip.'

24

'Tregunna? Sir? Have you got a moment?' DS Ollie Reed slides his arms into his jacket pockets with a mixture of reluctance and excitement, as though he has a pregnant wife whose waters have broken and he's so scared that he is seriously considering ignoring her call.

'Yes, Ollie?'

'We received a phone call that someone has recognised the photo of the facial reconstruction of the head. I'm going to see them.' He pats the breast pocket to check its contents.

'Has Maloney been informed?'

He shrugs, exchanging a meaningful glance with Sponge-Rob. 'Maloney is off duty tonight, sir. Some family do, I believe.'

Clearly Maloney's message about interrupting his meal hasn't got through to everyone.

'Jennette suggested I go alone, but perhaps you can come with me.' He hesitates, eyes lowered. 'You tend to get more out of people than most of us do, sir.'

My surprise must have been written all over my face, because Sponge-Rob grimaces slightly before rummaging through a pile of papers and documents on his desk

'It's in St Dennis.' He smiles, a yellow post-it note stuck on his fingertip with the name Price on it.

'Okay. You can drive and drop me off at home afterwards.'

The road brings us right to the middle of the county. The small town was originally built along the slopes of a hill, allowing most residents a panoramic view over the valley, perhaps even a view of the sea in the distance, but now their view is obscured by the shapes of the incinerator, decreasing the value of most the properties. The tall chimney has red lights on top.

'Mrs Price?'

Dressed in a top with a joyful abundance of bright colours over a pair of jeans, she has a dark skin and a halo of black Afro hair. Her smile is wide and white.

'You want to see my husband.' The love she must have felt on her wedding day seems long gone in her tone. She points along the hallway which is lined with shoes and wellington boots in all kinds of sizes and colours. My mother used to make me put my shoes on an old newspaper, but Mrs Price doesn't seem to be bothered about mud stuck on the floor.

We pass a kitchen that looks like it's been involved in a recent disaster. She sees me looking, but her face remains rather stoic about it. By the looks of it, the family has just had dinner. There are plates with unwanted vegetables moved to the edges, spilled milk lies around the plastic beakers with prints of cartoon characters on them. Cutlery is scattered across a red-and-white-checked plastic table cloth as though someone has emptied the contents of the cutlery drawer on it. There is a smell of an odd mixture of cabbage and bleach.

We enter the living room that reflects its title exactly: people are living in it, rather than keeping it tidy for possible guests. My parents have a living room like that. Cold and unwelcoming and undergoing a dutiful cleaning session every Friday, even though it's hardly ever used.

A man and six children fill the room. Two of the children are redheads like the man, the others must take after his wife, with darker skin but light enough to suggest a mixed race. The TV is loud, showing images I recognise, even at my age. Sesame Street. Tommie. Bert and Ernie. One of the dark little girls is clutching a soft-toy version of Bert – or Ernie? – under her chin, thumb of the other hand in her mouth. She's the only one staring at the TV screen. The other children are otherwise occupied: two boys of similar age but different skin colour are fighting each other that will no doubt end up in tears, another dark girl is trying to learn how to hula hoop, and an older dark girl is lying on her back across the top of the back rest of a flowery sofa, watching and listening to You Tube videos; a red-haired girl is arguing with Mr Price who's in charge over the remote control.

'Har.'

He looks up with relief. His wife has called him from the doorway. Putting the remote control in the breast pocket of his shirt, he rises to his feet, gently pushing the girl away as she tries to grab it. 'I said no, Wendy. Not until Rosa is finished watching Sesame Street.'

The girl pushes her lower lip forward, gazing around with uncontrolled anger, then sticks out an arm towards the girl with the hula hoop. It crashes on the floor, subsequently the girl bursts out in tears.

'Is there somewhere we can talk, Mr Price?' I say, raising my voice over the crying girl, You Tube songs, shouts of the two fighting on the floor, and Bert and Ernie singing a duet out of tune.

Inwardly, I feel for Ollie, hoping his new girlfriend has no plans yet to start a family with him. He'd be better off having a vasectomy after this visit, I think, but his face suggests otherwise.

Looking relieved, Mr Price exclaims: 'I guess the pub's the best option.'

As we follow him outside, I wonder briefly if he agreed to see us at this time of day for an excuse to go to his local.

'I'll tell my wife.'

We follow him back to the front door, where we wait and he disappears into the kitchen. His wife isn't very happy, by the sound of her raised voice. Next to me, Ollie stares at his feet and I fail to read his body language.

At the Boscawen Inn, the door shuts behind us with a bang, alerting a cluster of regulars standing at the busy end of the bar. Harold Price is quickly recognised. Smiles and greetings are shared, pats on shoulders exchanged, and remarks made about matters that are beyond me. The landlord nods and asks politely if he's all right. Harold shrugs and looks around him, uncomfortable to be seen in the presence of two strangers.

They say people can easily pick out policemen, who are often treated as enemies. I'm reminded of that when the landlord turns his back on us and signals to a big blonde woman, interrupting her conversation with a couple sat on bar stools.

I put a twenty pound note in Ollie's hand and he makes his way to the bar to place our orders. We take a table in the quietest corner, away from the large TV screen on which the inevitable football match is being shown. The sound is off and a handful of men are staring at the subtitles with little interest. Only one of them seems to get excited by the match, gesticulating frantically to instruct players what to do or not to do – in his humble opinion.

I wait for Ollie to return holding three pints of beer in two hands with the experience of a regular pub visitor. I pull the photo out of my pocket and place it on the table within the triangle formed by of our glasses on a rather sticky surface.

'You called us, Mr Price. Was it about this man?'

'The photo in the paper. Yes.' He nods, barely looking at it. 'I read the paper at work. In my break. I knew immediately that it was him.'

'Can you tell us his name?'

'Hugo Holmes,' he replies without hesitating and I see the grin of satisfaction on Ollie's face when he writes the name in his little notebook. Then he glances at me, pursing his lips, waiting for his cue. He knows me well enough to hold back and not instantly ask for Hugo Holmes's address. I sip my beer and carefully centre the glass on a beer coaster, quietly waiting until Price becomes aware of the silence. Breaks it.

'We used to meet in the pub. Not here. In Bodmin, where we both lived at the time. We had a group of friends.' He shakes his head with disappointment, silent for a moment as though we have interrupted his train of thought. 'That was before I met Win. My wife.'

He feels sorry for himself. But for her he might still be a regular pub goer. Now he is stuck washing the dishes. Reading bedtime stories. Watching whatever she prefers on TV.

'We were six. Me and my brother Des and three other mates. We had a great time.' He looks up and gazes around wondering how and why those wonderful times have gradually vanished from his life.

'Was Hugo a sociable man?'

If he thinks this is an odd question, he doesn't show it. 'Best mate I ever had.' He stops. Realisation dawning. He blinks a few times, forcing back sudden tears. 'I'm sorry to hear he's dead.'

'When did you last see him?'

'Oh! That must have been a while ago.' He is overreacting. Smiling. Hyper. Tears pushed back violently. 'Let me think. He did come to our wedding with his new missus. I guess she was his wife. Pretty girl. But after that. No.'

'When was your wedding?'

He chuckles with vague discomfort. 'Third of next month. Three years ago. Win reminds me almost every day in case I forget to buy her flowers. Or a present.'

'What happened?'

'With Hugo? Who knows? We used to meet quite regularly. A few times a week and of course at the weekends. My brother was single, still is, so were Toby and Ray, but me and George and Hugo had a family. I was still married to Ronnie in those days.' He falls silent and I wait patiently for him to go on, sensing that his divorced from Ronnie wasn't an easy one, that she was probably the mother of some if his children.

'She used to go out with her mates most Fridays and my time was every Saturday. We went to football matches sometimes, ending up in our local.' Silence again. 'Ronnie died. Cancer. Mal was only a baby.'

Ollie clears his throat. Lost for words. Harold Price swallows hard a couple of times. Reliving it.

'When did you move to St Dennis?'

'That was when I met Win.'

'Was that why you lost contact?'

'Not really. My brother also moved to St Dennis and in the beginning we still went to Bodmin on Saturday. Drove in turns.' He looks like he's lost something. 'At first, I didn't really notice that Hugo wasn't there every week until my brother joked about it. His missus seemed a bit bossy and we teased him a bit about that. Afterwards, I've often wondered if we might have offended him. He wasn't the kind of person to shy away from jokes at his expense though. Most of the times he laughed about it, but maybe … Sometimes when he came, he was like feeling guilty and he went home early.'

'Did he drink a lot? Too much maybe? And his wife wasn't happy about that?'

He chuckles. 'Hugo could swallow a gallon of beer and no one would notice.'

'Do you think his wife was keeping him away from you?'

'I honestly don't know. I'd met her of course, but she wasn't our type. Win thought we should maybe invite them for a meal at home, or meet them somewhere, but Hugo didn't seem very keen, so it never happened.'

'Do they have children?' I ask, hoping that the answer will be no.

'No, not him, but his missus had two already. A girl of the same age as my Wendy. The boy was a little younger than my Mal.'

'And Wendy and Mal are…?'

'Wendy's ten and Malcolm's seven.'

'No children together, though?'

'Not that I know of. But as I said, I haven't seen him for three years.'

'What else can you tell us about him?'

'Not much that may be useful to you, I'm afraid, inspector. We worked together in a petrol station with a garage attached. I'm a mechanic and he worked on the till.'

'Which company was that?' Ollie asks, the point of his pen ready on his notebook.

'They've closed down,' Price shrugs. 'New regulations

with health and safety were too expensive for them. My boss tried to keep the garage running for a while but he gave up a year later. I was made redundant.'

'Holmes as well?'

'Before me. As I said, he worked on the till. He did help us out in the garage every once in a while but he wasn't a qualified mechanic. Anyway, it didn't seem to matter to him that much. That he was made redundant, I mean. His missus had a good job, I remember him saying. He didn't need to work. Not with her salary. I think he looked after the children for a while.'

'Where do you work now, Mr Price?'

'In the garage here just outside St Dennis.' He points in a vague direction.

'Did you know Hugo's last address?'

'He lived in the street behind us in Bodmin before he moved away. I believe he went to St Austell.'

'He never gave you the address?'

'No.' He shrugs. 'I had his mobile phone number. I had no dealings with her.'

'When were you last in contact?'

'I can't remember that, to be honest. At some point we realised that he didn't come to the pub any more. That must have been a few weeks after Win and I got married. I can't remember the exact date.'

'And you haven't heard from him, or about him, since?'

'No.'

'Do you still have his mobile phone number?'

'The number isn't active anymore. Sorry.' He shrugs by way of an apology as if he's feeling guilty having let down his friend. Perhaps he wonders whether Hugo Holmes might still have been alive if he'd kept in contact with him.

'What was the name of his missus?'

'He called her Bee but that wasn't her real name. Apparently she was a big fan of Beyoncé, the singer, and I seem to remember that he said she wanted to be called the same as her.'

'No last name?'

'I'm sorry. He always referred to her as Bee, or his missus.'

25

'Mine is called Alistair.'

The woman's voice is a tad hoarse, as if she has recently suffered a bad cold and still has bouts of coughing.

She sits two seats to my left. A woman in her late fifties, knitting frantically, the needles clicking away furiously. Every now and then she pulls a thread of beige wool from the ball hidden in a cotton bag with crochet flowers sewn on it. Her smile is cheerful enough to tell me that she isn't a patient waiting for bad news from the consultant. As a result of this observation I decide that she is probably waiting for someone she drove to the hospital, someone she is not necessarily emotionally attached to.

I'm back in the waiting room in Treliske, where two volunteers, different from last time, negotiate the coffee and tea trolley. One is tall and slim, with thin greying dark hair and a yellowish tan, the other is short and stocky, constantly humming the same indecipherable tune. Duly waiting for Mr Cole to call me in, half of me is hoping that he will be called out again on an emergency. Sad. Foolish.

I accept a black coffee and a chocolate biscuit from the tin. The woman near me drops her needles in her lap to take a cup of white coffee and, after a shrug, two digestive biscuits. United in a coffee break, we sit and smile awkwardly, neither of us wanting to start a conversation about the weather, the kindness of the voluntary ladies or, if all else fails, the wait for our appointments.

The sun has disappeared behind a bank of clouds gathering above Truro. It's still dry, but only just. The temperature has dropped and there is a cold dampness in the air that sends a shiver along my spine.

'Alistair, I've named him.'

It takes a full minute to realise she is talking to me. 'I'm sorry?'

She chuckles, decides the coffee is too hot and bends over to place her mug on a small table. The digestives will have to wait also.

Then she picks up her needles and the clackety-clack continues.

'You'll think I'm mad.' She glances over a pair of reading glasses.

'Yes.'

She's obviously used to making statements that come from nowhere. What she isn't used to is getting a truthful answer. For a moment she stares at me, half in shock. Then she nods, contemplating what to say next.

I try the hot coffee in an attempt to obscure my face behind the steam that comes off it, almost deciding to get up as if I need to use the toilets.

'Has yours got a name?'

Curiosity sets in slowly. They say that mad people can be funny. Or that funny people are mad. Either way, I remain seated.

'I'm not sure what you mean.'

'I bet.' She drops her needles again and blows into her mug. 'At some point Alistair decided to assume squatter's rights in my bowel. Thankfully he was evicted by Mr Cole three months ago.' She smiles sadly when she looks at my face. 'Alistair is my tumour.'

'Oh.'

'He's named after a boy who lived next to us when I was a child. He made my life a misery. First by teasing me and nagging me every hour of the day, later by dating every other girl in our class, but not me. When I finally got his attention, I was so flabbergasted that he made me pregnant and left me when I told him.'

Another life in a nutshell.

'Is he still around?'

Her face breaks in a wide smile. 'Him or the tumour? Well, actually both are still somewhere out there. Although we've never kept in contact, the man Alistair lives with me through our daughter. From my scans three months ago, the other Alistair is still alive in all the nooks and crannies in my bowel, but I expect to hear from Mr Cole that the course of chemo tablets has annihilated the last traces of his malicious remains.'

The trolley with empty mugs rattles behind us. We are offered a top up, and more biscuits. We decline in unison. The interruption could have ended the conversation, but the woman isn't finished.

'I'm still feeling shell-shocked about all of this, you see. I never had any signs. They found out when I sent off that bowel cancer research thing. I'd nearly chucked it in the bin but my husband found it caught between other papers.' Her smile fades a little. 'My way of coping is by giving things names. I hope you don't really think I'm mad ... but maybe I am.'

'Everyone deals with it in a different way.'

'I guess.' She's had enough of her knitting. She sticks the needles in the ball of wool and wraps them in what looks like the bottom half of a small jumper. She gives me a sideways glance. I hope she's not expecting me to tell her my medical history.

'Has your tumour got a name?' She points at me with the needles sticking out of the ball of wool.

'No.'

'But what would you call him? Or her?'

'I've never thought about it,' I reply, giving the subject the benefit of a second thought. The thing with names is that you tend to associate them with someone you like or dislike with the same name. For me it's even worse. I hated Mr Jason, the teacher in my third and fourth year. He didn't bully or abuse me physically, but he managed to make me feel like nothing, a waste of space, by making my mistakes in maths public, and the whole class laughed. It wasn't because I couldn't do maths. Billy and Walter made more mistakes. For some reason, Mr Jason had decided that he didn't like me.

I'm not sure what came first when I met DCI Guthrie, whether I disliked him as soon as we met, or when I found out that his first name is Jason.

'There they are.' About to put her needles into her bag, she points, making it look as if she's thinking of sticking them into Mr Cole. He has emerged from one of the side rooms, followed by a smiling trio of young nurses.

'Andy Tregunna.' I'm not sure whether it's a good sign that he doesn't need to check his list of appointments to know I'm next.

'Good luck,' the woman whispers and I follow Mr Cole and his gang into an examination room that has a framed picture of a snow scene of Bodmin Moor.

'I'm sorry about the extra wait, Mr Tregunna,' Mr Cole says, shaking my hand as he studies the top sheet in my rapidly growing file. As two of the nurses leave, the third stays, her legs loosely crossed, leaning with her back against the door as if she expects me to make a run for it.

'How are you feeling, Mr Tregunna?'

He examines my stomach and his questions come in a rush, just a bit slower than the woman's knitting needles. I answer and he makes notes, nodding, frowning, every so often looking up to scrutinise my face to see if I'm telling the truth. I'd like to bring up a particular issue about a physical problem but find it too embarrassing to raise in the presence of the nurse. She's too young.

As if he can read my thoughts, he asks casually, 'You're not married, Mr Tregunna. Do you have a girlfriend?'

'Ehm … not really.'

'Are you having sex with anyone?'

I stare at him in shock and disbelief. He's still making notes, waiting perhaps, or giving me the opportunity to recover and formulate an answer. The young nurse smiles encouragingly. I can't say anything.

'Not yet?' He looks up and I manage to stumble, 'No.'

'Do you worry about that?'

'A bit. Yes.'

'Hm. It is one of the side-effects of the kind of operation you had,' he nods. 'But it is still early days. I can't make promises either way, I'm afraid.'

'I understand.' I suddenly feel very young and even more awkward. In my job I'm able to interrogate criminals in a tough, unfeeling manner, tough enough to put the fear into them to make them feel insignificant. In here, with the man who had my life in his hands, sticking a knife in my flesh, I'm on the brink of tears. At least the young nurse has the sensitivity to look down at her hands and study her fingernails. They are varnished a pale, orangey pink.

'You can try Viagra.' He doesn't see the expression on my face. Retrieving a small notebook from his breast pocket, he scribbles something on the top page and tears it off before I can muster an answer.

'I ... Thank you.'

He smiles, looks straight into my eyes as if he can see my soul.

'You can try it if you want. It's up to you.'

When he hands me a piece of paper to make my next appointment, blood tests and new scans, the prescription is on top of it.

26

Penrose was given the task of finding Hugo Holmes's wife, whom Harold Price had named Bee. She spent several hours on the phone and at her computer, getting fed up as she didn't seem to be making much progress. However, the fact that her colleagues were reaching dead ends with their tasks, made her all the more determined to press on. Eventually she found the date of Hugo Homes's marriage to Millicent Robson. After their divorce, which was filed by Hugo, Millicent started using her own name again and it didn't take Penrose long to track down her address.

Tired but contented with her results, Penrose made the phone call. A woman answered. Snapped aggressively as soon as Penrose mentioned Hugo's name. Would she know the whereabouts of Hugo Holmes? If anyone knew, who wouldn't be more entitled to know than her? The bastard had walked out on her, left her with two young kids crying for days and, on top of that, took some of her belongings with him.

'Does this mean that you don't know his address?' Penrose interrupted the rant carefully.

'That's what I said, didn't I? Why? What's up?'

'Ehm … I'm sorry but I'll have to inform you that he is dead.'

'Dead? What do you mean by that?'

'Dead as in … no longer alive,' Penrose replied curtly, expecting the other woman to start crying her eyes out.

Instead, Millicent Robson laughed.

'Well, I'm not sorry to hear that!' she announced happily and then hung up on Penrose.

It took half a dozen attempts on the phone to establish from Mrs Robson that she didn't have a clue where Hugo had been since he walked out on her. If she had, she would certainly have made sure that she'd got her belongings back.

Penrose still sounds tired and frustrated when she repeats the phone calls and I can sense her growing annoyance, and, more importantly, the reason why she is telling me all this, and not Maloney. My rather reluctant suggestion to go and see Mrs Robson personally, and that I would be willing to accompany her if she so wishes, is subsequently brushed off with a statement that I would do a better job of extracting information from Millicent Robson about her estranged husband on my own than the whole police force would. When Penrose is really angry, she tends to exaggerate.

I have just driven away from Treliske, a foul taste in my mouth and bitter with frustration. My appointment card and the prescription for the pharmacy are on the passenger seat. I have opened the window in the hope that they will get blown away, but they land on the floor and almost cause me to drive into the back of someone else's car when I pick them up.

Realising that I had set my hopes on the visit to Mr Cole, I am now more or less faced with the reality that I will have to accept the dysfunctional problem I've got. Mr Cole may think that it's a minor issue when you compare it to a fatal condition, but I beg to differ. Subsequently, I again find that I need something to cling to, which, as usual, is work. So, with mixed feelings, I circle the whole of the next roundabout and drive back in the opposite direction.

Tregony, I find as the information pops up on my mobile when I look up the address on the map, is a small town with a history that goes back centuries. These days, the river is silted up, but, amazingly, it was once a busy port of which I find no evidence when I enter the main street and pass an unusual clock tower. The address brings me to the outskirts, where modern bungalows are scattered along the road. Millicent Robson lives in an uninspiring bungalow. Large white-framed windows overlook a tiled garden with a sole palm tree half hidden behind a wooden fence and some dilapidated sheds that could even be old garages.

I park behind one of the old sheds and walk to the

square-shaped porch, which has the same white net curtains as the other windows. The door is open. Shelves covered with adhesive plastic material, white with tiny daffodils and daisies, are stacked with rows of shoes and boots. I have never seen a porch so neat and tidy.

The bell may be ringing somewhere in the bungalow when I press the polished brass button, but I can't hear it. Someone inside must have heard it because the front door is opened by a man in his early thirties, wearing navy blue shorts and a matching pair of original Crocs. A beige Weirdfish cardigan hangs open over a white vest and he has one arm in a sling of pink foam rubber. According to the expression on his thin face, it must be as uncomfortable as it looks.

Retrieving my warrant card, I offer a reassuring smile, aware of what is usually the first thought when police appear on someone's doorstep unannounced and uninvited.

'Is it possible to speak with Millicent Robson?'

Grey eyes with golden specks blink rapidly and despite my friendly tone I see panic rise in them. 'Millicent. Is she … May I ask …?'

'Don't worry, Mr Robson, I'm a police officer investigating the…'

He interrupts with a relieved but rather shy smile. 'I'm Jonathan Casey. Although Bee seems to prefer calling me Jonno.'

'And Bee is ….?'

'Sorry. That's Millicent, but she hates that name. She thinks it's too soft and girly. She prefers to be called Bee.'

'As long as she doesn't sting.'

'She wouldn't be alive still, would she?' he replies rhetorically.

'Unless she's disguised as a wasp.'

He's not amused. I can hear children laughing in the background. The high tinny voices of cartoons. Pressing his lips together, he contemplates how to respond. Clearly, he is not inviting me in.

'But Millicent does live here?'

'Yes.' He hasn't fully opened the door. 'She still uses her own name for her business. But … is she in some sort of … trouble?'

I smile. 'Not that I am aware of, Mr Casey. Is it possible to speak with her? I was hoping she could help me with an investigation. It's about …' I stop abruptly with the appearance of a young child. Half hiding behind Casey's skinny, hairy legs the boy has a grin on his face as though we're all involved in a game of hide-and-seek.

'You see, Deacon?' Casey says gently, wiping the curly fringe from the child's forehead. 'It isn't Mrs Morley at all.'

'Or Mr Morley,' I say helpfully.

'Mr Morley is dead.' This statement is said as if the boy knows there is no need to be scared by the mention of a dead person. Mrs Morley, in contrast, seems to be more of a danger to his well-being. He can't be much older that six or seven, yet he has broken through my vague attempt of reassurance like it was a thin layer of ice.

'I'm sorry.' I feel like getting back into my car and starting all over.

'Deacon, go back in the house.'

The boy doesn't move. 'If you're not Mrs Morley, why are you here?'

'He's here to speak to your mother.'

'Mum's at work.'

'Deacon!'

'Okay.' He disappears as suddenly as he had emerged from the rather dark hallway. I hear a door click in its lock, but I can't make out if he has gone to another room or is hiding curiously in the shadows.

'Sorry about that, Mr Tregunna. Deacon was right though. Bee's at work.'

'Where does she work?'

'Truro. She's an accountant.' He offers a wry smile. 'I'm the house man. I look after the house and the kids.' He motions

188

with his thumb over one shoulder. 'Deacon and Charlotte. Seven and ten. Charlotte is with a friend.'

'And you are … if you don't mind me asking … the father?'

'No. Bee's divorced. We've only been together for a year.' Pulling his sleeve in the arm with a sling, he glances at his watch. 'She'll be home in thirty minutes. You can come back later or I can make you a cup of coffee.'

'Coffee would be lovely.'

I follow him into a kitchen that looks more like a showroom. Modern. Black against white, handles in chrome. Even the cat has matching colours. Black, with a white foot as if someone, trying to be funny, has dipped it in paint. The only sign that it's a working kitchen is a saucepan on the hob. Its glass lid dances gently on wisps of steaming water. Casey busies himself with an expensive-looking coffee machine before switching off the ring of the hob. He stares at the contents of the pan intently, as though he's watching the water cool.

'Sorry,' he says, not looking at me. 'She likes her carrots soft and soggy. Mash.' The expression on his face puts me off asking who he means by 'she'.

'You broke your arm?' I ask casually, gazing out of the window at a narrow garden with mostly green shrubs.

'Yes. Three more weeks in plaster.' Lifting the saucepan with his right hand, he offers a wry smile. 'Very annoying because I'm left-handed.'

The coffee machine comes to life, hot water hissing and fresh coffee beans grinding. He gets two white cups and saucers and making sure he finds the exact spot to place the cups on the machine, he presses a button . The smell of strong fresh coffee replaces the sweet smell of the carrots.

'How did it happen?' I ask, making conversation. He seems a very quiet man and the silences between us are uneasy. Every so often we hear laughter in the living room, bouts of music or a tinny voice from the TV. Casey lifts his head, half hoping to escape from the kitchen and join in. Every now and then he glances at a clock above the fridge and frowns. He is uncomfortable, perhaps already regretting having invited me in, since I accepted the offer. However, the coffee smells good.

He hasn't replied to my question and I press on when he places our coffees on the table. Mine is black, his is milky and weak.

'Your arm. Was it an accident?'

'How can one break an arm when it is not an accident?'

'Surgery?'

'No. It was rather silly.' A smile. He sits down. The cat jumps on his lap. He lifts it up with one hand and puts it on the floor, stroking its head. Gentle. Caring. 'I washed the floor in the hallway and slipped on it while it was still wet. I landed half on the stairs and my arm got caught between the banisters.'

'Nasty one.'

'I was lucky not to break my leg. That would have been much worse. With a house that needs looking after. And the children.'

He opens the oven door and waves at a cloud of hot air, pulling out a baking tray with overheated oil. Then a quick glance at the clock. A frown, deepening. Worry.

'Something wrong?'

'No. Well, the oil has got too hot. I guess I'll have to start again.'

I almost feel sorry for him, struggling with pans and plates with one hand while the other is arm clearly still hurting. I pick up my coffee but it's too hot, otherwise I could suggest I'll come back later. Perhaps it might be a better idea anyway to come back when the children have gone to bed. However Millicent Robson's reaction to Penrose when she was informed Hugo's death will still leave her in shock, especially when she hears the details. Suddenly, I realise that I don't even know whether her children were fathered by Hugo or anyone else. I consider sending Penrose a text, but Casey's question interrupts me.

'May I ask what it is that you would like to discuss with

190

Bee, inspector?' He lowers himself onto the seat opposite me as though he's making up his mind that he won't do anything else before he knows exactly what is going on.

'Does the name Hugo Holmes ring a bell?'

'Should it?'

'Perhaps, yes.' I can't take back the question. 'I am informed that he was your wife's husband.'

His face is pale suddenly. 'What was his name again?'

But before I can answer, a mobile phone rings. Taking it out of his trouser pocket, he replies without even looking at the display. 'Yes Bee?' Apparently he has one of those sophisticated mobiles on which you can set a distinct ring tone for each person.

Turning his back to me, he listens, his face tight with concentration. Every so often he mutters something that seems to sound like some sort of reassurance or confirmation.

The conversation almost comes to an end when he turns and stares at me as if by doing so he can send images of me to Bee.

'Well, as a matter of fact, we have a visitor.'

I can't hear her reaction, but I can see his face blush as if he's been caught with another woman. 'No. He is a policeman.'

Another silence.

'No, I don't, Bee. He's here for you.'

Another silence. Shorter this time.

He lowers his hand. 'Mr Tregunna, who did you say this is about?'

'It's about Hugo Holmes.'

He duly repeats the name, and listens for what appears like a long time. Wisps of hot air seep out of the oven door and I fear that he has overheated the oil for the second time.

Then the conversation ends without another word.

'I'm sorry, inspector.' His eyes drift away from my face, scanning the kitchen walls to find a new vocal point. When he can't find one, he stares at the oven cloth in his hand. 'She ... called to let me know that she'll be home later. Some delayed appointment. It will take at least another hour.'

'All right. I can come back later.'

He looks worried. 'She seemed a bit uncertain about the time she'll be home. She said she would call you to make an appointment.' I can sense his unease about the whole situation.

'I see.'

Rising to my feet, I put my card on the table. 'Would you ask her to call me, Mr Casey?'

'Yes. Of course.'

'What about you, Mr Casey? Did you know Hugo Holmes at all?'

He is already opening the door for me. 'I'm sorry. I've never heard that name.'

27

I meet Millicent 'Bee' Robson in The Inner Tide café in Truro, which is walking distance from her office. She insisted on meeting me at lunchtime rather than later at home. Her children were very fond of Hugo and she hasn't come round yet to telling them about his death.

The cafe has jigsaw-type walls of old driftwood. Some of it is randomly painted in bright colours. Aqua blue, lime green, orange. Mismatched chairs are scattered around mismatched tables, a small glass bottle with a single white flower on each of them. Easy-listening music wafts through the premises like a gentle summer breeze; pleasantly unobtrusive in the background. There are two couples, and a trio of young women with toddlers clutching bottles in prams that obstruct the way to a corner in the back. A woman laughs too loudly in one of the window seats, her husband, embarrassed, urges her to quieten down.

Wearing a black dress with a silver scarf around her neck, Bee Robson sits at the far end in the corner. A beautiful, attractive woman. I look round quickly, but there is no other woman alone, not of the right age. She lifts her fingertips in a tiny wave as though we are having a blind date. I offer an acknowledging smile and, as I approach her, it occurs to me that I had more or less expected her to have honey blonde hair and freckles on every inch of her skin, and that she'd be dressed in bright reds or oranges. Her eyes are so dark I can't make out their colour and her shoulder-length black hair is loose. Large silver earrings peep through with every movement.

Sizing me up she reaches out a hand that feels a bit like jelly to the touch.

'Mr Tregunna. I appreciate you agreeing to meet me here.'

'No problem.'

'I'll have to be back at the office at two. Sorry.'

'That shouldn't be a problem.' I find a soft cushion and arrange it to sit on, propping another against my back.

'I'm really sorry, but ... there was no other way, really.' Her shoulders are hunched and a little vein throbs in her neck. 'I didn't want to upset Jonno. He was so shocked after your visit. He's very ... sensitive.'

'I understand.'

'Or the children,' she adds, as an afterthought.

'Of course.'

'It is a terrible thing.' She wipes a single tear from the corner of an eye. 'I just can't believe it, inspector.' Her lips tremble and she lowers her eyes, fingers fumbling with a paper napkin.

'How long were you married, Mrs Robson?'

She doesn't answer. Instead, a warm smile settles on her face and I become yet again aware of how attractive she is.

'I'm Bee, inspector ... what can I call you?'

'Tregunna.'

'No first name?'

'Tregunna is fine.'

Her eyes narrow. I can't see her expression, but her breathing has quickened. 'Is it too familiar to call you by your first name?'

'I just prefer Tregunna.'

'All right, Tregunna.' She smiles mockingly, making me feel like a silly child.

Partly to avoid her amusement at my expense, I glance at my watch. She seems to have forgotten that she needs to be back at her office in just over thirty minutes.

'What did you say? How long was I married to Hugo? Two years and ten months,' she answers promptly, making it sound as if she has rehearsed the question. 'It's horrible, when you think about his last ... hours.'

'You didn't come forward after we released a composite photo in the press,' I say accusingly.

She shakes her head, lifting a fingertip to wipe away another tear. 'I simply can't understand how I must have missed it. Obviously, I've heard about the body parts. Only I had no idea it was him! Hugo! Poor, poor man. Horrible!'

A young Polish girl with pinned-up dark hair and a grey apron that is so long as to breach health and safety rules appears at our table. Her English is fluent and with only a slight hint of an accent.

Bee Robson smiles, momentarily brushing aside her grief. 'What can I order for you, Mr Tregunna? One of these?' She has a green smoothie with a red and white straw in front of her. 'Kale and ginger and something else. Anyway, very healthy.'

'A coffee please. Black. No sugar.'

'On my bill, of course,' Bee Robson says casually, then adds swiftly, even though I have no intention to object, 'No inspector, I insist. I asked you to meet me here instead of at home.'

'Thank you.'

She leans over to put the straw between her full red lips. I catch a glimpse of a red bra with black lace edges. She looks up suddenly, knowing perfectly well why I look away so quickly.

I clear my throat. 'We are trying to find out where Hugo Holmes lived and worked in the period prior to his death, Mrs Robson.'

'I can't help you there, inspector.' For a split second her face hardens. I'm not even sure if I imagined it. 'Our divorce was rather ... unfriendly. One day he was there as usual, the next I came home from work and found his message that he'd left me. He didn't even leave an address!'

'That must have been quite a shock.'

'Of course it was. I wanted him back. I didn't understand why ... he said he didn't love me any more. Or the children. I couldn't believe that he walked out on us ... like he did. I've tried everything to find him, but he seemed to have disappeared.'

'When was that?'

'Just after Christmas.'

'And you haven't seen him since that day?'

'He'd made breakfast for the children. He kissed me, as he always did. I asked him to get me something; I can't remember now what it was. Something from the pharmacy. He said it was no problem. He would get it when he came back from shopping with the children.'

'And you never heard from him again? At all?'

'Well, obviously I called him that night on his mobile. Asking him, begging him to come back. But he said that he needed time to think about his life ... that sort of rubbish. He wasn't even forty! That's normally the age men start to wonder if they are leading the life they really want, don't they? He wouldn't give me his address, because he needed time and space and ... privacy. I couldn't believe it, Tregunna. He had all the freedom in the world.' Her voice switches from anger to pain, from fury to distress. And back. 'He had no job, he only had to look after me and the house and the children. He could do what he wanted when they were at school and I was working. I always encouraged him to make friends, go on courses, play golf or football ... Anything!' Tears are running down her face. The waitress has brought coffee for me and a plate with a Panini and garnish for her. She looks at in disgust and pushes the plate aside.

'He also took some ... things. My stuff!'

'What kind of stuff?'

'Well, you know, letters, photos. A ring he'd given me. Nothing valuable but emotionally it was very important to me.'

'If we find his address, we might be able to give it back to you.'

She nods and puts the straw between her lips, sucking slowly. I can see the green substance getting stuck halfway down the straw.

'That would be wonderful. Honestly. Besides, it's hardly of importance to anybody else, is it?'

'It may take a while, but I'll do my best, Mrs Robson.'

'Thank you,' she says solemnly.

'Did Hugo have any relatives?'

'I'm pretty sure he was an only child. I've not met many of his family members. His father left them when he was nine or ten. His mother … The bitch!' Her face has tightened, her eyes aflame with anger and frustration. 'I was never good enough for her precious little boy.'

'Hardly surprising.'

Her eyes narrow. 'What do you mean by that?'

'Just that it is commonly known that mothers-in-law are not very popular with the wives of their sons. And vice versa.'

'To be frank, that was definitely the case with us. In the end I didn't bother with her any more. Haven't seen her in years. I don't even know if the bitch is still alive. Wouldn't surprise me if she wasn't because she was always complaining about aches and pains.'

'Do you know where she lives?'

'No, I don't. I believe she moved somewhere else, but I've never been there. I was never included in any invitations.

'Yet, she deserves to know that her son is dead.'

'Oh, but of course she does! Poor soul! Her only child! But sorry, I can't tell you her address.'

'What about Hugo's friends? Is there anyone that you know of who he could have gone to stay with when he left you? Even it was only until he found somewhere else to live?'

Thoughtfully she stirs the straw in the smoothie. Her lunch remains untouched.

'It occurs to me how strange it is that I can't remember the names of Hugo's friends. And I assure you, there is nothing wrong with my memory. To be frank, I don't think he had friends. As such.'

'People he met in the pub?'

'He wasn't a drinker.' She chuckles, smiling suggestively. 'He wasn't used to alcohol. He got funny after a single glass of wine. Frisky. Horny.'

Harold Price told me Hugo could drink gallons of beer and you wouldn't notice anything. He must have changed his life style drastically after he met Bee.

'I presume he had his mobile phone with him when he left?'

'Of course he did. That's how I managed to speak to him.' She lifts her shoulders. Hurt. Incredulous.

'Do you have his number?'

She picks up her iPhone. It has a pink cover with a curly pattern of little fake diamonds. Then she shakes her head and puts it back on the table. 'No. I remember. I deleted it. He didn't want to explain why he left me. I tried several times but he wouldn't answer after that first phone call. In the end, I thought there was no point in even trying, so I wiped it.'

She picks up her fork and chews a slice of cucumber.

'You said he took some stuff of yours.'

'That was later. By the time I found out what he had taken I had already deleted his contact details. I didn't have a clue how to contact him. Very frustrating.'

'And you couldn't remember his number?'

'No.' She frowns. 'Do you remember phone numbers, Tregunna? We all rely on our clever devices nowadays, don't we?'

'Did he use a computer?'

'Oh yes. When he was made redundant, he spent hours on the internet to find a new job.' She frowns.

'Did you have access to his emails?'

'On our computer at home? I did. We shared everything, Tregunna. He could always see my messages, I could see his. We had no secrets.' Her frown deepens. 'At least that was what I thought. I discovered that he'd changed his passwords for his emails before he left.'

'Our technical department can work miracles with computers and phones. So, we would like to look at your computer, Mrs Robson. You will understand that it is important that we know his whereabouts before he died.'

She picks up her knife and fork and cuts a piece of her Panini. Melted cheese drips on her plate. She stares at it with disgust. 'When did you say he died?'

'We don't know exactly.

'Oh.' Her face grows pale and her eyes moisten. 'I'm sorry. That sounded awfully insensitive. I didn't ... I don't really want to know any details about his death.'

Her hand trembles and she grabs mine for support, squeezing my fingers as if she thinks I will retract mine. It's a weird feeling, as if we are a couple and she needs my comfort. Her hand is warm, her smile is intoxicating, her eyes full of emotion. Her thumb caresses my palm and I feel overwhelmed like a powerful jetstream is sending me in the opposite direction of where I want to go.

'Tregunna,' she says softly, her head moving closer is if she's about to tell me the secrets in her heart. She is so close now I can see that her eyes are grey. Dark. Dark shades of grey. The connection to the book that swept the world a while ago with its explicit sexual content makes my insides churn.

'I would like to meet you again, but under different circumstances,' she says softly, licking her lips in a suggestive way. I clear my throat, feeling like a schoolboy who has set his hopes on sneaking a kiss from the most beautiful and popular girl, behind the sheds in the schoolyard.

Briefly, guiltily, I consider going to the pharmacy to get Mr Cole's prescription after all.

'Are you married, Tregunna?'

'No.'

'Do you live with someone?'

'No.'

She smiles with a hint of triumph and certainly a promise. 'Me and Jonno, we have an open relationship. He has his ... moments and so do I. We are completely honest about that to each other.'

'That sounds unusual.'

'Do you think so? Have I embarrassed you, Tregunna?'

She leans forward again, her head only one or two inches away, her hand still holding mine. I feel like I'm trapped on an island with her, in the middle of a turbulent sea.

'I wish I could have you here and now, Tregunna. But I'm afraid I'll have to go to work.' She smiles with honest regret. 'Doesn't that sound awful?'

28

Trerice Manor is a romantic Elizabethan House just on the outskirts of Newquay. Owned by the National Trust it is a popular tourist destination particularly when the weather isn't warm and sunny enough to flock to the beaches in the county. As a great fan of romantic historical novels, Lauren has just been reading a novel based in and around the estate. She'd casually mentioned it on her birthday and I haven't forgotten.

We explore the parts of the house that are open to the public, listen to one of the many volunteer guides who has a font of information and a friendly smile. The main attraction of the house appears to be an historically important plastered ceiling in the great hall, but Lauren has more passion for the paintings and furniture, trying to work her way through the past centuries and imagine what life was like in the days of the heroines in her favourite books.

She searches the room containing second-hand books for sale and buys small presents in the shop for the boys: kits to explore the lives of birds and insects. I haven't visited a place like this since my younger years when my parents were determined that I should get acquainted with a bit more historical education than was offered at school. I must admit, I am pleasantly surprised how much I am enjoying myself here. Not least because of Lauren's presence.

We head for the cafe. Order lunch and take our drinks, mineral water for me and chilled white wine for Lauren, on trays outside. There is barely a breath of wind and the sun is warm. Wooden tables are full with couples and families with young children in prams. Insects buzz and birds sing in the trees of the sheltered garden. Everyone seems to be relaxed and happy.

Dressed in light beige linen trousers and a pale blue silk blouse, sunglasses perched on her head, Lauren lifts her face towards the sun in an attempt to relax. She was tense and nervous when I picked her up from home earlier, after she told me, in tears, that her sons had been taken out by their father for the weekend. The agreement had been that he would bring them home at the end of the day, but when he arrived and announced that he had a surprise for the boys that involved staying overnight, she felt she had no other option than bite her lip and hold back her comments. She is too sensitive to have a fight with her ex-husband in the presence of the boys, a fact I think he uses to his own advantage.

A rather loud group gather at a nearby table, headed by a tall, pink-nosed man in red trousers, a pale blue shirt and a navy-blue jumper draped over his shoulders as if he used glue to keep it in place. He looks like a retired banker who successfully negotiated the world's most treacherous financial waters, while his wife looks like her only goal in life has ever been to spend his money with gay abandon.

I walk round the building to the toilets for a safety check on my stoma bag, smelling the sweet scent of an abundance of pink roses climbing against the wall. When I return, Lauren is chatting to the couple on the table behind ours. The woman is stroking a tiny dog hidden in the folds of her cardigan. It has huge brown eyes and is trembling all over. The husband is looking at his mobile as if he is contemplating who to call and have a rant with about everything that has gone wrong in our society.

'She misses her little sister.' The woman's eyes flood with tears which drip onto her chest. Lauren grabs a small tray on our table, where a bundle of napkins is weighed down by a flat pebble with the National Trust logo painted on it.

I lower myself onto the bench, giving a sympathetic smile to our temporary neighbours, but not warm enough to invite the woman to include me in the conversation.

'The other little dog died yesterday,' Lauren says, offering support.

'A terrible accident.' The woman casts me an uncertain

glance. She sniffs and blows her nose in one of the napkins. A piece sticks to her bottom lip making it look like one of her front teeth is sticking out. 'Very sad.'

'Hm.'

A seagull hovers over our heads, scrutinizing the plates on the tables for a snippet of left-over food. The woman's plate is still full of chips, garnish and half a sandwich. The surviving dog is small enough to be mistaken for a chicken-wing.

'What's so funny?' Lauren asks, suspiciously.

'Nothing.'

'You rarely smile.'

Although she didn't mean it like that, I feel a stab of pain. 'Sorry.'

A waiter arrives just a split second before the seagull dives for the woman's plate, muttering a curse. 'Are you finished, Ma'am?'

'Yes thank you.' The woman looks embarrassed. 'I'm sorry I didn't have much of an appetite. It's because of Lillie you see, her little sister Ellie was run over by a car yesterday and I can't …'

'Maureen!' A single word is enough to silence her. 'I can't think why this man would be interested in your story.'

'Oh.' Her face grows pale.

'You're making too much of a drama of it. As usual,' he continues.

'Oh.' The woman looks like she's going to burst into tears again and Lauren is already reaching for more napkins.

The husband isn't finished. 'Besides, it was the little creature's own fault, running across the busy road like that,' he blurts out coldly. I can tell what Lauren is thinking by the look on her face: inconsiderate bastard, can't you have more sympathy for your distressed wife?

'I know you blame the driver, but he couldn't do anything to avoid the little monster.'

Comparing the nervous, trembling little dog with a monster is not helping.

'I don't blame the driver,' the woman whispers miserably.

'No?' he raises his bushy eyebrows. 'Well, if anyone was to blame, it's you! You let that lead slip out of your hands!'

Lauren's eyes are wide open, her lips tight in disgust. She's about to reply in the poor woman's defence, when the waiter reappears, placing plates in front of us.

'Anyway, Maureen, leave these people alone. They're not interested in a story about a pathetic little creature that was unlucky enough to be driven over by at least three cars.'

He thrusts his mobile phone into the breast pocket of his shirt and rises, looking at us with a mixture of disgust and apology. Before he can add any more to his wife's misery, his mobile rings and he turns away to bark a 'hello!' into it. His wife holds her breath, keeping it in her lungs for a while before she lets it out in a sigh laden with self-pity.

'That was unnecessarily rude of him,' Lauren says as soon as the couple has gone out of earshot as they walk towards a grass area where visitors are playing traditional games.

'Hm.'

'He's a bully,' Lauren observes, following the couple with anger in her eyes. 'It's obvious. I saw the fear on her face. Men like that just enjoy bullying their wives. Humiliating them in front of other people. Making them feel small and unworthy.'

We watch the pair disappear around the corner, the man with fury on his face, his wife, little Lillie in her arms, with eyes wide open trying not to allow more tears to fall.

'This is such a lovely place.' Lauren scoops coleslaw onto her garnish changing the subject to something less upsetting. We clink our glasses and make small talk and the atmosphere relaxes into a more natural conversation. The sun sparkles on her red hair, lighting up the space between us. As a result, I start feeling warm and dozy, as if I've drunk several glasses of wine or beer and the alcohol has just reached a comfortable level in my blood. I find myself staring at her lips, the gentle spot behind her ear, the curve of her neck. A warm feeling settles in my lower abdomen I wonder if it will go beyond that.

I feel like taking her in my arms and caressing her until she's out of breath, clinging onto me, begging me.

One can only hope and dream.

'Andy?' Her face is flustered and shy. She's read my thoughts and is now trying to find an excuse to go home as quickly as she can. I wish I could tell her she needn't worry, that the wounds of my operation are still fresh, and that the one bit that used to make me a man in every meaning of the word, hasn't had time for a full recovery. Yet, I hope.

Slowly turning her glass between her fingertips, Lauren is watching some children running along the hedgerow and a sad smile flutters on her lips.

'You miss them.'

She chews thoughtfully. 'I know I should be enjoying myself today, but I feel like … like I've forgotten something important. Like I forgot to get dressed.'

'I can assure you that you haven't forgotten that.'

Her eyes jump to me, her cheeks burning. The moment of longing for her children is over and I have her full attention. Perhaps more than I should wish for.

'In your dreams,' she says, after a pause.

'You can read my thoughts.'

We sit in silence for a while. Every so often her brows lift in a tiny frown, she sips her wine and turns her gaze towards the children, yet this time with as much interest as anyone who is a parent.

'It was very kind of you to bring me here.'

'No problem.'

'This' – she motions at the Manor house behind me – 'and that' – she points to the clear blue sky with only a whisper of clouds in the distance – 'makes me feel like I'm on a surprise holiday.'

'You deserve it.'

'But I have so many things to do at home that I feel guilty sitting here.'

'The likes of Henry can wait.'

'I've hoovered the house already this morning. I'm thinking more about a huge pile of laundry waiting to be ironed.'

I reach across the table and take her hand in mine. 'Lauren, stop it. You sound like my mother, and believe me, not a single man taking you out for lunch wants to talk about ironing boards or washing machines.'

She smiles. 'I'm sorry.' She doesn't pull back her hand and we sit in silence for a while, perhaps both a bit confused by the sudden change in the atmosphere between us.

It isn't long when the cosy warmth between us is interrupted. My phone is vibrating. I retrieve it from my pocket with regret and glance at the screen. Bee Robson. I decide to ignore the call. Somehow she's managed to get hold of my number. She called me earlier this morning, suggesting to meet at lunchtime, claiming she had news for me.

The banker's wife slips on her sunglasses and turns her head in our direction. I can't see her eyes but I know they are fixed on our hands; her husband doesn't seem to be the type who will ever ignore a phone call.

'Shouldn't you answer?' asks Lauren.

'She can wait.'

I stare in her eyes, realising what I just said. Gently, she releases her hand from my grip. My phone is vibrating again. Same name on the screen. Feeling Laurens eyes scrutinizing my face, waiting, I consider briefly to apologise, explain, but for lack of words, I choose the only other option.

'Mrs Robson.'

'Bee.'

'Can I call you back? I'm in …'

'No.'

'It's just that I'm in the middle …'

'You're busy. Yes, of course. I get the message, Andy, but it won't do. I know you won't call me back because you don't want to talk to me. You think I want something from you which you're not prepared to offer.'

'You're a mind-reader.'

I don't need to see her to understand that she's annoyed by my sarcasm.

'Are you afraid of me, inspector?'

'Should I be?'

'Of course not. And you aren't. It's just that you give me that impression.' I'm glad she can't see the satisfaction on my face.

There is an outburst of laughter at the table behind us. The banker, astonishingly, has made a joke.

'Where are you?' Bee Robson snaps.

I stare at Lauren's face. It has no expression but I sense she is regretting she accepted my invitation.

'Out.'

One of the men near us slams his fists on the table and glasses jump, one rattling against the other. 'Where are you, Andy?'

Lauren has lowered her eyes, fixing her attention on a stray ant finding its way across our table.

'How can I help you, Mrs Robson?'

'I won't tell you unless you call me Bee.'

'Bee.'

A knife or fork tingles when it falls on the tarmac. 'Are you with someone?'

'Yes. That's why I'm busy.'

'A woman?'

'Yes.'

'Pretty?'

Somehow, I am trapped on a treadmill of questions I don't want to answer.

'Pretty and attractive?' She sounds as though I'm now supposed to reply something like 'not as pretty and charming as you'. It would be a lie.

'Yes,' I say earnestly. And she cuts off the connection.

'Business?' Lauren asks in a casual tone.

'I think so, but she seems to believe otherwise.' We

continue to eat but the conversation isn't as easy as it was before. I want to tell her about Bee Robson, almost reassure her that she means nothing to me, but that would make the woman more important than I would like her to be. Yet, it feels like Bee Robson is taking hold of my life, dropping little markers because she wants me to follow her trail. Some are like bread-crumbs randomly snatched by birds or insects, some are like small pebbles. White and bright. Not to be missed.

'Pud? Or coffee?' I ask, when one of the student waiters has taken our plates, mine empty, Lauren's not.

'Perhaps we should go,' she says, but she doesn't move. I stare at her as the sun catches her red curly hair, setting it almost on fire.

'Lauren, I would like to invite you to a birthday party.'

'Yours?'

'No. Becca's.'

'But ...?'

'I know. The nurses want to do something special for her. Fill her room with bunting and balloons, get her a birthday cake.'

'And you're going?'

'I dismissed the idea when they first asked my opinion, but now ... I'm still in limbo.'

'Will she be aware of anything?'

'No change in her condition whatsoever.' I hesitate. 'They are talking about moving her to a care home now.'

'That'll be probably for the best,' she says, her eyes soft.

'I know you're right, but it makes it so ... definite. In hospital, you still have the feeling that someone might be able to do something for her. A miraculous cure, if you like. Moving her to a care home will mean accepting that she will never recover.'

'I'm sure they've tried everything.'

'Yes.'

'Do you think there'll be a small chance that ... something will happen on her birthday?'

'I hope not.'

Her eyes widen in surprise. 'Why?'

'There is another complication,' I say slowly, knowing deep down that this is information I should not share with anyone else. 'Her mother has requested to be present on her birthday and the request has been granted.'

29

Clearly, Gerald Davey enjoys the sense of conspiracy and secrecy. He unlocks a small office room between the PE halls and indicates towards a seat behind the desk, pulling down the yellowed blinds.

I called him earlier, half hoping that he had obtained some useful information through his own private channels. When he hadn't, I moaned more about the attitude of Siobhan Carter's father than anything else. He listened to my rant and suggested that if I still had something nagging at me about the case, and I wanted to speak to Siobhan without involving her father, I'd better come to the school again. Swiftly dismissing my concern about the school's rules and the school director's reaction if he found out, he repeated the offer, which I accepted more out of curiosity than expectation of getting anything useful out of Siobhan. I'm more intrigued by Davey's reason to allow me to continue with what is really an already closed case.

'Leanne's not here today,' he says.

'Any special reason?'

He shrugs. Not worried. 'Her mother left a message to say she was sick. The receptionist made the effort to return the call. Just in case ...' His voice trails of, expecting me to fill in the rest. 'It seemed to be true.'

'Not another secret trip?'

'No. let's hope it's taught them something.' He frowns. 'Not that it's likely to happen again. Siobhan is being watched almost every moment of the day. One of her father's men takes her to school and more or less waits until it is time to bring her home again. I can't see the point, but he seems frantic that something will happen to his princess.'

'He only has one daughter.'

'All the same. What is the point in keeping her in a gilded

cage? Poor girl. That trip to Plymouth has cost her dearly.'

Gesturing towards the window, he tells me matter-of-factly that he will tell the PE teacher that there is a phone call for Siobhan.

'I'll bring her in. Don't show your face. Siobhan's bodyguard knows she's got PE lessons. He might be smart enough to walk round the school building.'

He grins sadly and makes his way towards the sports field. Through the slats in the blinds, I can see a shed with open doors. Nets with balls in different shapes and colours spill out along with all sorts of poles and sticks. Young girls in shorts, shirts and trainers, hair tied up with elastic bands, gathered at the edge of a field that is equipped for a hockey match.

I watch Davey approaching a woman in a black tracksuit and a red baseball cap. They talk briefly, after which Siobhan Carter breaks away the circle and walks alongside him with a sullen expression on her face, reluctance increasing with every step.

Wondering if I'm wasting my time here, I offer a friendly nod when the girl appears on the doorstep. 'Thanks for seeing me, Siobhan.'

Her face is pale and her eyes are as scared as Bambi's. She smiles faintly, automatically looking round, but Gerald Davey is already assuring her that her bodyguard can't see us here.

'Why is that man waiting for you?' I ask casually, gesturing towards the chair opposite the desk. I perch on the corner.

Her surprise overtakes her cautiousness. 'He works for my father.'

'I am aware of that. But why? Does he have reason to believe that you and Leanne are planning another trip to a pop concert?'

'No!' Her face turns from pale to red then slightly purplish. 'Of course not.'

'Doesn't your father trust you?'

She shrugs, hiding her eyes behind her long lashes. 'I guess.'

Gerald Davey is hovering near the open door. Blinking, keeping his face down. I can sense his curiosity and glance over to him.

'Sorry, I'll leave you two to it.' He disappears, leaving the door open. I suppose it is best from his point of view. If someone catches me in a closed room with a thirteen-year-old girl, questions will be asked.

'Siobhan, I'll be honest with you. I have been trying to speak to you but your father won't let me.'

She nods seriously.

'Are you willing to answer my questions?'

'Depends.'

'Okay, I appreciate that. I only need some last dots on the i's.'

Her eyes drift towards the doorway. 'I thought Leanne ...'

I nod, interrupting her. 'Leanne's not at school today. That's why I asked Mr Davey to fetch you.'

She stares at me, scrutinising my face, unsure if I can be trusted.

'You two went to Plymouth to see that new pop star perform. Sammii. Was he good?'

She shrugs. 'Leanne wanted to go. She just loves Sammii.'

'But you were not so impressed.'

'Not really, no. I don't like ... his type.'

I've seen and heard some of his videos on YouTube. A lot of senseless noise from an arrogant little bastard. Just like so many others, except for his baby blue eyes, which may well attract girls like Leanne.

'Was it your first concert?'

'Yes.' Her eyes shine and I can guess what she doesn't say: she will go to other concerts and gigs as often as possible.

'So the concert was over and you got back to reality.' I smile encouragingly. 'What happened? You missed the bus?'

'Yes. It finished later than we thought and we couldn't find the bus station. When we got there, the bus had already gone.'

'Did you panic?'

'Yes, of course we did. We were supposed to get back to Newquay. We had to be back at school the next day.'

'What did you do?'

Uncertainty paints her face. 'Didn't Leanne tell you?'

'She did, but I'd like to hear your version.'

'We didn't know what to do. We waited for a while. I looked on my phone to check my bank account, but there wasn't enough to pay for a taxi. And my father checks my balance all the time.'

'Your father is a wise man.'

'I'm no longer a child,' she snaps, lips trembling with anger. 'I am almost fourteen!'

'Okay. Sorry, I shouldn't have said that. But go on please. You didn't have enough money to have a taxi. What did you do?'

She looks down at her hands, frenetically turning a small silver ring round her finger. 'Ehm … Leanne suggested we go back to the club. She thought she'd heard one of the barmen say that he lived in Newquay. We were hoping to get a lift if that barman was still there.'

'And was he?'

'No. We asked if there was anyone else, but … no.'

'Leanne mentioned a girl.'

'Yes. Stacey. She'd been there all evening and she was still there. She was … with one of Sammii's friend. I think he's the drummer in the band. She was …' She doesn't finish, blushing.

'What can you tell me about Stacey?'

'She … she was with, Larry, I think his name was. They were …. She said she could help us, but we had to wait. Ten minutes or so. The bar was closing. They went in a sort of a van. It had windows, but they were all dark.' She shifts. Uneasy. I can't work out whether she is lying and making things up, or just embarrassed by the whole situation.

'We waited. It started to rain. We were so cold! I was

almost suggesting calling my dad.' She offers a tiny smile. 'But then Stacey came out of that van and we … walked to her home.'

'How old is Stacey?'

'A few years older than Leanne and me, I think.'

'Okay. So she took you to her house. Do you remember the address?'

'No. Leanne said we should not tell anyone. We didn't want Stacey to get in trouble for helping us.'

'Of course not. I understand. But it was in Plymouth?'

'Yes. In a terraced house. She lives there with her mother.'

'Did you meet the mother?'

'Stacey said we'd better not make any noise. Her mother would be pissed off if she saw us. She told us that we had to wait until her mother went to work the next day, and we couldn't leave before her mother had gone.'

'Where did you sleep?'

'On the floor. Stacey gave us an extra duvet and some cushions from her bed.'

'Who is Lillie?' The question, and the name, jumps up out of nowhere.

'Lillie?'

'Leanne mentioned a dog. Lillie.'

She hesitates. 'Oh, yes, of course. I forgot about the dog.'

'What kind of dog was it?'

'I … don't know.'

'Big or small? What colour? Black? Brown? Spotted?'

'It was dark. I … didn't really see him.'

'Leanne heard him barking.'

'Ehm … yes.' She swallows. 'Stacey was afraid her mother would wake up.'

'But she didn't.'

'No.'

'Okay. Then, in the morning, you waited until Stacey's mother went to work?'

'Yes.'

'What time was that?'

'I can't remember.' Her eyes almost shut, but not because of sun or a bright light. 'Stacey made us a cup of tea, but she had to go as well.'

'She had to go to school?'

'I'm not sure. Maybe she had a job. I can't remember.'

'Okay. It doesn't matter. What time did you catch the bus?'

'Maybe ... between nine and half past?'

I nod, quickly making a mental note to have another go at CCTV from the bus. I'm pretty sure the images have already been checked, but I can't remember the girls were on them. 'So it was too late to get to school on time.'

'Yes.'

'What time did the bus arrive in Newquay?'

'It was a long ride. When we arrived in Newquay ... we didn't know what to do. Obviously, we couldn't go home. Or to school. And we were scared that someone would see us.'

'According to Leanne you went to the house where Sally Pollinger used to live.'

Her face flushes. 'Yes. We did. But as I said, we were scared that someone would see us. The house is on the same estate as Leanne's. Everyone knows her there.'

'And you stayed there until it was time to get yourselves to the bus stop?'

She straightens her back and looks up. Her confidence is growing. She is on safer grounds now. 'Yes. I went first, because my bus stop was further away. Leanne only had to walk for five minutes.'

'Through the back alleys, I presume?'

'She couldn't risk one of the neighbours seeing her.'

'Okay.' I nod, offering a friendly smile. 'I think that was all, Siobhan. Thank you.'

'You ... won't tell my father?'

'Tell him what?'

'That I talked to you.' His threat is conveyed in her voice.

'Of course not. Maybe it's in both our interests not to tell anyone about our conversation.'

'Not even Leanne?'

'You and Leanne are friends, Siobhan. I'm sure you'll tell each other everything.'

'Not everything,' she whispers, regretting it instantly.

She is uncertain again. This time, I don't understand why, but I let it go for now. I've heard enough. The dog, Lillie, was my little white lie. I made it up. If the bit about the dog was a lie, then so was the bit about Stacey.

'Let's call Mr Davey, shall we? He can take you back to your class.'

'I don't like playing hockey anyway.'

She rises, staring outside to the fields where her classmates are running around in the middle of their game.

'What's with Leanne today? She isn't at school.'

'I haven't had contact with her.' Tears moisten her eyes. 'My father has taken my mobile phone.'

30

'They are back.' Curtis calls over to me, cleaning the already clean windows of his car in the resident's car park.

I stop in my tracks. 'Who are back?'

'Those men in the car. Well, the car is back.' He drops his sponge in a bucket of soapy water. 'Are you going to do something about them parking there?'

'The car is parked on a public road, Mr Curtis. Anyone can park there. You don't even have to pay to park.'

'I thought you knew who they are.'

'I do, but it doesn't mean I can stop them from parking there.'

'Suppose they're terrorists?'

I almost laugh. 'They aren't.'

He persists. 'How can you tell? I saw it on TV. Last week. A terrorist was caught in the new shopping centre in St Austell. What if another one has come here?'

'To do what? Plant a bomb in the lake and kill the swans and ducks?'

'You aren't taking me seriously.' He eyes me up with a hint of a sad smile. He is used to not being taken seriously.

I sigh. 'I am, Mr Curtis, I am.'

'Then what …?'

'I will deal with this. I promise, Mr Curtis.'

He bends to pick up his sponge from the bucket and wrings it out forcefully.

'If you say so, inspector.'

It seems we're back to our previous cold war.

'You know who they are.? Do you also know why they're here, watching you? Or me? Or maybe Chloe, from next door?'

'Yes,' I say, although that's only a truthful answer to his first question. His face is sullen still. He doesn't believe a word of what I said. I don't really know why his opinion of me bothers me so much, but suddenly I feel angry.

'Okay. I'll deal with this. Now.'

I see shock in his eyes. 'I didn't mean …'

'I know, Mr Curtis, but you are right. It can't go on like this. I'll have to speak to the driver's boss. Now.'

I walk back to my car, but change my mind. Curtis is watching me. His mouth hangs half open and the sponge is forgotten in his hand. Water drips on his polished shoes, soaking one of his trouser legs. He doesn't even notice.

'Can I help?' He calls after me.'

I don't respond. I cross the road and the park, ignoring the paths, walking instead on the damp grass. The man in the car doesn't see me approaching. He is slumped behind the steering wheel playing games on his mobile phone. His index finger is moving coloured bricks across some fields to build an empire of his dreams. I startle him when I open the door on the passenger side.

'What the …?' He jerks upright, dropping his phone between his legs and reaching for the ignition keys.

'I'd like a word with your boss.'

'My boss?'

'Mr Carter.'

His face turns a pale shade of grey. 'You are mad,' he blurts, but there is an element of fear in his eyes. It is the same young blonde driver I've seen before. Plucking nervously at the stud in his eyebrow, he remembers our earlier encounter, when he believed that the car had a flat tyre.

'I thought you would say that.' I smile coldly at him. 'You don't mind if I get in, do you?'

'Well, as a matter of fact …'

'You're too kind.' I slump next to him and close the door, reaching for the seat belt.

'What the hell …?'

'I told you, I want a word with Mr Carter.'

'And who might this Mr Carter be?'

Producing my warrant card, I say curtly: 'Listen mate,

let's not play games, shall we? You know who I am. Detective Inspector Tregunna.'

'I'm sitting here waiting for my wife. She's …'

'If you are sure you don't know Mr Carter, then I'll have to arrest you on suspicion of theft. This car is in Mr Carter's name.'

He sighs. Defeated. 'What do you want him for?'

'It's about his daughter.'

He doesn't ask why. Nor does he come up with silly lies that Mr Carter doesn't even have a daughter.

'What about her?'

'That's between Carter and me.'

His hand is still on the keys, but he hasn't started the engine. It needs more pressure.

'Mr Carter won't be happy today,' I say casually. 'Did your colleague tell you about his little encounter with me today?'

'Ehm …'

'Clearly not. Shall I enlighten you? I was at Siobhan's school today. Your mate didn't see me go in. He only saw me when I came out. Too late. I think his instructions were to keep me away from his daughter.'

'Ehm …'

'Do you think Mr Carter will be pleased with you when he finds out that I am sitting in his car?' I ask rhetorically.

'All right. But I'll have to make a phone call first.'

Retrieving his mobile from between his legs, he wipes his game off the screen and presses a circle on the top of his contact list with a trembling index finger.

'I need to speak to Mr Carter.'

No explanation needed. This man's reason for the call is immediately trusted. No doubts or cautions.

'Mr Carter. I have Mr Tregunna here and … .' On second thoughts, he stops before explaining I am next to him in his car. 'He wants to see you.'

'What?' I hear the bark that must have hurt the poor man's eardrum. 'How can he …?'

I grab the mobile phone from his hand. 'Mr Carter, you know who I am. DI Tregunna. I have kindly asked your ... driver to take me to your house.'

'I see no reason for this visit, Mr Tregunna.'

'But I do, Mr Carter.'

A short pause. 'Listen, Tregunna, leave my man alone and tell him I'd like a word with him.'

I hang up and nod to the driver. 'Okay. Let's go.'

'I didn't hear him say it was all right ... '

'No. You didn't.' I fasten the seat belt and make myself comfortable on the seat. 'He said he wanted a word with you. It may be in your best interest if I come with you. Perhaps I can prevent him from firing you.'

Both options don't appeal to him, but unless he comes round the car and pulls me out, there is no other choice but to do what he's told.

Camellia House is bathed in the late evening sun. The walls have a welcoming golden glow. The gates open on our approach. I haven't seen the driver press a concealed button, so there must be an automatic device which opens them.

'I think it's best if you stay in the car,' I say. 'You'll have to take me home after my conversation with your boss.'

'I don't think ...'

'You're right. Maybe it's best if you stop thinking for a while.'

I get out and walk the short distance to the front door. It opens with a click and the same square block of a man appears in the doorway, stepping back with no expression in his face. The door to the living room is open. A woman in a plaid shirt and tight jeans sits on one of the white sofas. In her hand, she is holding a crystal glass with a pink clear liquid. Champagne?

'My wife, Fiona.' Nodding casually Carter moves towards a tray table with bottles and crystal glasses on a spotless mirror. 'What can I get you, Mr Tregunna?'

I must admit that Carter deserves some admiration. He's won the first point. His attitude of casual friendliness is the last thing I expected. I feel like a balloon deflating quickly, not having noticed the punch. My anger escapes with the air. 'No thank you.'

'You're not driving.'

'No. I'm on medication.'

'Tonic? Fruit juice?' He looks at me, his eyes avoiding the bulge under my jacket either deliberately or because he doesn't know about it. Or is just being polite?

'Fruit juice please.' My anger gone, I don't even know what I'm doing here.

'What is the nature of this visit, Mr Tregunna?' He smiles, but his eyes are stone-cold. Dangerous.

His wife sits quietly, her feet in black leather pumps, neatly next to each other. The glow of the setting sun is reflected in her eyes. Her blonde hair is cut in a bob, but she's left it too long to have it cut properly. She looks as if she doesn't care. Her mouth is tightened and a deep frown sits between her brows. She doesn't seem in the least interested in my presence. I simply don't exist.

'I have almost finished my enquiries,' I reply slowly, as if preparing for a long monologue. He doesn't interrupt, although his brows rise in an act of mock surprise. 'Almost. I need some clarification on one or two minor points.'

'You could have saved yourself the trip, Mr Tregunna.'

'I know what happened last week when your daughter and her friend were missing. I know where they went and why.'

'You've been working hard.'

'I have.' I feel like I'm a male tiger being let into the cage of a rival. We are circling each other, waiting for a sudden attack from the other one. Meanwhile, female tigers are dozing in oblivion.

'All I need to clarify is why you, or your wife, didn't report your daughter missing.'

'Nothing happened to our daughter, Mr Tregunna.'

'No. But you couldn't know that, Mr Carter. Or did you?'

Fiona Carter gulps her champagne, licking her lips. Her eyes are pools of contempt and pain. Her lips move, but as Carter flicks his fingers, no sound comes out.

I clear my throat and bluff. 'Either you knew exactly where she was, or I can accuse you of neglect.'

His wife has frozen still. An animal-like whimper comes from the back of her throat and her eyes shoot in different directions. She moves to the edge of the sofa, but her legs fail or she obeys an invisible gesture of her husband.

'You are right, Mr Tregunna. I knew where she was.'

'So why lie about it?'

'Shall we change the subject, Mr Tregunna? Do you like sport?' His smile hasn't reached his eyes. 'What do you think? Who will win this weekend's Formula 1 race?'

31

'You said you have remembered something about Hugo Holmes, Mrs Robson.'

She has come to Newquay but refused to meet at the police station. She doesn't like its dull grey outside walls and believes she won't be able to handle the official approach of the police officers. After all, she is very emotional about Hugo's death.

Instead, she directs me to a pub. It's too early for the evening rush of regular pub goers. We are the only customers.

'What is it that you remembered, Mrs Robson?'

She leans back, a hint of annoyance in her eyes. 'Are you in such a rush, Tregunna, that we have to skip the pleasantries? For instance, how was your day?'

'It's been busy.' She knows that I find her attractive, but that I would prefer to keep a certain distance between us.

'Ah well, time to relax then, now. What are you having? A pint?'

'Lemonade please.'

'Don't tell me you don't drink, Tregunna!' Her voice is low, full of mockery.

'I'm driving.'

'So am I. But that doesn't mean we can't have a drink. After all, we're not in a hurry!'

'I have an appointment later.'

Her eyes narrow. 'Well, we'll talk about that in a moment, shall we? For now we both need something stronger than lemonade. You've had a busy day. Stressful, I suppose. Beer? Wine? It will help you relax and feel much better.'

A girl behind the bar – mid-twenties, chubby-faced and plump - is polishing glasses. Her smile tells me she's heard Bee, and waits for me place our order.

'A lemonade please.' I lean against a bar stool.

'And a large red wine for me.' Bee's eyes feel like the tips of icicles hanging off the gutters as she puts her hand on my hip in a casual gesture. 'Shall we find somewhere more private to sit?'

The girl behind the bar stifles a grin. I feel I am in dangerous waters, unable to see the sharp rocks under the surface as Bee Robson steers me to the most obscure corner. She chooses a table furthest away from the kitchen and the bar.

'Is there anyone waiting for you with your evening meal, Tregunna?'

I hesitate. 'I have an appointment later.'

'So you said. A woman?'

'A friend.'

'Of course. A friend. Male or female?'

I can't mention Laurens name. I can't possibly drag her into this. 'Ehm ... female.' My hesitation is too obvious.

'Okay.' She chuckles. Her mood is lifting as mine is declining.

'Shall we get to the point, Mrs Robson? What have you remembered that may be important for the investigation of Hugo's death?'

'What time is your appointment?' she replies.

There is a sudden outburst of laughter as three young men enter the pub, yelling greetings to the girl at the bar and other invisible employees. Chuckles, giggles and voices come from inside the kitchen, with greetings back. Annoyed by the interruption, Bees gulps down a fair amount of her wine.

'My private life is of no relevance, Mrs Robson,' I say, ignoring signs that she is determined to follow her own rules in this conversation. 'First of all, we would like to inform the family about Hugo's death. And, secondly, we need to identify him officially. Dental records or other medical information will probably be the best way to deal with that.'

Elbows on the table between us, she leans forward, offering a clear view of the lace trim on her bra. Her smile is soft and warm. Her irritation has evaporated.

'I'll do everything I can to help you ... Andy.' A husky voice. Suggestive.

I am more and more regretting that I agreed to meet her again. Thinking about her has already kept me awake and I really don't want to add more fuel to the situation. I should have asked Ollie Reed to accompany me. Even better, Penrose. Or just passed the message through to Guthrie or Maloney and let either of them deal with her. Instead of listening to my instincts, I agreed to speak to her myself, sensing that she would tell me something important. Something to gloat about to Maloney and Guthrie. Pathetic. Silly.

'You don't mind me calling you Andy, do you? After all, this is our second date.'

'I wouldn't call this a date.'

'Technically not, but ... who knows?' She smiles broadly. Not in the least offended. 'But from now on I will call you Andy.

'If you insist.'

'I do, actually.'

Looking down, I centre my glass on a beer coaster. I formulate in my mind the words to get her on track, but she speaks before me.

'I didn't tell you the truth, Andy. About two or three months after me and Hugo split up, I saw him in Truro,' she blurts. 'He was waiting outside a ladies lingerie-shop. Most men don't like going in shops like that. Do you?'

'I have no reason to.'

'Oh Andy! I'm sure you have a lovely lady somewhere who would love you to bring her a little pressie from a lingerie shop.'

'Did you see who he was waiting for?'

'Hugo? I did. Not a very pretty girl, I regret to say. A bit of a grey mouse, unattractive. Unnoticeable. And to be honest, it made me wonder what reason she had to go in the shop in the first place. You know? From what I saw, she was hardly the type to wear sexy lace underwear to seduce poor Hugo.' She giggles, but without humour.

She opens her handbag, shiny black faux leather with big gold-coloured locks and a thick chain to hang over her shoulder. Producing a little box containing business cards, her other hand searches for a pen. 'I'll give you my card,' she says in a flippant tone. 'It's new. I just collected it from the printer. I had to order new ones. One of the disadvantages of moving house.' She shrugs off a hint of irritation. 'You are the first to have one.'

'I'm honoured.'

'So you should be, Andy. I don't hand out my cards to just … anyone.' She rolls her eyes, again suggestively.

I read her name and contact details. She is a senior partner of an accountancy firm which is based in the centre of Truro. More offices in Bodmin, St Austell, Redruth and Plymouth.

'My mobile number is still the same,' she says, secretively lowering her voice as though she thinks the three young men, now slumped around a table at the other end of the room, may want to have it. 'You can call me, any time, Andy.'

'Do you still have feelings for Hugo?'

Her chin comes up quickly, anger flares in her eyes. My repeated return to the murder inquiry confuses and annoys her. 'Feelings for Hugo? What do you think? He left me. One day he packed a bag and just left. Can you imagine how I felt? Being left like that? With two young children?'

'Was he their father?'

'Not their biological father, no. But he was a good father to them. They adored him. And that also made me angry, inspector, he didn't only leave me, but also my little darlings. And they are too young to understand.'

'How old are they?'

'Charlotte is ten and Deacon is eight.'

Deacon, the boy, scared of Mrs Morley. I wait for a moment, preparing for her reaction as I intend to change the subject again. 'So you met Hugo outside the lingerie shop. Did you speak to him?'

'Only for five minutes. I teased him a bit about the lacy underwear and stuff, but he said the girl only went in there because she saw someone she didn't want to meet. Her ex, presumably. She didn't want him to see her with Hugo.'

Her face is devoid of any expression, but I can't miss a glint of emotion in her eyes. Unfinished business,. Jealousy. Anger.

'He said it was her previous boyfriend. Apparently he was kind of a violent and obsessive man and he didn't agree with the break up. Couldn't cope with it. She was scared of this ex-man of hers and she didn't want him to know she'd moved on and was now with Hugo. I suppose she was afraid that he would turn his anger on Hugo. It wasn't like she'd been two-timing with Hugo or that kind of thing, but still she was afraid that her ex wouldn't believe it.' She pauses. That's what Hugo told me, anyway.'

'So, you and Hugo ... just talked. There wasn't a row, or a fight of some sort.'

'No. It was ... upsetting. I hadn't expected to see him.' Her voice is hoarse. She picks up her glass with two hands. Swirls the remaining inch of wine round. Unsteady. Then she gives a small smile and continues. 'Suddenly he was there, right in front of me. I was shocked. Maybe, if I'd had time to think about it, I would have turned on my heels, but he saw me and ... I couldn't just back of, could I? So I asked what he was doing there. I wanted to invite him for a coffee or something. I don't know why, to be honest. Perhaps part of me wanted him back, but then he told me about his new girlfriend and ... I suppose it was clear that there was no chance for me.'

'Did you ask him about the ... stuff he took?'

'No. This happened only about four or six weeks after he'd left me. Up to then I hadn't noticed that there was anything missing. When I got my head round meeting him again unexpectedly, I went back to find him. Get his phone number or something, an address, whatever. But I couldn't find him.' She pulls a face with disdain. 'His little mouse must have dragged him away, scared of her ex.'

I lean backwards. 'Are you telling me this because you believe this has anything to do with his death?'

'Well, it's obvious, isn't it? He has a new girlfriend. Her ex is a violent man. He must have found out about Hugo and ... well, I'm sure you can fill in the rest.'

'Do you have the name or the address of this girlfriend? And perhaps you know who this ex-boyfriend is?'

'I didn't ask. Hugo didn't seem very happy seeing me. He said he thought I might be aggressive towards the girl, but there was no need for him to be afraid of that.'

'You didn't feel angry any more?'

'Oh! I can't deny that I had murderous feelings when he left me so suddenly, but gradually I started to realise that he was right. We weren't good together any more and I thought it was best for all of us that we got separated.'

'What did your children say?'

'Obviously, they were sad, upset, but after all, Hugo wasn't their biological father. They were fond of him, of course, but ...' She gestures and doesn't finish the sentence.

'You found a new man.'

'Yes. Jonno. You've met him. He is a wonderful man. We're good together.' She smiles happily. 'Jonno's been in a relationship before. We both know what can go wrong, so hopefully we won't fall into the same trap.'

'Very wise.'

'Yeah.' She leans forward, her eyes dark and full of seduction. 'If you give me your number, Andy, I will call you as soon as I found out who that girlfriend is – or was – and more importantly, the name of that jealous violent ex-man.'

'I'd appreciate that.'

She has taken her mobile out of her bag and opens it. It's pink with a curly pattern of little fake diamonds. 'So, what's your mobile number?'

'It's best to call the station.'

'No, no, I insist that I only want to deal with you. It is

your case. I want to help you catch this awful killer.'

'Technically, it isn't my case.'

'Isn't it? Well, whose case is it then?'

'The senior investigating officer is DI Maloney. You can ask to speak to him.'

Obvious irritation lights her eyes. 'You're a DI. Why is he working on this case and why not you?'

'Maloney is also …'

'I've spoken with this Maloney-fellow. He didn't sound very competent. I think you would be much better leading that case. I'd be more confident that you will find Hugo's killer, Andy.'

Narrowing her eyes, she scrutinises my face, thinking, guessing, deciding. Then she breathes deeply, loosening her shoulders.

'There was an incident,' I say, finally, against my better judgement. 'I am currently … on sick leave.'

'Did you get shot? Hurt in a fight with a villain?' The idea seems to excite her.

'Nothing like that, I'm afraid.'

She narrows her eyes. 'But you are okay, now, Andy? Healthy and active?'

'You could say that.'

'But still someone else is doing your job.'

'Maloney is a good colleague.'

'All the same … I'd prefer to ring you, Andy. If not, I'll come to the station and insist that I only speak to you.' A smile breaks through and she looks like a completely different woman suddenly. Her eyes sparkle and her lips open a tiny bit and yet again something stirs in my abdomen.

She knows. She's well aware of the effect she has on men. Smiling with content and badly concealed triumph, she proceeds. 'Come on, Andy, I know your type. You want to be better than that Maloney. You're here because you want to solve his case.'

'I'm not that competitive.' I object, yet knowing that she

is quite right about me. I am almost ashamed about these silly thoughts, but the truth is that I don't like it at all that Maloney is the senior investigating officer of this case. I can't help but secretly hope that he won't be able to unravel the different leads in the case or find out who the killer was and scattered the body parts across the county.

'We haven't been able to trace Hugo's mother.'

'Mm. As I said, I can't help you there. But I see your point, Andy. You know what? I will have a look in the attic in case I still have some old address books and see if I can find her last known address.'

'I'd appreciate that.' I finish my lemonade, leaving the ice cubes melting on the bottom.

'Another one?' She drains her own glass and reaches for mine.

'No, thank you, I really have to go.'

Her face hasn't changed expression, but the sparkle has disappeared from her eyes. I shake my head, look at my watch as if I have already spent much more time with her than I intended to, yet wondering what to do next. I can tell Bee Robson wouldn't mind having dinner with me. Or something else, which I can't.

I look at her face. She isn't aware of my stare, as she is fumbling with something in her handbag. Her guard is down and I see a vulnerable young woman instead. Intuitively, I reach out my hand across the table, feeling sorry for her, although I don't exactly know why, wanting to touch her and give her some strength and comfort.

She looks up, stares in my eyes as if she can see my soul. 'Are you sure you don't want to give me your private phone number?'

'Yes.'

She smiles self-consciously. 'I'll get my hands on it somehow, Andy, believe you me.'

32

The drive to Helston is held up by a car accident that blocks the main road for most of the morning. Life seems to have come to a complete standstill. There are dozens of policemen in yellow vests with their arms folded across their chests, talking to colleagues or gazing at mobiles. Everyone seems to be waiting for something or someone, but there doesn't seem to be anyone in charge, let alone someone brave enough to give the order to move the damaged vehicles to the side of the road and get the traffic moving again.

As the accident happened less than a mile in front of me, there is no other option than to join the queue and be patient. I rest my head back, watching the activity in front of me. Drivers and passengers have got out of their cars and are standing around talking and sharing their impatience and annoyance, making it difficult for an ambulance with flashing blue lights to get through on the hard shoulder.

Retrieving my mobile, I check my messages. Cindy Ferris has reminded me of my appointment in Treliske. I don't need to be reminded; the date and time is etched in my memory. Facebook: an image of a dog dressed in a flowery apron, sitting up straight up open-mouthed as if it's smiling. Like. Share. Comment. I don't like and I don't see any point in sharing it with my so-called, but anonymous, friends. Comment. What would my comment be? I'm rather inclined to make a cynical statement, but I dread what the various responses will be. Another image: a city-view. Workmen standing on the flat roof of a five storey building. Not seeing the point of this, I read the original post: a retired lady with nothing else to do, apparently, moaning that the men aren't wearing helmets and safety gear. Liked by sixty-seven, shared by none, commented on by nine: oh's and ah's and fully agreeing. Only one woman says that she's zoomed in on the picture and wouldn't mind helping the second man on the left in – and out! – of his gear. I delete all my Facebook messages and end up with an alarmingly short list of four unread messages, one of which is a security warning about a bank-con urging me to follow a link if I want to keep my money safe. Another is a suggestion to buy more books in the style of the one I ordered online two months ago. The book was a present for my mother; the online shop won't give up. A message from a solicitor in Truro. Penrose sending a copy of a chart she's made with details about Bee Robson's previous marriage and relationships. I flick through the names. Archer. Whittaker. None is familiar.

And there is a saved message from Bee Robson last night. Which is why I'm now stuck on the A30. She's found a wedding announcement for Hugo Holmes's mother. The wedding was two years ago. Hugo was his mother's witness. Bee and her children were not invited. Glenda Holmes married David Morris and moved into his house in Helston.

More police cars are arriving. They block the other side of the dual carriageway, having diverted the traffic off at the junction a few miles further west. A second ambulance arrives. Men in green overalls with yellow vests scramble through bushes and climb over the barriers dividing the road.

A message pops up. Someone called Wendy Wilson wants to be my friend on Facebook. Curiosity mixes with boredom. I open her page and find her profile image. It's the woman from the waiting room in Treliske. Knitting. Telling me about her tumour, Alistair. Alistair, her latest post says, is now leading his remorseless army, but the defence is in place and Alistair had to retreat and hopefully hasn't got enough troops left for a proper regroup. I smile, reading her previous posts. Her life seems to evolve around Alistair and her daughter, who recently had her second baby, Toni. I press the button to accept the friendship request and I immediately receive a message that I am now friends with Wendy Wilson. I have two friends: Gerald Davey and Wendy Wilson. Sad. Pathetic.

When I finally arrive near the friendly looking cul-de-sac

where daisies dot the grass, I find my way blocked once more. A police car with blue lights flashing, is obstructing the street. I stop next to it and a uniformed policeman gets out.

'I'm afraid the street's sealed off, sir.'

'Why? What happened?'

He looks at my face as if he's politely going to tell me that it is none of my business. 'Do you live here, sir?'

'I am visiting … someone.'

'Who are you visiting, sir?' he asks almost sceptically.

'Sorry.' I gesture vaguely over my shoulder. 'I was just curious. I noticed the police.'

'We can do without curiosity, Sir.'

'Yes, you are right.' I offer a smile, wondering why I don't produce my ID card to let him know that I am a colleague rather than someone suspicious.

He nods. Points over my shoulder. 'You can park over there.'

'Thank you.'

I do as I'm told, park the car and get out. Branches of young trees are outlined against the sky and I can hear birdsong in the shrubs lining the pavement on one side. The street has been sealed off with blue-and-white police tape. A police officer with a serious face keeps everyone at a convenient distance.

Between two rows of detached homes is a public footpath leading into the park behind the houses. The entrance is blocked by more police tape stretched across between a fence post and a young tree trunk, fluttering in the gentle breeze. Square aluminium stepping boards lead to a white tent erected beside the gritted path. Forensic scientists are bending and crouching between shrubs and bushes on either side of the path. There is a uniformed policeman with a clipboard pressed to his chest behind firmly crossed arms, his legs spread as though to underline the importance of his presence. A colleague in plain clothes wanders in a small circle, head bent and speaking into his phone.

A dozen neighbours are grouped together around a

wooden bench on which sit two elderly men with walking sticks resting between wobbly knees. Faces white and eyes big and round, they look me up and down as though they expect me to be the bearer of more bad news than they can fathom.

'The street is blocked,' someone declares, trying to be helpful.

'More police?' A woman asks, shocked, yet excited at the prospect of being important enough to being questioned.

I shake my head. 'What's happening?' Police cars and an ambulance with its back doors open are parked beside the pavement that runs through the grass as if it was laid there by a drunken roadworker.

Nobody answers. I'm the outsider they don't know. Or trust. Following their gazes, I watch a policeman emerge from the second house in a row of six detached houses, erected in accordance with a government scheme to build more affordable homes for local Cornish residents. They seem to pop up everywhere in the county, in fields in the outskirts of towns and villages: small, narrow and characterless with postage stamp-sized gardens and white plastic doors and windows. Although they are meant to help young families get onto the housing ladder, they are just big enough for two or three people.

'What happened?' I try again.

I'm cautiously being sized up. Inspected. My importance considered, weighed. Dismissed.

'An accident,' someone says, but no explanation follows.

Glenda Morris's home is number 14, but the numbers beside the front doors are too far away to read.

'I am visiting someone,' I say slowly. 'Number 14?'

As if someone has pulled a single string that is attached to each of them, they all turn sharply towards me.

'That's where the ambulance went.'

'And where that policeman is.' One of the women points in the direction of the detached house where the policeman emerged a minute ago. He is rooted to the steps in front of the door staring over everyone's heads, giving the impression that he has been put there without being told why.

I get a feeling like a cold hand touching my back, crawling up my spine until it comes to a halt at my neck. 'What happened?' My voice must be laden with urgency and emotion.

This time a man replies. Wearing scruffy trousers and a sleeveless T-shirt, he has the muscular arms of a builder. He shrugs, perching a cigarette in the nook above his right ear. 'They say it was a heart attack.'

'Who is it?' I ask, with a sinking feeling.

'Our poor Glenda.' The woman shakes her head and wipes tears from her face with the tip of her sleeve. As though they've all been waiting for a signal, everyone is now talking at once, a mixture of wild assumptions and speculation. Only the builder is quiet.

'Why would there be so many police for a simple heart attack?'

Good question. I interrupt the discussion. 'Was she ill?'

'Not that we were aware of.'

'But she was sixty-five.'

'That's not old.'

'Still, it's a dangerous age.'

'That's true.'

'They haven't told us exactly what happened. And why don't they take her away?'

'Perhaps they are waiting for something.'

'Or someone.'

The conversation is probably a repeated version of several others, because they all seem to agree and none of them comes up with anything other than speculation. There is a movement in the area surrounding the white tent and everyone around me is silent. We look at a figure in a white paper suit, blue gloves and covers over his shoes. He waves and the photographer jumps forward to flash his camera in multiple directions centred on a spot in the tall grass.

A second figure, also dressed in a white paper suit, appears from the tent, carrying a clipboard, bending down, making notes and finally something is deposited in a labelled plastic evidence bag. Even though none of us can see the item, it is soon agreed that it must be a weapon. A knife. A pistol. The heart attack is dismissed.

The ambulance drives off without a corpse and two minutes later a dark van with obscured windows arrives, squeezing between the gates at the entrance of the footpath.

Tears flood around me. Glenda Morris seemed to have been a popular neighbour. Two years ago, she married David Morris, a widower who'd lived in Helston all his life. He owned a big house in the town centre, but when his daughter surprised the family with three sets of twins, he decided she needed more space than he did and they swapped houses. Sadly, he died about ten months later. Glenda inherited the house and stayed.

'Does she have children?' I ask casually.

'I think she had a son, but I've never seen him.'

'Hugo,' someone else says helpfully. 'Hope they find him, because she didn't seem to know his whereabouts.'

'The police will find him!'

I leave them to their speculations and walk across the street. The uniformed police man is sitting in his car, looking slightly embarrassed, and quickly turns off his mobile phone when I approach him more or less from behind. His instructions were to stop everyone but the police from entering the area; he's not interested in who is leaving.

'Who is the senior investigating officer?' I ask, offering my ID card.

'DI Corbett.' He sizes me up. 'Are you here to see her, sir?'

'I think I have some information to share with her.'

He writes my name and details on his clipboard and speaks in his radio to establish the whereabouts of the woman in charge. Listens. Nods.

'Right sir. DI Corbett is currently in the victim's house.

Number 14.' He indicates with his pen. 'If you can wait there, please, sir? DI Corbett will come to meet you outside.'

Through the front window I can see that Glenda Morris' house has an open-plan living room and kitchen area and looks out on a back garden that has a wooden fence brightened up with hanging baskets that still have an abundance of blue and white lobelia and some other pink flowers. I wait obediently in front of the three steps that lead to the front door until a hand invites me in.

DI Corbett is in her early fifties, short and stocky, with close-cropped grey hair and moist eyes. She shakes my hand with an unexpectedly firm grip and a smile that seems plastered around the corners of her mouth.

'Surprised to see you here, Detective Inspector.'

'I came to see Mrs Morris.'

'Then you're too late.'

'So it seems. Any idea what caused her death?'

Her grin makes dimples in her cheeks. 'You should know better than to ask me that, Detective Inspector.'

'I'm sure you have your thoughts and suspicions.'

'What is the nature of your visit to Mrs Morris?'

'I am investigating the death of her son.'

Her eyes narrow. 'Suspicious death, I presume?'

'I don't doubt you've heard about several body parts found scattered along the coast?'

She lets out a whistle. 'Her son?'

'Hugo Holmes.'

'Well.' She frowns, looking at a tall, slender figure who is examining the contents of a small desk in the corner of the room, a computer screen flashing on top of the desk. 'What's wrong with the computer, Sam?'

'Nothing, ma'am. I'm waiting for George to come and take it away. I don't want to turn it off and lose anything on it.'

'No. Listen Sam, I'm going to the crime scene with DI Tregunna. Can you manage?'

A flash of amusement on his face. 'Of course we can, Ma'am.'

'Come.' Expecting me to follow her, DI Corbett moves with the slightly sideways steps of a spider running away from someone with a dust cloth to remove them from the house.

'You'd better tell me everything about Hugo, Detective Inspector.'

'Equal share?'

She chuckles, walking swiftly towards the white tent. 'Has someone handed you a suit and shoe covers?'

'No.'

She gestures to no one in particular, and someone appears from behind the tent and offers me a plastic bag. 'Your name sir?' He scribbles my details on his clipboard, gazing at his mobile phone to check the exact time. Murder scenes have become a neutral area where everything has to be recorded in detail.

'You can see for yourself, Detective Inspector.' Corbett steps aside to let me in the tent erected around the scene of the crime.

Glenda Morris' corpse is lying on its side in the bushes. Her bare legs are wedged between two hedges. She's wearing a pink fluffy dressing-gown over what looks like a white cotton nightdress printed with yellow and blue birds. Her hair is untidy, partly covered by grass, a small twig sticking out of her collar. Her face is only visible on one side, but it's immediately obvious what caused her death: she has a clear plastic bag over her head.

'This wasn't a heart attack,' Corbett says wryly.

A figure kneeling down beside the corpse looks up. 'We can't yet rule out a heart attack, Dinah, but if it was, it has been caused by fear and shock.'

'What time?'

He shrugs. 'Sometime early this morning. She was found at half past seven by a woman taking a shortcut through the park going to work.'

I swallow. I received Bee Robson's text message with Glenda's address last night. Too late to get in my car and drive to Helston. It feels like I could have prevented her death.

33

Never have I felt so miserable and humiliated. There is no need to look down at my shoes to check if one of them has got dog poo on it. If anyone has noticed, I haven't seen them pulling a face behind my back, stifling a snigger. It's my own fault. For several hours, I have been preoccupied with DCI Corbett's investigation of the death of Hugo's mother, enabling me to search the growing files for information about Hugo's friends or other relatives. The good news is that it will be possible to compare DNA of both victims and hopefully to confirm that they were related as mother and son.

The bad news is that I completely forgot about my stoma bag until I walked back to my car and noticed the smell before I felt the wet stain on my white shirt.

Sitting in my car, I rest my head on my hands on the steering wheel, wanting to cry. My eyes are dry, gritty, but no tears come. Stay positive, I say to myself. Not being able to cry is a good thing. I can drive home. Nobody else but me will have to endure the smell in the car. I could even nip into the toilets of a petrol station; however I would hate to go into an unhygienic public toilet like that.

A knock on the window startles me. There is an elderly man on the pavement next to my passenger window, waiting for me to open it. A ripple of bitter laughter forms somewhere inside me, wanting to escape, but it mixes with a sob half way. The sound that escapes from my throat comes out as a shriek like some animal in distress.

I hesitate, staring into the man's face, imagining what his expression will be when I open the window. I can't avoid him.

Thankfully there is a button to open the passenger window on my side of the car and I fumble with both buttons, opening the window on my side, letting the worst of the smell out first.

'Is everything all right?'

I stare at his clean-shaven face. My jacket hides the stain on my shirt, but the smell is awfully pervasive. 'Thank you. I was just leaving ...'

'It's terrible.' He shakes his head incredulously. 'Were you ... a friend?'

'A friend?' My mind has come to a halt. All I can think of is the torn stoma bag, which is still half-attached to my body, and what it will look like. However much I try, I fail to shift my thoughts elsewhere, to safer grounds.

The man sniffs. 'A friend of Glenda Morris?' His head motions towards the cordoned off area where the blue-and-white police tape shines in the sun, sluggishly moving in a gentle breeze.

'No, I'm not a friend.'

'You look like you've had quite a shock.' He waits, considering his best option: retreat to his home, which appears to be second on the left to Glenda's. The front door is open, a green plastic watering can sits on the threshold.

'Can I use your bathroom?'

I don't know which one of us is more shocked by my sudden outburst. I regret it instantly, inwardly cursing myself for not having thought before I spoke. The expression on my face, or a tone in my voice must have sounded desperate to him. Two bushy eyebrows rise above watery blue-grey eyes. Hair thin and rosy blonde, a suntanned freckled scalp.

'Of course you can.' He steps back and I meet his gaze. He knows.

Holding the front of my jacket together with one hand, I retrieve a small navy blue emergency case from the dashboard locker and get out of the car. The uniformed policeman at the park gate watches stony-faced when I follow Glenda Morris's neighbour into his house as though I am a good friend or family member.

A sign next to his house, number 12, says that his house is called Sweet-Pea. Glancing over his shoulder, he chuckles, following my gaze. 'My wife's name: Petra Sweet.'

'Nice touch.'

He nods, but looking like he's regretting his rather hasty reaction to my request even more than I am. It suddenly seems to dawn on him that he's just let into his house a complete stranger with unpleasant stains on his shirt. Or perhaps the close proximity of the police officers has reassured him a tad. Yet, it is a bit foolhardy of him to invite me in, for all he knows, I could be the man who murdered his neighbour.

'Let me get you a clean towel.'

My hand reaches to the door handle. 'Are you sure about this, Mr Sweet?'

'Huntington. And yes, I'm sure.'

'Perhaps you should be more careful who you invite into your house. Glenda Morris has …'

'Don't make me change my mind, sir.' He moves towards the staircase with surprising speed and agility, gesturing to me to follow him.

Patiently I wait on the landing, staring at four doors, all ajar but not wide enough to see much inside. I hear him opening and closing cupboard doors and drawers. A glimpse of a guestroom with a single bed in the middle. Unmade. A small pile of bedclothes and a folded duvet. A suitcase with a leather address label next to it. He launches into the door opposite, opening onto a bathroom which is even more clean and shiny than my mother's. Stainless steel handgrips surround the bathtub and the toilet, a plastic stool sits in the shower cubicle. Clutching a small pile of things against his chest, he lowers the lid of the toilet seat and places the things on top of it.

'There you go,' he says almost cheerfully. 'I'll make us a cup of tea, shall I? Or would you rather have coffee?'

'Coffee would be lovely, but …'

'I hope you'll find everything you need,' he interrupts hastily. 'If not, give us a shout.'

I feel numb and humble, and it doesn't get much better when he disappears, his footsteps fading on the staircase. I find a brand new, white long-sleeved shirt still in its cellophane wrapping, along with some empty plastic bags and a white vest under two folded towels that smell, unsurprisingly, of sweat peas.

My eyes are still misted up when I meet him in the kitchen fifteen minutes later. The tablecloth covering a small square table matches the cushions on two wooden chairs. Two mugs, one china with red roses has milky tea, the other with black coffee, is a robust dark blue with wording saying 'I am the man in the house'.

'Do you take milk and sugar?' he asks.

'No, thanks.'

He sighs heavily, as if all the tension is now finding a release valve.

'Thank you,' I say simply.

He shrugs, not looking at me but staring out of the window. His back garden has a wrought-iron fence at the end, offering a clear view of the path in the park where the white tent is now deserted except for an officer standing guard outside next to the tape cordoning off the area.

'Did you see anything, Mr Huntington?'

'Sadly, no. I wish I had. I wish I could have helped her, before … Or at least help the police to catch whoever has done this to her.'

He doesn't ask what happened. Perhaps he has seen the corpse. Or the door-to-door officers have already enlightened him. Or he just dreads knowing the details, trying to cope with the death of his neighbour first.

'How well did you know Glenda?'

'From when they moved in. Her and David. He died six months after I lost my Pea.'

Which must have formed a strong bond.

'We look after each other,' he continues, as silent tears negotiate the creases on his wrinkled cheeks. 'We're going on a coach trip to Scarborough at the end of this month.' He can't speak in the past tense yet. 'She's always been healthy, you know, never showed any signs of heart problems.'

If he saw her lying half-hidden in the bushes, he clearly didn't notice the plastic bag around her head. Just as well.

'There will be a post mortem,' I say slowly. 'It's too early to say if it really was a heart attack.'

'That's what we heard.' Spreading his hands, he looks down at them, turning a gold wedding ring with trembling fingers.

The fridge next to him resumes a humming noise. A wooden-framed group photo on top of it shows him, laughing proudly, surrounded by two pairs of adults in their early forties and five children. The youngest is a baby anxiously staring at the camera, the others are three boys under the age of ten, and an older girl with a wide smile exposing braces to straighten her front teeth.

'Your family?'

A warm smile crosses his face. 'My son has two girls, my daughter three boys.'

'What about Glenda?'

'She has … had two sons.'

'Two?'

He nods, unaware of my surprise. 'Oscar and Hugo.' A hand clasps over his mouth. 'I'll have to let them know, won't I? Or will the police do that?'

'It is one of their tasks, but there's nothing to stop you contacting them, Mr Huntington.' I hesitate, 'Do you know Hugo at all?'

'I've only seen him once. Must have been a couple of months ago. Yes, I remember. My son's little one was just a week or so old. May Bank Holiday. We posed for the photo, which was a Father's day present.'

'Did Glenda say anything about him?'

'Not much. She loved him, but I don't think their relationship was very good.'

'Was he close to his brother that you know of?'

He shakes his head warily. 'Oscar lives in Australia. I must have his address somewhere.' He smiles sadly. 'I don't know about Hugo but I'm sure the police will find him.'

'We already have. Hugo is dead, Mr Huntington.'

34

.

People who are tempted to follow their instincts and act on the spur of the moment are never prepared. That is what happens to me when I hesitate before climbing the narrow concrete staircase to my flat. Behind me, my car makes a clicking sound as the engine cools down rapidly. A dog barks in the distance and a humming sound high in the sky, announces that the last plane from London is due to land at Newquay Airport. A footstep crushes a small stone on the slate path that borders the residential parking area. Instinctively. I turn. Nobody. Or is there a sharp intake of breath?

Once more I hesitate. However, I keep telling myself that it's becoming almost an obsession I can't resist to check if Carter's car is still parked on the road, if there is a man, or two, in it, keeping an eye on God knows what. Like a burglar in the dark on the way to his next robbery, I sneak away from the car park and round to the front of the building.

Dusk is setting in early this evening. After the overnight rain and a grey, overcast morning, finally the sun came out at mid-day, warming the wet earth. A mist hangs over the Gannel river like watery milk, reaching out towards the lake. I can just work out the shape of a pair of white swans floating on the surface, the air trapped in-between their well-oiled, water-repellent feathers. The water ripples in a widening circle as something moves under the surface.

The quietness is almost unnerving. Sometimes, I dream that I am walking through empty streets in a city centre where all the shoppers and shop-staff have disappeared, run away like in a disaster movie; I'm the only survivor and I am desperately looking for my family. Or someone else. Anyone. Like after a nuclear attack, or an alien invasion when everyone has been taken away except me and now I'm being spied on by big green eyes.

Sweat breaks out on my neck. I stand still on the tarmac path, my eyes darting across the lake. There are no dog walkers in the park. Not even the lady with the swollen ankles and white fluffy slippers. No one in trainers and tracksuit bottoms preparing for a charity run. A motorcycle passes on the road. A brief burst of the engine breaks the silence as it speeds up out of the roundabout until the driver has to slow down for the next one. Then it's quiet again. Something rustles behind me but when I turn there is nothing out of the ordinary.

There are two groups of trees marking one of the exits to the park. Within reach of their branches, five cars are parked on the road. One is a small white van marked Chloe's Cleaners, suggesting it employs more people than just Chloe Barnett, who lives one floor down from the flat next to mine. The other cars are unmarked, their colours subdued by the mist to various shades of grey.

The mist is damp and drenching cold and I walk quickly towards the exit. Reaching the pavement, I make up my mind that this will be the last time that I let myself do this, and that I definitely will not listen any more to Mr Curtis's suspicions about men sitting in parked cars with binoculars. A car passes. I can hear the bumping sound of loud rock music. The driver is a youngster with a baseball cap, his face a pale blur as he accelerates and speeds away.

There are footsteps behind me. This time it isn't just my imagination. As I turn my head to look over my shoulder, a car door is opened in front of me. I have to step aside to avoid bumping into it. I suppress an annoyed curse as the passenger sticks out his leg, half rising to his feet with the grunt of someone who's been behind the wheel for too long. His black shoes are polished and he's wearing jeans and a black leather jacket, his face hidden under a dark baseball cap.

'I'm so sorry.' His voice is faintly nasal as though he's just sneezed and is hiding his nose behind a hand. It sounds familiar, somehow, although I can't think where I've heard it before. There's no time to consider it anyway. Another man emerges from behind me, blocking my escape route. A firm hand grips my arm. Fingers lock.

'What ...?' I say, perplexed.

'Shall we?' He says almost politely, opening the back door as if I'm employing him as my private driver.

It happens so quickly that I don't realise the situation before I am sitting in the car staring at the back of the man with the baseball cap with my hands tied together with a cable tie that is looped through the buckle of my belt. I guess it would have been much less comfortable if they'd tied my hands behind my back, like the police do.

'I think you are making a mistake,' I say, trying to let my voice sound as casual as possible in an attempt to hide my fear. No answer to my question is given. Instead, the man who pushed me in the car, mutters something, folding up like origami as he leans over me to adjust my seatbelt. His face is obscured in the dim light and I don't recognise him. It's sullen and devoid of any emotions as he slides a simple white pillowcase over my head. I'm not exactly in the dark but it doesn't make me feel any more comfortable.

'No worries,' he says matter-of-factly. 'Just a precaution.'

I feel like I've just woken up from a deep sleep, slightly disorientated, wondering what day it is and what I am supposed to do that day, failing to comprehend where and in whose company I am.

Child safety locks click to lock the doors and the engine starts. We pull out and we pass the petrol station; I can see the red lights of the sign with fuel prices through the fabric of the pillow case.

'Where are we going?' I ask, trying to let my voice sound as casual as possible in an attempt to hide my fear. Unsurprisingly, again, no answer.

We drive round a few roundabouts as though we are retracing our steps all the time. A radio is turned on. Loud classical music fills the inside of the car, drowning out any sounds that might come from the rest outside. The pillowcase over my head, I'm trapped in a little cocoon wondering what's going on, where I am, why I'm handcuffed and who has instructed the two men to do this to me.

'Are you taking me to Carter?' I try, but either they haven't heard me or they choose not to reply.

Fewer roundabouts. I'm guessing we've left Newquay behind us though I haven't a clue in which direction. It seems strange but not being able to figure out where I am and where I'm going makes it difficult to work out how long we've been in the car. I try to count the seconds but the loud music annoys and confuses me so I give up.

Who is behind this? Carter, no doubt. These men have been watching my place for days. But why?

When I met Carter, he denied that his daughter was missing. He must have lied. It's the only explanation I can give for his behaviour. For some reason he didn't want to get the police involved when his daughter was missing. Perhaps he knew she'd been kidnapped. Perhaps he had contact with the kidnappers. In films and books, kidnappers warn the parents, or those closest to the victim, not to alert the police. Therefore some kidnappings stay under the radar. Ransom is paid and the victim returns home unharmed. Physically unharmed. Nothing is said about the emotional or psychological damage. Perhaps Carter thought it would be easier to follow the instructions if Siobhan had been kidnapped, pay the ransom money and wait for her return. Which she did.

She too lied to me about that night. They weren't offered a place to sleep by Stacey. There was no Stacey.

Stop. Rewind. Play again. Think about the facts. They left the school together. Leanne was seen in the bus by her mother's cousin. They both lied to their parents about the sleepover party at Carensa Pencreek's. Pop star Sammii, Leanne's idol, has definitely given the concert in Plymouth; I've seen a recording of it on YouTube. I have also seen the girls together on the images of Mirek Schmidts CCTV footage. About twenty hours later, they were back together, getting off the bus as if nothing had happened, as though they'd been to school as normal.

If Siobhan was kidnapped it must have happened during or after the concert. But what about Leanne? I can't imagine that Carter paid ransom money for her as well.

'I want to speak to Carter,' I say, but there is no reaction from the two men in front of me.

After a while, we turn slowly and drive onto a lane that seems to be scattered with potholes. The driver eases the car round them with care and patience. A country lane leading to a farmhouse or deserted village I wonder, which seems to be confirmed when the music is turned off and I can hear no other nearby traffic.

'Here we are.' It is declared with a hint of relief, and the car slowly comes to a halt. Once more the child safety locks click, and unlock the doors and the one on my right side is opened.

'Get out, please.'

I am no hero. I am not Bruce Willis fighting the evil in the world. I am not Jason Bourne trying to find out who stole his identity and why. On the contrary, I am a coward. Perhaps Jason or Bruce or any other movie hero would make a brave attempt to attack the two men, and win as well, but I don't even see the point in trying. I am not someone who will start a fight. I especially don't want to be kicked at, or land hard on the floor, bruising my body. Or have my stoma damaged.

Obediently, I get out of the car and wait, lifting my elbows as I am told to with my cuffed hands in front of me and I let them take all my belongings from my pockets. My wallet. Mobile. Coins and keys. Even the pen from my breast pocket. Becca's birthday card with 'Happy birthday, from Andy' written on it after I'd had a long think about what to write on it. 'Get well soon,' seemed the most appropriate line for someone in a hospital, but I couldn't bring myself to write such encouraging words laden with hope. I thought 'Happy birthday' was more appropriate. She wouldn't notice anyway. Not her birthday, not the card, not what is written on it. It mattered to me more than to her.

'Come.' The driver seems to be in charge; the one with the nasal voice keeps quiet. 'No tricks.'

As if I would consider trying to escape with my wrists in handcuffs and my head in a pillowcase so that I was unable to see where I was going. It almost makes me laugh.

We are in open air. I can smell the salt in the air, feel minuscule droplets on my skin, hear the waves crashing on the rocks. For a brief, devastating moment, I strongly believe that they are going to push me off the cliffs. Stage my suicide.

There are tall grasses beneath my feet. Wet and damp. Every now and then I manage to detect the remains of an old path or track, disused, with loose pieces of old tarmac and grits crunching under our feet as we walk. The low 'baa' of sheep comes from a nearby field. I count the steps. Twenty, thirty. We must pass a building or a wall because we are sheltered against the wind for about fifteen steps, and then a cold wind blows from across the ocean.

'This way.'

We turn left. A solid path. Concrete.

'Careful. There is a step here.'

I lift a foot, finding a threshold. A house. Relief settles in, but only very briefly. The floor is littered with debris and dust. We must have entered a barn or a shed.

I am pushed to one side and my shoulder touches the rough surface of a brick wall.

'Now. Sit down, Mr Tregunna.' If I still had any doubt about the reason for all this, addressing me by my surname confirms at least that I have been the original target after all. It's not a case of mistaken identity.

'On the floor against the wall.'

It may be my last chance to escape. I consider it briefly. Dismissing it. Stumbling blindly on my feet with my hands still cuffed in front of me will hardly give me the benefit of surprise. I may have more chance when they go away and leave me alone. After all, I am not a hero.

Carefully I lower myself to the ground, keeping my back against the wall. Pulling up my knees. I bow my head and the pillowcase hangs loose. I can see my hands, which is somehow comforting.

'Spread your legs.'

The upright foetus position was fairly safe; spreading my legs makes me feel more vulnerable than ever.

But the voice quickly puts an end to this train of thought. 'Here's some food and water.' There is a snippet of amusement in his voice as he tucks a plastic bag between my legs. You don't supply food and water to someone you're going to kill, or push over the cliffs or make otherwise disappear.

'Your right leg, please.'

I don't move, not understanding what I am supposed to do with my leg. He grunts, picks up my foot and wraps another plastic cable tie around my ankle and attaches it to a metal pole which is firmly rooted in the concrete floor, once probably holding a metal gate to keep cattle indoors.

'Good luck,' he says and I listen to their footsteps disappearing. The car engine is started and they drive off. I am alone.

Not alone. I feel the sweat prickle beneath my hairline. Something, or someone, rustles beside me.

35

I have been lying in the dark for most of the night, trying hard to stay awake, scared that the men might come back - for what reason I daren't think about. Every time I fear I'm drifting off, I jerk awake in panic. Most of the time, I'm trying not to think about the situation I'm in and what will happen next. Thinking about what lays ahead of me this morning leads to places I'd rather not visit. I once read that forty per cent of people sleep in the foetal position, which is on one side with arms and legs pulled toward the torso, which apparently makes us feel safe. This position is usually adopted by emotional and sensitive people and more often by women than men. Researchers even claim that this submissive position affects the way we think and feel: our bodies influence our minds, our minds influence our behaviour, and our behaviours influence our outcomes. However, lying in a prone position with arms and legs stretched out gives us more confidence. It makes us feel bigger and more powerful, and feeling powerful will make us more assertive, and self-confident. Still, knowing this doesn't make it easier to adapt the position in preparation for when the two men come back.

I check the plastic bag. It holds three bananas and three bottles of still water. Enough water to prevent me from dehydrating. Enough bananas to cause constipation.

The wind is cold, the draught feels unhealthy. It is quiet. It must have been an animal rustling beside me, because I haven't heard or sensed it after I kicked wildly in the air with my free leg. The sea can't be far away. I taste salt on my lips.

I bow my head down towards my stomach and finally manage to grab the rim of the pillow case with my teeth, wriggling it until I can pull it over my head.

It is with a mixture of relief and disappointment that I'm able to see my surroundings. I am in an old barn or outhouse, with grey brick walls and open spaces where there have once been windows, or perhaps the builders never got round to putting them in. I am sitting against the wall and my legs are stretched out in an opening between two low walls that surround two square areas. There is a faint smell of cattle and I guess I must be in a building that is occasionally used to shelter animals. Perhaps sheep are sheared here, or ewes are brought in when the farmer suspects a difficult birth. At the end of a passage on my left is a doorway without a door, to my right an opening for a window, without a frame or glass. It is cold and draughty and I shiver. Suddenly, I am overwhelmed by self-pity and despair.

I eat one of the bananas, not knowing when more food supplies will arrive. I drink one of the bottles of water. It is only when I wake up feeling dizzy and giddy, that I realise something I should have noticed before: the bottles had been opened and the water tasted slightly bitter. I hadn't paid attention to it but now it dawns on me that I must have been drugged.

Early morning and the sun is rising, casting long shadows on the floor from the open doorway. Now able to see in the early daylight, the small animal droppings on the ground confirms my suspicions that my nightly visitors had been mice. It was a less alarming and frightening thought than the possibility it was rats.

Along with the darkness going, my lack of action and unwillingness to be a hero have gone. I need to get out of here before they come back. I've spent hours weighing up all the options for the reason for my kidnapping and I am none the wiser. Victor Carter is the most likely suspect, only I can't see why he's made the effort. Besides, he isn't the type. If he wanted to cause me any harm, he would have had me killed, most likely in a road accident or a staged suicide. Who else? I'm hardly working on a case. I have no enemies, at least, none that I know of. The disappearance of Leanne and Siobhan is over. I'm only working on the case of the body parts from the sidelines; it would have been a better idea to kidnap Guthrie or Maloney if that was the reason. What else? Who else? Why?

There is a piece of rusty metal on the floor beside the low wall. In films the hero can reach it just, using conveniently placed equipment that is essential for success. I have no equipment and I can't reach far enough to get my hands on the rusty metal and use it as a saw to cut the plastic ties from my hands.

My belt. The cable tie is tucked through the buckle, but my fingers can reach it and I can undo the buckle. It feels like it takes me another half an hour to pull my undone belt of the loops of my trousers. I have no way of checking the time, other than that my sense of unease tells me to hurry. If the two men are coming back, they won't wait until the evening. More likely they will appear in the morning, early enough not to be disturbed by curious passers-by.

Which brings hope. Passers-by. Someone must come past this building today. I only need one person to help me. All I need to do is attract attention and someone will come and set me free.

Cable ties can be tricky. We use them in the police force and we are always aware that they can easily fail. You have to squeeze one end into a little eye box at the other end and pull it tight. When adjusted in the proper way, they are strong enough to hold heavy weights, surely too strong to break with bare hands. When you put the end in the wrong way up, it won't hold at all and it can be pulled out as easily as it was pushed in.

For some reason, the men haven't tested the one they used on me. Nor have I. I haven't even thought about the possibility that the men could have been so careless. Still, one pull of my foot and the black plastic strip lands on the dusty floor. No such luck with the ties round my wrists, though.

I kneel, crawl, and stumble to my feet. After all my inner cursing about the missing windows and door which have made me cold to the bone, I am now thankful that I am not faced with a locked door or barred windows.

The sky is pale blue and watery orange, deepening in colour as the sun rises over the hills. The old barn now looks as though someone started to build a house but gave up and ended up using it as with a shelter for sheep. I can see some in the nearby field, behind an old weathered dry stone wall overgrown with mosses and lichen. I retrace the route we came here last night, through the tall grass which is swaying in the wind. Below the cliffs, foaming white waves crash onto the steep rocks of a headland and my confidence grows when I recognise Trevose Lighthouse in the distance.

A fishing vessel passes in the bay. I can almost work out the shape of the fisherman in his cabin and for a moment I imagine it's Clem Trebilcock, returning to Newquay harbour after a night out fishing. I hope he's caught enough to have a proper meal on his table, as I know how difficult the life of fishermen has become nowadays, with environmental restrictions and ever-tightening regulations from Brussels.

The road is a single track alongside a dry stone wall overgrown with red and white Valerian and blackberry brambles, I pick a few, tasting their sweetness mixed with a touch of salty air. Weeds are forcing their way through jagged cracks in the crumbling tarmac and grass grows in the middle telling me how little traffic uses it. Which I find rather worrying.

I hear the sound of a car engine in the distance, imagining it coming closer. Mixed feeling make my mouth dry. Alarm. Fear. Comfort. Hope. I turn round, scanning my options. No shelter, nowhere to hide in case the approaching car means that my abductors are returning. I have no doubt that they will. Sooner or later. Another turn on my heels. An open field to my right ends at the cliff edges. To my left is a high section of wall overgrown with unforgiving branches of brambles. Too high to climb over without the proper use of my hands, the wall is not an option. Beyond is another field, sheep slowly waking up, staring at me with dull eyes. A track runs along the wall, both ends disappearing from sight round the bends.

The landscape is slowly emerging with the dawn and early morning dew. The sun is throwing long shadows over the ground. The sound of the car engine grows louder. I can't work out where it's coming from. Unless it's just my imagination, fuelled by fear. When young children get lost on long stretches of busy beaches, the best chance to find them quickly is to walk with the sun at your back rather than in your eyes. Reasoning that my abductors will instinctively do the same, I start walking away from the sun. People running usually attract more attention. I walk. Whether you walk slowly or run fast as if you want to win the London marathon, your arms swing automatically to keep the right balance. My arms don't swing with both my hands still tied up. Aware that my silhouette is etched against the sky I feel myself moving awkwardly, slightly sideways, correcting after each fourth step in a vain attempt to look like a casual walker. The car is still on the move but the wind makes it difficult to establish where the sound is coming from. After a while, I hear voices. A man. Not a nasal voice, or the other one, but that doesn't mean it's any less dangerous.

I duck behind the wall. Think. Wait. Relax. Best to check before I walk straight into the unwelcome open arms of my abductors. After the awfully long, cold and uncomfortable night, I feel I deserve some luck. I move forward, keeping my head down. Every once in a while, I can see slate rooftops and chimneys. I stop at a rusty metal gate which is closed with blue fisherman's rope. A sign on one of the tall stones on either side of the gate says 'Tregrells Holiday Cottages.'

However, the location won't be that helpful if it comes to a quick escape, I lower myself onto the grass as if I'm having a break from my walk. I peer round the corner. A farm has recently been renovated and converted into a collection of holiday cottages, the old cobblestones in the courtyard are glistening with dew in the early morning sunshine. There are two cars parked in the courtyard. One is a small red Vauxhall

Corsa, the other a black people carrier.

I can't remember the colour or make of the car had I was abducted in, but if it is Carter behind all of this, he has several vehicles to choose from. Although he doesn't strike me as a man who would own a bright red car.

Then suddenly a small dog comes running towards the gate as if it has set his hopes on playing with me.

'Dusty!'

Not a man's voice. A child's. A little girl appears in my sight. She is almost as startled as I am. Abductors don't tend to have a family. Or children.

'Dusty?' Her thin voice trembles, along with her bottom lip.

I stiffen. Probably, alarmed by her tone a man emerges from behind a wooden lean-to housing a coal box, a wood pile and an assortment of bicycles. Dressed in clean, new-looking jeans and a light blue shirt buttoned to the top he looks like he's trying to dress casually on holiday but he's missed the point completely.

The girl looks up at him, points towards me and asks, 'Daddy?'

'Yes, princess?' His voice has the authority of a man used to being the chairman in the boardroom. Bold. Ruthless. Making decisions in split seconds.

'Sorry to bother you, sir,' I say quickly, before he can form a bad opinion of me. 'I need your help.'

He looks round, searching for something, someone. His right-hand man. His loyal secretary. Or any other hired help.

'I've been kidnapped. And robbed.'

The statement is lost on him. I can't blame him. I wouldn't believe me either.

'They are after me.'

'I can't see anyone.' Disgust and disbelief in his tone. A protective hand lands on his daughter's shoulder. To him, I must look completely at odds with the norm of his neat suburban life. Unshaven. Dirty. Smelly.

'It's true, sir. I'm not making this up.'

He hesitates, uncertain how to deal with this unexpected situation, looking around for something to give him cause to believe me but the only track to the cottages is deserted on both sides. There is nothing that would support my claims.

'Please leave us alone.'

'They will come looking for me. I escaped.' I get up, holding my cuffed wrists towards him, hoping to use his still half-shocked state as a lever. All I need is to use his bathroom and his phone. 'They will come back for me.'

His focus is still on my face. 'Daphne, go inside the house.' His composure regained, his hand squeezes the girl's shoulder comfortingly.

'But daddy …'

'Do as I say, Daphne.'

She looks at me seriously, as if she's trying to tell me that she will come after me if I dare to hurt her father.

'Go to your mother.'

Obediently, she disappears between the two cars, then into the nearest holiday cottage, emerging at the window with her nose pressed onto the glass, an adult version of her standing behind her.

'Who are you?'

'I'm a policeman.'

His brows rise. I realise that it's the most unlikely of possible answers he was expecting to his question. 'Where's your uniform?'

'I normally don't wear one.' It feels like I'm digging my own grave.

'Your badge?' His hands are now in his trouser pocket. I suspect he's holding his mobile phone in one hand. Ready to use.

'They've taken everything from my pockets.'

'Including your ID card?'

'And my wallet. My mobile phone.'

'Very convenient,' he says suspiciously, but his face is

expressionless, his bright blue eyes alerted as if he's trying to read a business opponent's mind and true intentions in a big business deal.

'Not convenient, it's bloody annoying. I need to go to the hospital in Truro and I have no means of ...' I'm digging deeper. Start again. I can't undo the damage I've done. 'They left me in that barn last night. Look. I'm tied up. They ...' I stop as I hear a car approaching. 'That's probably them. They must have found out that I escaped.'

Once more, I hold up my hands and this time he allows his eyes to go down. For some reason, my tied hands are reassuring for him. A flicker of understanding appears in his eyes, but he is not moving. 'Where were you held?'

'I don't know. Beyond the wall.' I gesture vaguely with my head. 'In a grey brick building. No doors or windows. Bloody cold.'

He nods. At least he knows the building. Understands the remoteness of the draughty place.

'If they find me here ...'

'Will they kill you?' he sounds like he's ordering a pizza from Domino's.

'I don't think so. If that was the plan, they would have killed me last night.' I hesitate. 'But I really have to go to the hospital. A friend of mine is in a coma and today's her birthday and I ...'

One hand emerges from his pocket, as I assumed, holding a mobile. He is telling me he is not a push-over. Looking down at his feet in clean white trainers with an expensive logo on them, he thrusts his head forward as if he is battling against the wind. 'Then why did they ... kidnap you?'

'I don't even know who they are.' I gaze over my shoulder. The silver roof of a car appears where the wall is a bit lower. It won't take long before they will reach the old barn. Run inside. Scan the empty rooms, search everywhere . Jump back in the car. Drive. And see me standing at the gate, pleading desperately for help.

'So you claim you are a police officer and you have been kidnapped and robbed by two men you have never seen in your life. Might there be some motive for their actions?'

'Not that I'm aware off.'

'Okay.' He tut-tuts his lips. He too is now aware of the car approaching slowly on the uneven track. 'You think it is them?'

'It was a silver car I was taken in.' It's a lie. At least I believe it is.

'Okay.' Finally he has made up his mind. I am not a serious threat to his safety. I am still handcuffed. With his thumb, he motions over his shoulder. I can see a shape moving behind the net curtains of the small quartered windows.

He steps back and opens the gate as if he's inviting in a welcome guest, not bothering to put the blue rope back to secure it. I follow him as fast as I dare feeling exposed to anyone in the open courtyard, expecting my two abductors to emerge at any moment. However, he now seems willing to help me, I can't afford for him to get into the position of discussing the situation with the men in case they make him believe a story about an escaped prisoner, or a psychopath looking for his next victim, convincing him that it would be in everyone's best interests to take me off the premises before I can cause any harm to him or his family. His lovely little princess.

'What is your name?' As if on cue, the dog comes forward, sniffing at my feet with curiosity rather than suspicion. Gazing up at me with lively brown eyes for a few seconds, the dog turns to find a sheltered spot in the sun and lowers himself on his chosen spot.

'Tregunna. Andy Tregunna.'

'James Banks.' To my surprise, he offers me a hand. Realising mine are tied together, his face turns pink. 'However odd your story is, I do believe you.'

I take a deep breath, unsure if he is trying to help or laying a trap. Perhaps he knows my abductors, perhaps he is part of the whole plan and is inwardly laughing at my attempted escape, then running straight back into trouble again. 'Thank you.'

'Now,' he says, as though it is only just occurring to him. 'What can I do for you, Mr Tregunna?'

I glance over my shoulder. The car is uncomfortably close. 'First, I need to get home.'

'Ehm. Yes. Of course.'

He has almost reached the door and I am scared suddenly that he will lock himself and his family inside the cottage and call for help. The police, maybe. Uniformed officers who won't know me will arrive sooner or later to take me away and lock me up on the grounds of trespassing. Or worse. I doubt he is a liar, but if necessary to protect his family he would exaggerate the situation.

'And ... is it possible to use your bathroom?' Stopping mid-step, his hand reaching for the door handle, he looks at my crumpled trousers, my unshaven dirty face, my unkempt hair, and the smudges of blood on my hand where I hit the rough concrete blocks when I tried to rip open the cable tie. I am well aware of my appearance and I can understand his concern but I really need to have a proper look at my stoma bag. Check the damage, see if I can empty it and stick it back onto my skin. It won't be an ideal solution, but it would be better than nothing. From now on, I promise myself, I will make sure I carry an emergency kit with me all the time. It won't be that difficult to store a spare stoma bag and a small adhesive's bottle in a bumbag like a tourist hiding all their valuables from pickpockets.

'Wait here please.' The silver car has reached the gate. It stops and, with a sinking feeling, I hear a car door opening. James Banks may be a friendly and helpful soul, but he doesn't understand how scared I am that the men could persuade him that the best option is that they take me away. Perhaps they will even come up with a story about a joke that got out of hand, a training exercise which made me too disorientated to find my way back to base camp.

My face must be an open book to him. 'Okay. I think you'd better come in.' He motions over his shoulder to follow him. 'No tricks.'

I step inside. The cottage has plain white walls and a varnished wooden floor. A kitchen is separated from the living area by two large beams in the middle holding up the low ceiling. A young woman is standing at the sink in front of the window. Her blonde hair a mess, face pale and brown eyes sleepy. She's dressed in a fluffy white bathrobe with the logo of a hotel on the chest pocket. Her feet are bare, nails painted bright red.

'James, what's happening?' She sounds husky, as if she'd just been making love. 'Daphne said …' She stops when I come into her vision, raising her eyebrows, and her small nose covered with freckles.

He smiles quickly, putting his arms around her and resting his chin on her head for a moment. 'This is Andy Tregunna. He's asked for our help,' he says, his mouth making in a wry smile.

Her face is one big question mark. 'Is everything alright?'

'Of course, my darling.' His hand slides down her back, stopping briefly at her bottom. 'He would like to use our bathroom and make a phone call to someone to pick him up.'

36

A few years back, I used to have everyone's phone numbers stored in my head but since mobile phones have become so universal, the ability to remember contact numbers is now redundant. At least for me. I can't even remember Lauren's number. Or Guthrie's.

What I do remember is my parent's landline. I can't possibly bother them with this. They'll be sick with worry about what's happened, what could have happened and even more so what will happen to me next.

Oddly, the other phone number I do remember is that of my neighbour, Mr Curtis. It's not even an easy number to remember, but somehow the rhythm of it has got stuck in my mind.

'Hello?' A deep voice grunts at me. He sounds sleepy and suspicious.

'It's Tregunna. Your neighbour.'

He's so silent for so long that I think he's hung up on me.

'Well, you surprise me, Tregunna.' His chuckle echoes spookily as if he's standing in the centre of a big empty sports hall.

'How do you mean?'

Another chuckle, this time with a hint of embarrassment. 'You wouldn't speak to me when I called you last night.'

I must have missed something. 'When was that?'

James is waiting. Frowning. I promised him I would call for someone to collect me, now he seems unhappy as it occurs to him that he might get stuck with me after all. His nostrils flare and his eyes only drift off briefly when his wife comes down from upstairs. She's combed her hair and applied some light make-up. Not too much, only enough to give her self-confidence. She's now dressed in white trousers and a loose, navy blue blouse, printed with white dots. Her curly hair is pulled back and gathered on top of her head with a elasticated band, looking like she has a fountain on her head.

'Last night of course,' Curtis says in my ear, enough irony in his voice to alert me. I can't remember he's ever called me before, so why would he have tried last night, when he could have seen the lights in my flat were off and he would have known that I was out.

'Everything all right?' James Banks' wife asks without looking in my direction.

'Sure.' Her husband sounds as unconvincing as the expression on his face suggests. 'Where is Daphne?'

She shrugs as if the question is too ridiculous to answer seriously. 'In the courtyard.'

He stiffens. 'Alone?'

'Of course not. Julie is there to look after little Ash. I asked her to keep an eye on Daphne as well.'

'What time was that, Mr Curtis?'

James is moving awkwardly, clearly wondering why I don't ask Curtis to come and fetch me. He has a point. Pointedly, he ducks to look out of the window, as if to remind me that the silver car is still there.

'Half nine. Ten. Eleven. Midnight?'

Something is very wrong here. I must have missed something. My head isn't working as well as it should do, as though my senses aren't connected to my brain any more.

'Why did you call me, Mr Curtis?'

He chuckles incredulously. 'Because of the noise, of course. That Chloe girl, yes, she can turn the music up, or that other chap, that new guy, isn't his name Mark? Anyway, I hadn't expected it from you and ...'

'What noise?' I interrupt, staring at James who is clearly contemplating grabbing his phone from my hand.

In the kitchen area, his wife gasps, her body freezing, a jar of coffee granules in her hand. Beside her the kettle is coming to the boil.

'What's wrong, darling?'

'A man is coming through the gate.'

'Your Mr Curtis?' James asks hopefully.

'No.' I'm half hidden behind the net curtains. He isn't. We follow his wife's gaze.

'Are they police?'

'No. I am police.'

Once more he frowns, doubt filling his mind. In fairness, I don't look like a policeman at all.

'Mr Curtis?'

'Mr Tregunna.'

His voice is not exactly unfriendly and I take a deep breath. 'Mr Curtis, is there a possibility that you could come and pick me up? As you can probably see my car is still outside my flat in the car park and I'm kind of stranded here. I'm ...'

'Why would I do that after you've ruined my sleep?'

There he goes again. Hinting at something I'm missing. Perhaps people with dementia suffer from missing connections like this. I am beginning to understand how unnerving and frightening it must be to lose the ability to understand. One look at James's face and I dismiss the idea of asking Curtis what he means. James is staring outside. A man has got out of the car and is holding a mobile phone against his ear, listening with concentration. He is too far away to recognise his face and I hope he can't see mine through the net curtains. The only thing that he may find a bit suspicious is the fact that he can see James's wife staring out of one kitchen window with a hand over her mouth and James looking out of the other. The silver car is parked near the gate, but so that it's impossible to see whether there is another person in it.

Two children are playing in the courtyard, laughing, running after a bright red plastic ball. The girl, Daphne, and a toddler on unsteady, chubby legs. A young woman with short blonde hair is smiling, looking at her little one with pride and love. Suddenly she halts. The man must have called out something to her, she walks closer to the gate, her little boy forgotten for a moment. The man gestures at her, his phone still in one hand. He motions towards the holiday bungalows and she nods vigorously.

Has she seen me? Has James's wife told her about me? Is the man now enquiring if she saw a strange man in dirty clothes and where might he be now?

'Mr Tregunna? Are you still there?'

'Mr Curtis,' I say urgently. 'Do you remember the two men who were watching our building from their car?'

'Of course I remember that.' Doubtful but intrigued.

'Well, you may think I'm mad, but I'm telling you the truth, Mr Curtis. Those two men kidnapped me last night.'

'Sure they did.'

Outside the man is still talking to the young woman. Whatever she's told him, he seems certain that he'll find me here.

'Mr Curtis, I can't explain it right now, but I really need your help.'

'Why don't you call the police?'

Good question. 'They won't believe me.' The truth is that I don't want any of my colleagues to find me. Not in this situation. Not like this, not with the bulge of my stoma bag sticking out under my shirt. I have emptied it and closed the hole with plasters I found in the bathroom, but I doubt it will hold as long as I need it to. And I am too dammed proud and have too much dignity to face any of my colleagues, and to have to listen to muttered voices and laughter behind my back.

'What makes you think that I will believe you?'

'Because you saw those men. You know they were there. They were watching our apartment building. You know that. You said so yourself.'

I glance at James's wristwatch. 'At this moment I have no time to explain everything, but I need to be in Treliske in about one and a half hour's time.'

'Do you have a doctor's appointment?' He sounds like it may be the only reason why he would come and get me.

'Not exactly with my consultant,' I reply truthfully. 'But there is …'

'A psychiatrist?' he insists.

'No, but I'm ...'

The young woman has picked up her little boy. He has fallen and is crying, a red graze on one of his knees. The man is turning away from the gate. His body language is telling me that he is arguing with someone on the phone. I can hardly believe he is backing of.

'No Mr Curtis. I have a friend who is seriously ill in hospital. Today is her birthday and I promised the nurses I'd take her a birthday cake.'

'Oh. Okay.' It is clearly not the answer he expected, but it increases my credibility and his curiosity.

'They're leaving,' James's wife announces, relieved, nodding her head as her world begins to return to normal. She flicks the button on the kettle and for the first time she looks straight into my eyes. 'Coffee?'

'That would be lovely.'

'I would be really grateful if you could come and fetch me, Mr Curtis.

'Okay Mr Tregunna. I must admit I am rather more curious than kind. After all, that noise you made kept me awake half the night, but I guess I don't understand how you young people live. Everything is so different from when I was young.'

'Yes.' I still haven't a clue what he is talking about, but the best option right now is to agree with everything he says.

'I will explain everything on the way home, Mr Curtis, I promise.'

He takes the bait without hesitation. 'Okay then. Tell me where you are.'

Helpfully James hands me a brochure of the company that manages the holiday lets and I read the details out loud, imagining the expression on Mr Curtis's face.

'All right then. But I'd like you to apologize for the noise last night.'

'I'm sorry if you thought that the music was ...'

'Music?' He chuckles. 'Believe you me, Mr Tregunna, even loud music would have been better than having to listen to your neighbour making love to his girlfriend all night long!'

37

'How will you get to Truro?' Curtis asks practically, frowning but with an unexpected sparkle in his eyes.

'Good question.'

He has parked his car in its usual space and it has just dawned on me what it means to have lost my keys. It's one thing that I can't get into my house but I'm more concerned that I can't have a quick wash and change. In the worst case scenario I can visit the stoma nurses tucked away in a backroom in the Treliske tower block, but I also need a shave. Brush my teeth. Clean clothes.

'I can drive you to the hospital,' he suggests, probably thinking about my offer to reimburse his fuel costs. Or perhaps I am reading him wrong.

'That's very kind of you, but …' I stop. I have this habit of not locking my car overnight. There is an emergency kit for my stoma bag in it.

'… I need to change first.' I don't think he knows about my condition and I won't fill him in unless it's necessary.

'I think you do,' he nods, more honest than helpful to my self-confidence.

'I guess I can help you with a shirt, but my trousers will be too short for you.' And probably too wide, I think to myself.

'You can't go to a birthday party in the state you are,' Curtis continues, sniffing and making me feel even worse. 'Come on, old chap.'

He makes it sound as though we are planning a secret schoolboy's prank, putting glue on the teacher's seat, adding salt to a cup of tea or putting worms in someone's lunchbox.

He makes tea and toast as I use his bathroom and put on a shirt that is too wide around the neck. When I come back into his kitchen crammed with crockery and unused utensils, he sits at the kitchen table waiting with two steaming mugs on a tray, apologising that he doesn't have any biscuits as he decided long ago that was a luxury one can live without.

We sit facing each other, nursing our hot drinks, me wanting the warmth to seep back into my body. When I open my mouth, he speaks first. 'You should have paid more attention. You didn't believe me when I told you it was suspicious. Dangerous.'

'You are right,' I say obligingly.

He finishes his tea. 'So we are off to the hospital now?' he asks, cheerful as though we're off on a school trip.

'If you don't mind.'

'Of course not.' He gestures round, his mouth twisted in a piteous expression. 'I've got nothing else to do that is more important.'

'We will need to pick someone up.'

He frowns. Then nods approvingly. 'Good that you've found a girlfriend, Mr Tregunna.'

'Lauren isn't …'

'Of course not. Shall we go? I'll need some petrol for my car. Ehm … would you mind…?'

'I have no money on me, Mr Curtis, but I will pay you back, I promise. As soon as we come back, I will sort things out with my bank. I'll need new keys for the front door and …'

'Perhaps you'll need a new lock as well,' he says pragmatically. 'If they still have your keys, they may come back.'

It hasn't even occurred to me that they might. Hiding my shameful smile, I look away and ask if he's got a telephone directory. Unsurprisingly, he has one and I dial Lauren's number.

'I'm a bit late, Lauren. But I'll be on my way in a minute. Eh … I'm with Mr Curtis.' I explain that I have lost my car keys and my neighbour has kindly offered to drive us to Treliske. Her replies are curt and clipped. The idea of having Curtis for company doesn't appeal to her and I have the feeling that she will opt out if I add something like 'unless you'd rather not come.'

'What time will you be here then?'

Spot on ten minutes later, Curtis drops me at her house and we stand awkwardly on the pavement waiting for him to come back from refuelling his car.

'Is something wrong, Lauren?'

'No.' Her answer is too curt.

'Have I done or said something to upset you?'

A blush of pink spreads up her neck, bright red spots on her cheeks. Her eyes are like daggers as she looks at me with a mixture of anger and despair. 'I tried to ring you a couple of times last night,' she says, her words clipped and tight, the bitter accusation barely hidden.

She looks as if she's unsure whether to slap me in the face or start to cry. I can see her chest rising and falling with the effort of controlling her anger.

'I was going to tell you what happened last night,' I say miserably, realising that she has drawn her own conclusions and it is too late to set things right.

'You don't have to,' she replies sharply.

'I was abducted by two men.'

'I have no right ...' she stops mid-sentence, eyes wide in disbelief. 'You what?'

'I thought you wouldn't believe me.'

'That's right.' She turns on her heels and marches to the door, taking her keys from her handbag. I feel like she's walking out of my life and I know it would be my own fault. I haven't been honest with her. I tend to tell her half truths, just because I am too scared to let her come too close – and then lose her again.

'I tried to call you, but I got your answer machine,' she says when I catch up with her.

'I wasn't at home, Lauren.'

She doesn't listen.

'Several times I called you because I didn't know what time we were supposed to go to the hospital and I needed to make arrangements for the boys in case we would be back later than I expected.' She stops to take a deep breath. 'You didn't answer.'

'They took my phone.'

Still she doesn't listen. 'Except for one time,' she continues, staring at me with big eyes and a very pale face. 'Only one time I got connected,' she continues with a flat voice, her face stony. 'A woman answered. She said "Sorry, but he's not available for you at this moment". And then she laughed as though ...'

'A woman?'

'She didn't say who she was. And I didn't ask.'

I fall silent. Two men abducted me. Carter's men. They took my wallet and keys. And my phone. Someone answered. A woman. Who is also involved in my kidnapping? Not Mrs Carter. I can't believe she's got anything to do with this. Not her. She is too ... posh, well groomed. Siobhan? No, she's only a very young vulnerable teenager.

Lauren's mood lifts as she accepts with a smile Mr Curtis's courteous bow and kiss on her hand. However liberated and opinionated about women's rights she is, she's pleased by such conventional courtesy.

She notices the scratches on the back of my hand. 'What happened?'

'It's a long story.' She notices my dismissive tone.

'He was kidnapped,' Curtis announces cheerfully, as if it's all one big joke. 'Would you believe it?'

I wouldn't. Nor does Lauren.

Curtis is holding open the car door for her, another small courtesy which I seldom bother to extend. 'Kidnapped?' she asks, incredulously, turning towards me, searching my face, hoping that I will laugh about Curtis's joke. I can't.

'Andy will tell you everything about it,' Curtis continues, looking at me expectantly. But my mood has changed at the prospect of having to meet Dorothy Trewoon and I keep quiet.

We drive in silence, each of us occupied with our own thoughts. I can't deny that Curtis tried his best with old-fashioned jokes but Lauren only smiles faintly and I can't even force myself to listen. In the end he turns on the radio and the car fills with classical music. It is loud and melancholy, and too depressing for my taste, but he doesn't seem to care. When we reach Treliske, Curtis drives into the main car park and finds a space almost next to the entrance of the hospital. Some people are always lucky. I am very tempted to ask him to wait in the car, but Lauren, reading my thoughts, shakes her head and picks up the plastic bag containing a big chocolate birthday cake and two bunches of flowers. One from me and one from her, the argument being that one bouquet wouldn't be sufficient for the birthday celebration of a pretty young woman. As if to confirm her point, despite telling him he needn't to come in with us, Curtis buys a bouquet in the hospital shop and tucks it under his arm with the determination of someone who can't be persuaded to stay behind.

It's a bit too early for visitors and our footsteps echo off the walls. Nurses push medicine trolleys with boxes of pills, checking the clipboards at the foot of each bed before handing out tiny beakers with the precise amount of pills to each patient. Volunteers push similar trolleys with mugs and thermos flasks to serve coffee and tea. A group of young doctors go from patient to patient, studying the clipboards, exchanging comments with each other in terms which the lay person would not understand. Dr Elliott is one of them. He smiles and nods, recognising me, and gesturing that he will join us later. The fact that he will, puts a small lump in my throat.

The door of Becca's room is slightly ajar. I hear murmured voices.

A man in a dark suit is sitting on a solitary plastic chair outside the door to Becca's room. Looking bored, he rises to his feet as we approach, squinting against the light shining on the linoleum floor. He is stiff and awkward.

'Sorry. You can't come in here,' he says bluntly, stretching himself up to his full height and giving us a very serious look.

'Please enquire at the desk for the person you wish to visit.'

'We are here to see Becca Trewoon. It's her birthday.'

He doesn't move. 'And your name is?'

My ID card is in my wallet. In the possession of my abductors. It's starting to feel more like a conspiracy to keep me away from celebrating the birthday of a young woman who doesn't even recognise the world around her.

'I am Detective Inspector Tregunna. I have organised this little … party.'

'We have a birthday cake,' Curtis says, pointing at the plastic bag dangling from Lauren's hand.

'You are?'

'Harradine Curtis.' His shoulders are square with pride as he produces his driver's licence with a flourish as if to convey his importance. The man barely looks at the little pink card that shows Mr Curtis as he was years ago: with a tuft of blonde hair and a happy smile across his face.

'Are you here because … Dorothy is here?' I ask.

'Yes sir.' He smiles faintly. 'We are … accompanying Ms Trewoon on this occasion so that she can be present at her daughter's birthday.' I stiffen. I open my mouth to correct him: Dorothy is not Becca's mother, but her sister. In fact, she is both.

The door opens and a nurse appears. Mirabelle. 'Oh, there you are Mr Tregunna. We're waiting for the cake.' She grins. The guard shrugs and sits down as if defeated by a superior.

There are dozens of silver and other brightly coloured balloons tied to the head and foot of Becca's bed. Some hang steady in the air, held up by helium gas, others move gently in the faint breeze that comes from an air-conditioning outlet in the ceiling.

Plastic seats and uncomfortable tripod stools are arranged around the bed as if it's been set up as a stage for some kind of act. I count at least half a dozen people in the room but the first face that catches my eye is that of Dorothy Trewoon. Close enough to the bed to make me want to pull her away immediately, she sits between two other guards, a tall and muscular man who would have a fair chance of being on TV to compete as the strongest man in Britain, and a tiny, skinny woman with eagle eyes and a hooked nose. Not strong but mean.

'Andy!' For an instant I believe it's Becca calling my name and I am perplexed, shocked by the possibility that she has suddenly come out of the coma.

'Andy! Inspector!' Dorothy almost jumps to her feet, smiling with a mixture of triumph and an emotion that I would be inclined to call suppressed hatred or disgust. 'I didn't expect to see you today!' she exclaims with a strange flicker in her eyes.

I take a deep breath, steadying myself. 'Why not?'

She smiles slyly, recognising my feelings and pitying me for them. 'You blame me for what happened.'

'I do, but let's …'

'You know I never meant to hurt her.'

I ignore her. Lauren stiffens beside me and Mrs Curtis's eyes shift back and forth as if he's lost control over their movements, meanwhile trying to work out the relationships and underlying currents of emotion.

We put our flowers in glass vases and add our cards to the board behind the bed. Nurses and doctors flock in. I wonder if they have just come in for a short break in their busy daily routine or for a piece of cake. Does it matter? The main thing is that Becca is certainly not forgotten on her birthday. We're here for her today and I know she'd be pleased if she could see or hear us – or even be aware of us. Which I start doubting more and more. The bleeps and lines on the monitor don't change. Her breathing is shallow but steady. At no point does her heart rate increase, let alone jump around. Not even when Dorothy bends over to kiss her to wish her a happy birthday and whispers something in her ear. I try to hear what she says, but Dorothy smiles secretively when she straightens up and our eyes meet.

'As I said, I didn't expect to meet you here, Andy.' With a meaningful smile, she moves from between her guards and sits on the chair next to mine. The question, repeated, suddenly strikes me as odd.

'What makes you say that, Mrs Trewoon?'

'You seem to avoid me. You refuse to see me.'

'I don't see the point in seeing you.'

Lauren is slicing cake and serving portions on paper plates, and napkins printed with red balloons.

'I have sent in a request to discuss my case.'

'You are waiting for your trail, Mrs Trewoon. It's up to the jury now.'

'What if I have new information?'

'Speak to your lawyer.' I want to turn to the person who sits down next to me, but she persists.

'You know you are the only one I wish to speak to. My lawyer is a waste of space. She doesn't believe in my innocence. She won't do anything to help me get out of that prison.'

'She's a professional lawyer, Mrs Trewoon. She will do what she is supposed to do. Defend you. She's not meant to like or dislike you. Whether she has an opinion about you or your case, or not, that won't make any difference to your case.'

She lifts her eyebrows in an almost comical way. 'I didn't do it, inspector.'

I shrug, relieved to be able to turn away from her when Lauren touches my arm. 'There isn't much cake left, Andy. Shall I go to the shop and see if I can get some more?'

It isn't the cake. She wants to get out of here. 'Good idea. I haven't even had a piece yet.'

Dorothy's eyes follow her as Lauren tosses her bag over her shoulder and leaves the room hurriedly with relief. I regret that I didn't consider her feelings when I invited her to come with me. I should have been less selfish.

'She's lovely, inspector,' Dorothy sneers.

Her hand grabs my arm. I can feel the pressure of her

fingertips. Her nails. One of the guards moves. 'Mrs Trewoon, please?'

With a disappointed smile, she pulls back. 'Sorry,' she says, not meaning it.

'It's okay.' I move slightly away from her, trying to get involved in the conversation between Dr Elliott and Mr Curtis, the latter with multiple questions about Becca's condition and her chances of recovery while the doctor tries to avoid giving direct answers.

'It's a sad story,' Curtis says. If he is aware of the circumstances that led to Becca's situation, it certainly wasn't me who told him. Thinking of him using binoculars to spy on Carter's men in the car, I'm inclined to believe he is fishing for information rather than making polite conversation.

'Indeed.' Elliott manages to get the attention of a nurse, Mirabelle, who has just walked in. He rises from his stool and I'm left with Dorothy on one side and an empty seat on the other. As much as he has proven to be a helpful neighbour, Mr Curtis is turning his back to me to chat with another nurse.

'Are you two in a relationship?' Dorothy asks.

'Sorry?'

'You and ... the little redhead.'

'Her name is Lauren.'

'Are you?'

'Mrs Trewoon, I do think it is none of your business.'

'But it is, Andy. I care about you, you do know that, don't you?'

'Mrs Trewoon ...'

She leans sideways, her cheek almost touching my shoulder. One of the guards shifts, alerted, so she sends him a flashing smile, acting innocent, and he leans back but keeps his eyes on her.

'Please call me Dottie.'

Somehow I feel trapped. In the room, in the hospital, in her sight.

'I don't think ...' I start, not knowing what to say.

'I'll send another request for you to see me, Andy.'

'Ah, Mr Tregunna! I knew I'd find you here. Eventually.' A nurse appears in the doorway, a worried look on her face. 'I've tried several times to call you, Mr Tregunna. It's about Mr Grose.' It's Rosie. I remember her.

'I've lost my mobile.' I get up, stretching my back, unclenching my hands which I wasn't even aware had been tightly clenched.

'How inconvenient,' Dorothy Trewoon chips in from behind my back. 'I'm sure you'll find it soon. Things don't get lost. They just mislaid.'

Stolen more likely.

'What's up with Mr Grose?'

The nurse turns her head to suggest we go over to the far end of the room. More private. I'm glad to escape, albeit short-lived, from the close proximity of Dorothy Trewoon.

'He isn't getting better,' Rosie says, lowering her voice. 'He's asked for you. He seems … restless and uneasy about something, but we don't understand what he is talking about.'

'His wife?'

'Something about ringing someone, we think. Anyway, I know you didn't intend to, not today, but is there a chance you can pop in to see him? He's asleep most of the time, but you can wake him up. It will only be for a few minutes.'

'Of course I can.' I look round. The nurses are chatting and laughing. The guards look stoic, interested only in the prospect of Lauren returning with more cakes. Dorothy has managed to attract the attention of Dr Elliott. Although I dread the idea of her discussing Becca's condition with the doctor, I don't want to get involved in the conversation and get trapped with her again. Somehow that woman is dangerously intoxicating. She's a like a fix of drugs taunting an addict desperately trying to become clean.

I follow Rosie through quiet corridors, past an empty desk where the phone has no doubt been forwarded to someone's pager, someone who has sneaked away for two minutes and is now attending the birthday party. I can't blame them. All we can hear is the sharp click-clack of our heels as Rosie quickly explains that Mr Grose has had several minor strokes and his condition has deteriorated.

'He doesn't seem to care any more,' she adds, halting at a closed door. 'Moving him may very well cause his death.'

Her gaze is serious and I keep to myself what I'm thinking so as not to shock her. What is the point in keeping Mr Grose alive? He won't recover. He won't be able to return to his home. He won't even want to.

She opens the door, whispering, 'I'll leave you to it.'

The curtains are drawn and there is a light above Mr Grose's head. A single card wishing him to get well soon is stuck on the otherwise empty board. I recognise my mother's handwriting. A vase, a discarded glass jar that once held a healthy juice of the kind you buy when you visit someone in hospital, is empty on the window sill. His brown check slippers are under his bed but I doubt if he will ever use them again.

His mouth is half open. His breathing is heavy. Difficult. Every so often, he seems to stop breathing, then there is a deep sigh and his eyes open, staring, wondering perhaps where or who he is, closing them again as he can't find the answer.

'Mr Grose.' I grab a chair and sit down, placing my hand on his arm to make him aware of me but not to startle him. 'Mr Grose, are you awake? It's Andy Tregunna.'

There is a movement at the door. Perhaps Rosie wants to make sure that I am OK to be left alone with her patient before she heads back for the cake. Lauren should be back with new supplies by now.

'You wished to see me, Mr Grose.'

There is no response. He is asleep and there seems no point in staying to wait for him to wake up which could be any time. Yet, I stay and bend over close to his head. And I talk about a boy who once sat next to him and listened to his stories with a mixture of curiosity and horror. I tell him about my nightmares. There is a faint movement in his face when I

279

add that I laughed about the nightmares later. One eye opens and I imagine I see the same sparkle in it from all those years ago. A rumble like a deep earthquake comes from his throat. One corner of his mouth twists into a faint smile.

'It's Andy.'

Another rumble, followed by what sounds like the start of a bout of desperate coughing.

'No, don't speak, please.' I can sense his unease. He wants to say something but physically can't. He is too weak.

'I did everything you asked. I went into the kitchen. I cleared everything away. No one will find it. It's all gone Mr Grose, you needn't worry about it any more.'

His hand reaches out with surprising strength. He grabs my fingers with a weak, trembling and cold hand. He is trying to tell me something. A mixture of faint coughing and whispering. Single words. I don't understand any of it.

'I took the wedding ring and I put it where you wanted it. Everything is all right.'

'Oh. Aaah.'

His hand drops and his face relaxes. He is asleep again, peaceful, and somehow I am confident that I have told him what he wanted to hear. I get up and look at my mother's card above his head, and I say an inaudible farewell to him. I know I won't see him alive again.

38

I use Lauren's mobile to call the station. Disgruntled, I tell the desk-officer that I've lost my phone and I'll let him know as soon as I have a new one. He smirks, finding it funny rather than sharing my annoyance. Sponge-Rob would have been more understanding than this new recruit.

At my request, he connects me somewhat grudgingly to Penrose.

'Sir, I've been trying to contact you,' she says before I can get a word in.

There must be a long list of missed calls and messages in my phone.

'Well.' She lowers her voice. 'Guthrie is not happy with you.'

'I've already spoken to Maloney. He said DI Corbett has been in contact.'

'Yes. She is very helpful.' She hesitates. 'Sir, are you expecting a bomb to go off?'

'A what?'

She chuckles. 'A bomb.'

Suspicion. Paranoia. A bomb. The bomb threat springs to mind. It could never happen here, not in Cornwall, not on my doorstep. Yet, I can't dismiss the feeling that I am slowly being trapped into something, slowly pulled towards a situation I won't be able to handle any more.

'Why do you ask, Jennette?' Perhaps last week's bomb threat in St Austell has had more impact on her than I expected. After all, initially the threat was taken seriously and officers must have had serious fears that something major was about to happen.

'We have a parcel here at the station, sir. It was delivered at about noon.' She pauses for dramatic effect. 'It's for you. It says it's private.'

'And you think it may be a bomb?'

'Well, I hope not sir, because it's in front of me on my desk.'

'How big?'

'About half the size of a shoebox.'

'Not big enough for a bomb, Jennette.'

'Depends what that bomb is made of, Maloney said.'

'Oh. Clearly you are not treating it suspiciously.'

'It's been on my desk for hours.'

'You've taken a big risk on behalf of me.'

'Sure have!' The whole issue seems to amuse her. 'I think I know what it is, sir.'

'Have you opened it?'

'Of course not! Such a breach of privacy would cost me my job.' She chuckles. 'But I am a good detective, sir.'

'You are, Jennette.'

I hear her rummaging through papers on her desk. 'Have you lost your phone, sir?'

'How do you know?'

'I said I am a good detective.'

'Indeed, Jennette, I was just calling you to let you know that I've lost it. Along with some other items.'

'Hm. I've rung your number because I wanted to ask you something, sir. It took me a while before I realised that the phone I thought I heard ringing on someone else's desk wasn't a distant phone. Actually, it is your phone, sir. In the parcel.'

The events of the last few days have been so extraordinary that I am hardly surprised.

'Would you mind opening that parcel, please Jennette? And tell me what else is in it?'

'Probably only your phone, sir. Someone who wanted to remain anonymous must have found it and didn't want the hassle of reporting it found.'

'Please, Jennette.'

'Did you just say that you lost some other items?'

'I did.'

'I'll have to put you down for a minute, sir. The parcel is wrapped in tape.'

'I'll wait.'

'Sir.' She's back three minutes later. Perplexed.

'It is your phone sir. Along with a set of keys. Your ID-card. Your watch. Your wallet with £40 in bank notes and some loose coins. Bankcards. A Tesco loyalty card. A pen engraved with your initials. And a birthday card.'

'That's good news, Jennette.'

It saves me a lot of hassle, especially with the more private items, but I don't understand it.

'Have you lost all these items, sir?'

'Ehm ... it was all in the pockets of my coat and I must have mislaid it.'

'Well, you're lucky, sir.

'I suppose there isn't a note from the sender so that I can thank them for their honesty?'

'No sir. And I've asked Sponge-Rob. He says it was delivered by two schoolgirls. Teenagers. You know Rob, he wants to know everything. He wouldn't let those girls go before they answered his questions. I think they must have been pretty scared, anyway. Apparently there was a woman who asked if they needed some money and promised to give them £10 each if they delivered the parcel to the desk at the police station.'

'A woman?'

'A very vague description, sir, sadly. The girls were rather nervous. One says it was a dark blonde woman in her thirties, the other thought she was at least ten years older, with dark hair and a mole beside her nose. The other girl hadn't noticed the mole.'

'Thanks, Jennette. Do we have the details of those girls?'

'No. Sponge-Rob was called to the phone and his colleague didn't see the point in asking for details.'

'Thanks, Jennette. I'll come in straight away.'

I disconnect and hand Lauren her phone. She's heard my side of the conversation.

'Don't tell me. Your belongings have been returned.'

I nod, grinning. 'It seems I don't have to buy a new mobile after all. Or call the caretaker for a new lock.'

'I'm not so sure about this,' she says thoughtfully. Perhaps they copied your bank card. Or your keys. I think it would be wise to have a new lock on your door for starters.'

I nod, already having made up my mind to do exactly that.

'Thanks for your company today, Lauren,' I say, holding her hand. 'If Becca has been aware of anything, she'd be pleased with the attention, the presents and the party atmosphere.'

'Do you think she is aware of anything?'

'I don't know. Sometimes, I have the feeling she is awake. I talk to her, you know. Nothing important, just my daily routines. Sometimes, I think she is trying to tell me something, but I'm sure that is only in my imagination.'

'I found you on Facebook,' she says suddenly.

'Did you?'

She smiles briefly. 'I've sent you a friend request.'

'I haven't seen it yet.'

'You have two friends.'

'Two? I thought my only friend is Gerald Davey, which is debatable anyway.'

'The other is a woman called Wendy Wilson.'

I grin, pleased by the look on her face. 'I forgot about her, to be honest. Lauren, Wendy Wilson is …' I pause, not really wanting to explain about 'Alistair' and his impact on her life, as it will undoubtedly end up with her asking me if I have a similar character nagging me. 'She means nothing to me, Lauren, I will …'

'It's just something Dorothy said when you left the room for a while.'

'What did Dorothy Trewoon say about me, Lauren?'

Her face goes red and she looks down, fingers fumbling with the top button of her shirt.

'She said you are a dangerous man.'

'And you believe her?'

'No, but … she also said I should ask you where you were last night. And with whom.'

39

Siobhan Carter waits for me in a small room behind the entrance of Tregarrett school. She called me with panic in her voice, half in tears. I couldn't work out what the problem was, but I could sense her despair.

'I'll bring you some tea,' Gerald Davey says, casting a glance at Siobhan's face.

I nod and take a seat opposite her. 'How can I help you, Siobhan?'

'It's Leanne. She's ...' Her voice breaks in a sob.

'Is Leanne here, Siobhan? At school?'

'Yes. She was. I don't know.' She looks down at her hands and adds miserably, 'We've fallen out.'

'Why? What's wrong, Siobhan?'

'Leanne, she's ... she says she's going to find Barry.'

'Who is Barry?'

She hesitates. 'He is one of the guys ... we went to Plymouth with.'

'Her boyfriend?'

'Well, that's what she thinks.'

I sigh. I was right. They didn't spend the night with a girl called Stacey. They were with friends, most likely the two young men behind them in the queue waiting for BarZz to open. 'How did you meet him? At school?'

'No We met in town. In Newquay. He ... I believe that he used to go to our school because he seemed to know Mr Davey.'

'What about the other guy?'

A flicker of surprise in her eyes. 'Ronald.' Her mouth tightens. 'He is a bit older than Barry. Not as good looking. Barry really is a looker. I could understand why Leanne was so keen on him, but I didn't like his ... manners. She said I was being arrogant, just like my parents, but it wasn't that. I just didn't think it could be true that he really loved her. But Leanne laughed when I said we were only children compared to him. She said her father is eight years older than her mother, and it worked out well for them.'

'Depends on what age they met.'

She shrugs, uncertain if she understands. 'Leanne hasn't heard from Barry since that night. She wants to go back to that house and see him. I can't let her go back there. Not on her own.'

'Of course you can't,' I say reassuringly, trying to remain patient.

'But she doesn't want me to go with her. She is so angry, because I tried to stop her. I can't believe Barry will want to see her and she'll be so ... hurt, when he rejects her. I'm sure he will do that!'

'What can I do to help?'

'Maybe, if I can find that house again, and you come with me ... we can find out if Barry really loves her or not ... then I'll know she'll be alright.'

Hearing a fourteen-year-old talking so seriously about love can be sad or amusing but also dangerous. Teenagers have committed suicide for less. Unfortunately, suicide is no longer a rare incident these days. We hear of suicides so often that it's almost become a trend and we're so used to stories about it appearing on the internet that we barely flinch any more. For young people, the number has increased even more. One of the main reasons is bullying at school, and cyber bullying. I'm not sure whether Leanne would go that far, but discovering that the boy you think you love has made a fool of you, can make you feel that your life is no longer worth living.

'Do you know when Leanne will be going there?'

'She said something about missing school. Pretending she's unwell.'

'Today?'

'I don't know.

I hesitate. 'Whereabouts is that house, Siobhan?'

'I think ... it was somewhere on the Camel Trail. But it was dark and ... everything looked the same. Woods and fields.'

'Will Leanne be able to find it?'

'I hope not.' She has fallen silent. Frowning. Contemplating the options. Weighing up her chances. 'I can skip classes. I can say I'm having my period or something like that,' she says naively.

'Is your father's man still parked in front of the school?'

'I suppose so.'

'You think you'll find the house?' I ask casually, careful not to imply that she and her friend have been lying to me all along.

'I believe so, yes.' Her voice is low and full of guilt.

'Okay.'

Fifteen minutes later, she gives me a vague smile as she walks quickly through the back alley, undoing the lock in the gate with more experience than I care to know.

'Are you sure about this?' I ask, not yet starting the car.

'Yes. Of course.' She's almost as nervous as I am. 'I have to help Leanne. She's my friend.'

The statement tells me a lot about her friendship and loyalty and I envy her.

'Let's go then.' I start the engine and put my hand on the gearstick. 'Do you know where we're going?'

'Yes.' She's holding her mobile in her hand. It's switched on. I can see a map on the screen.

'It's a con, you know. I think that Barry's just been using her. Now that he's had ... what he wanted, he's not interested in her any more. But she won't believe me. We fell out when I told her.'

I pull out and we drive past the entrance to the school building. The car with her bodyguard in it is still in the same spot. She ducks down by way of precaution, but he doesn't notice us. His head is resting back, earplugs in his ears, staring out of the window without noticing anything that he should be alert to. Being a bodyguard isn't as exciting as it seems to be. The poor man must be bored to death sitting here while the girl he's supposed to be guarding is sneaking out like Matt Lucas in the wheelchair sketch in Little Britain.

She's spent hours on her computer, searching on Google Earth, retracing their steps from the house where Sally Pollinger used to live with her mother to the house they spent the night in. Staring alternately at the map on her mobile phone and out of the window, she guides me towards a lane in Wadebridge, alongside the river Camel, where our car journey ends. We park in a small car park between two other cars and she leans back with a deep sigh.

'Is it here?'

'No. I need to use street view to recognise anything, but the Google camera doesn't go any further.'

I try to hide my disappointment, but seeing her bottom lip tremble, I say encouragingly, 'Where shall we go next?'

'I'm not sure.' She looks uncertain, eyeing the area as though she is Little Thumb looking for the trail of breadcrumbs he left behind to find his way back. Amazingly, she recognises something. With a broadening smile, she points to an old wooden post that once bore a sign indicating the trail.

'This is it. I'm sure.'

She gets out and I follow her as she stops at the old sign post, sliding a fingertip down the weathered wood. 'I stuck my chewing gum here.' A faint smile lights up her face as she points to a faded pink piece of rubbery stuff clinging to the cracks on the post.

'We came from there.' She gestures in the opposite direction to Wadebridge.

'Okay, let's start here, shall we?' I spread out a map on the bonnet of my car, but she shakes her head.

'I think we'll have to walk. Otherwise, I won't be able to find it.'

'The Camel Trail is about 18 miles long from Padstow to the end at Wenford Bridge. It will take us several hours to walk it all. You'll be too late back to school and your father's man will raise the alarm.'

It works. She's too scared of her father and his repercussions.

'Okay then, what do you suggest?'

'We drive to the next place where we can access the trail. If you recognise it as a place you came past, we'll go further on, if not, we'll walk back to this point, hoping we find it on our way.'

'Okay.' She hesitates, her shoulders sagging. 'What else can we do?' she asks miserably.

We follow the river and turn right on a narrow single track that leads up the hill. Siobhan shakes her head. 'I can't remember a hill so steep.'

'We'll find the Camel Trail on the other side.'

'Do you know this area?'

'I have been here before.'

'Do you know where we're going?'

'There is a car park is across the bridge. We'll get out and find the trail. Perhaps you'll recognise something.'

She is silent, growing restless as we start to go down hill after a while. Dark and damp woods, where the sun barely shines, obscure the area. We pass a few buildings, but nothing familiar. 'The house was close to the trail,' she remembers. 'I don't think we had to climb a steep path. Or go down one.'

'The trail is almost flat as it's a disused railway line that once connected Padstow with Bodmin.

'There!'

She remembers the old bridge spanning the trail and the river. With a groan, she recalls slimy water dripping from between the old bricks. When she complained that she was thirsty, Leanne suggested opening her mouth and catching some.

Slowly, we drive over the bridge and park between puddles that are in too much shadow to dry out. Getting out, Siobhan shivers, although the valley is sheltered and the sun is warm.

'I think it is here,' she repeats.

There are a few buildings on the sunnier side of the valley. One has a yard littered with motor parts and old fences. Hens pick their way between shrubs and a dog sniffs along a half-paved path leading to a garage. The other building is a two-storey house with a tall chimney and walls painted a light colour between yellow and green. The curtains are drawn and the short driveway is empty. On a fence is a sign. 'Polbrook Cottage.'

Siobhan ducks behind me. 'This is it,' she whispers with a mixture of excitement and fear.

'Are you sure? Shall we have a look?'

She stops mid-step, hesitating.

'You can wait in the car if you like,' I suggest, but the thought of being alone, albeit in a car locked from the inside, is less appealing.

Grabbing my hand, she gives me one last anxious look, then nods. 'Okay.' There is no one around. We approach the house and find a key under a flowerpot containing pink geraniums.

'Is this it, Siobhan? Do you remember this door?'

Sliding the key into the lock, it's my turn to hesitate. The lock clicks. The door opens. We shouldn't be doing this. Entering a house without the permission of the owner is an illegal act. Even for a policeman working on a case. We ought to call the police and let them handle it but Siobhan is already ahead of me.

I am beginning to regret this. I should have backed off as soon as Siobhan confirmed it was the house they spent the night in. I didn't listen to my instincts. Sometimes, I wish I could turn off my impetuousness and think things through before I leap into action. This situation is a good example. The problem is that now I can't turn back. Even if I wanted to. Once again, my curiosity takes over from common sense.

'Hello?' Siobhan's voice echoes against the bare walls of a narrow hallway. There is no response.

There are no coats on the hooks, no shoes, boots or wellingtons on a metal grate underneath. A single pale blue umbrella sits in a ceramic vase. The house is cold and damp. The heating is off. Nothing to indicate that the electricity is on either.

I push open the first door and enter a kitchen. Bare shelves. The fridge door is ajar, with a neatly folded checked tea towel draped over to keep it open. The fridge light is off. Dark. Empty. Deserted. No electricity. The house must be unoccupied. Unless by coincidence there is a power cut.

Siobhan doesn't bother with the living area. Climbing the steep, narrow staircase, her footsteps are hollow and loud on the painted steps. Reluctantly, I follow her, gazing at a door to the living room which I would have liked to check before going upstairs.

All the doors are open. One is a newly refurbished bathroom with white tiles from floor to ceiling and blue sanitary ware. The other rooms have double beds made up; in one room, there is a cot in the corner with a wind-up mobile hanging motionless on a plastic ring above it. Small piles of blue bath towels and face cloths are on top of each bed.

'This was my room,' she says softly, stopping just before the threshold, pointing at a key in an old rusty lock. 'You can't take the key out. I locked the door from inside.' Her face is pale and her eyes are restless. Every so often she licks her lips as if the atmosphere makes them dry. She didn't want Barry's friend to come into her room.

'And Leanne was in the other room?'

'Yes. With Barry.' Her eyes fill with tears. 'I got away with it because I was angry. They didn't like that.'

'The other guy?'

She nods. 'Ronald. I locked myself in the room and they left me there. I guess they could have kicked the door, or something, but they didn't. Barry made Leanne promise that she wouldn't tell anyone.'

'So Leanne and Barry were in the other room?'

'Yes. I could hear them. First, she was laughing, but then I heard her crying. She asked him to stop. But when I asked her later, she said it was alright. She said he was ... kind to her. He understood that it was her first time.' She smiles sadly. 'I wanted to come out to help her, but I was scared of the other guy. I think he was meant ... for me.'

Entering the room Leanne shared with her so-called boyfriend, I check the bed, the wardrobe and chest of drawers, then the bathroom. Someone has done a perfect job of cleaning. Siobhan follows my movements with an expression that tells me she is regretting she'd brought me here. It brings back memories and she knows her nightmares about it will only get worse for having come back.

'You are a very brave girl, Siobhan.'

She looks doubtful. Whispers. 'I'm doing it for Leanne.'

'I know you are.' I lift the corner of a mat covering the wooden floor under the bed. Not even the tiniest speck of dust.

'Someone has cleaned up very thoroughly.'

'Don't you believe me?' She sounds tired and disappointed. Defeated.

'Of course I do. I was thinking of forensic evidence. If we can find traces of DNA from Leanne and you, then I'd also expect to find some of Barry and his accomplice. If they're in the police database, we'll be able to find them.'

'And then what?'

'I understand that Barry was in bed with Leanne. She is only fourteen. It's illegal to have sex with under-age teenagers.'

'She wanted to do it. She said she loved him.'

'Did he know her age?'

'I don't know. Maybe she lied to him.' She hangs her head, staring at her feet. Her voice is almost inaudible. 'Will he be punished?'

'Probably. But we'll have to find him first.'

40

Penrose drops a yellow post-it note on my desk. It flutters until it lands on top of my keyboard, sticking to the escape key. It's upside down. I can't read her scribble.

'What is this, Jennette?'

Her cheeks are flushed and there is anger in her eyes, but mixed with triumph.

'Sometimes people can be so clever that it's no surprise that we can never catch them,' she announces.

'Most people make a mistake. It only takes one to get caught.'

She shrugs, quickly dismissing my interruption. Getting back to her original train of thought, she grins. 'But sometimes they can be so utterly stupid that it's unbelievable.'

I pick up the yellow note. It has several initials written on it. SB. BS. FB. MR? 'What is this, Jennette?'

She pulls a seat from beside someone's desk and lowers herself onto it, planting her elbows on my desk and lowering her voice as though she might be overheard. There is nobody else near us other than two colleagues staring at computer screens deep in concentration.

She nods, more patiently now that she has my full attention.

'I googled the address of Polbrook Cottage. The cottage was bought three years ago by a businessman from London. He had it refurbished and tried to sell it. Now, an estate agency that also specialises on holiday rental handles his behalf.' Her breath is quick and shallow. Her face grows an unhealthy red and her eyes are shining. We are nearing the climax of her story.

'I was going call the agency and ask them which cleaning company they use for the house in Polbrook. But I didn't need to ask them anything. I found this website. I'd like you to look at it.' Her head jerks towards the yellow note. The initials haven't become any clearer.

'KeyhomesinCornwall?'

'Yes. One word. Dot com.'

Staring at the screen with eyebrows almost touching in concentration, she pushes the keyboard in my direction. I type the url of the website and a homepage gradually opens. On top of the page is a row of tiny thumbnail images of keys and properties of varying kinds and the name, Key Homes in Cornwall.

Underneath is a box where potential customers can fill in the details of what they are looking for so that the site can find all the properties they may be interested in. The kind of property. Location. Price range. Next to this box is a snapshot of a man probably in his fifties, David Green, grey hair and black eyebrows, looking at ease into the camera – definitely not a distorted face like on a selfie - smiling broadly as though he is completely trustworthy. Under his picture is some text saying why he is the best man to approach if someone is interested in buying a new home.

Homes for sale. Penrose sees the words forming on my lips. Tells me, 'Further down.'

The site is having technical problems and like a rollercoaster slowing down, it is now moving so slowly it has almost come to a halt. As Penrose is usually the impatient one of us, I try to hide the feeling that she is wasting my time.

Another box comes up to fill in with another range of preferences. Bald and bearded Benjamin Hill is the person to contact for residential lettings. He is younger than David Green but his face has the same sort of broad smile. It makes me feel that estate agents are a bit smarmy.

'Go down further,' Penrose says.

We finally reach the right place, but I'm still not excited enough yet to scream and shout as though we are loving the ride, but are really scared inside. At least I would be.

The bottom part of this page is for holiday lettings.

Another box with more options. Number of beds. Near the coast or inland. With a swimming pool. Wheelchair access.

I read on. Holding my breath. It is staring me in the face. Literally. A picture of Barry.

His face is as handsome as Siobhan described, with his hair dyed and trimmed to perfection. The same broad smile as his older colleagues, but with a hint of charm and amusement.

Barry is the perfect man to contact if you would like to have your property listed as a holiday home. The agency will take care of everything, from contacts with customers and taking bookings to cleaners and insurance. All you need to do is wait to receive the money in your bank account.

'We will have to show this to the girls.'

'Yes.' Somehow Penrose seems to think that my reaction is not excited enough. It feels like the rollercoaster isn't going as fast as it should do. Instead, the brakes are controlling its descent.

'We need to have a word with him, Jennette. This is brilliant.'

She smiles, blushing, but shakes her head. 'There is more.'

I wait. 'His name is Steven Barry.' Her index finger taps on his smiling face. 'I've looked at Leanne's Facebook page. He is one of her friends. On Facebook.'

'Show me, Jennette.'

She taps three keys and a Facebook page unfolds. It has the same photo as on top of the property website. Only here his name is Barry Stevens.

'How did you know he uses an alias?'

'I didn't. I recognised his photo.'

'And Leanne is one of his 'friends'?'

'Yes. Her name is ...' She finds a small notebook amongst the papers on her desk. '... Leanne Jayne.'

I could have saved her the trouble of finding Leanne's page. 'Can we print a list of all of their 'friends'?'

She motions towards the printer. 'I've already done that, sir. In fact, I've done more.' She clicks the keyboard again and a simple spread sheet comes up. Two columns, disappearing below the screen. 'These are all the friends of Siobhan, Leanne and Barry,' she explains. 'I sorted them and came up with mutual friends.' She glances at my face. 'You know how Facebook works, Sir?'

'Yes Jennette. I have a Facebook page myself.'

Her surprise is written all over her face.

'Really, sir?'

She grins. I see in her eyes that she will have a look at my page as soon as the opportunity arises and I feel awkward realising that she will find out that I have only two 'friends'. Maybe I should make more of an effort. Find old school friends. Previous colleagues. Yet, what would be the point? I haven't missed any of my schoolmates, or contact with former colleagues. Why would it be necessary to keep in touch with them?

'Anyway, here is a smaller list of people they have in common. Barry Stevens, or Steven Barry has quite a few girlfriends.'

She is now rummaging through the mass of documents and newspapers that cover her desk and gives me a sheet of paper with twelve names. Sally Pollinger is amongst them. Janice Lobb, Leanne's sister. And another name I recognise.

41

Gerald Davey is standing close to a younger man, holding a pint of lager in one hand, laughing cheerfully. Relaxed. Not blinking. He could be leaning towards the young man because he can't hear himself speak over the loud music, but I notice his hand on the other man's arm, his thumb caressing the soft skin of his inner wrist.

'Inspector.' His eyes narrow and the smile dissolves into a more worried look. 'Is this a coincidence?'

I shrug, not telling him that I went to see him at home in the first place. His neighbour, who kindly directed me to the pub, Davey's local apparently, will let him know soon enough.

'You're not after Gerry, I hope?' the younger man asks with a mischievous wink. He already has visions of his mate being locked behind bars.

In his late twenties or early thirties, he has a tanned face with startling blue eyes and a mischievous grin in them. A tuft of dyed blonde hair seems to be kept in place with yellow gel. He is wearing casual, well-fitting jeans and a white shirt with rolled-up sleeves, unbuttoned to reveal a muscular chest with just the right amount of hair.

'Sorry inspector.' Gerald Davey remembers his manners. 'This is Alan. A friend of mine. Inspector Tregunna.' He hesitates, uncertainly. 'Detective Inspector Tregunna handled the case of the two missing schoolgirls.'

'Ah. Good of you to bring them back safely, inspector.'

'Thank you.' There is no point in correcting him.

'Can I buy you a drink, inspector?' Davey asks.

'A soda. Lemon, no ice.' I retrieve a twenty pound note from my trouser pocket. 'This round is mine.'

He accepts without objecting. 'Just soda? Nothing stronger?'

'No.'

Putting his glass on a nearby table, he elbows his way through the crowd, leaving me with his friend Alan.

'Is Gerry a suspect?' he asks lightly.

'Why do you ask?'

My response takes him aback. 'I suppose it's the way normal people like us see the police. It's either that they are there to help us, or they are after us for something to do with a crime.'

'And you think Gerry is in which category?'

'I hope the first.' The glint has disappeared from his eyes and is replaced with concern. 'Are you here in particular to see Gerry?'

I nod, accepting a glass with a slice of lemon and a black plastic straw as Gerry returns with our drinks, holding all three glasses confidently.

'I understand the inspector has come to see you.' Alan says, his glare directed at me accusingly.

'Really?' Davey replies, not addressing anyone in particular.

I take a sip of my drink, pushing the straw aside with my nose. 'I have some questions.'

'You mean now, here?'

'I tried you at home.'

His eyes narrow, his face tightens. He blinks five time. It occurs to me that this habit must drive him mad sometimes. A possible reason for being made fun of by a room full of cruel and inconsiderate pupils. 'How did you know where to find me?'

'Your neighbour.'

'A woman? A fat woman in a tracksuit?' His look shows disgust and contempt.

'That must be her.'

'She's the proverbial nail in my coffin, inspector.' He offers a lopsided grin. 'Always sees and hears everything. Always commenting on everything I do.' He jerks his head towards where his friend is now talking to an older couple. 'Alan says we would never have bought the house if we'd known about Mrs Pig.' A rueful smile. 'Polly Piggott.'

'We can't always choose our neighbours.'

'Like we can't choose our family.' A world of experience behind his words.

'Very true.' I pull the straw out and dump it in an empty glass on the table beside us.

'How can I help you, inspector? I take it, we can talk here? You're not taking me to the station?'

'I'd like to know about Barry.'

'Barry.' The name floats from his lips to his brain. He blinks. Thoughtful. 'Barry who? I know three Barry's.'

'A young man. Eighteen or so. Good-looking.'

'That rules out my fifteen stone uncle of fifty-three.'

'And the other two?'

'I guess the same applies to the caretaker at the school. He must be in his mid thirties. Can't say he's good-looking either.'

'Which leaves us with the third one. You seem to know who I'm talking about.'

'Maybe.' He looks in his beer and doesn't find what he's looking for. 'What do you want to know about Barry?'

'His full name, for a start.'

'Steven Barry.'

'Address?'

He lifts his shoulder in a half-shrug. 'Somewhere in Newquay, I think.'

'How do you know him?'

'Know him isn't really the right word, inspector. He used to be one of my pupils. Left Tregarrett School three, four years ago. He must be twenty years old now, I presume.'

'Do you happen to know where I can find him?'

'He used to work in a shop. Clothes, of some sort. Men's fashion, sports stuff, that sort of thing.'

'Did you introduce him to Leanne and Siobhan?'

'Me?' He stops and tilts his eyes towards the ceiling as though he's having to dig deep in his memory.

'What exactly do you mean, inspector? Are you accusing me of something?'

His matter-of-fact tone suddenly angers me. I punch my index finger in his chest. 'I believe you are involved in this, yes.'

'In what?' His expression changes to disgust.

'You know a lot of young girls. From school. It's easy for you to pick out the right ones. All you need to do is introduce them to some good-looking charming guy. The girl falls in love with him and she will do anything for him. Anything. Once she's introduced to having sex, got some experience, she's ready for any other man who is willing to pay for her. All very discrete. The girl is scared to death and will obey her charming lover boy for as long as he chooses. Once he's dumped her, she'll be too humiliated and scared to tell anyone.'

'This is ridiculous.' His face is chiselled like stone. His eyes are staring at me with contempt.

'Or is it money? Do you receive a share?'

'This is getting even worse.'

The atmosphere between us is stone cold. He has created a distance between us. Emotional distance. It feels like we are on different planets, drifting away from the sun into a cold, dark space. I am the one talking, but he is moving further away from the subject. Erecting a shield. Hiding behind a brick wall. With a sense of regret, I realise that, at some point, I had thought Gerald Davey might be close enough to become a friend. Or at least an acquaintance. Someone you might meet up with a couple of times a year. Not close, but ... there. I had liked him. It stopped when I saw his name on Penrose's list of mutual friends.

'You have a very bad taste in jokes, inspector,' he says coldly, as though he has been watching me on stage at Live at the Apollo, feeling sorry for me because nobody in the audience has laughed.

'Tell me if I'm wrong.'

'I don't think I have to tell you anything.'

I feel a wave of despair growing in my throat. I am right about him. I know I am. He knew Barry. Leanne. Siobhan. His knowledge and experience of the girls would have made it clear to him that Leanne would be a perfect match for Barry. An ideal situation. All he had to do was make a casual introduction. The good-looking, charming lover boy did the rest.

'Tell me if I'm wrong, Mr Davey,' I repeat.

'No.' He shakes his head vehemently. 'No. I don't have to tell you anything, inspector. In fact ...' he pauses, fumbling in his trouser pocket and retrieving a crushed twenty pound note. All of his attention is drawn towards the note as he straightens it slowly. 'In fact, I would like you to take this back, inspector.'

He is already turning away from me, launching a missile that is programmed not to miss me. 'I'd rather not be in your debt.'

42

The interview room is deserted. I stare at the white board where someone has drawn a spider's web with the picture of Hugo Holmes in the middle, surrounded by names of which I recognise several. Glenda, Hugo's mother. Oscar Holmes, his brother who has boarded a plane to bury the mother and the remains of his younger brother. Jonathan Casey. James Archer. Millicent Robson. Jenna Morris. Harold Price. Kylie Stark. Matt Prowse. Known relatives and other acquaintances.

I came to the station to check some names and places that have popped up in my mind during yet another almost sleepless night. I am in desperate need of something to do, something to focus on, concentrate, get obsessed by if necessary. I am tired, but I can't relax. Images are flashing in my head incoherently. Some make sense, others don't. Faces. Names. Snippets of information. Even a single word. But nothing makes sense. I was kidnapped. By whom? Why? Someone stole my valuables and handed them back the next morning. Who? Why? Carter's men have been watching me. Why? I'm a police officer, why was he interested in me? Carter denied that his daughter was missing. Yet he thinks it necessary to have some of his men watching me. Why? I'm doing my job. Most of the time, I follow orders from Guthrie. Whenever I can, I work alongside Maloney. Is Maloney being followed? Has he been kidnapped? Or any of my other colleagues?

I was too late for the morning briefing, but Penrose left a message for me asking if I could get some information about James Archer and Jonathan Casey. I write the names on a piece of paper and sit behind my desk. It is cluttered with piles of paper, which is rather surprising now that everything is stored digitally somewhere on countless computers full of useless information.

Jonathan Casey has a clean sheet. No convictions. No

drugs or alcohol-related issues in his teenage years. Adopted son of an elderly couple, mother died 6 years ago. Jonathan inherited the family home in St Austell, which he was forced to sell when his father was taken into a care home suffering from Parkinson's disease. He did a traineeship with a plumber, but never finished his education. Had some odd jobs in the tourist season which must have left him enough money to survive the winter with only a small job as a delivery driver. No known relation to Hugo Holmes, other than that he met Bee Robson after Hugo left her.

James Archer is more interesting. He married Millicent 'Bee' Robson and was the father of her two children, Charlotte and Deacon. He died in a road accident.

Jimmy Archer ran out of the roadside bushes and, without looking, crossed the A30 near Bodmin. The driver of a heavily loaded supermarket lorry saw him coming but couldn't avoid him. The crash caused the road to be closed in both directions for the rest of the day as Jimmy's remains were removed from the scene and the police sealed the road off. On the other side of the road, the driver of a small white Ford Ka saw it happening and braked suddenly, skidded on the road and hit a red car he was overtaking. Jimmy Archer died. The driver of the red car died: a woman in her late seventies on her way to look after her grandchildren while her daughter and husband were going on holiday. The driver of the white car was taken to hospital with major back injuries but recovered surprisingly quickly. His passenger, his 16-year-old son, came out of it with only a scratch on his hand. The supermarket lorry driver never got back behind the wheel and ended up filling shelves in the early hours of the day, when he wouldn't have to talk to his colleagues. His wife left him three years later.

For a minute, I sit and stare at all this information, grieving for the lives of innocent people who just happened to be in the wrong place at the wrong time. If the lorry driver hadn't stopped for a pee at a service station, if the driver of the white car hadn't looked sideways for a second and saw Jimmy

Archer being crushed by the lorry … If. Too many if's.

Whether Jimmy Archer ran in front of the lorry because he wanted to die or because he was being chased by someone and thought he could escape, has never been proven.

'Tregunna?'

Maloney peers over my shoulder. 'What are you doing?'

'Reading the post mortem report of Jimmy Archer.'

'And who is Jimmy Archer?'

I click the button to print and close the attachment.

'He was the first husband of Millicent or Bee Robson. The father of her children.'

'So?'

'I was following one line of enquiry, sir. The possible connection with Hugo Holmes. Archer could have been a jealous ex-husband.'

'But he is dead.'

'Killed in a road accident. No proof if it was suicide or not. The driver of the lorry seemed certain that Archer jumped out into the road deliberately. There was no suicide note. The investigation was inconclusive.'

'Dead end.' Maloney pulls his face in frustration. 'We could do with some really useful information, Tregunna. Especially now that the police from Helston are involved.'

'We're all doing our best, but it is difficult with no motif and no more accurate time of his death.'

He nods. 'I just had an update from Champion. She's been looking into freezers. Do you have any ideas how many freezers have been sold that are big enough to hold at least a torso? Between the time that Mrs Robson last spoke to Hugo and when the first of his body parts was found? I don't have the exact number but it is far too many to continue with that line of inquiry. Anyway, it could well have been a second-hand freezer, a bargain on eBay from outside the region.' He shakes his head. 'I'm not so sure if we will ever solve this one, Tregunna.'

'But the death of his mother must tell us something. Their

305

murders can't be a coincidence.'

He snorts. 'According to DI Corbett, there have been quite a few break-ins lately. She believes that Mrs Morris must have heard someone, went down to check and caught the burglar in the act. He threatened her and she ran off through her back garden which leads into the park. He was scared that she would be able to identify him and pulled the plastic bag over her head.' He pauses. 'Corbett's theory based on the port mortem report and forensics.'

'Have they caught anyone?'

His mouth twists in a bitter expression 'Not yet and to be frank, I don't think they will if the burglar lies low for a while.'

'I don't know. I may have something here.'

'What?'

I point to the screen. 'This is the PM report on Jimmy Archer.'

He stretches his shoulders and chin, moving his head from side to side. Something in his neck cracks. 'Don't waste your energy going over that report about Archer, Tregunna, When did he die?' His neck cracks once more. He winces, closing his eyes.

'More than six years ago.'

'Then he can't have murdered Hugo, can he? Or his mother.'

His mobile bleeps with a message and he takes it out of his pocket with a touch of relief. He slides through the menu options, looking through his text messages hoping to find one announcing a break through, then puts it in his pocket dismissively.

'Well, you carry on, Tregunna. I can't stop you from doing things your way.' He smirks, then slams the door shut behind him.

The PM report says that Jimmy Archer had multiple old bruises. Mostly on his lower back and shoulders. Around his wrists that suggested he'd been handcuffed. But he has never been in contact with police other than one fine for parking and one for driving 6 miles over the speed limit. He broke more bones in his life than a team of rugby players. His left arm twice, once below and once above his elbow. His clavicle on the right-hand side. Toes. A wrist.

I stare at the screen, knowing instinctively that the answer lies here. I read and reread the lines and suddenly it dawns on me. The absolute certainty of what had happened to Hugo – and Jimmy Archer is staring me in the face.

I print the report and make a few phone calls. I rise to retrieve the print from the printer. I check my watch. With a bit of luck Jonathan Casey will be at home. Or will be soon, after he's taken the children to school.

I call his mobile but get a message that I dialled an unregistered number. I call the landline but get connected to an answerphone. A voice from the phone company asks me if I want to leave a message after the tone.

'Mr Casey, this is Detective Inspector Tregunna. Can you please call me on this number as soon as you get this message? If not, I'm coming to your house. And we'll speak later.'

Ten seconds later my phone rings. No caller ID. As ever, the first thing that springs to mind is it's the hospital. Bad news about my blood test, my scan, anything? Jonathan Casey, returning my call?

Mirabelle.

It takes me twenty seconds to realise who she is. Mirabelle. The nurse. When we drove back from Becca's birthday party, Curtis was able to tell us that she had two pieces of cake.

Becca.

She is breathless, as if she's been running round all the hospital buildings trying to find a phone. 'Sorry to interrupt you, sir, but Dr Elliott has asked me to call you straight away. It's Becca, sir. Ehm … there has been a change in her condition. Dr Elliott would like you to come as soon as you can, sir.'

43

She is surrounded by people in blue and white uniforms. Someone, a young doctor I don't recognise, turns his head and frowns, opening his mouth to stop me entering the room. He turns on his heels as I come forward. 'I'm sorry, sir, but you can't come in.'

Moving towards me, he leaves a gap between his colleagues, wide enough for me to see the white face on the white pillow, the tuft of hair, growing, falling over the scar where she was operated on, where the bullet went in.

Dr Elliott notices me, gesturing me in. I can't move. After all these weeks, she has half opened one of her eyes. Or at least the one I can see.

I can't be certain, but I imagine that some of the lines on the monitor are forming different patterns.

'Hi Andy.' Dr Elliott offers his warm open smile. 'She's a little fighter.'

It's not the first time he says that. And from my experience of him, he never says anything he doesn't mean.

In the beginning, she wasn't breathing on her own but connected to a life-support machine. After a while, they believed they could wake her up by reducing the medication that kept her in an induced coma. They stopped the medication but nothing changed. She didn't wake up. A few weeks later, they suggested disconnecting her from the life-support machine and letting her die peacefully. It was all set up, authorities informed, documents signed. They stopped the machine and Becca started breathing herself.

When they took Becca off the machine, Dr Elliott was almost a hundred per cent certain that she would die. I told him she wouldn't. I told him that she was a little fighter. I proved him wrong and he admitted it. Not that I needed a humble or unnecessary apology. At that moment in time, I was just glad and hopeful that Becca would recover and live happily after.

That was nine weeks ago, six weeks after the emergency operation when she was taken to hospital.

'Come in, Andy.' Dr Elliott turns his head and the nurse next to him steps aside. Mirabelle. She smiles encouragingly, but I can sense that the initial excitement has reduced a bit. I listen to Elliott addressing a handful of young doctors and Becca's regular nurses. She has opened her right eye, but although the monitors show some activity in her brain, there appears to be no sign that she can see out of her eye or that the optic nerve is sending the right messages through to her brain.

'It is rather disappointing,' Elliott says later, when the crowd has disappeared and we both stand at the end on the bed. The balloons are still attached to the back of a chair. One of the birthday cards has escaped from its pin and is stuck between the headrest and her pillow.

'But we can't give up hope,' he adds. 'It can be a sign that something is happening in her head.' I'm not sure which of us needs encouragement most.

His pager bleeps and he excuses himself. I reply with a short nod, telling him silently that I understand. He retreats swiftly and I sit on the chair beside the bed, the balloons swaying behind and above me.

44

I stay with Becca for an hour. She hasn't moved since I came in. No significant brain activity is visible on the monitors. Dr Elliott comes in several times, his hopes fading each time he disappears in the corridor, where hospital life is business as usual.

My phone vibrates. No caller ID. I almost ignore the call but then remember I left a message for Jonathan Casey.

'Hello?'

His voice is so low, I barely recognise it, but he sounds familiar.

'Jonathan? Jonathan Casey?'

'You called but … and we … I got your message.'

I stare at Becca's hand. Has there been a slight tremor in her index finger?

'I am in the hospital at the moment, Mr Casey. But I need to speak to you.'

'No. no. not now. I'm not … I can't get away from the children.' I hear something in his vicinity but it is too subdued to make out what it is.

'Are you at home, Mr Casey?'

'Yes. Yes of course I am. The children … we have a bit of a situation here, inspector. Charlotte is sick. And Deacon isn't feeling very well. I just collected them from school.'

His voice is a combination of anxiety and pragmatism.

'Something they've eaten? What about yourself?'

'No. I'm all right. Nothing wrong with me.' He pauses. 'What makes you think …?'

'The children may be ill because of something they ate. I wondered if you had eaten the same as them.'

'No. No. It must have been the milk. For their cornflakes, maybe, I don't use milk.'

I remember him with his expensive machine. He had milk in his coffee.

'When can we meet, Mr Casey?'

'Err ... tonight?'

'Of course. If that is more convenient for you. What time?'

'Half eight? The children will be in bed by then and Bee won't be here. She's working late tonight.'

'Okay. Your home?'

'Well, yes, if you don't mind? I can't leave the children alone. Can I? Bee will kill me is she found out.'

'Of course.'

'Err ... what is it about, inspector?'

'It is about Hugo Holmes.'

'I told you, I have never heard of him.'

'And I don't believe you, Mr Casey. Hugo was married to Bee for almost three years. They divorced before you met her, but all the same. I can't believe his name has never been mentioned in your presence.'

He is silent for so long that I start thinking he has cut me off. Then his voice is a whisper, almost inaudible. 'Yes. You are right. And I can tell you something about Hugo Holmes.'

45

The house is enveloped in darkness. Birds and insects and neighbours are all asleep. A black cat moves sinisterly across the road, stopping for a moment when the sound of the engine dies. As the headlights fade in his eyes, he turns quickly and disappears in a gap in the hedge.

I sit and wait. Trying to remember the exact words he said before he hung up on me abruptly.

'And I can tell you something about Hugo Holmes.' Urgency in his lowered voice, a hint of breathlessness, as if he'd just come home and remembered he forgot to buy something important. He gave me no opportunity to ask him what he meant. Just those whispered words.

I stare along the deserted street. I'm tired. I can't think properly. I can't concentrate. I see wires tangled into one huge ball of different colours. Logically each colour represents a line with two ends. I can't find any of them. It's like a nightmare in which I need to untangle the wires before I fall into a deep black hole in which I can't see the bottom. I am scared I'll keep falling forever. I want to escape and stop my racing heartbeat.

I need to sleep. The last couple of days have been nerve-wracking. The case of the disappeared girls who hadn't exactly disappeared. The sight of the body parts. The idea that there is someone living here somewhere who has the ability to kill someone, cut the body up in pieces and chuck them anywhere like unwanted pieces of equipment. My own night in that cold barn, cold, scared, desperate. Meeting Dorothy Trewoon again, looking into her shark-like killer-eyes. Becca, surrounded by balloons and cards because she's passed one more milestone in her miserable little life. My scan. The appointment for my results hanging over my head like Damocles' sword. Mr Grose and his pathetic little life indoors, keeping his kitchen door locked to hide his secret.

I am tired. I want to pull the duvet over my head, forget the world and sleep for a week. I want everything to be sorted and over when I wake up.

Rather than going to bed early, I made an appointment with Jonathan Casey. He knows something about Hugo Holmes, but surely, it could wait till tomorrow?

I got in my car and drove over. Finding he isn't here. His car is not on the drive. The house is dark and somehow it feels like it's empty.

I am tempted to start the engine again and drive back home. Another forty minutes and I'll be home. In bed. Asleep. But his voice is in my head. Nagging me. I can't leave without at least having looked for him in the house. He might have got fed up waiting for me and went to bed. I will wake him up and demand to know what it was he needed to tell me that couldn't wait until tomorrow. I can't let him sleep while not being able to sleep myself. It isn't fair.

I reach and undo my seatbelt. The click and the clunck of the metal part against the window are like gunshots in fog. The cat is back. It is moving along the hedge for a few meters, then it crosses the road. Away from me. Some people say that if a black cat walks towards you, it brings good fortune, whereas it takes good luck with it if it walks away from you. My mother always laughed about it, saying, 'Look away and you won't see it'.

I close my eyes when he is in the middle of the road and he's gone when I open them again. My talent for hiding my head in the sand must come from her.

I leave my car unlocked but put the keys in my pocket. In my other pocket is my hand, holding my mobile as though it is my only connection to life. Silly. My grip relaxes, but I don't take my hand out of my pocket.

The porch door is ajar. Against my better judgement, I push it open with the tip of my index finger. No sound. The children must be fast asleep. The coat hooks are empty, save for a pink plastic raincoat. The shoe racks are empty; coloured boots, black shoes, coats and jackets, hats and scarves have all gone. Not a tiny speck of grass or dust or dried mud off shoes. The front door has a key in its lock, like someone forgot something and ran in with haste, leaving the key in the door to lock the door quickly on leaving.

'Hello? My voice echoes against the walls. I hope I'm not waking the children. The house is dark. Cold. And empty. The kitchen is clean, the fridge is empty. Not even a milk bottle in it. TV light is off, the Wi-Fi box doesn't flash. The heater has been turned off. Mattresses in the bedrooms are bare. Wardrobes and drawers are empty. Not a damp towel in the laundry bin. No toothpaste or brushes or bottles of shower gel in the bathroom. The toilet seat is down, the lid closed.

They have left. Moved to who knows where. The first question is: why? The second question is more important: why so quickly? It isn't so long ago that I had stepped over children's boots and shoes and coats in the porch. Now they have gone without a trace.

I go back to the hallway. Anger and frustration about the wasted trip. Inwardly, I repeat his words: 'You are right. And I can tell you something about Hugo Holmes.' Rewind. Play again. 'I can tell you something about Hugo Holmes.' Whatever he meant at that moment, he changed his mind

I leave the house as I found it, the key in the front door. Pull it closed. Was the porch door open? Ajar? I can't remember.

There is a noise behind me. I turn and see a dark shape approaching me, eyes with a develish shine as they are caught in the light of my mobile. The cat. Black and eerie. Foreboding.

Something else stirs in my brain. A cat flap in the door. They have left the house as if nobody has ever lived here. They forgot the cat. Something tells me that they won't come back for it. No doubt the cat will survive on its own. Unlike dogs they are perfectly capable of finding and catching something to eat. Or perhaps someone will take pity on it and take it in.

The cat has stopped on the tarmacked front garden.

Looking at me as though it's waiting for me to go one way and it will go in the opposite direction. It sits down, licks the white toes of a front paw.

I retrieve my car keys and somehow I must press the button, as the warning lights of my car flash and I can hear the click of the automatic locking system. Startled the cat jumps up and vanishes. More bad luck. I hear the cat flap bang when it enters the shed.

I don't know what to expect in the shed of a house that has been abandoned by its residents. Nothing. The odd box of unwanted items. Left rubbish. I follow the cat, thinking it's cruel leaving it behind and expecting other people to take care of it. Perhaps Lauren would like to have it. Her boys. If not ... can I keep it in my flat? It would be nice to have someone to talk to. Someone who won't nag me, force me to do things I don't want to do. Remind me to eat and drink on time. Caring. Loving.

The cat flap bangs when I open the door. Immediately, I am almost overwhelmed by a bitter, sour smell. Not the smell of cat litter that hasn't been changed for weeks. Something else.

Vomit.

I find him behind a wheelbarrow with folded blankets and a bicycle with two flat tyres and no seat. His hair is damp and his left cheek is in a puddle of vomit. Eyes are staring at me and this time it isn't just the cat.

46

The next morning I watch the dark sky lighten to a pale glow as the sun rises over the horizon. Dark, navy-blue clouds are silhouetted against a warm glow that turns from yellow and orange to pink to pale blue, gradually gaining strength of colour.

Today is decision day. Several unrelated issues, but some definitely need a decision, though I have no idea yet how I will deal with them. The strange brooding dawn gives away to the reality of the day. I want to pull the duvet over my head and close my eyes. Sleep. Sleep until the day is over. I want to ignore everything, forget what I'm supposed to do today. I don't want to make any decisions. Yet, as someone told me long ago, even not choosing between A and B is itself a decision. The decision to postpone what I must do today will only cause me discomfort and anxiety.

I get up with an undeniable sense of foreboding. Brushing my teeth, I wander through my flat, switch the kettle on, check my phone for messages. I shower and attach a clean stoma bag to my stomach and check the drawer under the sink to see if I need to order new supplies. Not yet. Postponed.

I try to put into some order today's issues that are bothering me most. The scan. Hugo Holmes's case. Lauren. Carter. I owe Gerald Davey an apology. I have suspected him, accused him, wrongly; he had nothing to do with Leanne's and Siobhan's ordeal. I will have to go and see him and apologise, as he deserves. Bee Robson. Bernie Whittaker. Jonathan Casey. The scan is clearly on top of my list, but I decide on an alphabetical order and it comes, happily, last. Last but not least. I shake my head, angry with myself and turn off the kettle as it comes to the boil.

Not on my priority list, but I decide to have breakfast at The Tearoom in the Garden. Not because there is no food in the fridge, but because I am too nervous to be on my own. I know I can call Lauren or my parents but I'd rather not tell them that I have an appointment in Treliske to get the results of my latest scan. Perhaps people are right and I am a sad, pitiful loner. Perhaps dealing with the worst things in life will seem less awful if you share them with other people, loved ones, or even people you barely know. I can't. However much I would like to, I can't share or be open about my emotions.

If I'm told that the original tumour – I haven't named it yet – is still growing, or has spread elsewhere in my body, I don't want anyone else to know. Maybe later, but not today. I will have to deal with the horror of chemotherapy, radiotherapy, more surgery even before I will be able to talk about it. And in the worse case scenario, if I'm told that there is no treatment available to stop the process, I won't tell anyone before I've dealt with the implications of this myself, and the prospect of my shortened future.

The minutes tick by with the speed of a sleepy tortoise. The girl behind the counter who failed to have a cheerful conversation with me is now in the kitchen, chatting and laughing with her colleague, and preparing for the busy hours ahead. I am the only customer in the tearoom and I feel lonelier than I would have been at home.

My phone rings and I pick it up quickly, hoping for a miracle. That my feelings have been conveyed to Lauren by some sort of telepathy and she's enquiring how I am. Maybe, just maybe, I'll be able to tell her ... something, part of the truth. Enough for her to offer to come with me. Or another miracle, the hospital, cancelling the appointment because the scan is clean and I need not come back. The idea is as childish as it is stupid.

No caller ID.

The need to speak to someone, anyone, makes me answer, rather than curiosity.

'Hello?'

Behind me the door opens and the cold morning drifts

in along with an obese family. Four children between 5 and 10 and their parents. They move with the awkwardness of carrying too much flesh. Or maybe fat is the right word. I feel sorry for the children. Obesity is not in their genes but in the way they've been brought up, educated, taught what to eat. They sit and grab menus. I can already see 'full English breakfast' glimmering in their eyes.

'Are you at the police station?' I recognise the voice because of its arrogance

'No, I'm …'

'Home?'

As if on cue, a saucer crashes to the floor. For the superstitious, shards of broken crockery are a sign of a happier future.

'Not at home,' he concludes contented.

Something makes me stare out of the window. I see Carter walking on the path in a grey coat that looks expensive even from this distance. 'Were you coming to see me, Mr Carter?'

'You're in the tearoom.' It is a statement rather than a question.

'I am.'

He chuckles and as I gaze past the obese father's head, I can see Carter changing direction and putting his phone in his pocket to prevent me from objecting. He walks swiftly towards the small bridge in front of the building. An autumn leaf lands on his shoulder and he brushes it off with a hint of annoyance.

He comes in, a swirl of wind and leaves round his feet, shaking his head as though the leaves are stuck to it as well. Birdsong dies as he shuts the door. He orders a double espresso and sits opposite of me.

'You are a strange man, Mr Tregunna' He untangles his burgundy scarf, leaving it hanging loose in front of him.

'And you aren't?'

He chuckles. 'But I must say I quite like you.'

'I'm afraid I can't say the same, Mr Carter.'

He shrugs. My opinion doesn't matter to him.

'So why are you here?'

'I thought we'd better have a word.'

'About?'

'You are an intelligent man, Mr Tregunna. Don't treat me as if you think I'm stupid.'

'Siobhan.'

Even mentioning her name brings a smile to his face. He adores the girl. Perhaps that's why he is so unhealthily possessive.

'You went to her school. You spoke to her.'

'Hm.' He could cause a lot of problems for me if he brings this out in the open. Especially when he finds out about our trip to Polbrook.

'I am aware that you don't have children, Mr Tregunna, so I suppose you can't understand my feelings for her. I love that girl to bits.' His face darkens and his eyes glaze over. 'Especially after ... three years ago we lost her sister. She was sixteen. She was caught up in an accident. The driver hit her and left her on the verge. She was found the next day. The driver has never been found.' He straightens suddenly. 'I don't know why I am telling you this.'

'I listen.'

'Yes.' He narrows his eyes, scrutinising my face but in a positive manner. 'You do. You seem to be able to read people.'

'I read their body language.' I wish I could read myself as well as he suggests I can read other people.

'I would like to know what Siobhan told you.'

'That is private.'

'I thought you would say that.' He pauses. 'I could have had you charged for that. You questioned an underage girl without consent.'

I nod, suppressing my smile, but he is not that bad reading other people either. 'I thought you would say that.'

'Point taken, Mr Tregunna, but I would still like to know what she told you.'

'Maybe you ought to ask your daughter.'

'I did.' He smiles faintly, wary, uneasy. 'She's a brave little girl, I can tell you that. Gave me an ultimatum: she would tell me everything if I promised not to send her to another school. Mind you, my wife and I were seriously considering boarding school, but she pointed out to me that a boarding school doesn't necessarily mean the pupils can't sneak out. And I wouldn't even know because I suppose the school wouldn't tell us everything.' He shrugs, annoyed by his inability to control everything to do with his daughter. Or maybe to do with life in general. 'Anyway, her second condition was that we accept Leanne as her friend.'

'And you have?'

'Of course I have. Does that surprise you? I admire my daughter's courage to stand up to me.' He has some odd values.

'If she told you everything, why are you here?'

'I have a feeling that she was ... let's say, a bit creative with the truth.'

'Perhaps that's in her genes.'

'You may well be right there, Mr Tregunna. That's why I came to see you. I would like to compare our versions of her story. Find the discrepancies.'

'Or perhaps she didn't tell you anything.'

'I am not a liar.'

'You lied when I came to see you when she disappeared.'

'Mm. I can see your point. But let's not beat about the bush, Mr Tregunna. You called me about my daughter. You knew she wasn't at home. You knew she hadn't been home all night. Nobody knew that. I hadn't told a soul. So, how did you know?'

'Because Patrick and Elsie Lobb, Leanne's parents, were worried to death when they found out that their daughter was missing. Unlike you, they called the police.'

I pause. He has the decency to avoid my eyes for a single second.

'Leanne and Siobhan are best friends. They are always together, except when she's at home, for obvious reasons. Best friends, especially girls of that age, tell each other everything. I couldn't believe that Leanne would go to that gig to see that pop idol all by herself. I was certain that Siobhan would have gone with her.'

'You seem to know my daughter better than I do.'

'Children don't tell their parents everything, Mr Carter. In fact, parents are often the last to know their children's little secrets.'

'Hm. My wife says the same thing.'

'So that leaves us with the question of why you lied to me, Mr Carter.'

He leans back. 'That is not the reason why I came to see you.'

'I guess not, but I want to know everything as much as you do.' I look at him, searching his face for a clue. Any clue to help get to the truth.

'To be frank, I feel quite embarrassed by this. I thought you kidnapped her. When you phoned me, I had your number and I traced your address. I found out that you were a police officer, but you weren't officially working.'

'Is that why you kidnapped me?'

'Kidnapped you? Why would I do that?' His surprise seems genuine.

'To teach me a lesson?

'Honestly, Mr Tregunna, I don't know what you are talking about.'

'Why did you think I kidnapped your daughter?'

'Because I had … a dispute with someone a couple of weeks ago. A very nasty man. He claims that I have robbed him but … anyway. He warned me that the whole affair hadn't been settled to his satisfaction and he said there were other ways to get his money back.'

'And you thought he took your daughter.'

'When she was missing? Yes. I didn't want to call the police because I didn't want to make things worse.'

'What's the man's name?'

'I don't ...'

'Off the record.'

'Hunter.'

Not a name that had popped up during the investigation. 'Well, I can't disclose the whole matter to you at this moment, but I don't think it is your Mr Hunter. In fact, and now I am being very honest with you, and maybe also very stupid to tell you this, but when I spoke to Siobhan at her school the other day, we didn't stay in the school. I don't think your bodyguard noticed that we went out through the back exit and we drove somewhere.'

'What! Why ...'

'If you want to keep your family safe, perhaps you need to consider your security arrangements. But that is by-the-by. I am just telling you, off the record, that with the help of Siobhan, I will soon be questioning two young men who were involved in ... the trip to that gig in Plymouth.'

His face is ashen. I gesture the girl from the café and order another double espresso for him and a large glass of mineral water. 'I lied to you,' he says softly. 'She didn't tell me anything.'

'Siobhan will keep her secrets. Especially as you ignored her friendship with Leanne Lobb.'

'I am sorry about that too.'

'I'm glad about that, Mr Carter. Those girls have had quite an adventure and they need each other. Leanne is still devastated about what happened to her. Oh, it wasn't as bad as we all feared, but still it has had an impact on a young girl's life.'

'Do you know ...?' He can't speak the words.

'Leanne was deeply in love with someone. She lied to him when she told him she was seventeen, almost eighteen. Although he must have known that she was younger, he didn't care. I don't think he loved her. Let's just say he was flattered by her adoration and he took advantage of that. Not of her, though. Everything happened with Leanne's full consent. And your daughter, well, she was brave enough to lock herself in one of the other rooms. Apparently, the other guy didn't like her enough to persuade her to let him in.'

If his face hadn't already gone pale, he would have gone even paler.

'And that is the truth, Mr Carter.'

He is silent for a long time, sipping his strong coffee and staring into his empty cup afterwards as if the dregs could tell him something. Or, perhaps, he sees himself reflected in it, and is disgusted with himself because he had it all so wrong.

'Mr Lobb is an extraordinarily generous man, Mr Carter. Leanne has confessed everything to her parents. Obviously they were furious. They pressed her to tell them the name of the young man involved, but when they realised that she was just as guilty by lying about her age, they decided to drop the charges against him. They hope he will have learned from all of this. And Leanne and Siobhan too.'

'How much of this is your doing, Mr Tregunna?'

'Err ...'

'I thought so.' He smiles vaguely. 'I owe you an apology, Mr Tregunna. I was ... wrong.'

The obese family are leaving, replaced by two ladies in their late sixties, chitchatting like sixteen-year-olds and arguing furiously about whether or not to indulge themselves with a piece of Victoria sponge with their tea.

'Siobhan is a lovely girl, Mr Carter. Please don't make the mistake of keeping her away from her friends.'

'You are a wise man.'

'Not as wise as I should be, Mr Carter. I have ...'

He interrupts, holding up his hand. 'Please call me Victor.'

'Okay. I'm Andy.' We shake hands across the table.

'I'm still not much the wiser,' I say slowly, 'If you didn't kidnap me, then who did?'

47

There is something familiar about the tall and rather skinny man seated on the far side of the bed. He rises quickly when I enter the room, taking two steps towards me and then realises that his escape route is blocked.

'Inspector,' Jonathan Casey hisses, eyes almost panicking as I stop to view the situation. 'My friend is just leaving.'

He is in the bed, upright, his arm still in a sling, dried blood on his forehead, purple bruises on his arms sticking out of a hospital gown. Perhaps I should have bought him pyjamas instead of a bag of fruit and magazines.

'I don't want to interfere.'

'No, honestly, he was just leaving.'

There is something in his eyes as they shoot towards his visitor.

'And who is this, Mr Casey? Won't you introduce us?'

His shoulders sag as the tall man accepts defeat. He slums back in the chair between Jonathan's bed and the window.

'This is Bernie, my mate. Detective Inspector Tregunna.'

The name sticks in my head. Bernie. 'As in the former partner of Ms Robson? Whittaker?'

'Yes.' Jonathan smoothes out his blanket and makes sure it is straight. Bernie straightens his back and has his hands on the armrest of his chair. Ready for take off.

I lean against the foot of the bed, blocking his escape route. In films, he might have jumped over Jonathan, but this is the real world. He knows that I will catch him eventually.

'How are you feeling, Mr Casey?'

'How do you think?' He sounds bitter. Piteously. 'I've just lost everything.'

'I am sorry you feel that way.'

He shrugs, stares out of the window, following the silver dot of an airplane high in the sky.

'It's good to see you, Mr Whittaker,' I say casually, turning to his visitor. 'You were not aware that we were trying to find you?'

He doesn't ask why. 'No.' He shakes his head uncertainly, not knowing what to think about me or the precarious situation he finds himself in.

'I believe you can enlighten me about what happened to Hugo Holmes.'

Shock and disbelief cloud his eyes. 'I don't …'

'No, please, don't treat me as if you think I'm stupid, Bernie. I know what happened. I only need you, and Jonathan, to fill in some …. minor blanks.'

The word minor does the trick. It sticks in his brain. He relaxes.

'And by the way, the French police have been very helpful. They found Mrs Robson's car just off the ferry in Calais. She should have taken the train, then maybe it will be more difficult for us to find her.'

'She was always scared of tunnels,' says Jonathan, almost sympathizing with her. 'Where is she now?'

I shrug, as if it doesn't matter to me. 'Somewhere in France, I suppose.'

Surprise. Then fear, as it dawns on him that it might not all be over. 'They haven't found her?'

'Not yet.'

A short silence. Bernie Whittaker opens his mouth like a fish gasping for air, his hands clasped over the arm rests of his chair. His knuckles are white. Jonathan speaks, clearing his throat first.

'What about the children?'

I swallow. I can't make this easier for him. 'They were found in the car.'

I'm not so sure if I believe the French police, who assume that Bee must have got out for an errand, leaving Charlotte and Deacon asleep. I am more inclined to believe that she made a run when she found her car surrounded by police and

325

realised she had more chance to escape without them.

'In the car? Are they alright?'

'Yes. They are travelling back to as we speak, Mr Casey. They're being taken care of.'

'Can I see them?'

'They'll be taken to a foster home. A temporary solution.'

He starts to sob. 'I will never see them again, will I? I'm not their family.'

I doubt he's in a mental state to look after himself, let alone two young children whose mother is a suspect in the murder inquiry of Hugo Holmes and his mother. Who attempted to kill Jonathan as well.

'I'm sure they will be alright, Mr Casey. Social Services have only one priority and that is the children's safety.'

'But they will be safe with me! I have always made sure that … she'd never hurt them. Not them.'

I try to catch his gaze, but he looks down. 'Did she hurt you instead?'

'No, she only hurt me when I deserved it.' He is obviously determined to stick by her side.

'You accepted punishment when she said you did something wrong?'

'It wasn't her fault, inspector. It was mine.'

His friend stirs next to him, looking down. Understanding. Keeping his mouth shut.

'You can't honestly believe that, Jonathan,' I say.

'It's the truth!'

'She abused you. She beat you. Not once, not accidentally. She hurt you because she wanted to hurt you. We found records of you attending A&E. Your broken arm, for starters. Previously you were there with broken ribs.'

Stubbornly he shakes his head. 'I'm clumsy.'

'Jonathan,' I say, trying not to appear patronising. 'You are not clumsy. It is maybe what she wanted you to believe, but you are a normal human being.'

'No I'm not. Sometimes, she shouted at me that I'm a

waste of space and she's right. It was me. I made a mess of it.' His voice trails off in a half-sob.

'I know what you've been through, Jonathan. I promise you everything will be alright.' His friend taps his arm clumsily.

More frantic shaking of Jonathan's head. 'If I've said something about her then I'll take it back. I'm not having her charged and accused of something that is my fault.'

I turn to Bernie for support. We exchange looks. I can see compassion on his face. Whereas I find it difficult to comprehend that Jonathan is still defending Bee, Bernie understands.

'Jonathan.' Bernie Whittaker clears his throat. Tears glisten in his eyes and his bottom lip trembles like that of a young boy who isn't allowed to play with his older brother's toys. 'Jonathan, please, I know exactly how you feel. I have been there, you know that. But once this is all over ... you will see that it's all for the best.'

'I can't ... I'm sorry.' Closing his eyes, he rests his head on the pillow and sobs. There is a jug half-filled with water and melting ice cubes on his bedside table, along with an empty glass with a yellow straw in it. I pour him another glass of water and hand it to him. He accepts it as if he isn't sure what it is.

Bernie speaks to him in a soft voice. Comfort. Understanding. Support. Shared hurt and pain. Humiliation.

I've never been able to understand why someone can be abused and still love the abuser. Or at least stay with them. I remember the couple in the supermarket car park, the woman sheltering in the car from the rain, while her husband got soaked, with resigned acceptance. The couple in the at Trerice, where the husband publicly humiliated his wife which she just accepted, probably finding excuses for him, and telling herself that it was all her own fault. Jonathan still loves Bee. Adores her. Worships her. Up to a point, I can understand that he stayed with her for the sake of the children, but he could have ended the relationship in the very beginning, when he was first subjected to her violent beatings. He should have realised that it was a pattern, not a one-off, and more importantly that he would never be able to break the pattern. People like Bee Holmes are often victims of abuse themselves. A vicious circle rather than the end of the line.

Bernie turns to me, his eyes clear. Relieved that it is over. 'Has she been arrested?'

'Not yet. But soon. She will be charged with murder, attempted murder and physical and mental abuse.'

'Will she go to prison?' Jonathan asks slowly, incredulously.

'You won't have to see her again unless you choose to yourself.'

Looks are exchanged. 'Do we have to go to court?'

'I think we can arrange a video hearing for you. You are traumatized victims.'

Jonathan starts to sob again, but this time it is more to release of the tension and fear. Bernie grabs his hand. United in fate, fear and finally in freedom.

I feel almost sorry to interfere but I need to know the truth. 'What can you tell me about Hugo's death, Bernie? I will need you to come to the police station for a formal statement, but I would like to ask you some questions now.'

He hesitates. 'It is a long story.'

'We have plenty of time,' I say casually. I'd rather not look at my watch. I left Lauren with a cup of tea and a magazine in the café at the entrance where I will collect her after I have spoken to Jonathan and Bernie.

'I've just seen your doctor, Jonathan. He said you'll be here for a couple of nights. And I have … time to spare.'

Bernie's story is much the same as I had figured out myself already. He met Millicent after the death of Jimmy Archer. In the beginning, he felt sorry for her and her young children but gradually he became involved in her life. She asked him to move in with them and he did. By then he was over the moon. He loved her. Adored her. Worshipped her. He lived in a dream. He couldn't believe his luck that a woman so beautiful and attractive and successful in her job had fallen for him. The abuse started slowly and so gradually he hardly noticed. First, he thought she wanted rough sex and he was willing to go along with it. But bit by bit, he learned more about her relationship with Jimmy. She could hide her past from him, but the oldest child couldn't be silenced. Charlotte loved her daddy and missed him every day. Bernie started asking questions and it didn't take long for him to understand what Millicent's real character was like. Unpredictable. Abusive. Violent. She could smile one moment and burst into a rage the next. He never knew what triggered her rage and he started to avoid her. He thought of leaving her, but he'd grown fond of the children and there were times that she was really good to him.

Eventually, he left her. He couldn't take it any more after she'd beaten him so hard that his ribs were broken but she wouldn't let him out to go and see a doctor. After ten days of agony and having difficulty breathing properly, he managed to escape and went straight to the hospital. He attempted to lie about his injuries, but one of the nurses gave him the number of a safe house for abused men. He knew there were homes like that for women but it had never occurred to him that there were other abused men like him. It gave him the courage to make the call and he stayed there for eighteen months. They helped him get back on track, find him a job and a roof over his head. He was happy, thinking he was safe, escaped from the evil woman, until he met her coincidentally. She followed him, found out where he was living. Three months later, she visited him. Needed his help. Forced him to go with her on the pretext that she needed his help with the children. He went with her and found Hugo in a pool of blood in her kitchen. The scariest thing, he thought at that moment, was the fact that the knife that she'd used to slit Hugo's throat was simply lying on his chest.

I interrupt him to ask what date it was and he doesn't need to think about it. 7th May, 10 past 12.

She was panicking, in tears, she was desperate for his help. And his love. He was under her spell again. He went and bought strong plastic sheets from B&Q and they wrapped Hugo's corpse in them. Cleaned the kitchen, burned their clothes. Together, they stored the body in a wardrobe and she insisted he went with her to fetch the children from the school. Coming back, she sent him to buy a big freezer, which was delivered the next day and was installed in the shed. She took the children to the nursery and they dumped the body in the freezer. She wanted him to come back to her, but he knew what she was capable of. He'd become even more scared of her after she'd killed Hugo during one of her outbursts of uncontrolled rage. He tried to hide from her, find a new address, a new job, but she knew very well what he was trying to do and she threatened him that he was guilty of being an accomplice to the murder. Then, to his horror, she made him buy a chain saw to chop firewood – they didn't even have a fireplace – and she cut ... it ... Hugo's body in pieces.

'She did that?' I interrupt.

'Oh yes. She may be a woman, and not a big one, but she is very strong.

'Go on please, Mr Whittaker.'

She had quite a shock when there was a big storm and we had a power cut that lasted twenty hours. She knew then that they had to dispose of the contents of the freezer. It was her that dumped the hand when she went for a bike ride from Wadebridge to Padstow. She was intrigued by the idea of what would happen if someone found the hand. She followed every article in the press and was furious when she couldn't find anything about it in the papers. A week later she dumped two parts of the leg. One in Newquay, one in Port Gaverne.

Then she met Jonathan. He lived in Tregony and she managed to persuade him to let her and her children move in with him. Obviously, she couldn't get rid of the freezer at that point as part of Hugo's corpse was still in it.

Bernie stops, recalling the sight of the torso and the head, still in the freezer which had been bought in his name. The horror is etched on his face and in less than ten words he finishes how she made him dispose of the last and most difficult parts. He was so scared, he didn't have her ruthlessness and, he just got rid of the remaining parts as quickly as possible.

Then he sobs and Jonathan taps his shoulder comfortingly, supportively.

'Why did she kill Hugo?' I ask when after a while Bernie has calmed down. 'What was her motive?'

They look at each other. A conversation unspoken. Eventually Bernie answers. 'Hugo was about to leave her. He'd spoken to friends and they had advised him to start proceedings for divorce. She was furious. She didn't want that. But most of all, the fact that he had spoken to a friend, or friends about her, people she didn't know, that was a threat to her as well.'

I nod. Turn towards Jonathan, whose face has grown a few shades paler. He is probably realising what a narrow escape he had.

'She forced you to take those pills did she, Jonathan?' I say gently. 'She left with the children and set things up like you had committed suicide because she'd left you.'

'I was sick.' He nods miserably. 'As soon as she left, I managed to throw up. Get the pills out.'

Bernie is shifting nervously on his seat. 'Will you charge us, inspector?'

'I have to abide by the law, I'm afraid, Mr Whittaker, but I'm sure there are certain circumstances that will work in your favour.'

'Like what?'

I offer a vague smile. Jump in the deep end. 'Like you came forward voluntarily to make a statement.'

'But I didn't …'

'I intercepted you, remember? We saved Jonathan from drowning in his own vomit.'

'Oh. Did we?'

I nod seriously. 'We did.'

They both look relieved. I feel a lump in my throat as I see them exchanging glances, wiping tears from their eyes.

'Inspector.' Bernie touches my arm. 'I have to tell you … it was us, sir. Jonathan and me. We kidnapped you. She wanted to get you out of the way, but it all happened so quickly. I think she never thought Hugo's body would be found. And so quickly! We'd barely disposed of those … parts. And then you came along and asked her all those questions. She panicked. She tried to … seduce you. She wanted to control you as she had controlled us. But you were not interested. Which infuriated her even more. That night she sent us to kidnap you. You had treated her badly, she told Jonathan and me and she needed to teach you a lesson. It was on the spur of the moment, I suppose. She knew it wouldn't take long before you got on her tail. She needed time to think of a way to kill you and … well, maybe Jonathan and I were supposed to do it. But I wouldn't have done it, inspector, honestly. I am guilty because I helped her with Hugo's body but I have never killed anyone and I never will, I promise.'

'You came back the next morning. I saw you from where I was hiding.'

His eyes widen in surprise. 'You knew it was us?'

'I didn't recognise Jonathan when you kidnapped me. It happened too fast, I guess. I only saw you, Bernie, but I didn't know who you were.'

'I'm glad it's over,' Bernie says, patting Jonathan's arm.

'What I don't understand,' I say slowly, 'is why you went into my flat and put a rather loud porn DVD on. Why did you do that?'

Once more they exchange looks. The surprise on their faces I genuine: they don't know anything about a DVD that caused Mr Curtis a sleepless night.

If it wasn't them, I can only think of one person. Bee Robson. I find it unnerving that she is still out there somewhere. A mad woman. An invisible adversary who will certainly have plans to return and take revenge.

48

My phone bleeps. It's time to collect Lauren from the café at the entrance and go to the all-too-familiar waiting room and wait for my results from Mr Cole.

I never thought I would have Lauren by my side today.

As I make my way to Treliskes' busy entrance, I recall the last part of my meeting with Victor Carter. Strangely enough, we settled for a preliminary stage of friendship. It was him who saw through me, saying without thinking, 'I know about your stoma. And your cancer. I made enquiries about you when I suspected you of kidnapping my daughter.'

'I see.'

'Are you going back to work soon?'

'I hope so,' I replied slowly and, meeting his eyes, I felt my defences crumbling. Before I knew what was happening, I found myself telling him about this morning's appointment with Mr Cole.

'When is the appointment?'

'Quarter to twelve.'

'And you're going on your own? Don't you have … someone? A girlfriend?'

'There are … some issues, complications she isn't aware off.'

'And you'd rather not tell her.' A bald statement. Not a question. It makes me wonder what else he knows about my condition, but I daren't ask.

'Yes.'

'It's never good to keep these things to yourself, you know.'

Keen to escape, I excused myself and went to the toilet. I rested my forehead against the door. Squeezed my eyes shut as they were brimming with tears.

When I returned, he had ordered another double espresso

and a cappuccino for me.

'Your phone,' he said, stretching out an arm with a stubbornness that couldn't be ignored.

'I beg your pardon?'

'Your phone. Make that call. Be as brave as my 13-year-old daughter. Call that woman of yours. Ask her the question.'

I blinked at him, knowing he wouldn't let me go until I'd made the call.

She answered before the second ring, as though she'd been waiting.

'Lauren. Err … ' I started, then blurted, 'I have an appointment in Treliske. The results of the new scan. They've had a meeting about me.'

'Is it bad?'

'My appointment is today. At 11.45.'

'Would you like me to come with you?'

'Err ...please.'

'Okay.' No fuss. 'I'll arrange for the boys to go home with a friend.'

'You don't have to …'

'No,' she interrupted quickly, cutting me off before I could refuse her offer. 'But I'd like to. I'm glad you called, Andy.'

'Yes. Me too.' My voice cracked. A tear escaped. The very act of admitting that I needed her company today, more than ever, was releasing some of the tension in me.

I stared at Carter. He stared back. I couldn't find the words to thank him.

We walk through the corridors. Lauren's heels click-clack on the floor. Somehow, it is a reassuring sound. I don't have to look to know that she is by my side.

We enter the waiting room. Lauren accepts a cup of tea from the volunteer trolley ladies while I tell the woman at the desk that I have arrived. It is too late to turn and walk away.

Ten minutes later, I can barely look him in the eye when Mr Cole motions us into an examination room, shaking my hand and smiling vaguely at Lauren, He doesn't ask to be introduced to her. He only nods by way of acknowledgement. He is interested in my file. In me.

'Good news, Mr Tregunna.' He looks up, the point of his pen resting at where he's just written down today's date. 'The tumour hasn't spread and we found no signs that we hadn't been able to remove the whole thing.'

His voice echoes in my head. I find it difficult to concentrate on his words and understand what he is saying. He talks about the prognosis and future management of my condition. About regular check-ups and blood tests and scans. Lauren asks questions and I stare at his lips as they move. Answering. Explaining. Then the consultation is over. My knees wobble when he rises and I try to follow his cue. Time to go. Time for his next patient.

He shakes my hand and, this time, Lauren's too. 'We'll see you in three months time, Mr Tregunna. Of course, we can't be certain at this point, but .... It's a start.'

Lauren is quiet, squeezing my hand, gently leading me away from the hospital, back to where we parked the car.

I can't see through a mist of tears.

ACKNOWLEDGEMENTS

This is a work of fiction. The idea for this book is remotely based on the true story of *The Girl from Nulde,* a little girl who was murdered, her body parts scattered around the countryside in The Netherlands, a few decades ago. If it wasn't for her former teacher, the Dutch police would probably never have found out her identity – and those responsible for her death.

I could not have achieved this without the help of Magda Pieta and Hannah Vaughan of TJ Ink, Jeff Bell for sharing his memories and anecdotes of his work for the police, Sue Black for explaining some specific forensic issues, Neil Harding for help on police procedure, Margot Coleman for legal expertise, Wendy Wilson and her 'Alistair' and last but not least my editor Mollie Goodman. A big thank you also to the group of Cornish authors, the wonderful lunches and tips and do's or don't's. Mike for listening to my crazy ideas and supplying me with enough black coffee and Cornish sandwiches to keep me going,

All mistakes are mine.